Praise for Jason Phillip Reeser's

Lazaretto

"The Lazaretto is more than just a place of exile, it is a state of mind. Part psychological thriller, part murder mystery, part bitter-sweet romance, the *Lady in the Lazaretto* is always science fiction at its best." — A.C. Flory, author of *Vohktah*

"The *Lady in the Lazaretto* takes readers back to the gritty moon-world that serves the space-faring universe as a quarantine station. Why do I like going there when it's so dark and unforgiving? Because I love a good mystery, I enjoy listening to two of my favorite future detectives poke at each other with classic comradely sarcasm when they aren't facing lethal dangers; and because, most of all, the Lazaretto is a unique creation. There is only one Lazaretto. Another first-class intriguing noir science fiction mystery from Jason Phillip Reeser." –S.J. Hunter, author of the *Longevity Law Enforcement* series.

I0629470

Books by Jason Phillip Reeser

<u>Fiction</u>
Jury Rig

Cities of the Dead

The World that Slid Downhill

<u>The Lazaretto Trilogy</u>
Book One: The Lazaretto

Book Two: Lady in the Lazaretto

Book Three: Kiss of the Lazaretto

<u>Non-Fiction</u>
Room with Paris View

Kiss of
the Lazaretto

a novel by

Jason Phillip Reeser

First Trilogy Edition, April, 2014
Copyright ©2014 by Jason Phillip Reeser
Cover Art Copyright ©2014 by Jason Phillip Reeser
First Printing April, 2014

ISBN: 978-0615976099

Rocket Fire Books
Westlake, Louisiana
rocketfirebooks.com

Acknowledgements: Writing a book can be a lonely journey. There are, however, people along the way who not only break the isolation but lend a helping hand to ensure the destination is reached. This trilogy would not have been possible without the keen insight and the sharp eyes of my wife Jennifer, my children Kathryn, Maxwell, and Simon, and my good friends John Z. and Paul B. Their time and attention are greatly appreciated. Their contributions have made this a better novel and a fun journey.

For Paul
A tough critic.
A shrewd reader.
An honest friend.

"My Sweet, so do I.
But I would kill you by petting you too much.
Good night. Good night.
Parting is such sweet sorrow."
— *Romeo and Juliet*, William Shakespeare

"Good night, sweet prince
and flights of angels sing thee to thy rest!"
— *Hamlet*, William Shakespeare

"Sacrifice turns to revenge
and you would hear the voice that would say:
I love you…I'll kill you…
but I love you forever."
--*I Love You…I'll Kill You…*, Enigma

The people of Earth had never given the Lazaretto system serious thought. The quarantine moon was not hidden from public view, though it did suffer from a collective ennui in society which had grown so bored with anything remotely connected to bureaucracy that all government functions were virtually ignored. Those aware of the Lazaretto took the usual, cynical view of government programs and assumed that it was either an excessive budgetary drain or inefficient and inept process worthy only of disdain and a certain macabre derision.

The inception of the Lazaretto controls had become necessary in the wake of rampant interplanetary epidemics. By the time the Lazaretto system had brought a measured control over the migration of interplanetary diseases, the great interplanetary travel age had ended. No longer did the average man seek to fulfill his wanderlust by booking a flight to the outer planets. Colonists found fewer reasons to visit the home world. Technology had stepped in where angels and tourists had feared to tread. Virtual Vacations replaced actual off-planet larks and there were even segments of the population who had rediscovered the joy of reading about far-off lands. Travel writers like Gloria Dempsey and Pete Nguyen risked the dangerous trip to the stars and wrote poetically of Phasis, Dnepr and the other exotic planets in the Euxine system. The Lazaretto came too late to save the massive travel needs of the early, heady days of space travel.

Interplanetary travel, however, was far from dead. The business of trade was far too lucrative and necessary to die from fear. Death and disease could not stop men from plying their trades in the dark recesses of the universe. The dangers only served to decrease supply and increase demand. Profits soared. The implementation of the Lazaretto built and toppled empires in a matter of months. Old bastions of finance came crashing down while enterprising young upstarts built upon their ruins.

It was this association with massive trade empires that ensured the Lazaretto's corrupt and distant reputation with the general population. And if the corrupting influences of business were not enough to keep one away, the second dominant presence in the Lazaretto was equally distasteful: the government.

The Lazaretto was a throughway for government diplomats, military leadership and personnel, and a myriad assortment of lesser members of the massive central governing institution. Although there were fewer government employees traveling through the Lazaretto than employees of the trade conglomerates, their penchant for corruption was on an equal scale.

It had been the needs of both business and government that had finally convinced the government to spend the money to establish the Lazaretto. At first, small lazarettos had been built on as many planets as possible. They were small facilities, designed for minimum traffic. There had been too many sites to build to allow for any sizable Planet Lazarettos. Before they had been built they were outdated, run down, and in dire need of upgrades. All of them were too small to handle the regular flux of travelers. It took two years of crippling logjams at the lazarettos before the central Lazaretto was given the green light.

Built in the center of the Euxine system, on the largest of Sinop's moons, the Lazaretto was a gateway. All traffic into and out of the system came through the gateway. Any traffic headed back into Earth's Solar System had to leave through the gateway. Any traffic connecting a planet to another planet within the Euxine System—Bukovina, Dnepr, Phasis, Arcobia, and Sinop—had to pass through the gateway without exception.

Once the government had issued the directive to build a central lazaretto, there was a surprising lack of conflict over where it should be based. Sinop's moon, Aegean, was an optimum choice that found nearly universal favor.

Aegean was an anomalous moon that had surprised early space explorers. Though clearly a moon of Sinop, it was found to have its own atmosphere. Moreover, nearly 98% of its surface was covered in water. Its one continent, nothing more than an island, was originally named Far Britain by its founder, British astroexplorer Sir Edward Brown. Though smaller than his homeland, Brown was astounded at how identical the weather patterns reminded him of home.

Far Britain was never settled due to the overabundance of good land available on Sinop. A gentler climate and less hostile environment made the colonists on Sinop forget all about their odd little moon. The decision to build the Lazaretto on Aegean changed all of that. Suddenly, that odd little moon was the center of attention. Despite its rainy atmosphere, it gained a population as workers descended on its wet island to build the interstellar quarantine port.

The Lazaretto was built as two separate ports: one for travelers, one for shipping. Both ports had profoundly different procedures for controlling the spread of contagions.

No human was allowed to enter the shipping port. This restriction also applied to animals, although by this time most of the planets had adopted a ban on the transshipment of livestock between planets. The entire operation was controlled and operated by machines.

As freighters arrived at the quarantine port, all crewmembers were required to disembark and transported to a ship that was leaving quarantine and destined for their planet of origin. In this way, the crew avoided quarantine.

The freighters that entered the shipping port were sprayed down with a toxic biocide that could guarantee the eradication of all known contagions. The toxin was lethal to all living beings. This toxin, once applied, remained on the freighter for twenty-four hours, after which it was deactivated with a heat wash. Nine days were set aside as a safety measure to ensure the toxin was no longer a threat. Although this method of decontamination was expensive, it had a valuable benefit: all freighters were allowed to leave quarantine after this ten day period—one-fourth the time required for humans in quarantine.

Human travelers were required to participate in a more passive quarantine system. Upon arrival at the Lazaretto, all travelers were processed and placed into one of four quadrants. Each quadrant was on a fifty-day cycle. Each quadrant was open for ten days to allow travelers to arrive. Once that quadrant shut its doors, it remained sealed for forty days. No one was allowed in or out.

The travelers who were in quarantine were not treated with any vaccinations. A careful study of the contagions known to be found on the various Euxine planets had determined that any contagion already infecting an individual would manifest itself within ten days. But travelers were forced to wait another thirty days. This was the most important precaution taken by the Lazaretto protocols to make certain that no passengers carried the Euxine Spirare.

The Euxine Spirare was an influenza strain that had once nearly wiped out one-quarter of the populations of the Euxine System and was the final factor in the decision to build the lazarettos. The Plague, so named by a fearful populace, was deadly to nearly eighty per cent of those infected with the virus. The virus had one predictable trait: it could not live beyond four weeks. IHS added two days to the four-week period and required the thirty days of quarantine.

There were no treatments used on sick travelers. IHS had recommended that treatments and vaccinations be avoided as cost-prohibitive. While shipping must be expedited, travelers could wait. The time wasted in quarantine meant nothing to IHS.

Book One

Ghosts

Heavy fog crawled across the broken, paved surface of a narrow alley in Alpha Quadrant. On one side of the alley, wet glass formed the walls of one building. Stark shadows appeared as heavy, thick spider webs, formed from the ironwork of fire escapes clinging to the brick building on the opposite side, fed by the yellow glow of lamps shrouded by filthy windows. The thick white fog rose from the ground, thinning as it dispersed into the black, late-night sky, obscuring the shadow play.

Frobe entered this mix of white mist and black, wavering shadows; his steps slow, hesitant, unsure. He moved deeper into the alley, pausing every few steps to look behind and to the side. At times he would tilt his head to scan the suspended iron ladders.

At the sound of approaching steps, Frobe, a lock-pick by trade, pulled back against the glass wall, his figure marred by ripples of white vapor and black stencils. His own silhouette grew fat then thinned out as a cold breeze blew in more fog from the adjacent streets. His hand slipped inside his coat. His eyes glowed pearl white.

The footsteps tapped out a solid, steady rhythm. Just as he discerned a wide form in the billowing morass, the tapping ceased. The black form held still. Frobe's hand remained glued to the inside of his coat. His fingers were wrapped around the handle of a Para-Lazar, but he did not withdraw it. He did not move. He hardly dared take a breath.

The fog washed over his face; chilling condensation dribbled down the slope of his jaw. With his free hand he wiped away the wet of the night. He continued to stare at the form in the fog.

"Jardyn?"

No response. It was too big to be Jardyn. The massive man-shape remained immobile. Or had it? He wiped his face again. Each time he did, the form appeared to be closer, even as the fog seemed to thicken. He could make out the shape of a man with impossibly broad shoulders. He could even see the silhouette of a wide-brimmed hat on a head that also seemed too wide. It had to be the man he'd seen in the hotel lobby. The one with the brutal eyes. Rivulets began pouring down Frobe's pockmarked cheeks—now from sweat, not condensation.

His nerves shot, Frobe made a decision and snatched the silver Para-Lazar from his coat. Arm extended, he fired. Deep, rich blue streaks cut through the fog without leaving a wake. One, two, and two more. The fog swallowed them with ease. He did not wait to see if they hit their mark.

Frobe jerked into motion.

He did not run down the alley. He certainly didn't rush straight at the form in the fog. Jamming the Para-Lazar into an outer coat pocket, he lunged across the alley. Extending fully, he jumped, his hands just catching the bottom rung of a fire escape. Scrambling feet found purchase against stacked wooden pallets and he was able to let go with one hand to reach higher on the cold, iron frame. He kicked off from the pallets, felt the stack come apart under him, but managed to lever himself higher still.

He bent upwards, jamming a knee into the space between two rungs. From this awkward position, able to free a hand yet again, he grabbed the railing that guarded the first landing. Holding tight with both arms, he coiled himself, then kicked his feet up and over.

It had taken no more than five or ten seconds from the moment he dove across the alley to the time his knees crash down on the iron landing. He had to catch his breath. He hadn't expected to make it across the alley, let alone reach the first landing on the fire escape. He had no plans beyond this point.

But his silent pursuer was not to be left behind. Scrabbling at the base of the brick wall, it tried desperately to reach the ironwork above. Frobe knew how difficult it was—he was a tall man, and had barely been able to make the jump. The man-shape was obviously heavier. Perhaps it would not be able to reach the iron.

Who was this massive shadow? It had stopped its frantic efforts to reach the high ladder rung. It was difficult for Frobe to see it, so well did it blend with the fog and shadows. He listened carefully; heard nothing. But his unknown stalker did not remain unseen.

The scraping of wood on stone forced Frobe to peer more intently into the alley fog. The big man was moving, dragging the pallets back into place, working with steady purpose.

Now, the ice-cold beads of sweat coursed down Frobe's wide forehead. His hands, shaking, slick with sweat and fear, felt for the Para-Lazar. Which pocket? The slim mechanism was still warm as it slowly recharged. It would take too long to reach full power. His pursuer had already used its rebuilt platform to grab the lower iron, its gorilla shape swinging amidst the swirling miasma of fog.

With a quick, powerful jerk, it pivoted up, wrapping itself around the vibrating frame. Frobe backed up the steps of the escape, aiming at the form, now just a meter away. If the Para-Lazar's charge were sufficient, and he hit the pursuing form at the right moment, it would fall back to the alley. He might possibly injure the thing. It might never recover.

If.

One. The Para-Lazar's jolt of electric blue sparked brilliantly against iron. In the golden flash, in the resulting prism of jagged vision, a man, his eyes filled with the promise of violence, was clearly visible. Two. Frobe's aim was no good. The shot sliced tendrils of fog, missed iron and flesh, vanished beyond. There was no third shot.

He fled up the stairs, hand cracking hard against the rail. The useless Para-Lazar clattered loudly, bouncing once on the landing before slipping down through the fog.

Pounding up the steps, he no longer wondered at the shadow's identity. One look in those eyes was enough for Frobe to know he was dealing with a seasoned killer. The man's eyes told all. This was personal. This was no random mugging on the streets of a quarantine zone that was about to lock down. That mad, colossal killer was hunting Frobe. He knew about the theft. He was there to take back their prize. Had he and Jardyn ever had a real chance?. What were the odds this killer would have found them this quickly? They'd covered their tracks, hadn't they?

Had Jardyn betrayed him? Was that the simple answer? Or was Jardyn already dead? Had they already recovered the stolen artifact? Was the man below just tying up loose ends?

At the top of the escape Frobe knew he would have to make a choice: flee across the roof or hope to jump to an adjoining building. Maybe he could find another fire escape and try to beat the killer back to ground. But what then? Even if he escaped, he couldn't stay in Alpha as it locked down for the next five weeks. And fleeing the quadrant was just as pointless. Out in the city he would be found. They would never let him get into another quadrant.

There were no easy escapes from the Lazaretto.

Legs burning, lungs out of oxygen, he paused a few stories shy of the rooftop. It was too dark, too foggy, to see his pursuer. But the low, steady thrum of vibrations told him the killer was coming. At least he was far below. He was in no hurry.

A noise from above shocked him. He craned his neck to see what had made it. One light at the top of the escape was enough to outline the oversized man who had just stepped out onto the escape. How had his pursuit ended up ahead of him? Frobe wondered if he were losing his mind. His senses were surely not to be trusted.

He leaned over the rail and looked down. No, he was not losing his mind. The big guy below was still slowly climbing. One more quick look above confirmed it; there were two pursuers, each one as big as the other. He should have guessed the killer would not be alone.

From the landing, Frobe could see a second fire escape across a gap of thinning fog. Four meters, maybe more. The distance was impossible to judge in that light. But the solid black frame was his only option.

The killer called out. Above, the second man answered. They called Frobe by name. The second fire escape called to him silently. The gap was too much. He might make the jump. But could he grab the iron and hold on? It seemed impossible.

There was no time to think about it. Jump—escape. No jump—no escape. He'd worry about getting out of the Lazaretto later.

Clutching a support iron, he put a shoe on the thin, black handrail, pulling himself up until he was balanced on top of it. He had regained enough breath to slow down and inhale deeply.

Four meters. Maybe more.

From above, the vibrations increased as the second man could see what he was about to attempt.

Legs bent, arms out, fingers tensed, ready to grapple with the unforgiving iron, Frobe pushed off as hard as he could. To his shock, he cleared the four meters easily. Too easily. His outstretched hands flew beyond the iron and his chest rammed into it unexpectedly. Pain shot through him even as he realized he was dead. His fingers never wrapped around the iron as they slid back past it. He narrowly missed smashing his head against the iron.

Gravity jerked hard at his body. This time, as he dropped past the next landing, his head did not miss the iron. It hit hard. He felt rather than heard his skull crack. To his horror, it did not knock him unconscious. Instead, Frobe watched the iron frame rush by him, saw the swirling white vapors part before him, and watched in terror as the alley floor leapt into the air like a tiger eager to devour him.

2

Gregor Lepov lay on his back, his head resting on air with the backdrop of a hotel lobby over a hundred feet below him. Grounded bits of glass dug into the back of his neck as he reached wildly for anything to grab in order to stabilize his body and keep it from slipping out the shattered window.

The crazed little killer Chitti Sienté just kept coming. Lepov had already kicked her twice, rolling her across the room. But each time he did, she scrambled to her feet and tore after him like a rabid dog. Lilly was screaming, her broken body discarded near the front door where she'd been slashed with Chitti's knife.

Chitti no longer had the knife and Lepov was glad of the fact. She was too much to handle even without the knife. She'd managed to bite him once, on the hand he had used to hold her at bay. Her long fingernails had scratched cruel red gashes on his forearms and neck. A strong smell of iron clung to the room. Sweat ran down his temples.

Chitti finally stopped, down on hands and knees, to catch her breath. It should have allowed Lepov time to right himself and prepare for her next attack. Should have even allowed him time to find that damned shockhammer and slam it against the side of her head. That was the best idea he'd had all day.

But her breath caught much too quickly and she tilted forward, regained her feet and lunged at him once more.

Lepov had only been able to sit up halfway before she struck. He was up enough, enabling her to hit him hard with her body weight, scant thought it might have been. Lepov felt her impact the center of his chest and heard his own sickened groan. He slid further out the window, the shards of glass shredding his back. He bled stark fear.

Wait! He rammed the palms of both hands down into the shards of glass. I'm not ready! The absurdity of that thought was not lost on him. He simply had no time to consider it. Instead of blocking her attack, he'd allowed her to win the strategic battle of position. He had no leverage whatsoever and it meant the death of him.

Chitti gripped him with her arms and no amount of force could separate her from him. Lepov was aware that she was driving her legs against the floor, deliberately shoving him out the window.

Wait! Lepov tried to shout, but the pressure she applied to his chest made the effort useless.

"Cut that out!" Lepov's words were barely recognizable.

"Gregor!" Lilly's scream rang out clear. "Chitti! Don't! Please!"

"It's not Chitti!" Lepov growled, tearing at the Chitti-thing with both hands as he felt his shoulders drop off the edge. Its teeth began snapping wildly, biting at his fingers and hands and arms. "She's already dead for God's sake!"

"What is it?" Lilly sobbed.

"It's her damned ghost! How the hell should I know?" Lepov felt hair in his fingers and he clamped down his fist and yanked the fiend's head back hard enough to break its neck. "Get off, dammit! Stop pushing!"

He tried to sit up, had to sit up, there was nothing solid under him north of his stomach. But no matter how hard he tried to curl up, the weight of Chitti, or whatever she was, pressed him back out the window.

And each time she did, he felt his body creep more and more over the edge.

Lilly kept screaming. Lepov was able to look over at her but all he could see was blood on the walls around her.

He saw the shockhammer too, but by then it was too late.

His weight, combined with his attacker's, was too much. He broke free of his contact with the solid world and they fell. No longer a part of the world he had known, Lepov accelerated into a deep and noisy void. What had once been reality instantly became air and vapor. And the struggling vicious animal that had been Chitti Sienté fell apart in his hand, and turned to dust and ashes and memories.

He fell to his death alone.

3

The phone did not wake the New Yorker, who was lying in bed, waiting for the call. He answered immediately, though he did not speak. The voice on the other end of the transmission was curt.

"The German is dead. An accident."

"You have it?"

"No. And we missed his partner."

So the Frenchman had escaped and his co-conspirator had died. The New Yorker sighed, resigned to the errors. The men committing them could worry about that. They did not answer to the New Yorker. The Australian would judge their excuses. But it did not mean he was happy with the outcome.

"You'll keep looking, of course." He added: "I'll let you know if I hear from the other one. He'll probably call me after he hears what happened to the German."

Would the Frenchman still trust the Englishman? Or did it mean they had blown the Englishman's cover when they had tried to grab the Frenchman and his partner?

The caller terminated the connection without another word. It was to be expected. He was known for his actions, not his communication skills. For the New Yorker, it was time to communicate with the Australian. He would have to be told. He always had to be told. He could never allow the New Yorker to take care of the job on his own. It was insulting, but there was no alternative. The Australian did not care who he insulted. Truthfully, he wasn't even aware an insult was being made.

But the Australian's insulting habits were not the New Yorker's immediate problem; that the Frenchman had escaped with the artifact was. If these men failed to find him, the New Yorker would have to keep the Englishman in line. He would have to be sure the Frenchman and the Englishman did not start working together again.

He turned over and put his arm over the woman beside him. This one he liked. She had surprised him with her strange chatter. The New Yorker had found it oddly fascinating. Never before had a woman spent a night with him prattling about religion. No, she hadn't tried to convert him. She hardly knew enough about it to try it. And if she had, he'd have sent her on her way with a good hard smack across the teeth. But she had merely shared her own eagerness to discover if there were something more to life than food and clothes and booze and sex. The New Yorker was sure there wasn't for a woman, but it was strangely entertaining to hear her speculations on the subject.

This one he would keep around for awhile.

At his touch, she pressed close to him, even as she continued to sleep. He pushed her away and slipped out of bed, pulling on pants, a sweater and shoes without bothering to find his socks. The Australian was just down the hall. The woman would never know he was gone. Let her dream about facing God and all that jazz.

Facing the Australian was his immediate concern. And no golden cross was gonna protect him from the man's anger.

4

A flame broke the darkness. Gregor's face held deep shadows under his cheekbones and jaw. The image became obscured by smoke and the flame disappeared. Lilly was left with only his silhouette in the doorway.

"I didn't hear you come in." She sat up, the cold air hit her shoulders and she pulled a blanket over them.

"You were sleeping hard. I've been standing here awhile." His black form stepped out of the doorway and she did not see him until he switched on a lamp. His bare head was wet; his thin hair pasted flat.

She slipped out from the blankets and into a silken robe. She pulled a belt tight at her waist, walked across the room and held out her hand. Gregor took a last drag on the cigarette before he handed it to her. Lilly wrapped two fingers around it, put it briefly to her lips, then ground it out on a silver ash tray on a nearby table.

"Thanks, I was smoking that."

"You don't smoke, remember?" She disappeared through a doorway then returned with a towel and covered his head with it. "And you wear a hat."

"Maybe you're thinking of another man." He pulled away from her but she held onto the towel and pushed it down the back of his neck.

"My luck's not that good." Leaning forward, she kissed him. "You've been dreaming again."

"I'm beginning to like it. It's a lot easier than reading books."

Lilly ignored his banter and kissed him again. She knew he was upset. The dreams had been wearing him down. She'd only learned about them when she discovered he had taken up smoking again. He wasn't smoking on a daily basis, but he needed one or two cigarettes to calm him down after each dream.

He wasn't being haunted by the same nightmare. From what he'd told her, they were always different. They always woke him. And they always shook him hard. Gregor Lepov did not shake easily.

They went into her kitchen where she began to make coffee. He pulled off his coat and left it hanging on the back of a chair.

"So do you want to tell me about it?"

"I'm sure you're tired of hearing this kind of thing. Let's pretend it never happened. Instead you could kiss me again. Only this time try to not do it like you're my mother who's upset to see I've been out playing in the rain."

"If you want to play in the rain I'm not going to stop you. But you didn't come over here in the middle of the night to get fresh with me. So why don't you take this cup of coffee, drink it, warm up, and tell me about the dream."

"As a favor to yourself, never underestimate how fresh I want to get with you." Gregor sipped the coffee before continuing. "That makes the walk over here worth it."

"It's freezing outside, Gregor. Are you trying to catch pneumonia? Tell me you didn't walk all the way here."

"It's not freezing outside. This is the Lazaretto. It never freezes, remember? And if it makes you feel any better, I only *tried* to walk here. I didn't make it two blocks before I called for a TransitCar. It may not freeze here, but it sure felt like it was."

Lilly had almost begun to believe Gregor was feeling okay. He had fooled her right up until the moment his hand shook hard enough to crack the coffee cup against the side of the kitchen table. He set it down and flattened out his hand, looking at the back of it as if it were the wrong color or size. He flexed it twice then began making circles on his fingertips with his thumb.

"What's wrong?" she asked.

"Nothing." He made a fist and held still for a moment before putting the hand down out of sight. "You really want to hear about the dream?"

"No. But I get the feeling I'm going to hear about it anyway."

Gregor brought his hand back into sight and grabbed his coffee. "You've got to be getting tired of hearing this every night. You ought to take me off your door list. Keep me out of here."

She watched his head sink as he spoke and wondered when he had last had a full night's sleep. The coffee wasn't doing him any good. She slid the cup away from him before he could knock it off the table.

"I dreamt that you were dying, and I couldn't help." Gregor lifted his head enough to see that the cup was no longer in his hand. He accepted this without looking to see where it had gone. "We were back at the hotel, where Chitti threw me out the window. The day I died."

Lilly knew he was talking of the day they'd stopped Chitti Sienté from escaping through Delta Quadrant. Of course, Gregor hadn't been thrown out a window. It was Chitti who had gone out the window. It was Chitti who had fallen to her death.

Lilly guided Gregor into her living room. Without saying a word, she removed his shoes, his belt, and the last of his resistance as she stretched him out on her sofa.

She switched off the light and sat in darkness. It was difficult to watch him twist and turn, to struggle to sleep. She had once believed that Gregor Lepov was a man who was merely a little boy who had lost his way. Early perceptions can derive from great intuitive leaps that later prove to be astoundingly accurate. And sometimes they merely fit for that one early occasion. The later had proven to be the case with Gregor.

The man who lay on her sofa was very rarely lost. He was, more times than was good for his health, all too cognizant of where and what he was. A laborious weight dragged at him. The reality of sorrow surrounding him was all too clear. His investigator's mind was too practiced at tallying the score and computing the logic of a world like his. He was not simply a cynic. He was not lazy enough to draw such an effortless conclusion. His ego had never grown large enough to blame the darkness of the world on man. Yet he once admitted to Lilly that he couldn't quite give in to the belief that Fate was to blame for the evils that assailed men. Men were too skilled at tearing each other's throats out, and too happy to do it, to believe they were forced to take such actions.

For that moment, the world around him had ceased to be haunted by the phantasma of selfish, violent men and grasping, treacherous women. Sleep had finally taken him. Lilly dared not withdraw for fear she would wake him. She watched over him patiently, intently, as if she might be able to intercept the first specter that threatened to invade his brief respite.

5

A hand grabbed Lieutenant Ed MacNally in mid-sleep. He knew this after he'd clamped his own meaty fingers over the strange hand

and twisted it hard in hopes of snapping the wrist to which it was attached. The hand was too elusive and slipped from his grasp. MacNally rolled over, his fingers now curled into a fist as he sized up the shadow that bent over him, backlit from the early morning light barely visible through the edges of his drawn shades. The figure was long and thin and MacNally had just decided he held the weight advantage and curled forward in hopes of bull-rushing his assailant.

"Morning, Pops." The hand was splayed across his head now, holding him down with what had to be minimum effort. His partner, Menya Russell, might have been long and thin, but he was strong enough to keep his bull of a partner down on the bed.

"You tryin' to get your hand snapped off, boy?" MacNally reached up and swatted Russell's hand away. "You're lucky I didn't break your wrist."

"I'm sure you gave it your best try, Pops. Now get up and get dressed. Unless you want me to dress you."

"I *will* break your hand if you try that—hell, what time is it?" MacNally ran the palm of his hand across his forehead as if he were trying to reshape it. He stood up and both men looked down at the sheet as it fell away.

"Thank God you're not sleeping naked these days," Russell muttered.

"I wish I did, it might teach you to stay out of an old man's bedroom." MacNally had, in fact, fallen asleep fully clothed. He'd even left his tie on. He brushed at his shirt and then grabbed his tie, unsure of whether he should pull it off and change or simply tighten it and throw on his jacket.

"If you stand still I'll iron that for you." The kid was having too much fun.

"You stand still, I'm gonna take a shower." MacNally yanked down on the tie and it whipped out of his collar. Russell walked off mumbling something about coffee. "Why do I get the feeling there's a dead body waiting for me to finish my shower?"

There always was. MacNally stepped under a cold spray. His chest clamped down hard over his lungs and he fought to take in air. His lungs, finally inflated to their maximum, were emptied in one quick burst. He had to do it two more times before he was fully awake. There wasn't enough of his closely-cropped hair to bother scrubbing it with anything more than water.

He could vaguely hear the young Arcobian in the other room, probably explaining why he had fetched MacNally so early. MacNally couldn't make out a word the boy was saying, but then, MacNally regularly missed the boy's mumbling that was suppose to pass for communication. He'd given up asking Russell to repeat himself. For the most part he could guess what his partner was gonna say.

And at that moment, Russell was telling him that a body had been found in some apartment, or warehouse, or on a street corner. The initial report would be sketchy, cause would be undetermined, and the lab boys from Interplanetary Health Services would be on their way to lick and stick the body before Visuals were taken at the scene.

Russell's coffee was decent, a big improvement over his earlier versions of that essential beverage, and MacNally walked out the door without eating anything. His appetite had diminished a great deal as he'd grown older. He'd also learned not to fill his stomach before viewing a crime scene that involved a corpse.

Russell kept the car at street level, explaining his lack of speed as he drifted in and out of early morning traffic.

"There's no real rush here. The body was only reported just under an hour ago. I doubt IHS had a chance to get there yet. Who's up this early in the morning, right?"

"Russell," MacNally glared at the kid, "I'm up this early."

"Yeah, well fact is I couldn't sleep this morning, so I was up, heard the call, and figured I would come on over and get you out of bed. I couldn't see any point in waiting for you to wake up."

"Yeah, that makes sense, you Arcobian *boutrach*." MacNally had been picking up Arcobian swear words in an attempt to find more meaningful forms of communication with his young partner. It seemed to be working. Russell smiled at him and made a gesture that would have earned him a knife in the ribs in an Arcobian barrio.

"Thanks, Pops."

MacNally was learning to adjust to Menya Russell as a partner. He'd spent over twenty years with Arturo Fenelli as his partner, and they'd been great friends who held too much respect for each other to throw crass slurs back and forth. They had tossed out the occasional insult in order to prevent them from admitting just how much they meant to each other, but for the most part their insults were half-hearted.

It had taken a while, but MacNally had finally figured out how to breech the age gap that had initially kept him and Russell from working well together. As the senior detective, MacNally was too old to be a good-old-boy friend with his fresh-from-the-Academy partner. And Russell's age made it hard for the kid to accept any criticism without taking it to heart, as if his father were correcting him instead of a co-worker. It had puzzled MacNally for months, watching the kid squirm under the slightest sarcastic comment.

It had not taken MacNally long to realize his new partner was over-sensitive about his heritage. Arcobians were seen throughout the Aegean System as lower-class citizens. Though most of that was in the past, there was still an element of it that survived among a great portion of the planetary populations. They were still often the butt of many jokes, many of which started with the ever popular phrase *an Arcobian walks into a bar...*

In order to settle the kid's nerves, MacNally had made a conscious effort to avoid that kind of thing. But the more properly he addressed Russell, the more self-conscious and tense the youngster seemed to grow.

It wasn't until MacNally was actually angry at his partner one day that he'd hit upon the best way to deal with the young man's inability to loosen up. MacNally didn't like to admit it, but he wasn't out to help Russell loosen up that day. He'd simply become exasperated with him and let fly with a mouthful of cruel epithets that should have burned through the kid and left him crying like a baby.

Instead of falling apart, Menya Russell broke into a smile, followed it with a laugh, and in lieu of mumbling, simply said "Okay, Pops."

No scold of a father figure was MacNally: just a bad-tempered crazy old Grandpa.

The traffic picked up as they made their way through Center City. The morning light, or what little of it filtered through the overcast sky, had grown to full intensity, though much of it was blocked out by the towering buildings that lined the streets. On any other planet, the day would have been considered cloudy and sullen. In the Lazaretto, where the sun rarely penetrated the dense clouded atmosphere, it was practically a sunny morning.

Despite the auspicious beginning to the day, MacNally began to feel a knot in his stomach as he became suspicious of Russell's route out towards the east side of the city.

"I hope you aren't heading where it looks like you're heading."

Russell drove on without a response.

"Russell, don't tell me we're doing this. You lied to me. You did get me out of bed early for a reason, you ass. Why didn't you say something earlier?"

The car came to a halt and settled down off its air cushion at the entrance to Alpha Quadrant. Russell climbed out and looked rather pleased with himself. MacNally struggled out of the passenger side as he tried to choose just the right word from his list of Arcobian slurs but couldn't decide on one before Russell finally spoke.

"What's the matter, Pops? You got something against wearing a decon suit?"

"Oh, hell." MacNally gave up on choosing a slur and spit at the ground. "I hate breaking lockdown."

"Yeah, I know, MacNally. But that's where the body's waiting."

6

Travelling with a child is never easy. Children are restless, need space in which to burn off energy, and at the end of the day need order and familiarity. Lara Dassin knew this. She was doing all she could to help her child through the difficulties of travel, especially the peculiar difficulties one encountered in the Lazaretto.

Lara and Frank Dassin were en route to a new life on a new planet. Frank's decision had been quick and unexpected and Lara was still reeling since Frank had announced this move. A job had lured Frank from a comfortable life on Bukovina to the frontier world of Dnepr. Not many people were doing this anymore.

The colony worlds had become nominally civilized, their populations stable, thriving, and self-sustaining. Aside from the corporate war on Arcobia, the worlds were peaceful and required little interference from the home world. Most jobs were filled in-planet, and the majority of interplanetary travel consisted of businessmen who were willing to risk the Lazaretto gauntlet. These men were called Lazars, and they were well-paid for their willingness to endure the quarantine.

Frank Dassin was no Lazar. He had been an accountant, and had shocked Lara by accepting a teaching job at a Dneprish University: the oldest one on the planet. He'd never taught before. The job did not pay well but the Dneprish cost-of-living had dropped dramatically over the years as the colony gained self-rule and had ceased to rely on imports for its daily needs. Dnepr was still a wide-open frontier on many of its overgrown continents, but there were many solid nation-states that enabled the planet to be self-sustained. Frank's only explanation had been a desire to get away from the Earth-like claustrophobia of the overcrowded Bukovina. He swore he'd always wanted to move to one of the frontier planets—Dnepr or Arcobia—and life wasn't getting any longer.

Lara was slowly adjusting to the idea. By the time they boarded their transport she was excited at the chance to start anew. Both of their parents were dead; her mother the last to die a year before Frank had announced his intentions to move. All of their research assured them that their new home would be a wonderful world in which to raise their son.

Jett turned five on the trip out. There had been much discussion on whether they ought to celebrate his birthday before they arrived in the Lazaretto or after. Lara had wanted to throw her son a party before they left, Frank had made them wait until they were settled in the Lazaretto. In fact, their departure had been so sudden, there had been little time for a party before they'd boarded the transport.

Lara regretted Frank's decision.

No amount of research could have prepared them for the stark reality that was the Lazaretto. Its dank, gray atmosphere hung over them with a menace she would never have considered to be possible regardless what any of the travel publications had said. It was simply too queer to believe without experiencing. It mattered not whether they stayed indoors, with heavy drapes drawn across the windows or wandered about in the damp streets. There was no escaping the oppression that ruled from above.

Lara tried to ignore it. She knew it was impinging on their little party, and she did her best to hold it back.

"Isn't it wonderful?" she asked her son, smiling despite her unease.

"What's it?" Jett held a metal figure at arm's length. He was still in his gold and black pajamas.

They had decided to give him the party as soon as possible, but their arrival at the Lazaretto had been in the middle of the night, and they had dropped into their small suite well after midnight local time. Lara had no idea what time their bodies would think it was— interplanetary jetlag was not comparable to simple jetlag. What she did know for certain was that after arriving at their quarantine apartment they had all slept hard but awakened after only four or five hours sleep.

"That's a robot, Jett." Frank said, his voice lacking in enthusiasm. Dark bags under his eyes told Lara he had gained nothing from his few hours of sleep. "It's just a robot."

"What's it robot do?" Jett bit his upper lip and examined the gift in earnest.

"He's like all robots, little man. You command him. He has no say in what he does."

Jett, eyes wide with wonder, pointed at his brand new minion. "Jump up!"

The robot remained on the ground.

"Well, look at that," Frank's voice carried a hint of bitterness. "Maybe we got a smart one. Maybe this one don't want to be your slave."

"Frank, don't." Lara picked up Jett and ruffled his hair, diverting his attention away from the toy.

"A dose of reality wouldn't hurt the boy."

A knock on the door interrupted the party. Lara continued to hold Jett as Frank hesitated at the door, unwilling to open it. He finally gave in, and two men in white IHS uniforms stepped into the room.

"Mr. Frank Dassin?"

"Is there something wrong?" Frank's frosty manner suggested to Lara that their unusual surroundings were wearing on Frank's usual good manners. Lara could feel the same tension, though for her, it might have been a mother's instinct, or it might have easily been her natural pessimism; something had set off an inner warning. She held tightly to Jett.

"We are here to escort your son to IHS Alpha Central." The man raised his chin as if he expected an argument.

"I don't understand, we already submitted our samples and took all of your tests. Wasn't that enough?" Frank looked at Jett and Lara then swung his eyes back to the men in the doorway.

Lara didn't need to hear their answer. She knew right away what they were getting at. Without quite realizing it she had begun to squeeze Jett more tightly, as if the room had begun to spin and centrifugal forces were attempting to pull him out of her arms.

"Sir, I can only tell you that your son is to be escorted to IHS Alpha Central." The IHS man's voice betrayed not the slightest emotion. He stared at Jett and Lara and waited patiently. It was obvious he intended to take Jett immediately.

"Sure." Frank's voice lacked any measure of strength. "We'll all go."

7

Opening his eyes, it took Lepov only a moment or two before he recognized where he was. But recognizing that he had awakened in Lilly's bed afforded him no understanding at all.

He sat up, his mouth tasted like ashes. His head felt like boiling oil had been poured into his sinus cavities. The ashes he understood; he'd been smoking. The oil was something he'd have to think about.

A shower was running in an adjacent room. That would have to be Lilly.

He stood up and the oil sloshed from left to right then vanished in a startlingly brilliant flash. Lepov shoved the base of one palm into his right eye in an attempt to free the eye from an overpowering pain.

"You awake?" Lilly asked from the shower. The sound of running water ceased. She had heard him curse at the pain behind his eye.

Before he could answer he tripped over his shoes. His jacket and tie were hung on a chair beside them. He looked down and saw he was still wearing his shirt and pants. The cuffs on his sleeves had been unbuttoned.

"There's breakfast in the kitchen." Lilly leaned into the room as she pulled on a robe. "And coffee."

She smiled without using her eyes. Lepov did the same in reply. He began to roll up his sleeves. "Am I the only one here?"

She nodded, her eyes said she didn't understand the question.

"I just thought.—never mind. I'll pour you some coffee." He left from the bedroom and shut the door.

Chewing on a piece of dry toast, he sipped at black coffee until she joined him. He liked the bitter taste of coffee. It hit his stomach with all the compassion of an abusive step-father, forcing him to wake up enough to fight off the urge to spit it back up.

When she walked in and sat at the table, she was dressed with her hair held back in her usual pony-tail which seemed to rise straight from the top of her head. The coffee he'd poured for her had already grown cold but he knew she wouldn't care. She never hesitated to drink it, even at room temperature.

"I was just sitting here wondering how much fun we had last night."

"It's always fun with you, Gregor. Especially when you wake me in the middle of the night to tell me your amusing dreams."

"I know, but if memory serves me right, I did try to warn you."

A small collection of containers sat in the middle of the table. Lilly's long fingers closed over one and she slipped off its cap and slid two small capsules towards Lepov.

"Take these."

"I haven't had a decent night's sleep in weeks and you're worried about me taking vitamins. Even my wife wasn't this thoughtful."

"You don't ever see sunlight, Gregor. Fatigue, depression, I've told you all of this before. You don't sleep because you live in hell."

"I don't sleep because every time I close my eyes some crazy little fiend keeps coming after me. Speaking of wives and fiends, you know two nights ago *she* was in my dream?"

"Which *she*?" Lilly picked up the capsules and forced Lepov to take them in his hand.

"My wife."

The room grew alarmingly silent as Lepov tried not to look at Lilly. He had never said much about his ex-wife before. He'd let Lilly know early on that he wouldn't talk about her. In her usual way, she'd accepted that without comment. But now he knew he'd have to say something. It wasn't fair to weigh her down with his latest trials without telling her what it was all about.

"What's her name?" It was a simple question that Lilly had to ask with the greatest care. Lepov could tell she knew that to ask the question was to break their rules, but he could also see that she wasn't going to let him hide behind those rules anymore. He tossed the capsules in his mouth and dry-swallowed them.

"Her name was Gloria."

"You mean is—her name is Gloria."

"No, she's past tense now. Always was, always will be. Even when she was with me. I just didn't know it."

Lilly didn't ask what he meant only because she obviously expected him to continue.

"You probably think there's some big mystery here. Some sad, deep little story that will leave you in tears for me."

"I don't think about it one way or the other, Gregor. I do know, however, that most stories like this aren't interesting to anyone except for the husband and wife."

"You're one to talk. You've got a story that's better than any I've heard before. Not every woman turns her husband in for smuggling."

"But in the end, it's just another story of two young people who break their promise. That's not only boring, it's common." Lilly lifted her chin, and for that moment, Lepov could see she resented him for bringing Shay into their conversation.

"Gloria was common too. She married a boy she knew little about, but quickly learned she didn't find him the least bit interesting. The kind of girl who didn't know when I came home and didn't care."

"Ran off with the plumber?" Lilly's question carried a hint of malice. She'd been hurt by his comment about Shay more than he'd realized.

"No, she didn't run off. She very logically sat me down and told me one day that she had concluded there had to be someone out there that would be more interesting than me. Point of fact, she was fairly sure than anyone would be more interesting."

"And that was it?" Her eyes had softened and the coldness had left her voice.

"Not a chance. She then set about looking for someone. Stayed with me until she found him. When she left, he came to the house and helped her load up her things. When he asked for help carrying a few pieces of furniture he couldn't handle on his own, I actually think I smiled and said 'no problem'. The furniture had been one of our first big purchases. We'd spent hours picking it out. I helped him load it up in less than ten minutes."

"That's not boring, Gregor." Lilly leaned forward and touched his hand. "That's lousy. What was the dream about?"

"I was back at the window."

"And Gloria was attacking you instead of Chitti?"

"No, Gloria was in your role, she was bleeding, crying out for my help. Pleading. Begging."

"And did you help her?"

"No. I couldn't, really, but that wasn't the part that disturbed me. When I woke up, I knew that even if I could have, I wouldn't have. I would have let her bleed to death right there. I would have let her go on and on, whimpering, screaming for me. I even knew what I wanted to say to her. Knew I wanted to ask her why she suddenly found me so interesting. I liked the way that felt."

"Maybe you were right to ignore her." Lilly stood up and set their plates in the sink. "Don't let it worry you. It was only a dream."

The talk of spouses left Lepov wondering just what he and Lilly had become. Despite his crack about their having fun during the night, he knew well and good that if he'd awakened in Lilly's bed, she had either been up the rest of the night after he'd fallen asleep, or she'd gone to sleep in her front room. It wasn't that they were too old to feel the lure of physical desire, but they'd both grown old enough to recognize that neither one of them was interested in those kinds of complications.

At least Lepov was sure that Lilly had. His own views on the subject were less than definitive.

But in the absence of adolescent romance, Lepov had found Lilly to be a necessity in life, much like a roof over his head in bad weather. She was more than just companionship. She was balance. Something was always wrong when she wasn't there.

"Tell me to keep my problems to myself and I won't show up like this again." Holding his coat on one arm, he rubbed at his peppered short hair with his free hand, wishing he hadn't left his hat back at his place. His hesitation at the door, and his offer to stay away, was more than just an attempt to hear her say she wanted him to come back at any time. He didn't need her to insist he return. He just wanted to hear something in her voice that would assure him that she did not think he had lost his mind—that his torment held no substance.

He wanted to know that she understood his ghosts were real.

"Show up like that again, and I'll call the cops and claimed you raped me and I'll send you to prison like my last lover."

Lepov walked towards the stairs with a smile. It was more than he had hoped for. Not only did she understand, but she wanted him back.

 8

The IHS men, with no show of warmth or concern, acquiesced when asked if they would allow Lara and Frank time to change the boy out of his pajamas and into warm clothes. Though the words were unspoken, Lara knew the men wanted them to hurry. She didn't care what they wanted. She took her time. Frank must have sensed her mood as well as the two officials; no one dared speed her along.

"Wait," she said, as Frank picked up Jett and turned for the door. There was no reason to say it. She had dressed the child in nearly everything she could think of. She almost broke into tears when her mind formed the thought—*don't want him to catch anything*. But what had he already caught?

"Did you forget something?" Frank's arms were wrapped around the boy and for a moment, she saw him as an abductor, not the boy's father. The mother in her became something more, rattling her with anger, readying her to grapple with the enemy.

And then she saw fear in her husband's eyes, something she'd never seen before. Her attempt to think of an excuse—anything to keep Frank from taking Jett out that door—had failed as soon as she focused on his eyes. If Frank could look that afraid, how terrified must she look? And what would Jett think of it all if he realized both of his parents were too petrified to face what was coming?

They followed the men out, Frank holding Jett, Lara walking a step behind them, her hand lightly touching the small of Frank's back. By the time they reached the street, she had found a more balanced rhythm to her breathing, despite the cold air that hit them all. An IHS vehicle awaited them and the cold was shut out for a time as it whisked them along the empty streets of Alpha Quadrant.

It seemed odd to Lara that the streets should be so empty. Though it was early morning, there should have been people out heading to work. Several blocks rushed by her window before she realized her mistake. This was a quarantine zone. Few people had jobs to attend. No one wanted to mingle with their neighbors. Public gatherings would be non-existent.

Chills attacked her as a picture formed in her mind. There was no living in the Lazaretto Quarantine—only hiding. There could only be a sort of suspended animation as each traveler held his or her breath, wondering if they would ever get a chance to leave this hard, cold, nether world. Wary shadows of what were once men and women would cling to their hiding places, determined to conceal themselves from bad luck and cruel fate.

If Lara had realized it sooner it wouldn't have mattered. They could have done nothing different to change what had happened. If Jett tested positive for any one of the communicable diseases that would trap him in the Lazaretto, it would have been cruel fate indeed; the worst luck imaginable.

And just maybe it was simply her imagination. She was

overreacting as only a mother could. Perhaps the IHS men were only bringing him in to clear up a clerical error. A test sample might have been contaminated. Or even dropped on the floor. Surely that type of thing could happen? Perhaps more than one would ever guess?

They would know soon enough. The white, clean—irritatingly sanitized—vehicle rushed to a stop outside a glistening façade that was IHS Alpha Central. The sterile letters gleamed impossibly above the building's doors. In this dingy, grayed-out world, the International Health Service stood out like a beacon of goodwill and order. For the first time since they'd arrived the night before, Lara began to hope that her family would be safe.

Inside, the feeling intensified. Their escorts, men who had seemed more like prison guards than health officials had softened once everyone had passed through the entrance doors. Their faces, devoid of all emotion during the ride through the Quadrant, took on expressions of care as they steered the Dassins to a set of free-standing seats.

"If you will please wait here, Mr. and Mrs. Dassin, someone will be with you as soon as possible. Would you like something to drink? Something for the boy, maybe?"

Frank said no. Lara shook her head. She was eager to allow the men to withdraw and leave them alone. Both men did just that, disappearing as soon as they were assured that the Dassins were in need of nothing.

It seemed like Lara had been right. They had been brought here to clear up a mistake. This explained the men's odd, detached behavior. Someone had made a mistake, and no one wanted to be associated with it. Frank shrugged as she suggested the possibility.

"Don't you think I'm right?" she asked.

"Maybe."

"Don't do that," she took his hand and squeezed it. "You're the optimist in this little family. If you can't be positive right now, we're in real trouble."

"Okay, I won't do that. Now that you mention it, I think you're right. This is someone's lame attempt to cover up their mistake."

"Me too." Lara reached over and stroked Jett's mess of sandy hair. "Just a simple mistake. Dear God, please let it only be a mistake."

"Just a mistake, Babe."

She loved Frank for lying to her. He knew how much she needed that. Of course he wasn't deceiving her, just giving her something to focus on other than her own easily nurtured doubts. It was the reason she'd so quickly fallen in love with him. He felt no innate, masculine need to force his wife to face reality. He knew she understood the real world all too well. Knew that she would face up to it as soon as it was necessary.

And in this she would as well. The bright, ordered world of the IHS had momentarily lifted her out of reality and allowed her a respite from the despair that had begun to envelope her. She wanted that. Wanted it to last as long as possible. Taking Jett from Frank's arms, she cradled her child as if he were only five months old instead of five years. She would hold him, and hold on to that slim hope for as long as she was allowed.

It had to be a mistake. Because if it was not a mistake, then even Lara couldn't ignore the fact that their life had just been stolen from them.

9

The New Yorker sat in the wide, soft chair, glad that at least the chair was comfortable. The Australian was talking, which was one of his strongest traits. It did not matter what he talked about. It did not matter that the New Yorker knew the Australian was spinning stories that could never be true. What did matter was that the Australian expected him to sit and listen, regardless of what was being said.

And so he did. He tried to pay attention. He tried to nod when it seemed appropriate. He would even make an occasional comment.

At the moment, the Australian was explaining how disappointed he was that the men had failed.

"I can't understand how that happens. It's a simple thing. You have to move fast. Before your mark knows you're coming. When I was just starting out, I did that sort of thing for my first employer. Six years I was his enforcer. You can't do something that dangerous for that long if you make mistakes. But if you stick with simple, well-defined procedures, you don't make mistakes."

The New Yorker, despite his efforts to appear to be listening, wasn't believing a word of it. The last time the Australian had spoken of his first employer, he'd said he was his driver. The time before that, he had said something about a five year stint as his employer's legal counsel. All of these jobs he claimed to have during his first years in the business.

If the New Yorker had charted it all out, the man would either have to be ninety years old or he was clearly lying. And the New Yorker knew perfectly well the Australian was only fifty years old.

"Now I can't complain about the men you sent. At least I had better not complain about them. They're good men. Family. Don't I know it?"

Damned right he'd better not complain. The Australian had all but ordered the New Yorker to use those men. Nepotism wasn't just a problem for the police.

"What I'm saying is that someone tipped off at least two of these guys. You can't tell me otherwise. It's as plain as day. So what we gotta do is find out who it is. Who do you think it might be?"

This was a trick question and the New Yorker wasn't going to get caught by it. As with any operation like this, very few people knew what was going to happen. The only people who knew were the Englishman, the Australian, and the men — the *family men* — who were sent. There was only one safe suggestion to make: The Englishman.

"Yeah, I think that's possible," the Australian nodded. "But why would he do it? He came to us. Without him we might not have known who to go after. Including him. So why would he tip off the very people he double-crossed?"

At that moment, a young man dressed in a white suit entered the room. He paused until he was asked to approach. With a nod, he handed the New Yorker a screenpad.

More bad news. The Swede had disappeared as well. The artifact was still missing.

"You see what I mean?" The Australian was getting angry. His amiable chatter slowed, his full face grew red. His eyes bore into his right hand man. "Somebody, somewhere, is playing games with me. And it has been my experience that games never end without somebody getting killed. Know what I mean?"

The New Yorker knew what he meant. His boss had a very limited sense of humor, and an even more limited sense of fair play.

"He conspires to steal from me. He comes to me then and wants to double-cross his partners and return my property. At no cost, keep that in mind. So now, when I send in my people to complete the deal, someone tips them off, helps them get away from me. That's just stupid. You know?"

Yeah. He knew.

MacNally knew his nose wasn't really itching. But what did that matter? It felt like it was itching. And only because the decon suit had a hard-cover over his face. It hadn't started itching until the seal had been set on the suit.

Russell smiled at him from his own decon suit. MacNally was damn sure not going to let the kid know how bad he wanted to scratch his nose.

The open-air shuttler slowed down as it approached the site where the body awaited them. As it came to a stop, the whine of its teardrop engine ceased, and MacNally shook his head to clear it out of his ears. The decon suit provided amplified sound and it was already giving MacNally a headache. This was a prime example of why he wouldn't wear hearing aids. Sure you could better hear what people were saying but you also were assaulted with every little damned sound that tore through the air around you.

"Detective Edward MacNally." A quadrant cop, *not* in a decon suit, looked up at the shuttler with a big grin on his face.

"Don't look so surprised, Greenie. You guys call for help, and here I am." MacNally climbed out of the shuttler with a noticeable lack of grace. The decon suit was heavy, and not originally made for standard gravity.

"You've put on some weight." Greenie watched with amusement.

"Now that's real humor, Greenie. You hear that Russell? Take notes. That's the way to prove to the world how simple-minded you are." He shook hands with Bob Green, a long-time quadrant veteran who'd been a rookie with MacNally back in their youth. "Long time. You been okay?"

"Wondering what I'm still doing here." He pointed towards the alley and guided the two unwieldy detectives in that direction. "You heard that my wife died, yeah?"

MacNally managed to nod enough that the gesture was seen outside his bulky shell.

"Well, we knew it was coming, you know. She'd had it for maybe seven or eight years. Just took its time. We had more than enough time to say goodbye. So why do I stay here in this crummy job? That's my point."

MacNally understood. The man's wife had come down with cancer of the liver and it had taken her an inordinate amount of time to die. Treatments weren't readily available in the Lazaretto, and although cancers were not controlled by the quarantine policy, she had elected to stay on the quarantine moon. From what MacNally had heard, Greenie had tried to force her to leave but she had refused. She wouldn't leave him or their home. And now that she was dead, Greenie was still there, doing the same thing that had consigned his partner to her death.

The man had little choice in the matter. He did not make enough money to retire early, and the stigma that clung to any Lazaretto worker ensured that no one would hire him on one of the Euxine planets, let alone anyone on Earth.

"You stay because this place would fall apart without you, Greenie."

"You hear that Russell?" Greenie winked at the youngster.

"Take notes. That's the way to prove to the world how big a liar you are."

The alley was nearly as wide as a street, littered with dumpsters, vac-bins, and even a stranded freight sled. Above them, black iron shapes clung precariously to the brick and mortar walls on the north side. The south side looked as if it were a single slick wall of glass, eerily reflecting the iron across from it.

Thirty yards into the alley, two quadrant cops formed a barrier of sorts whose purpose was to keep out the curious. This was, however, a quarantine quadrant, and no one in their right mind would have considered coming near a dead body. Even the officers had positioned themselves far from the actual site of the corpse. They made no effort to stop the two decon suits from advancing further into the alley.

"We've got it, Greenie. You can hang back." MacNally put out a hand to block Greenie's forward momentum.

"What the hell for?" he asked, pushing MacNally's heavily gloved hand aside.

MacNally turned to look at his former fellow rookie. In the suit it required more of an effort. It was never a good sign when someone in the Lazaretto began to ignore precautions when dealing with possible contagions. It was like seeing a friend wander into heavy traffic. Like watching a friend play Russian Roulette.

"Bob, hold up. We got it."

"Mac," Greenie pulled away from MacNally's attempt to grab him, "I ain't that far gone. Not trying to go out before my time. Not yet. But I'm the one who found him. And I was right on top of him before I saw him. If he's contagious, it won't matter how much I stay away from him now. But this wasn't a pathogen. Least I don't think so."

"Well, if you don't think so..." the sarcasm was heavy enough that MacNally did not need to finish the quip.

"IHS been here?" Russell asked.

"Oh yeah, you know it. IHS never misses their chance to lick and stick the dead."

Lick and stick the dead was not a technical term. It was, however, a fairly accurate description. IHS officers first laid an adhesive strip on the neck of the corpse. After a count of fifteen it was removed, often taking with it more than just a chemical profile of the skin. After sealing the strip in a plastic envelope, the official would stick a hypodermic needle into the same area of the flesh and extract two vials of blood.

Lazaretto protocol was unique at a crime scene. If a body could not categorically be identified as a murder victim it first had to be sampled and removed for testing. The threat of disease—whether from virus, pathogen, or biological origin—had to be assessed and identified immediately. Even if a detective declared a death to be homicide, the on-site IHS representative had to sign a waiver releasing the body to the police. Tests would be conducted on the blood and the skin swatch at IHS, but the body would be taken to the police lab for the investigation.

"And since you're gonna ask, one of yours came in and handled the Visuals already."

Crime scene visuals were taken with a multistage camera that recorded six aspects, or levels, of the crime scene. Aspects one and two were a range of physical surface images that allowed investigators to view all images at their original aspect or magnified up to 48 times their original size. The clarity of the magnification was dependent on the High Data rate used in the recording. The greater the HD rate, the deeper the visuals were taken. But for each increased level of HD there was a corresponding increase in the cost to process the larger storage cells. The remaining four aspects recorded thermal images, chemical scans, CT scans, and radiation scans.

Chemical scans could tell an investigator the exact chemical makeup of any substance found at the scene. CT scans allowed them to see beneath the layers that could not be seen by the naked eye. Radiation scans were most often used to determine the rate of decomposition, the age of anything at the scene, as well as chronological sequences of injuries or damage.

"This some kind of holy day or something?" MacNally reached up and touched his clear faceplate instead of his nose. "Everybody's so efficient all of a sudden? Makes me feel slow and useless."

"They were just in a hurry to beat lockdown. Didn't want to don the decon suits. At any rate, this guy is all yours."

"And why is that, Greenie? This guy could have just been a jumper."

"Nah, it don't fit. Take your time, Mac. You'll see why we called you."

MacNally took his time. He had recently been allowing Russell to take the lead on cases like this in order to force-feed him some experience. But not this time. MacNally not only wanted to make sure there were no mistakes to avoid the necessity of coming back into the quarantine, but he also wanted to make sure they finished as quickly as possible. Not only was the decon killing him, he needed a cigarette more than he needed to scratch his nose.

The body lay on its right hip, the torso twisted so that the chest and both shoulders touched the ground. The head was twisted back to the left, resting on the right side of its prominent square jaw and cheekbone. The mouth was slightly open, as if the corpse were making a token gesture to take in one last breath. Back down the body, the legs stacked neatly, knees locked straight. The arms were trapped beneath the torso as if they had been hidden away in an effort to hinder identification.

The body was fully clothed: a synthetic suit, cheap but respectable.

"No PDT?" MacNally wished he could take off the decon for just a few moments, to smell the alley, judge the amount of humidity and mildew in the air.

MacNally tugged at the neck seal on his decon. He looked back down the alley the distant officers. It must have been obvious what he was thinking because Greenie put a hand to his shoulder and shook his head.

"Don't, Mac. We may not be hotshot detectives, but we take this damn lockdown seriously. If you break that seal, this place will go nuts. You remember the last time a quadrant had to break lockdown and restart? You might not end up fired over it, but I would be."

"Yeah, I know. I remember." MacNally shook his head and growled. "Doesn't do me any good to be here without being able to see and hear and smell this place. I might as well be back at the precinct watching it all on Videoscreens."

"At any rate, no, there was no PDT. And we did a basic scan on this guy, he's beat up pretty bad."

"So you assume murder." MacNally knelt beside the body.

"Actually, I assume he hit the ironwork above us on the way down." Greenie nodded, "but keep looking."

"How the hell am I suppose to look at anything?" MacNally tried to turn to one side to look at Greenie and nearly lost his balance. Russell grabbed his wrist to steady him. "I suppose I might see what you're hinting at eventually, but I'm not gonna stay in this lead-weight decon suit any longer than I have to."

"Turn around and face the bricks." Greenie did a poor job of hiding his amusement. "I'll help you."

MacNally looked like a baby unsure of his newly acquired pivot skills. With one foot locked to the ground, he swung precariously around. The large helmet he wore only added to the image.

"Now look down."

"Para-Lazar." MacNally's heavy boot had nearly stepped on a silver-plated Para-Lazar. He reached out a hand but did not bother attempting to bend down to actually touch the weapon. "This belong to the corpse?"

"We don't know that yet. We did check it for numbers. As you can guess, its signal has been jacked. Yet another example of the pointlessness of weapons ID regulations. Any bad guy with half a brain knows how to jack a signal."

"Well, we know that, but it keeps politicians and professors happy."

"Which seems important." Greenie produced a mock look of sobriety for Russell before continuing. "I also had them put the Para-Lazar back in the exact same position for you. But let me give you some specifics:

"Techs found four scorch marks off to your right, on the brick wall. They also identified one behind you, on the glass. A very weak signature. Above, on the fire escape, not this one, the one to the left of us, we found a scorch mark on the iron landing. There, that first level. There were no other signs of weapons fire."

"So," MacNally carefully turned his head to take in the alley as he thought through the shots. "Maybe it started down here. Fires four times at someone…"

"Or someone fired at him four times." Russell offered.

"What direction were the shots, Greenie?"

"Techs said it came from here. Shots went out, toward the end of the alley.

"Like I said," MacNally repeated, "fires four times at someone. Then he gets up on this fire escape, to the left. I would guess the marks on the shot on that first landing were fairly extensive?"

"Yeah, they made a mess of the iron."

"Right, but not a full charge. He was firing close. At someone coming up after him."

"The hit on the glass?" Greenie prompted him.

"A wide shot, from up on the iron." MacNally leaned back, straining to see the top of the escape. "Is there a way I can get up there to the top?"

"There's no elevator." Greenie eyed him with one good eye closed tight. "You want to walk up all those stairs?"

"How about someone else goes up there with a camera and gives me video of everything."

"Now that sounds like a good idea." Russell patted MacNally on the back of his decon suit. "For once, I like your ideas, old man."

"That was the wrong comment." Greenie shook his head.

"Don't worry, sir. I knew he meant me. I would have been insulted if he hadn't suggested it." Russell tried to walk away with as much grace as he could muster. MacNally knew Russell was simply trying to annoy him. Watching him exit the alley, MacNally knew that his young partner had succeeded.

"Is he a good detective?"

MacNally turned just enough to make eye contact with his former comrade. He nodded.

"And how about you? Are you a good detective, MacNally? Can you tell this guy didn't just jump?"

"I will concede it is in no way a clear case of suicide. Someone was out here with him. After that, it is hard to know what happened. But we'll give it some attention. And I'll get back to you."

"That's what we wanted to hear," Greenie put out his hand and grabbed MacNally by the shoulder. "Let's get you out of here, and out of this suit."

They stood back as a team of MedTechs arrived to collect the body. MacNally could see their breath as they set up the gurney and prepared to load the body onto it. MacNally had to admit the decons had one sure benefit. They were self-heating, and neither he nor Russell could feel the sharp cold of the morning.

Again, his hand went to his nose and found instead the faceplate. Frustrated, he rubbed the clear plate and tried to imagine he could feel it on the tip of his nose.

Settling into the chair behind his desk, Lepov laid his head back and briefly considered killing the office lights and waiting to see if he would fall asleep. He had no clients to appease, and he could shut down the office door, no one would know he was there. It wasn't like he was dying for a job.

He had forced himself from the start to show up early at his office regardless of his client list in an attempt to alleviate the lethargic spirit of the Lazaretto. To date, it rarely helped. Sitting in an empty office inspired depths of lethargy that Lepov had never known existed. At least back on Bukovina, the sun occasionally shone through a window, encouraging one to feel alive and look sharp. But in the Laz, where the sun never penetrated its abominable atmosphere, Lepov never even felt inspired to clean his windows.

He closed his eyes and tried to make a decision — make coffee, or let himself fall asleep. Coffee was tempting. There was no guarantee that he could actually fall asleep; or stay asleep. Why did he think he could sleep in the office when he couldn't sleep through the night in his apartment?

The thought of Lilly's bed came to mind and he allowed it to linger there. Waking up there was a habit he wouldn't mind developing. She was comfortable. She set the world right, even when he knew it wasn't.

Gloria had felt the same way. Even more. What made him think that Lilly would turn out any different than Gloria had?

Lepov stood up to make coffee. He sure wasn't going to mope all day about an ex-wife.

His coffee machine, an ancient boiler that never actually boiled the water unless Lepov only filled the pot halfway, struggled to reach a temperature above tepid. He'd been told it had something to do with the fact it had been designed and manufactured on Phasis, or maybe even Earth. It wasn't intended to operate in the Lazaretto's atmosphere. The pressure was a little higher here.

Lepov knew exactly how the coffee machine felt.

Before he could pour a cup, his door opened, and Lepov watched a real honest-to-God client walk through the door. Well, Lepov would have to hold judgment on just how honest-to-God he was, but the man did at least appear to be a possible client.

"You're Lepov?" The man stood in the doorway, as if reserving the right to turn and flee.

"Sure, that's my last name. Step all the way in the room and I'll tell you my first name."

The man took two steps inside, each step evidently painful. He pulled his hat off his head, wincing as if he were pulling off a bandage that had dried against a bloody cut. The door, now free of his interference, swung shut. The man jumped at the sound.

"I'm Gregor Lepov. Coffee's fresh, just not very hot," Lepov held out a cup in one hand and offered the man his other hand. It was Lepov's way of quickly sizing up a man in the Lazaretto. If he declined to shake hands with any hint of shame, he had been labeled with a pathogen. If he indignantly refused, it meant he was terrified of catching a disease. If he declined to shake hands with a dignified apology he was reasonably cautious. If he shook hands quickly he was a risk-taker, but no fool. If he accepted the handshake and returned it with a firm, even pump, it meant he was intelligent enough to realize that Lepov was clean and there was nothing to fear. If he shook Lepov's hand without the slightest hesitation and pumped it again and again, then the man was either reckless or just a plain idiot.

The reluctant man stared at Lepov's hand and deliberately stuck his hands in his pocket. Lepov would have won a bet on that response.

"No offense intended, of course," the man mumbled.

"None taken, sir. I'm not fond of coffee at this temperature either." Lepov poured the whole cup of coffee down his throat and set the cup on his deskscreen which powered up on contact. The man jerked back and Lepov thought he was going to back straight through the closed door.

"You need to take a few deep breaths and get a hold of your

nerves, then tell me your name and tell me what's got you so jumpy." Lepov sat down and gestured for the other man to do the same.

"Do you believe in ghosts, Mr. Lepov?"

"Let's just start with your name. After that we can share religious beliefs and metaphysical observations."

"I'm Miklos Nerrudah." He finally dropped into the chair Lepov had indicated, jamming himself in one corner of it. "Do you, Mr. Lepov? Believe in ghosts?"

"There's a few I wouldn't mind running into, and a few I hope to never meet in a dark alley. Is this a metaphysical discussion or metaphorical?" He tried not to think about Chitti and his dream. She was no ghost. Just a bad aftertaste.

"You're making jokes, Mr. Lepov. You obviously don't believe. I should leave." He grabbed the armrests and leaned forward.

"You can leave, Mr. Nerrudah, but I doubt that's going to help you any. Like I said before, take some deep breaths and calm down. Then let's have a logical discussion about whatever it is that's got you so wound up."

To his credit, the man tried to take a deep breath. He didn't do so well but he got better at it after the second and third try. It gave Lepov time to examine his nervous visitor.

Miklos Nerrudah was white-skinned, pale like a man who's spent his life in deep space. Lepov had known trade-sailors who'd been in stasis more years than they'd been awake. Guys from the old days whose ships had not been equipped with artificial solar rays. Nerrudah's skin wasn't quite as mucus-colored, but it was close. Like ice, it was stark white on the inside and nearly translucent at the edges. His thin hair could have been drawn on the crown of his head with a black marker.

"I made the most terrible mistake, Mr. Lepov. I've—I've killed my son. I know I have. I've seen him—his ghost."

"Let's stay logical, Mr. Nerrudah. Pretend I don't know what you're talking about and tell me the whole story."

"My son was stuck here. *Nullus Exitus*. But it was a mistake! He wasn't sick!" He squeezed his hat and it looked like he was going to tear a hole in it. "A clerical error, you know? A victim of a cruel joke!"

"Aren't we all, Mr. Nerrudah?"

"He's only seventeen years old. Seventeen! I couldn't allow him to be stuck here for the rest of his life. I had to do something. And I did. I met a man. He said he could get Nikosz out. He would be free. It was expensive, but that was okay, he was my son!"

The man's attempts to justify his actions were coming out in a torrent that Lepov didn't care to hear. So the man had done something stupid. He'd been taken in, sure, but willingly. Lazaretto officials spent a great deal of time warning travelers and exiles on the many scams that they would encounter. This Nerrudah could never claim that he hadn't been aware of the dangers of his actions. And Lepov didn't care either way.

"Just tell me what happened, Mr. Nerrudah." Lepov stopped the man from spouting more excuses. "He said they could smuggle him out. You paid him. Why do you think your son is dead?"

"He's appeared to me. I've seen him, continue to see him. He stares at me. Begs me undo it. I know what he wants. He wants to come back, to never leave. Knows he's dead because I trusted the wrong men!"

"How long ago did you give him to them?"

"A week." Nerrudah's voice faltered.

"He'll probably show up — where were they taking him?"

"Arcobia."

"Well, that's no comfort to any father, I'll admit. But give it time. They can't just land at the first Arcobian port and announce the boy's arrival. It takes time for this kind of thing to happen."

"You aren't listening. He's dead. I've seen him. I want you to find these men and kill them." Nerrudah's eyes, until then wide with fear, narrowed under black hatred.

"I don't believe in ghosts, Mr. Nerrudah. That was your first question. And since the rest of your — request hinges on that belief, I will have to politely turn down your proposition. I also don't believe in revenge. And I sure as hell won't kill someone based on your silly mistakes and superstitions. Get out."

It was the closest Lepov could get to politely turning down the man's offensive proposal. The man had screwed up so badly his son might be dead. But that was no reason to drag Lepov into a cock-eyed plan to murder those responsible. If that's what Nerrudah really wanted, fairness, then Lepov would be justified in killing Nerrudah. Eye for an eye. Sure, Lepov had killed men before, in self-defense, but he had never gone out of his way to murder a man for the sake of revenge.

It was becoming a habit for Lilly. A few hours into her day and she began to feel restless.

The bleak world of the Lazaretto was not the cause of her discontent. She had never felt the effects of its unwelcoming atmosphere nor its psychological detriment that so easily eroded the vast majority that dared to descend upon its slopes. This was no testament to an unflagging optimism or an extraordinary *joie de vivre* on her part. Optimism played as little a part in her life as pessimism. Neither one nor the other was a factor in her daily perspective. And no one had ever accused her of possessing a joy of life. Quite the contrary. She had been accused of being a cold woman: a woman who knew neither love nor passion.

There was truth in that, Lilly knew. But there was the added irony that a cold woman had a much better chance of surviving the Lazaretto.

Lilly only began to regret her life in the Lazaretto when she began to think of how much she missed her nomadic life among the planets of the Aegean system. The freedom to change scenery, to move from the supercities of Phasis to the underground communities of Arcobia.

The wall panel beside her front door announced a visitor and Lilly brushed her pony-tail by hand. A quick check in the mirror confirmed that she looked presentable.

"Good morning, Pete."

"Morning, Lilly." Pete Landon stepped into her apartment with his ever-present smile. His own great head of hair looked as if he'd ridden on the roof of a SubTransit on his way across town.

"Cold morning, too." Lilly scolded him with the same tone she'd used on Lepov hours earlier. "Don't men know how to dress around here? Why aren't you wearing a coat?"

"I don't need a coat, love, I've got you, and you've got coffee." He leaned forward and kissed her pony-tail where it seemed to sprout out the top of her head, then he pushed passed her and headed for the kitchen.

"You too?"

"Me too what?" he called from the kitchen.

"I don't need another man to get fresh with me this morning. Make me a cup while you're at it." Lilly sat at the table and watched him pour both cups.

"Another man?" Pete paused in mid-pour. "Lepov ought to be ashamed of himself, making fresh with my boss."

"And Sun would be ashamed of you for the same thing." She accepted the cup from him. "Thank you, young man."

"Thank you, boss, for both reminding me I'm just a youngster to you as well as reminding me that my real love is far away."

"Poor, poor, Pete."

Technically, Lilly was not Pete's boss. Pete was still employed with the Lazaretto police. Known as Puzzle Pete, Landon was an underachieving beat cop who'd been pulled from the streets when it had been brought to his superiors' attention that he was a puzzle whiz. His name was a misnomer; he didn't play at old-fashioned jigsaw puzzles. He was a word sleuth and numbers wizard.

With the math skills of a professor, and the word skills of a linguistic genius, Pete had no desire to make a living from either one of his gifts. He enjoyed being a cop, and spent his off days solving meaningless puzzles. He had been forced to leave his patrolman's position by the Precinct's Captain. From Pete's point of view, the increased stress from a job with greater responsibility was never worth the increase in pay. It was a simple equation that Pete could see clearly in his head. But the Captain had refused to take no for an answer. Before long, Pete was working special assignments puzzling out innumerable enigmas for nearly every department at the Precinct. Secretly, he loved it.

As often happens to men who are happy in their singular lives, a woman had come along and changed everything. Pete had befriended a young Army officer named Sun Uijong. They had met and become friends during the woman's convalescence after she had nearly been murdered by Chitti Sienté, the same she-devil that had been plaguing Gregor's dreams.

Pete was now looking to find a job outside of the Lazaretto, in order to join Sun in a healthier atmosphere. It was one of the reasons Lilly had been able to quit traveling abroad. She had hired Pete to take her place. She would still conduct most of the research needed to locate and acquire the antiquities that she handled for her clients, but now Pete could do the field work.

Pete was about to relocate to Beta Quadrant, which was only a few days from going into lockdown. Once he was out of the Lazaretto, he would first travel to Phasis to meet with several clients, then go on to Arcobia in order to physically locate the pieces their clients were seeking.

"Are you still sure about this?" she asked him.

"I'm not about to back out. This is really what I want." He stood up, unable to sit still with his usual energy. "It's a funny feeling, having been lethargic in life for so long, to suddenly need to get moving. But I can't stay here. And I can't ask Sun to come and live here, not after what happened. Besides, she shouldn't be here. It's not the place for a woman."

There was no awkward pause after he had said it. Lilly knew what he meant and took no offense. Pete did not need to explain himself. Sun was a gentle spirit that needed sunlight and goodwill. She had proven to be tougher than expected, but it had not been her nature.

"I wondered if you showing up here meant you were changing your mind. I guess not." Lilly led him into the main room and sat down at a large, charita style desk. She had bought it for a client on

Bukovina, but the client had died before she could move it through the Lazaretto. It was not her personal style, the large hand-carved rosettes were a bit much, but it was well designed for efficiency.

"Actually, I was worried about you." Pete dropped down on her sofa and kicked his feet up on one of the cushions. He lay back and stared at the ceiling. "I'm about to go into work and resign. I wanted to make sure you hadn't changed your mind."

"I am making the final entry on your account. The money will be transferred within the next few minutes. You are, Pete Landon, now obligated to make this trip."

"What I'll never understand is why you and Lepov decided not to leave. You were there, in the quadrant, ready to get out—"

"Call it nostalgia, Pete. This is where we met. Maybe you could say we just felt it was right to be here."

"Maybe I'd say I thought you were crazy."

"Isn't that the usual definition of love?"

"Hmm," Pete closed his eyes, mulling over her words, "I suppose. But it doesn't seem to be the sort of thing I'd expect from you. Lepov, yeah, I could see it. But not you, Lilly."

Lilly knew Pete would never fully understand their decision since he did not have all the facts. She did not, however, wish to correct that. This was just one puzzle he would have to give up on.

And he did. She enjoyed listening to him chatter on about his plans to reunite with Sun.

At some point while he was talking she had stood up from the desk and made her way to the front windows. Below, she could see the dingy street between the overshadowing buildings. For a moment, she was shocked to see a man who closely resembled her ex-husband Shay Stewart. It was impossible to even consider that it was actually Shay on the street. She was seven stories up, the air was heavy with mist, and the surrounding gloom did not allow for any sunlight to force its way through the cloud cover.

Pete must have noticed her reaction and asked her if she was all right.

"Just a man down there that looks like Shay. It's nothing." Lilly lifted her head and gazed across the street. She could see herself reflected in the opposite window, the light of her apartment creating a silhouette that was highlighted by her pony-tail. And then, taking her by surprise, she saw another outline beside her, and for a brief, terrible moment, she knew it was Shay.

This time, Pete could not have missed her reaction as she moaned as if in pain.

"Lilly!" Pete jumped up and rushed to her side.

"It's nothing. Nothing." Lilly could still see two figures in the reflection, though now the second figure was Pete.

"Did you say you saw Shay? He's your ex-husband, isn't that right?"

Lilly backed away from the window and did not answer until she had found a place to sit. Then she could only nod.

"He's in prison in orbit around Sinop, right?"

"Yes, the Conde Sur prison holds—and he's not eligible for parole. He is where he'll always be. I was just seeing things, you know? It doesn't mean anything." She was lying and he had to know it. Her hands were shaking. She slid them between her legs and the chair seat and still she could feel them quiver.

"What a mess we are," she said softly. Here she was imagining Shay had been standing beside her, an apparition brought on by Gregor's incident with the phantom of his ex-wife combined with a lack of sleep. To be sure, she went back to the window and searched the street.

"Are you sure you're okay?" Pete watched her intently. "You really look as though you've seen a ghost. Did you see him?"

"No, I told you, it couldn't be him."

"Parole is not impossible. Even at Conde Sur. Jeez, Lilly, you look scared to death. Would this guy be dangerous?"

"Well, I sent him to prison. Husbands don't usually like that." She did not see anyone on the street that even resembled him. She had to summon willpower to lift her head and look at her reflection. But when she did, there was no sign of Shay there either.

"Would I have been informed if he had been paroled?" Lilly began to doubt her insistence that he would never be paroled.

"Well, that's not easy to say." Pete, slipping into the mode of a policeman, began to speak in a more measured tone. "Depending on the circumstances, his evaluation profile upon exit, and any number of other factors—there really is no simple answer."

Lilly shook her head and forced herself to laugh. Pete's concern had contributed to her momentary paranoia brought on by lack of sleep. She wanted to forget about Shay. She'd seen nothing. The worst part of it was that once the idea came into her head, it was going to be impossible to ignore.

"We should go over your itinerary, Pete. I'd rather not continue to discuss the probabilities of Shay arriving in the Lazaretto. The next thing we'll be talking about is whether or not he might have escaped."

"Okay," Pete said unconvincingly.

Lilly realized that she was still searching the street for signs of Shay. It took significant effort to pull back from the window and return to her desk.

13

Sterility is a virtue for hospitals and surgeons. It is a curse to couples who want to build a family. As an office motif, it is numbing. Lara felt every bit of her inner being grow numb as they were ushered into the sterile office of the IHS official who had identified himself as Dr. Borshem. Lara had actually examined the man's credentials, as if she knew what she were looking at. As if she might find some discrepancy that would void anything he might tell them about Jett.

Dr. Borshem, a young doctor who could have graduated from medical school just days prior to this interview, frowned with just the right amount of concern as he waited for the Dassins to take their seats before sitting down behind his massive desk. He paused before beginning, paying careful attention to a smudged portion of his deskscreen. Wiping at it with a finger, he began to speak without looking up.

"Mr. and Mrs. Dassin, I apologize for your extended wait. We do our best to keep people moving as expeditiously as possible, but that can't always be the case. The gentleman ahead of you was difficult to deal with. As was the lady before him."

Lara watched him turn his attention to a file on the deskscreen. He pulled it to the center of the screen and proceeded to push it a finger's length to the right, then back to the left. He repeated this again and again.

"Your son," he said, "has been diagnosed with Caliphate's." He finally looked them in the eye as he silently allowed them to process the information.

Lara had been ready to fall apart as soon as the bad news was delivered; had anticipated the emotional breakdown with more fascination than dread. But now that the words had been irretrievably spoken she discovered that she was in no danger of going to pieces. To the contrary, she needed order, craved it, and focused on the facts to maintain it.

"I'm not familiar with—what was it?" she asked.

"Caliphate's. A disorder of the blood."

"That means it is not on the exile listing, right?" Frank's response seemed well-informed and it gave Lara a great boost of confidence. "Blood disorders aren't contagious."

"Most of them aren't, that's true, Mr. Dassin. Unfortunately, Caliphate's can be spread by pathogen, not just by genetic transference."

Frank retreated behind a granite expression. Lara could do no such thing. She leaned forward to add weight to her words.

"He isn't sick." It was the most obvious argument to make. "He's been just fine. Healthy as ever. What exactly are we talking about here? A recessive gene? A dormant virus?"

"Jett won't show any symptoms for a very long time, Mrs. Dassin. Possibly years before you'll be able to tell he is sick. But that is not the issue. Because it is contagious, any subject who tests positive for Caliphate's will not be allowed to continue through the quarantine."

"So, now what? We go back to Bukovina?" She turned to look at Frank. Frank didn't answer. She wished that Jett hadn't been left in the care of the IHS nurse.

"Oh, no ma'am. I'm afraid that's impossible. It was in all the literature you were given." Dr. Borshem narrowed his eyes at her, as if he couldn't see her clearly. "You understand that, don't you? You signed forms that explained IHS policies."

"Yes, but how did this...has he just contracted this?"

"I don't think so, Mrs. Dassin. More than likely he had it before transit."

"That doesn't make sense, Doctor. Wouldn't this have shown up on the tests we took back home?"

"I'm sorry to say that not all of the tests are regularly run at the pre-transit sites. Lazaretto testing is far more thorough." He began to fiddle again with the file in front of him.

"But wait a moment," Lara realized there was a simple way out of this, "if he'd been tested for this back home, and it had been found, we'd still be back there, right?"

"Oh, most definitely. You wouldn't have been allowed to transit."

"So going back wouldn't create any kind of danger on Bukovina. He already had it there, so we ought to be able to take him back."

Doctor Borshem shook his head. Lara was most unnerved by the lack of life in his eyes.

"That makes no sense." Lara sat forward, eager to explain the mistake the doctor was making. Frank put out a hand to hold her back. She pushed it away. "We can't go back now, but if we had stayed, he could live there?"

"That's policy, Mrs. Dassin. You of course have the option to appeal."

"How does that work?" Frank asked.

"A Board of Review will look at your case if you so request it." The doctor's tone was as somber as when he first told them of Jett's test results.

"Okay, then. How do we do that? Where's this board?" This was something Lara could do. She wouldn't have to sit back and watch helplessly.

"The Board operates out of Baltimore, at IHS headquarters. You will be assigned a case officer who will assist you in filing the required paperwork. But a little advice, Mr. and Mrs. Dassin: I suggest you don't put yourself or your family through that. The Board will not interfere in this case. I feel I can say that with confidence."

Lara tried to focus on the doctor's words. What did he mean? Put her family through what? Surely the appeal process couldn't be as bad as simply accepting exile?

"The appeal process is extremely slow, and at the same time, it will seem like you will have an actual chance to win your appeal." Dr. Borshem, despite his youth, sounded as if he were an old colony doctor dispensing more wisdom than medicine. "I don't expect you to believe me. But you need to. No matter how reasonable your appeal might seem, the Board never makes exceptions. You will waste more than just money and time, you'll waste an immeasurable amount of hope."

"You're saying we need a miracle. But you don't believe in miracles, do you Doctor?"

"As a medical professional, I actually believe very much in miracles, Mrs. Dassin. Doctors see miracles far more often than even preachers see them. But that's not the point here. Miracles are commonplace compared to the chance you have with the IHS Board of Review ruling in your favor."

Lara did her best not to lose her composure. She looked to Frank to keep her calm, but his distant eyes scared her. She could see him ticking off their limited options and knew he had understood this situation far more quickly than she.

"With the formal declaration of *nullus exitus*, Jett will be indefinitely exiled within the Lazaretto perimeter. As an exile, he will be allowed a modest stipend with which he can purchase shelter, food, and basic healthcare. He might qualify for aid from several private agencies, depending on your financial situation as well as how you decide to proceed."

"Proceed?" Hearing the doctor speak of Jett as if he were a prisoner of the state made her sick to her stomach.

"You will have to decide whether or not you will continue on to Dnepr or if one or both of you will remain here with Jett."

Lara stared at the doctor in horror. Was he serious? Could he honestly believe they might leave their five-year-old son behind? She wanted to laugh. It would be the only way she could avoid screaming at the ridiculous man.

"And before you very courageously tell me you intend to stay with your son, please take some time to consider this carefully." Dr.

Borshem put up a hand to keep them from interrupting. "Jett will not be released from this quadrant for two days if you request it. He'll be kept here in our facility, and you can take time to decide if you will remain with him. At the end of that time, you will either have to leave the quadrant with him, or he will be escorted into a processing center in the Lazaretto alone. It is important you understand that if you stay with him, you will not receive a stipend for your survival. You will have to find work, you will have to find a place to stay. And every day you stay with him will increase your chances of becoming sick as well. If that should happen, you too will be unable to leave the Lazaretto."

"What kind of policy is that? How perverted is the IHS to even suggest that we might leave our son—our sick son—here alone?" Lara wondered if this were some kind of elaborate joke.

"This has nothing to do with IHS policy, Mrs. Dassin. Our policies deal only with the individual who is ill. I was only pointing out options for you that travelers have taken in the past."

"I don't believe you." Lara knew even as she'd said it that it wasn't true. As impossible as it seemed, she was certain that children had been abandoned in the Lazaretto.

"The hard truth is, a healthy couple, once through the Lazaretto and safely at their destination, can have any number of children to replace the child they might have to leave behind. It's not as uncommon as you might think."

"I want my son." Lara stood abruptly. It was suddenly important that she see Jett, that she take hold of him and never let go. She'd been holding off a growing panic in her breast but it would not be denied much longer. "Take me to Jett, right now."

Frank stood up beside her. He had hardly said a word, but she knew he would feel the same way she did. There was no chance he would dare consider leaving their son alone on this moon. She turned to him for confirmation and was shocked to see his expression. No, she knew he wasn't thinking of leaving their son. But the panic evident on his face was immeasurable.

She felt her stomach convulse and the room lost its balance. Lara fought off the nausea and concentrated on one truth. Right then, more than anything else, Jett needed her to be strong.

14

It had taken all afternoon for the Vtechs to finish processing the Visuals. Russell had spent the day interviewing what were supposed to be witnesses from Alpha Quadrant through a video link. According to his summary report, the witnesses hadn't witnessed a damned thing. MacNally had spent the day finishing up paperwork on a simple murder case—man strangles wife's boyfriend and then takes the wife out to dinner. If only all of his cases were so simple and logical. And it had been a logical murder. If MacNally had been dumb enough to get married, and his wife had been dumb enough to start running around with an idiot like the victim, MacNally would have strangled him too. Might have been tempted to strangle his wife as well. He did not add these observations to his report.

By the time the Visuals came through to his deskscreen MacNally was sleeping in his chair. The notification chime was loud enough to wake him. His neck hurt like someone had stuck a pencil into it. When he sat up, Russell was standing over him with two cups of coffee.

"I see you're still sleeping in your clothes, Pops."

"I don't like the way you're worrying about how much clothes I'm wearing when I'm asleep, Russell. Let's try to keep our relationship professional. Put my coffee down, and pull up a chair."

The Visuals report could be overly technical at times, and MacNally preferred to let Russell go through it carefully while MacNally usually only scanned the report for the major headlines. But this was going to be different. Unable to glean many details on his own while in the decon suit, MacNally had to rely on the digital scans. He increased the magnification on the report to better read the details.

"Head trauma," Russell picked out the physical evidence first. "Visible scratches on the skin. Body temp confirms that Officer Green found him six or seven hours after he'd died."

"Well, from the looks of things, there isn't much here. Nothing sticks out, anyway."

"There's no lucky breaks here, Pops. Why don't I take this home and go through it in hopes of finding anything worth discussing in the morning. By then we ought to have an autopsy from IHS."

"Yeah," MacNally had already closed out the file and pulled up their own videos taken at the scene. He stared at the body as the view panned from its head down to its feet then pulled back for an overview. With no lucky breaks from the Visuals, it was time for basic deduction.

"So I'm gonna head home, okay?" Russell pushed back from the chair he'd stolen from a nearby desk.

"Russell, you have what you took from the roof?"

Russell leaned over on MacNally's desk and stabbed in a command. The center of the desk cleared and a view of the roof became visible.

"You can see it all here. Basic setup: the roof is fairly empty, there was a door to the stairwell, the adjoining building to the east is two stories higher, with no access point from this roof. The building to the west was the same height, and they shared access."

"How many fire escapes?" MacNally asked as he panned the image from left to right.

"At least a half dozen. Double that with the building to the west."

"So what does that tell us?"

Russell bit the inside of his lip and studied the moving image.

"Come on, kid. The answer isn't in the video."

"If we are right, and someone was pursuing him, he could easily have reached the roof first and took the stairs. Unless he was hurt. Which aside from the trauma and scratches, all of which happened in the fall, we know he wasn't hurt."

"So why didn't he get to the roof?"

"He panicked."

"Look at it this way," MacNally offered, "he could have made the roof, gone either for the stairs or another fire escape, buy himself time until his Para-Lazar is fully charged. Following is always more dangerous than being followed. With a fully charged Para-Lazar, he becomes the hunter."

"You're assuming he's smart enough to figure that out."

"I'm assuming he's not dumb enough not to. There's a difference."

"So he should have gone to the roof, but…"

"He can't. Someone else is blocking the way."

"A second bad guy." Russell nodded after a few moments to think it over. "Logical. Probable even."

"Now he can't go up. Can't go back down."

"They catch him and throw him off."

"Maybe. You're thinking of this from the pursuit point-of-view. You've got him trapped and you expect to be able to close the trap."

MacNally snapped open a visual of the fire escape. He zoomed in on one of the landings, then twisted it to the right, allowing their view to shift to the fire escape beside it.

"You think he jumped?"

"Wouldn't you?"

"I'd shoot the bastard below me and head back down."

"No, forget the Para-Lazar. It's dead, or you threw it at the bad guy when it went dead. There were no more shots. So ignore it. Wouldn't you jump across to the next escape?"

"What you're suggesting is there was no crime. This is an accident. Guy jumps, misses, dead."

"Oh, there's a crime. We just don't know what the crime is. But it would be safe to say it wasn't murder. Our two bad guys might have *wanted* to murder this guy. But maybe the klutz beat them to it."

"Your buddy Green will be happy to hear it," Russell concluded.

"I suppose he will. Let's give it a day or two before we tell him. They might come up with something new, or we might realize our conclusions are stupid. Anyway, there's no hurry to tell him. But once we do, we need to be sure. They aren't really equipped to track down killers. It's why they called us. If we tell them this was just a game of tag that got out of hand, they'll let it go. At least it would mean there's no murderer—or two murderers—running around Alpha."

"You know," Russell said, lingering over the image of the alley below the fire escape, "I sort of hope the poor guy really did fall to his death. At least he went on his own terms. Cheated these guys out of killing him. Or course, that means we can't hunt them down and make them pay for it, either."

"Oh, I wouldn't be so sure about that, Russell. Before this is all over, we may do just that: hunt them down and make them pay. You never know."

15

The woman lay on the bed, propped against a pile of pillows, her long legs white against the black satin sheets. The New Yorker watched her, amused yet again. She was talking, chattering, her legs sliding back and forth along the satin as if she were treading water. He could have watched her do it all night.

"Just imagine, all this time, all these people, living their lives, every day, with nothing to make one day any different from the next. You do this for twenty, thirty, forty, how many years? And you worry about getting sick, or losing your friends, or worry that your parents think you're wasting your life. But what life are you wasting? If we really do think nothing matters. If we really think there's no big guy out there watching over everything—and when we die it doesn't matter what we did—who's to say we wasted our life? I don't get it. Does it make any sense to you?"

She rolled forward onto her stomach and looked up at him. She clearly expected an answer.

"I don't know." He looked down at her and shook his head before he slipped off his jacket and pulled at his tie. The Australian had never stopped talking. Now, finally able to get away, he was yet again listening to someone ramble. At least this one was worth looking at. And despite her bizarre subject matter, he couldn't help but think she was fun. A little crazy, that was easy to see. But maybe he was going a little crazy in the head too. Why else would he let her keep on like that?

"What do you mean you don't know? I didn't ask if you could explain the meaning of life. I just asked if you thought it made sense to think someone could waste their life when we've been told life is nothing more than the time we have from the day we're born to the day we die. It either makes sense or it doesn't."

"Like I said, I don't know."

"If you don't know if it makes sense to you or not, who's gonna know for you? Pick one. It's easy." She made a funny face and rolled again, this time onto her back. She was looking up at him with her head hanging off the bed.

He bent low and kissed her. She rolled away from him.

"Nope, don't start that. Answer the question."

"So I pick one. If I say yes, it makes sense, you'll want me to explain it. If I say no it doesn't, you'll say it proves there's some kind of afterlife or it proves there's a God." He grinned and laughed as she retreated to the pillows, pulling the sheet up and over her body. "I'm not gonna pick one. Instead, I'm gonna ask you a question."

"Okay," she held the sheet tight. "Ask."

"Why do I let you keep talking about religious nonsense when you won't let me near you? I don't invite you up here for theological debates. I invite you up here for something else entirely. Yet there you are, talking, asking questions, and all of a sudden you won't let me touch you. Why wouldn't I just throw you out of here? There's plenty of girls like you all over Bukovina."

"Maybe it's because you know I'm right." She came forward again, still wrapped in the sheet, eyes bright with excitement. "You do, don't you? You know it doesn't make sense!"

Her smile was so big, so genuine, and so fragile that the New Yorker couldn't bring himself to disappoint her. He reached out and tapped her forehead twice.

"Okay, you win. I ain't saying I think there's a God, but I'll agree that it doesn't make sense. You can't waste a life that doesn't have any meaning in the first place. Fair enough?"

She nodded and her look of sheer happiness caught him off guard. What was he supposed to do with her? She was more child than mistress. The sudden trust in her eyes made that perfectly evident.

"Move over, my little religious zealot." She did, and he slid under the sheet with her. She did not recoil from him this time, though he could feel she was tense. "Relax, would you? I've had a long day. My boss wore me out with his jabbering, and so did you. I'm tired. Kill that light."

She did. And in the darkness she put her head against his shoulder. He could feel the tension leave her body. Before too long, she was asleep.

She was an odd bird—a real nut. But then again, so was the Australian.

It had taken most of the day for Lilly to shake off the chills she'd felt at Shay's appearance. Of course, he had not really appeared to her. But the optical illusion that had caught her attention had been real enough to short circuit her nerves for hours. She'd been forced to leave her apartment, just to remove the temptation of repeatedly peering out the window to confirm that Shay was not in fact hanging around outside her seventh-floor suite.

She should have stayed home. There was work to do. She had to begin sending out inquiries on her latest objective: the Levy Fragments. Her Phasian clients had heard the quaint stories of the Bukovinan Exploration Party. How the pilot, Chas Levy, stuck in orbit while the BEP began the first forays onto the planet's surface had filled several notebooks with hand-drawn illustrations of Bukovina's unusual surface patterns. Along with his artwork were supposedly many broken bits of verse and other marginalia that have since become the source of folklore. Many trite and sugar-sweet quotes have inevitably been pawned off as Levy witticisms.

No one had seen the books in many years, since an unnamed collector had bought them from the Levy family. (Not the whole family, Lilly seemed to remember, but one greedy minor cousin or step-child.) The few pages that had been copied and remained available for public perusal had never impressed Lilly. From her point of view, the Levy Fragments should have been called the Levy *Scribbles*.

But her clients had become obsessed with them. And Lilly was more than willing to track them down for a fee. Her initial research suggested the books were on Arcobia, and if all went well, Pete should be able to take possession of them as soon as he could arrive on-planet.

But first she would have to contact the current owners. Something that would never get done if she didn't go back to her apartment and stop acting like a child. A phantom had run her out of her home. It was time to put Shay behind her. He was safely locked away at Conde Sur. No one escaped from their prison barges. No one. She knew she needed to lock her memory of him away in the same manner. If only she could do so with the same assurance that her memory would never escape its prison cell. How much easier it would make her life.

She had never allowed the sordid ordeal that had been her marriage and divorce to weigh her down with despair and agony as if she were a tragic character in an ancient British tragedy. Lilly was not made to wring her hands and cry out in futile supplication. She had made up her mind to betray her husband and had never looked back.

But that didn't mean that a phantom rumbling did not draw her attention away from her self-confidence once every black moon. The voice was always recognizably Shay. It could just as easily accuse her as it could beseech her with words that cried out for mercy, for revenge, for simple explanation.

She ignored them always. And they never lingered. Lilly's granite resolve would never crack under such obviously selfish reproach. Yes, she had once loved Shay Stewart. But his guilt had driven a stake through her, not just breaking her heart, as if it were simply broken in two and could be mended with time and goodwill, but it had punctured her, draining the very life from deep inside her. She did not hate Shay. But neither could she love him again. Nor anyone.

Not even Gregor.

As she hailed a TransitCar, Lilly wished she had never looked out that window. Why had she allowed Shay to enter her world? One comment from Gregor about an ex-spouse and she had conjured the image of a man best left with the rotting carcass of the past.

It was easy to lay the blame at Gregor's feet. It was unfair but easy.

It would also have been easy to claim his mention of Gloria had not bothered her in the least. It would have been a lie but easy to claim. Lilly had no desire to take over the role of a jealous lover. Especially in light of the fact she had just acknowledged her inability to love anyone. But that did not mean she welcomed the idea of someone else loving Gregor.

"I can't take you straight there, lady."

"I'm sorry?" Lilly's thoughts were interrupted by the Transit driver. She raised one eyebrow and waited for his explanation.

"They got four or five blocks barricaded up ahead. Some big little festival going on in this neighborhood. Every year they do this. All they really do is screw up traffic for two days."

Lilly felt the TransitCar slow, lurch left, then lift with power as it picked up speed.

"I just didn't want you to think I was taking you on the long-pay, you know?"

"That's no problem," Lilly reached down and put pressure on a small ceramic panel in the door. The window on her left, smoked-white for privacy, cleared enough for her to be able to see into the street. A mass of people filled the streets, a scene one did not often encounter in the Lazaretto's Center City.

Raised above the crowd were effigies that Lilly did not immediately recognize. The bodies, for indeed they were made to look like human bodies, were lumpy misshapen things that hung from metal frames as if the life-size dolls had once been alive but had since died from some ghastly form of execution. The procession that bore these counterfeit cadavers moved with a drunken pace that allowed the hanging dead to swing over the crowd. Each of these effigies had bloated heads, exaggerated in size to allow primitive faces to be painted onto them. Many of those who carried the bodies had similar markings splashed across their faces.

"No point in looking, lady. That's just pagan crap from Arcobia. Mostly just people looking for a chance to protest our exile practice." The driver cut through a darkened alley and had to slam to a stop to avoid hitting a police cruiser that was dropping down from its patrol lanes. They had to back up and find a different way through the city grid.

Lilly knew more about the procession than the driver, though she said nothing to ruin his belief that his knowledge was both superior and in need of being shared. Calacas Mueros, while popular on Arcobia, had originally come from Earth. Some said it had been around for four thousand years, though Lilly understood that it had been celebrated in a slightly different fashion. The current name was a derivative of several older names, but the basic tenets fed the same appetites of its participants, both then and now. People always lived with the knowledge that death might be waiting around the corner. One could hide from this fact, or one could accept it and stare it down. Those parading through the streets and around Lilly's TransitCar went a step further. They felt compelled to honor death and those who had already become a part of it.

There were more complex issues associated with it, and Lilly had become something of an expert on the subject many years ago when she had researched and tracked down some highly prized clay figurines that had been crafted for a Mexican variation of Calacas Mueros in the 21st century. Her client had insisted that the figurines he had been looking for were handmade. It had taken Lilly a great deal of research and heavily documented due diligence to convince the man that the figurines had been mass produced, as had nearly everything else in that century.

"Damn!" The driver spit out the invective with embarrassment. "I'm sorry, that cop blocked our way and now we're stuck here till this thing is over."

The throng had indeed blocked their chance of getting out of the alley. Lilly smiled at the driver, more to calm him down than from a real feeling of goodwill. If they were going to be stuck there until the parade finished, there was no point in sharing the TransitCar with an emotionally charged stranger.

"I don't mind," she lied. "Who doesn't love a parade?" She twisted around until she could see the spectacle passing along the street. There was no loud raucousness from the mass of death acolytes. They moved in silence, the only sounds coming from the clanging of the metal frames that both held the puppet dead and fell into other metal frames as they tottered down the street.

"I could smoke out the windows if you like." The driver looked back over his shoulder and stared at the parade with what Lilly recognized as contempt and fear.

"If you would like to. In fact, I'm going to step out and smoke a cigarette while we wait. Don't leave me when the way is clear. I'll get back in."

The windows had turned solid white before she could open the door, exit to the alley and close the door.

The first thing Lilly noticed was the smell of Arcobian food. An opportunist in the crowd had set up a food stall and was selling fatty fried foods. At the same time, she saw that the procession of effigies had been followed by a parading group that carried large death masks, each one bigger than the full effigies that proceeded them. These grim facades swung slowly from left to right, as if massive bony judges stared into the crowds seeking guilty souls to devour.

Lilly lit a cigarette and turned her back on the bleak festivities. But she never fully turned her back. Out of the corner of her eye she had seen him. There was no mistake. There was no great distance to convince her she had imagined the vision. And this time, she knew that he knew she had seen him. A spectator in the crowd had also turned away from the massive disapproving skulls. He had been staring at Lilly. She was certain of it. Even as the man raised a death mask and seemingly fell back into the maw of the chaotic procession, Lilly knew she had truly seen him.

Shay Stewart had been standing but a few TransitCar lengths away from her. Lilly did not hesitate to dive into the crush of the multitude that had swallowed Shay. Her cigarette had fallen from her lips as she opened her mouth to shout Shay's name. But the fact that he had slipped away from her assured her that he would never answer her call.

For a brief moment she thought she had seen him again, heading into the forest of hanging effigies. Lilly struggled to make her way through the mass but quickly decided that she had no chance of catching up to Shay. She stopped moving forward and picked her way back through the marching dead in search of her TransitCar.

It had happened all too fast. Once their decision—Frank and Lara's only possible decision—had been made, IHS had moved quickly. Processing Jett as if he were a criminal, they completed his paperwork, photographed him, created a PDT for him that identified him as *nullus exitus*, then herded the Dassin's into a MedTransit and transported them to the wall of Alpha Quadrant. There, four white-jacketed IHS men escorted them to a small gated exit. They stepped through the gate alone. Outside the walls, yet another MedTransit awaited them.

All of this occurred under the blanket of night. Few streetlights were working along the route they followed. The night sky held no stars. What lights the city had to shine reflected dully off the lowered ceiling of clouds, just enough to make the swollen bruised stratosphere visible.

For Lara, it all felt designed to keep her head down, to not allow her the dignity that should have come with staying loyal to her family. As if the Lazaretto itself were attempting to scorn her efforts to stay with her doomed son.

The heavy transport fell to the street surface and abruptly stopped. Doors rolled back and a lone IHS officer stood looking at them. He backed up quickly as Frank stepped out with Jett hugged to his long frame.

Lara nearly cried at that. It was the future that her son would know: men afraid to allow him to draw near. A five-year-old boy who would never know acceptance from the world at large. She shuddered to think what his life would have been like if his parents had been selfish enough to abandon him. She tasted bile at the thought.

"Please follow me," the IHS man said, backing up even further before turning and heading towards the entrance to a building. Frank hefted Jett higher on his hips. Lara put a hand on one of Jett's legs and stayed close to her husband.

They were on a darkened street with nothing noteworthy about the buildings that lined it. Each building looked the same, lightless windows marked the many apartments that faced the street. Steel-caged stairs zigzagged up the side; black scars rising and disappearing into the upper darkness. In places, Lara could see stains that streaked down the walls that could easily have been bloodstains oozing from the malignant scars.

She paused at the entrance in time to notice a glow that began to increase from an intersection off to her left. Great shadows danced in the light, distorting shapes of creatures that bobbed in and out of the growing ring of light. A swelling roar seemed to bubble out of it.

Frank called to her from inside and she did not have time to understand what she had just seen. Instead, she entered the building and saw that the building's lobby was nothing more than an empty room, lit with a single grid-light, with corridors leading off in three different directions. In one of the corners she saw a darkened abyss that turned out to be a stairwell.

The IHS man began to explain.

"This is home for you, for now. We keep these apartments available for your situation. You can, of course, look for better rooms depending on your financial state. You have no obligation to stay here, nor do you have a termination deadline. As long as you occupy the rooms, they will remain yours."

Frank looked at the corridors, at the stairwell, then back at the official.

"And what apartment was assigned to us?" Frank's expression was neutral. Lara was grateful that he could remain so. She needed that.

"You're seventeen floors up. 1764 is the room number."

"Elevator?"

"At one time there was...but no. It's not in working order." The man, for the first time, seemed ashamed at the duty he performed. In need of a distraction he strode to the stairwell's entrance and felt along the wall for a light switch. "As I said, this is generally meant to be temporary."

"We won't need the light." Frank shifted Jett enough to allow him the use of one arm. He reached out towards Lara and squeezed her hand. "I'll take you to a hotel."

"I can call a TransitCar for you." At this point the man would not even attempt to look at them. He kept his back to them as well.

"You're joking, sir." Frank's neutral demeanor was becoming less so. He handed Jett off to Lara. "Take him outside, honey. Get him out of here."

Lara could still hold Jett, though he was getting too heavy for her to walk any lengthy distance with him. She had no problem, however, getting the boy out of the building. She could have done it even if she had been forced to carry him up seventeen flights of stairs.

Just before she left the room, she heard Frank, his voice more solid and demanding, speaking to the IHS man.

"Now look here, man..."

Lara stepped out into the street, the night chill a welcome relief to the stifling atmosphere of that bleak lobby. For a moment, she had the feeling that Frank would make everything turn out all right. But her brief delusion came crashing down when she saw the skulls heading toward her and Jett.

"Frank!" She squeezed Jett tightly, yet was unable to turn away from the sight before her. The hypnotic advance of the grim procession froze her in place. She pushed Jett's head against her breast to shield him from the sight. A second attempt to call out to her husband failed, her words a scratched whisper.

A mass of walking dead shuffled up the street. Lara felt Jett slipping lower in her arms. She backed away from the startling sight of the oncoming parade unaware of the street drain behind her until one heel of her shoe caught in it. For an absurd moment she thought someone—some*thing*—had reached out and grabbed her. She tried to wrench away from its hold only to fall sideways. Jett, sensing that she had lost her balance, jumped off to one side. Lara let go just long enough to put her hand out and catch her fall.

She pushed herself off the grimy street before the grinning assemblage engulfed her. She pulled her foot free of the entrapped shoe and reached out to take Jett's hand.

He wasn't there.

Lara called to him. She lunged forward, frantically sweeping her hand in case he was just a few inches out of reach. A large bony figure pressed against her and she smelled mildewed cotton. She shouldered the black-draped form aside.

"Jett!" This time she practically screamed his name. Those in the parade near her turned to stare. A large papier-mâché skull ogled her. Its black eyes laughing at her distress. Lara fought to regain her composure. She ignored the massive mask and spoke to the black-robed puppeteer that controlled it. "I'm looking for my son. He was just here. He's a small boy. Help me find him."

Lara tried not to panic as the skull-man turned away. She tried to grab another member of the procession but this one also pulled away and hurried off down the street. She spun around as the crowd passed by. She was surrounded by the dead, and like those who have actually died, they neither heeded nor bothered with the troubled woman who still possessed life.

Lara sucked in deep breaths and tried to calm down. Jett could not have gone far. But her mother's mind was already devising dark and disturbing scenarios in which she would never see the boy again. She had to smother her imagination. She had to take control of her reason before she lost it completely and allowed her panic to transform into frenzy.

"Frank!" She needed him. She couldn't do this alone but she couldn't go back into the building to get him. She dare not leave the spot where she had lost Jett. He might find his way back.

If she wasted time waiting for him to come back she might miss a chance to find him. If Frank came out he could search for their son while she waited. Without him she wasn't sure which was the best choice to make. She felt like a rocket whose engine has fired but was still clamped to its gantry. She wanted to move—had to move—but couldn't.

How long she stood there she never knew. But when the crowd shifted enough for her to see the woman with the white hair, she felt an inexplicable relief. The woman was obviously not with the parade. Though surrounded by the procession of the dead, the woman was standing still, her white hair shining as if sunlight glared off its silken surface. This angel, dressed in white, was staring straight at Lara. Her hands rested on Jett's shoulders.

Lara rushed into the throng and scooped her son into her arms, whispering his name repeatedly.

"I hardly need to ask if you're his mother." The woman put out a hand and gently pushed Lara out of the parade and onto the sidewalk. "That look on your face was proof enough. I spotted this little man in the middle of the procession and had an idea he was not a true adherent of Calacas Mueros. He looked a little too alive for that."

"Thank you so much. He—" Lara put her lips to the boy's hair.

"It's okay. I'm glad I could help. I have a soft spot for lost boys."

Lara, her panic gone and her breathing back to or at least close to normal, took a moment to really look at her son's guardian angel. The woman was taller than Lara by a few inches, her body long and willowy. She looked as if she might be easily swayed by the wind, but Lara also had the idea that no wind could ever force her to move if she didn't want to. Her hair really was white, it had been no trick of the light when Lara had first seen her, and it was secured into a pony-tail near the top of her scalp, dropping down below the woman's shoulders.

"I don't think he enjoyed his moment of freedom. He's clinging to you like there's no tomorrow. Yet more proof that you two belong together."

The woman was right; Jett was holding her so tightly his arms were hurting her. But she was not about to push him away. Her own arms might be causing the boy some discomfort, though if they were he made no effort to break free of their grip.

"No more running off, young man." The woman tousled his hair with her slender fingers.

"Wait, before you leave," Lara finally let go enough to reach out and stop the woman. "My husband would want to thank you. He'll be here in a moment. I'm Lara, by the way. Lara Dassin."

"I'm Lilly. And like I said, there's no need to make a fuss about this. Boys get lost all the time, and they generally get found too. But as you probably know, the Lazaretto is not the best place for a boy to run around. Come to think of it, he's not the first lost little boy I've come across in this city." Lilly smiled at what was obviously a private joke. "I need to get going. It was nice to meet you, Mrs. Dassin."

This time, before Lara could stop her, Jett's guardian angel stepped away from them and disappeared down the street. Lara looked down at Jett and nuzzled him, smelling his hair and allowing its scent to reassure her that her son was alive and well and safely tucked into her arms.

The Dead walked on, disinterested in the drama that had unfolded within their midst.

18

It would have been better if Lepov could have stayed busy all day. After that pathetic proposition from Nerrudah, Lepov had spent the better part of the day trying to rinse the sour taste of it out of his mouth. It surprised Lepov to discover how upsetting it was to be mistaken for a murderer. Sure, his friend McNally down at Lazaretto Homicide had accused him of it in the past, but that had been a mistaken idea that Lepov *had* killed someone. He couldn't remember ever having met someone who had assumed Lepov *would* kill another man for a paycheck. It not only suggested Lepov was a killer, but it clearly said he was the kind of man who could be manipulated into evil strictly for money.

All the coffee in the Aegean system couldn't wash out the taste of that. No doubt Nerrudah had come upon Lepov of his own free will and idiocy. There wasn't anyone who knew Lepov who would have led Nerrudah into thinking Lepov was capable of being a paid killer. But Lepov couldn't shake the hint of guilt that came with the crass offer.

A former client had shown up after lunch to make a final payment on a case he had finished several months ago. It was always nice to be able to clear a file out of his collection box. It was hard enough finding most of his clients once a case was over, let alone the near impossibility of extracting money from them.

When no one else had activated his office door by four in the afternoon Lepov shut down his deskscreen and grabbed his coat and hat. Once the decision had been made to leave for the day he was in a hurry to get out of the building before a late visitor might ruin his plans.

He took the stairs in order to avoid anyone that might be coming up in the elevator.

Stepping out into the late afternoon, Lepov felt a stiff wind tug at his hat. He jammed it down hard enough to hold it in place and turned into the wind with his head down. A favorite restaurant of his was just around the corner and he would have time to eat and run before the dinner crowd ruined the atmosphere.

He was at the door and through it before he had to push his hat back down. Once inside, he touched the front of it with the palm of his hand to loosen it. A red haired waitress sat on a stool, leaning against the front counter. She had been reading a newsservice screen on her countertop.

"Shut down early, Lepov?" She pushed away from the counter and arched her back, stretching with both hands in the air. The action drew attention to the tight sweater that was wrapped around the ample composition of her breasts. If Lepov had been twenty years younger he might have enjoyed the sight. Instead he couldn't help but think the image looked merely foolish. And in his opinion, the woman was old enough to know it, which she probably did, and simply figured it did no harm either way.

"Rubee, I was sitting in my office and got to thinking about you sitting here all alone, with only Jack to keep you company, and I didn't want Jack to have all the fun." Lepov hung his coat on a frail aluminum coat-tree then dropped his hat on top of it. He grabbed a pen that lay on the counter and looked at Rubee. "You mind?"

"Go right ahead. And you shouldn't have worried about Jack. He don't know how to have fun. I know 'cause I've tried. I think there's something wrong with that man."

"Or he might just be too old and tired." Lepov tapped an icon on the counterscreen and scribbled a note on the small white rectangle that appeared. When he was finished, he stuck the point of the pen in the center of it and slid it off the edge of the counter. The note disappeared.

"Let me guess," Rubee stuck a finger into her red hair and scratched her scalp with one of her bright red fingernails, "Lilly's invited for dinner."

"Nope. I'm just planning to eat quick and get out of here before all the other office bums show up for dinner."

"So that means you sent Lilly a note that said you were heading to her place after this and that means you ain't' got time for ol' Rubee." She pointed behind her to the room of empty tables. "So go find you a seat and Jack'll send you out a sandwich."

"Rubee, you take it well, girl. Sometimes I wish I'd met you before Lilly."

"That's only so you could ease your guilt over the many times you've broke my heart."

"You know," Lepov stopped walking towards the tables and turned back for a moment, "that note could have been to MacNally."

"The cop? Nah, I know better'n that. You don't get that same moony-look on your face when you're with the cop as you get with Lilly."

Lepov hadn't been aware he ever had a look on his face besides the one he always wore. Anytime he ever looked in a mirror all he ever saw was the same thing—a worn out version of the face he'd known since he was a little kid. The amount of wear and tear was the only thing that changed over time—sometimes alarmingly so—but he couldn't remember seeing any kind of *moony-looking* face. Ever.

No, Rubee was just being messy. She was always eager to flirt with him. Most likely because she knew Lepov was too tied up with Lilly to ever actually take her up on her flirtations. Besides, he had been reading people long enough to know that despite Jack's apparent disinterest in Rubee, the old cook definitely had the look of a man who felt possessive enough of Rubee to seriously injure any man who tried to come in between them. And Jack was big enough that his idea of serious injury could very well prove to be fatal.

"You alone, Lepov?" Jack, the potentially dangerous cook, stepped out of the kitchen and dropped a plate on Lepov's table. A sandwich sat in the center of it.

"Unless you see someone else at this table." Lepov caught the look Jack gave Rubee and tried to divert the man's attention. "You still out of beer?"

"I ain't' out of beer," Jack looked sharply at Lepov but it was evident he wanted to look back at Rubee. If Lepov couldn't keep the man's attention, Jack was in the kind of mood that could easily lead to a jealousy-induced argument.

It wasn't that Jack was wrong about Rubee's flirtations, it was that Jack had little right to take the path of the jealous lover. He acted more like a jealous father, though he had even fewer rights in that role.

"You were out of beer yesterday," Lepov said with a hint of accusation. The beer had run out due to a transport crash earlier in the week. Everything in the Lazaretto had to be imported from the colony planets. The crash had been no fault of Jack's, but Lepov had offended the cook by suggesting it had been his fault for not ordering enough. That had been two days ago, not just one, and Lepov was sure Jack would still be sensitive to the suggestion that he had made a mistake.

"I was out of beer *two* days ago because some dumb kid screwed up a simple transport program and directly caused a full transport of beer to land in and sink two full kilometers off shore. My beer, the beer I ordered, is sitting at the bottom of the sea. Damn thing's probably not even dropped off the shelf, but just sitting in about a hundred feet of water. And as if you didn't know, I arranged for a shipment from a warehouse here and had beer available the very next day."

"That's good, Jack. Glad to hear it. My mistake."

"So, you want a beer?"

"No," Lepov shook his head, "none for me. Seems to be bothering my sleep lately."

Jack opened his mouth but shut it before saying anything more. He glared at Lepov, did not look back at Rubee, and then rammed his way through the swinging kitchen doors.

Lepov might have been offended at Jack's surliness if he hadn't known that Jack's wife of twenty years had died in the Lazaretto from what should have been a mild case of pneumonia. Having contracted it just a few days short of the end of their quarantine period, she weakened quickly in the Lazaretto without proper medical care. Jack did his best to help her but ultimately had to watch her die. Angry, bitter, and fed-up with the IHS and their bungling of her case, Jack had stolen an IHS MedTransit van and driven it into the entrance of IHS headquarters. How he had been able to disengage the safety protocols Lepov had never heard. Instead of jail time, a judge without an ounce of mercy had sentenced Jack to exile in the Lazaretto, effectively imprisoning him within the system that killed his wife.

The man had a reason to be a pain in the ass.

Lepov was sticking the last of the sandwich into his mouth when the front door opened and Lilly walked in. Rubee smiled at her, not with anything close to real affection, then went back to reading her counterscreen. Lepov wiped crumbs from his lips and pointed at the empty chairs around his table.

"You're just in time. Still seats available."

Lilly sat opposite him. She did not smile at his little joke.

"Jack! Two coffees!"

"Who said I got coffee? I said I had beer!"

"I just sent you a note that said I was coming over after I ate."

"I know, I read it. I was close-by though, and thought I'd join you. I'm hungry. I guess you were too." She ran one finger along the rim of the plate.

"I just figured I'd eat quick and get out of here. You don't look so good, my dear."

Jack brought the coffee and Lilly ordered a cup of soup. The old cook softened his crankiness a little around Lilly. He too could see that Lilly wasn't feeling well.

"I better not go to your place tonight. I have a feeling that my late-night wanderings have left you too tired to deal with me anymore today."

"What I really want," Lilly sipped her coffee, then set it down and looked Lepov in the eye, "is to know more about Gloria."

So the old rules had been completely rewritten. Lepov wasn't angry about that. He wasn't happy about it either.

"I told you this wasn't interesting."

"Gregor, we have a very loose understanding between us. We might even properly call it a misunderstanding."

Lepov waited. He could see she wasn't done.

"What I mean is, maybe we don't have an understanding. We might have more of an assumption. What, for example, would you do if Gloria came back to you?"

"If you're worried I'd kill her and end up in prison you shouldn't. I'm in better control than that." Then it hit him. He could see it in her eyes. She wasn't scared that he'd end up in jail. She was afraid of something else. "I wouldn't go back to her, Lilly. I'd tell her I was already with someone."

"No you're not, Gregor. Neither of us really are."

Lepov had an idea he was not following the conversation accurately. He decided to hit the brakes before he ran into something in the dark. He reached out and took Lilly's hand.

"I know I'm a detective, and that I can think pretty quick on my feet at times. But this ain't the kind of thing I'm good at. In fact, when it comes to you, Lilly, I more often guess wrong, as you've painfully learned. So take a step back and tell me what's on your mind."

"Do you believe in ghosts, Gregor?"

Lepov sat back in his chair and tried to shake off the feeling of having been hit in the nose by a left jab. "You're the second person to ask me that today. I hope this means you aren't going to ask me to kill someone for you."

"I saw Shay again." She stared at Lepov, though when he tried to make eye contact with her he saw that she was in fact staring off to the side of him, as if someone were behind him. He deliberately had to not turn around to see if Shay were standing behind him. "I almost hope he is a ghost. Because I don't want to deal with the idea that he's out of prison and back in my life."

"Would he hurt you?" asked Lepov.

"You sound like Pete. No. He wouldn't hurt me. I'm more

worried that he'll want me back. That I'll—"

"Take him back?" Lepov was not surprised to see her nod. As a detective, he was all too familiar with the wild and twisted ways that husband and wife relationships often took. That never changed, even if they were officially divorced. Divorce might have become socially acceptable, but it had never found a way to solve every problem between spouses. It was fortunate that his professional persona was kicking in. He didn't want to dwell on what she was saying from a personal point of view.

"I wouldn't, Gregor. I wouldn't really take him back. It's why I was asking about Gloria. I need to hear it from you. That she's really gone. That we're exclusive. I'm not trying to get a marriage proposal out of you. I don't think I'd say yes, and that's unfair of me, I know. But I need to know what we are."

"It's not as complicated as you fear, babe. To me, Gloria's a ghost, and I know full and well she's alive. But she can never be more than a ghost to me now. So maybe I do believe in ghosts. But maybe that's all ghosts are, just an image captured on video, to be pulled up and watched occasionally to remind a man just how bad his mistakes have been." His mind cut to an image of Nerrudah in his office and Lepov had an idea that Nerrudah had been seeing a ghost after all. As if it were an afterthought, Lepov answered her question. "Hell yeah, we're exclusive, woman. If Shay tried to take you back, ghost or not, I'd kick his ass."

"My hero." Lilly watched Jack set the soup down in front of her and picked up a spoon.

"Just not your husband," he added. Before Lilly could apologize, Lepov cut her off. "So if that answers your question, I've got a question of my own. Do I look like the kind of guy you would hire to commit a murder?"

The question had been meant as a diversion, to draw them away from the serious nature of their conversation. Lepov had never expected an answer.

"Yes," Lilly nodded, "I could see that."

"I look like I could be hired to murder for money?"

"Not money," Lilly held a spoonful of soup just inches from her lips. "But for the right reason, yeah I think you could."

19

Night had finally claimed what was left of the day and MacNally should have gone straight home. But for reasons often blamed on the alignment of planets or some other astrological factor, MacNally decided not to go straight home. He went crooked home by way of a little bar just around the corner from his apartment.

MacNally had been stopping in at *The Mad Russian* since he was a beat cop fresh out of Alpha Quadrant. He was not a regular, not one of the guys who sat on one of the genuine wooden barstools that lined up along the bar's counter. He wasn't one of the women who came in every night to look for companionship and a few free drinks. He was simply an occasional customer who sat in a corner booth long enough to down two or three drinks before shoving his way back through the heavy steel door.

He never spoke to anyone except that night's waiter. And only then to order his drink.

He'd been coming long enough that he was recognized as wanting to be alone and no one ever attempted to give him less than the privacy he required. He was sure they knew he was a cop. He didn't have to tell them and they didn't have to ask. The women at the bar had figured this out as well and never approached him.

It was an old routine that had been established when he was young and in need of solitude. As MacNally became increasingly older he was not so very sure it was what he really wanted anymore. But those at *The Mad Russian* had seemed proud of their training and MacNally felt it would be a shame to ask them to change now. And so, he sat in a corner booth, facing the bar and the front door with a drink in his hand.

The waiter came over to MacNally's table once the drink was emptied and placed a second drink down while removing the first glass. MacNally nodded his thanks without making eye contact.

MacNally had been thinking about the man in the alley. It bothered him that Greenie had been the one to find him, without one person coming forward to say the man had been missing. No one had cared. Maybe no one even knew he was missing.

It made MacNally wonder just who would ever come looking for him? At one time, his old partner Arturo Fenelli would have raised an alarm. But Fenelli had died alone, when MacNally should have been out raising an alarm for Fenelli. Had Russell become the kind of partner that MacNally could rely on? Would the young Arcobian notice MacNally's absence and send the Space Cadets out on a rescue mission?

He would, of course, because it was his job. But would he beyond that? They had no interactions beyond their working relationship. Why should MacNally expect any more from the kid than that?

Gregor Lepov might come looking for MacNally. But that would only happen if Lepov wanted something. The fact of the matter was if MacNally didn't go home that night no one would even know to raise an alarm.

But that was how he had always played it. Alone. No one to interfere. No one to hinder him. No one to give a damn.

He slung the second drink down and waved the waiter away before he could arrive with a third. He needed to go home. He needed to quit feeling sorry for himself and get some sleep. He needed to leave right then.

Leaving proved impractical when the door opened and two guys who looked more like Transit buses than men crowded the front end of the bar. They walked fast. Straight at the bar, as if they weren't going to stop when they bellied up to it. MacNally's head was swimming a little from the two drinks and he had a sudden wish he'd never downed them. He watched the bartender and knew Bus Number One and Bus Number Two were not there for a few friendly drinks.

MacNally sat perfectly still.

Bus Number Two, with no distinguishing marks to set him apart from Bus Number One save for the fact that he was standing on MacNally's right and MacNally had learned to read in that direction, looked around the room and stopped when he saw MacNally. It was obvious to MacNally this guy's scrutiny had not come out of fear or even a mild sense of danger. It was more a simple case of curiosity. The tough guy made an invisible note of MacNally then scanned the rest of the room.

Bus Number One was doing his own thing. He had extracted a photograph from his coat pocket and held it out for the bartender to see. Reluctantly, the red-headed bartender stepped closer to peer at the image. Bus Number One took offense at the reluctance. He grabbed the man's red hair and yanked him off his feet.

Bus Number Two was staring again at MacNally.

MacNally tried to remember the Arcobian word for *idiot*. Because that's what he was about to become. Instead of sitting still, he stood up.

Bus Number Two had been expecting it. Without saying a word he shifted into powerdrive and accelerated straight for MacNally. MacNally wasn't armed. He had a police-issue service weapon in his car. He kept a riot-tamer standing beside his front door. His car was sitting outside the bar. His front door was two blocks away. And the on-rushing Bus was nearly within arm's reach.

MacNally stepped in close and kicked the right knee of the Bus with the heel of his shoe. He made contact just as the knee had fully extended in its stride. Before he could tell if the Bus-sized man was going to fall, MacNally slammed a fist into his front grill. The man, for at that moment MacNally hoped this was just a man and not a machine, gurgled out a curse as he came to a full stop.

Just past his cursing adversary, MacNally could see that Bus Number One had let go of the bartender and was pulling a weapon from his coat. The fight wasn't going to last very long. And MacNally was about to die because he couldn't sit still. Because he had to stand up.

He was all in now. And as he saw the flash of silver in Number One's hand, MacNally grabbed Number Two by the belt and shoved him backwards, using their combined weight to propel them back towards the bar.

Number One had raised his weapon but fired too soon when he saw both his partner and MacNally rushing at him. The distinct whine of an electrically fired volley split the air and MacNally ducked into the man he was pushing, putting as much of the man's mass between him and the incoming star pellets as time allowed.

He felt Number Two shudder and smelled rather than heard him grunt. Before he could allow the other man to fire again MacNally dug his heels into the bar's sticky floor and increased his speed.

All three men collided before the second volley was fired.

Whether he was conscious of it or not, the impact had thrown him to the ground. What MacNally did know for sure was that when he opened his eyes, Bus Number One or Two—did it matter?—was standing over him. A glint of silver pointed down at him.

A riot-tamer blew the Bus sideways because the waiter had been too nervous to attempt a shot from any distance. He had very bravely walked up to the massive man and put the muzzle of the riot-tamer into the man's ribs before pulling the trigger.

MacNally clawed himself to his feet and yank at the riot-tamer, freeing it from the waiter and swinging its barrel around until it was in line with the other Bus. He did not fire. The man was face down, his back a mess of shredded coat and blood.

Bus Number One had been firing an electrically powered star pistol. It was far less powerful than MacNally's service weapon, designed mainly to cause a lot of damage without deep penetration. Instead of slugs, they fired bursts of thin star-shaped pellets that shredded clothes and skin. They were painful, numerous, and considered more humane and therefore more acceptable to the politicians than the blunt power of lead bullets propelled by gunpowder.

He examined the man on the ground and wondered what was supposed to be humane about that kind of damage. MacNally kept the shotgun aimed at the wounded man as he backpedaled to the waiter.

"You alright?" he asked the waiter.

"Yeah, I'm fine."

"You okay down there?" MacNally turned and peered over the bar at the bartender who was still crouched behind it.

"Sure." The man spit as he grabbed the bar and pulled himself back up. "Damned Arcobians."

"What makes you think they're from Arcobia?" MacNally couldn't see any reason to suspect such a thing. When the bartender just shrugged, it confirmed MacNally's suspicion that the man was just a little too familiar with blaming Arcobians for anything he didn't like. He obviously needed a lesson in manners.

MacNally turned his attention to the riot tamer. It was a mid-gauge, which suggested that the damage done by the waiter was due to the shells it had been loaded with. Four-shot, probably, which was not even close to legal. "You know, if someone examined the shells that were still in this riot-tamer, he just might have to file a report. Perhaps when my partner gets here—he's an Arcobian, by the way, did you know that?—I might just let him take a look at this thing."

He lifted the riot tamer and sighted down its barrel.

It was MacNally's fault. He'd been distracted by the bartender's rude behavior. When the first pellets whistled past his ear, and he heard the whine of the star pistol, MacNally realized immediately he'd failed to disarm the Bus on the ground. Dropping to one knee saved his life. A second volley flew over his head and the bartender screamed. MacNally fired the riot tamer from the hip.

The Bus with the pistol burst into a pink mist. It didn't kill the man. But he dropped the pistol and clutched at what was left of his stomach. MacNally pulled on a bar stool to regain his feet and kicked the pistol away. He pinned the muzzle of his riot tamer to the man's chest.

"What's your problem, buddy? Your life been too long? You looking for a quick way out?" MacNally tried to allow his adrenaline to thin out as he caught his breath. "Who was it you were looking for?"

The Bus, now just a bloody man, sneered but said nothing.

"I couldn't hear you!" MacNally redirected the muzzle of the gun to the man's neck and pushed just hard enough to make the man squirm. The smell of burning flesh told MacNally the barrel was indeed still hot.

"Dassin!" the man hissed. Blood began to bubble from his mouth.

"Who's Dassin?"

The rattle of air through the man's windpipe was answer enough. MacNally wasn't going to learn anything more from this corpse.

By the time the uniforms arrived, MacNally was too tired to talk.

He gave his story to the first detective to arrive, then promised he'd be down at the precinct early enough for more questions in the morning.

Later, as MacNally climbed the stairs to his apartment, he wondered at his bad luck. Why had those guys come through those doors right then instead of two minutes later? MacNally wasn't sure, but he had an idea it had been his own fault. He certainly deserved such a scene, after sitting around and whining and worrying to himself. Maybe Lepov had begun to rub off on him.

It was easy to blame Lepov for what had happened. But the diversion didn't help. MacNally locked his door, pulled off his long coat, brushed his hat onto the coat, then sat down at the small kitchen table in the middle of his apartment. He watched his hands. Clinched fists trembled just as easily as open palms—at least when they were attached to a man who was badly shaken.

MacNally had spent too much time thinking about Fenelli's death. But he had never spent any time thinking about his own. He didn't want to start now. He hadn't wanted to stand up from that corner booth either.

And he sure as hell didn't want to sit in the dark and cry.

20

Lilly had left Gregor at the restaurant. She could see that he was tired, knew that she was tired, and she decided for the both of them to spare each other an emotional night. Better to retreat to their own rooms. Better to end the night early.

Lilly made a cup of tea, fully intent on getting to sleep as soon as possible. There was no use in staying awake. No use in sitting up and thinking about what she had seen. No reason to give Shay a chance to reappear.

She kept her shades drawn. Kept the lights turned low.

The tea helped. Slowed down her heart-rate. Slowed down the thoughts that had been racing through her mind. Slipping into bed, she cut off the lights and closed her eyes. She was tempted to open them, to see if Shay was standing beside her. To see if his image might hover above her, glowing with its own fury. She did not give him the chance. She had ceased giving him chances long ago.

Chances had been what he'd needed when she had met him. He was always in need of a second and third chance. He was always in trouble. She had actually liked that about him.

They had met on Phasis while boarding a flight bound for the Lazaretto. Shay's passport had become expired.

"Hold on, just wait a minute," Shay fumbled with his PDT, as if shaking it might correct the problem, "try it again. Everything is up-to-date."

"You need to reset your status, sir." The gate agent was not amused by Shay's stalling tactics. "You'll have to take this to a State Department office. Clear this up, or you won't be traveling anytime soon."

Shay looked as if he were about to begin shouting but the look on the gate agent's face was enough to keep him in line. Shay's shaggy head dropped in surrender and he backed away from the ticket counter. He stepped on Lilly and nearly fell over backwards on her.

"Oh, hell, I'm sorry" he muttered. He tried to turn around, to see who he had run into.

Lilly didn't say anything. She just raised an eyebrow at him. He took a good look at Lilly, muttered something completely incoherent then hit several more people as he rushed out of sight.

Encountering the same problem with her own travel status, she left the boarding area and followed Shay to the terminal entrance. She found him walking in a tight back-and-forth pattern, still muttering.

She had to insert her body into his path before he noticed her. When he did, he merely looked annoyed and tried to move around her. Lilly put up a hand and stopped him with the brush of her fingers against his arm.

"If you don't mind my saying so, you look like you could use some help."

"Yeah? Unless you work for the State Department, you're wasting your time and my time." He pushed her hand away. "If you drive a TransitCar that would change everything."

"You don't need to leave. If you come with me, I'll fix this."

"You work here?" He had not really paid attention to her until then.

"No, but if you'll trust me, I can get us on that flight in time."

"Lady, Shay Stewart don't trust no one."

"Trust me, Shay."

By the time they were married, she'd said that to him too many times to count. "Trust me, Shay." It had become an endearment. A line whispered between lovers. A phrase that brought a smile during a crisis. A simple code that reminded them both that they would always be there for each other. That no matter what happened in the world around them, they could always count on each other.

The last time they'd seen each other, the night he'd been arrested, Lilly had watched as Shay had been escorted out of their hotel room. That night, it had been his turn to speak the words. His turn to take those words of love and twist them into an accusation. His turn to look into her eyes and say "I know, Lilly. *Trust me, Shay.*"

Lilly opened her eyes expecting to see Shay in the room. She'd heard his voice. He must have been just a few feet from her. She'd heard him say it. Heard the pain in his voice. He was close enough to touch her. She looked around in the darkness. Looked for his silhouette, a shadow amongst darker shadows.

She held her breath. She had seen Shay earlier in the day and she was now convinced that he was there, in the room. Shay had returned.

She waited, wanting to call his name, but afraid to do it, afraid it might conjure what was not really there. Minutes passed before she found the courage to activate her lights. When she did, she found she was alone.

She refused to go to the shades and look out the window. Regardless of how foolish she felt, she was not going to look. She would not give Shay the chance to appear.

Lilly left the light on. Falling asleep, she heard Shay's voice twice before finally losing touch with the night.

Trust me.

Lepov had been right to insist that Lilly go home without him. He could see that she was upset about Gloria and he was in no mood to continue defending himself. There were only so many ways that he could say it plainly: he would never allow Gloria back into his life. Lilly had no idea what she was suggesting. The idea was an impossibility. There was a better chance that Lepov would get together with the ghost of Chitti Sienté .

Lilly was showing a side that Lepov had not yet seen. It might have been endearing to see her so jealous if Lepov had not been annoyed at the suggestion that he would take Gloria back. It was easiest to just go home alone and not allow the conversation to continue for the rest of the night.

Mercifully, he'd slept the night through without a dream that involved Gloria or Chitti. He'd awakened refreshed and feeling that he might just have a chance to get his life back on track. Maybe he could move on to something new and positive.

Lilly had mentioned the one subject he'd been avoiding but now had to admit needed to be considered. Could he and Lilly actually marry? Would that be so wrong? Wasn't it possible that they could find a way to be happy together? After all, it only made sense for them to marry considering that Lilly had nowhere else to go.

Lepov cleaned up after breakfast and went in to the office. He was proud of himself; he'd actually shaved and dressed in a clean suit. He'd even gone so far as to wear a tie. If he wasn't careful, he might be caught whistling as he entered his building. Even the rain in the streets didn't bring him down.

In his office, he brewed coffee, raised his window blinds for the first time in who-knew-how-long and wiped down his deskscreen. Rain ran gently down his windows. It might as well have been streaks of sunshine. Lepov had a feeling that this was the start of a very good day.

He should have known.

When the man tapped on his door there was still a minute left before the door would unlock automatically for the start of the business day. Lepov saw the man's outline in the frosted glass and decided he'd go ahead and let the man in.

He was long and imposing and stepped in as soon as the lock disengaged. Lepov knew right away this man came from money. His cloth overcoat—nothing synthetic about it—was well brushed, as was the felt hat he wore. As he reached up to remove the hat, Lepov could see that the man's hands were manicured. His hair was perfectly cut. A touch of grey could be seen around the ears as well as in the eyebrows.

All of this made a good impression on Lepov. The man might have been the perfect client save for the smug expression he was poorly hiding.

"Good morning," Lepov moved forward, holding out his hand. The man took the proffered hand from habit. He was definitely new to the Lazaretto. "I'm Gregor Lepov. What can I do for you?"

"My name is Dannen. Kry Dannen. My wife and I would like to hire you, if you'll allow us to explain, we hope you'll agree to help us."

"Okay." Lepov hesitated a moment before adding, "Mr. Dannen, you do realize you are alone, don't you?"

"Droll humor, she said to expect that." Dannen smiled without enthusiasm. "My wife is waiting in the hall."

"And what is she waiting for?"

"I'm to pave the way for her. She asked that I do this."

"I don't bite, Mr. Dannen."

"The fact is, you know my wife, Mr. Lepov. And she is concerned that when you see her you will react badly to her. I could have come alone and you would never have needed to know she was involved. Remember that, Mr. Lepov. She insisted she come. She refused to deceive you. She said that regardless of how unhappy you would be to see her you would most certainly be angry if you discovered you had been deceived."

"I get it, Dannen. You can stop paving." Lepov turn towards the still opened door and raised his voice. "You can come in, Mrs.

Dannen."

A click of heels in the hallway proceeded her. When she came around the corner Lepov knew he had guessed right. A slim blonde stepped into the doorway and raised her chin to look into Lepov's eyes. Her eyes, golden brown, were a mixture of anxiety and defiance; a woman looking for a fight and a way out all in the same glance.

"Hello, Gloria."

"Hello, Grey."

She stepped the rest of the way into the office and leaned forward. Raising her chin a few more degrees she kissed Lepov on his cheek. He twitched as her lips touched him, then fell back a step and stared at her.

"You should have deceived me." He turned his back and returned to his desk.

"I never lied to you before. I'm not going to start now."

"I won't either." He sat at the desk and rested each hand on its surface. "I won't work for you. No matter what you want from me."

"I know, Grey. But I had to try." Her voice didn't crack. She wasn't trying to lay it on too thick.

"If you'd let her explain, Mr. Lepov," Dannen spoke for the first time since she'd come in the room.

"She can explain all she wants. I'm just telling you ahead of time what my answer will be."

Rain battered the window, aided by several gusts of wind. So much for the feeling of sunlight. Lepov felt as if his day had been interrupted by a tragic accident. Maybe it had.

"If you don't want me to explain, I'll leave. I'll leave it up to you."

"I don't want you to explain." Lepov watched her, waiting for the tears that must inevitably fall. How far was she willing to go? How much would he listen before he threw her out?

"Please, Mr. Lepov." It was a nice touch. The appeal came from Dannen. Her husband's eyes carried a hint of desperation that piqued Lepov's interest. Dannen did not appear to be the sort of man who routinely gave in to desperation.

Lepov should have recognized her husband. After all, he'd helped the damned fool move her furniture out of their house. But this wasn't the same man. She'd probably grown tired of husband number two. It would certainly suggest a pattern. It might at least provide the proof Lepov needed that he wasn't the cause of her restlessness.

Little good it would do him now.

"I'll tell you what, Dannen. Why don't the both of you take a seat and you tell me why you're here. But I want to hear it from you, not her."

Gloria sat down immediately without argument. Dannen looked as if he might protest. He checked with her and she nodded. He placed himself in the remaining chair but did not sit back in it, holding himself on the edge of the seat instead.

For a second Lepov was afraid that Lilly would arrive during Dannen's little speech and she'd find the one woman whose return she feared. He'd been unlucky enough to find Gloria in his office that morning. Why wouldn't Lilly show up as well?

Dannen brushed back the hair around his ears with his fingertips and began to speak.

"I helped finance a deal that was to be completed here in the Lazaretto. My partners, Frobe and Jardyn, brought a certain piece of merchandise here in order to transfer it to our buyer. Due to unexpected changes in the buyer's traveling status we had to change the plan, and my partners went into a quadrant in order to take the piece to the buyer on Phasis. We were to meet up with them before the quadrant closed. Our own travel obstacles forced us to arrive nearly a week late and we were unable to join them."

"I don't do that kind of work," Lepov cut in. He wasn't about to aid someone illegally entering a locked quadrant.

"Just give me a moment. There's more. You see, Frobe has had a rather terrible accident. Incredibly, he died. We've heard no word from our man Jardyn and we are concerned. We need to find him, at least speak to him, and we had hoped you would have an idea of how that could be accomplished. We do not believe he stayed in the quarantine zone. It just closed today. I'm afraid the two men might have quarreled. If so, and if Jardyn feels that Frobe's death is his fault, well, you can see how he wouldn't want to speak with us."

"Is it stolen?" Lepov tried to keep his eyes fixed on Dannen but several times he gave in and glanced at Gloria. She kept her eyes fixed on the hem of her dress.

"I'm sorry?" Dannen seemed more amused at the question than insulted.

"The certain piece of merchandise. That's what you're after. Jardyn, I imagine, is not your primary concern. I want to know if it is stolen."

Dannen locked eyes with Lepov and neither man spoke for what seemed like fifteen minutes. A slight chuckle from Dannen broke the silence as well as their eye contact.

"That might have been an accurate guess if this had been a deal of mine twenty years ago. I do not, Mr. Lepov, get involved in that sort of thing anymore. You'll have to take my word on that."

"Will I? I think you'd best go to the police."

"You'll also have to take my word that it would be extremely inconvenient to involve any official agency. My financial backing on this endeavor was not to be made known to the buyer. I'd like to keep it that way if the sale can be salvaged. If it cannot be, then I at least need to procure my property in order to seek out another buyer."

"What are we talking about here?" Lepov should have just said no and ended it right there. But the sight of Gloria had unsettled him and he was having trouble keeping his balance, let alone his determination. "Drugs? No, don't protest. You haven't come to me for help to recover a wristwatch or a child's toy. So get very specific or walk out the door."

"Yes, you're right. I'll be specific. The piece is a German-made pistol, from around 1938. A 9mm Parabellum Luger. To be more specific, it is the gun that Adolph Hitler used to commit suicide." Dannen smiled and held his hands out, as if to say he had nothing to hide.

Lepov kept a sarcastic remark about suicide to himself. He closed his eyes and waited for Dannen to continue.

"I said it wasn't stolen. That is not technically true. I can say that me and my associates did not steal it—technically. It was already stolen, far in the past. It has since been floated around from one collector to the next. In our case, we removed it from the present collector, who has no legal claim to it whatsoever."

"And neither do you."

"That is quite true. However, as long as a buyer is willing to pay for it, I do not intend to quibble over such details."

"So this Jardyn has the gun now?" Lepov tried to skip ahead in the story.

"I hope. That's why we need you. We suspect that Jardyn is hiding because he is afraid of being blamed for the death of our partner. We'd like you to get word to him that we don't."

"Print up some signs."

"That's amusing, Mr. Lepov."

"And so are you, Mr. Dannen. If you can't tell me the whole truth, get out."

To Lepov's ever growing agitation, Dannen turned to Gloria for yet another look of approval. She nodded in consent.

"We suspect that Frobe might have been murdered by men acting on behalf of the man who last had possession of the Luger. If they are here, looking for Jardyn, he might be afraid to trust anyone at this time. It will be hard for him to distinguish friend from foe."

Lepov stared at his two visitors and tried to determine what he was missing. Their story was plausible. The accidental death of the partner and the fact that the whereabouts of the second partner added a touch of improbability to it all — added enough to give Lepov second thoughts about believing their story. The only thing that really bothered him was the fact that he was actually looking at this as if he were considering the case.

Who really cared if Dannen was telling the truth or not? Lepov was not going to take Gloria on as a client. He had done what he said he would: he listened to their story. It was time to tell them to get lost.

"Go to the police, or don't, Dannen. And I sure as hell don't want to work for you."

He didn't throw them out but he didn't make nice with them either. He made sure to say very little after that. For their part, they did not stick around to bargain with him. They simply thanked him and walked out of the office.

After they'd gone Lepov resisted the urge to leave the office in search of a bar. No matter how much he wanted to get drunk it would do him no good. Gloria had returned and for the time being she was back in his head. Maybe his nightmare had been a premonition. Maybe somewhere in the near future her arrival would bring bad things to Lepov's life.

He briefly considered asking MacNally to find a way to run Gloria and that smug husband of hers out of the Laz. He had to remind himself that not even the cops could run a man or woman out of the Lazaretto. No one ever left in a hurry.

22

Bad news was becoming a habit. The New Yorker did his best to balance the good with the bad, to keep the Australian satisfied, but there was not much good news coming in. Yes, the German was out of the picture — he'd paid for his sins in a roundabout way — but that was the only good news to come out of the Lazaretto.

Now, he had a feeling something else had gone wrong. The Australian's men could not be reached. The New Yorker had hoped they would call with news that could be added to the pitifully short list of good news. But they had been silent. No word. And for far too long.

The New Yorker spent the morning making calls. He had to exhaust his resources before he took this latest news to his boss. There were a few people he could contact who should be able to find the missing men. They were most likely drunk, wasting away their time because they couldn't find the Frenchman or the Swede. And though they had a job to do, they would not fear the Australian in the same way most men would fear him. After all, they were family. They had certain protections.

And this also meant that the New Yorker could not take their disappearance lightly. There was no room for error here. He couldn't walk into the Australian's office and announce that his men had disappeared without taking every measure possible to locate them.

The first thing he did was activate another team. They were on site, in the Lazaretto, and could be counted on to stay sober and focused on their mission. They had, in fact, been the New Yorker's first choice for the mission to recover the artifact. A married couple, they worked well as a team. They were swift, ruthless killers who recognized opportunity and acted without waiting for confirmation. And best of all, they feared no one.

If the missing men could be found, they would find them.

His next move was to contact the Englishman. If he were playing games, as the Australian suspected, it would be important to keep him on a short leash. Talking to him on the phone would put pressure on him. The New Yorker would have to make the Englishman aware of his precarious position. He could not afford to allow the man to relax.

After that he would spend a little time searching a few databases — police and NewsVision records — in case the missing men had been arrested. It was unlikely. The Australian spread enough money around to keep law enforcement disinterested in his people. But it would not hurt to check. Until the men were found, it was best to look under every rock; keep asking questions until he finally found an answer.

Just like the woman. He smiled when he thought about her. She hadn't been content with her *simple* question. She hadn't been satisfied with his answer the night before. When they had awakened to the bright sun shining through the windows of his forty-fourth floor penthouse, she started in with more questions. It had gone just as he had predicted. She'd focused on his admission that the traditional idea that life had no meaning made no sense. Strictly speaking, she had twisted his words. But he had to concede she was basically right. He hadn't said as much to her — no use encouraging her — but he'd spent the morning intrigued by her theory.

But that would have to wait for a later time. He had set up the call to the Englishman and the connection was complete. It was time to apply a little pressure. It was time to get to work.

The hotel had been adequate, though far from comfortable. Three hotels had indicated they had available rooms until they had acquired the Dassin's PDT readings, after which they amended their availability status. Frank had attempted to argue with the second hotel manager after it became obvious that Jett's status was the reason for their refusal to provide rooms. His efforts did nothing to change their situation, and it seemed that Lazaretto law allowed hotels to refuse rooms to any person who was labeled *nullus exidus*.

They had finally been allowed to rent rooms at a motel located in an older section of Center City. Frank insisted that the room's bedding be changed out and an indifferent housekeeping employee dropped off a folded set of bed sheets. It was difficult to be sure if they had recently been cleaned but Lara had assured Frank they would be sufficient.

She had stayed awake to watch over Jett and make sure he stayed in bed until he fell asleep. Frank, irritated from contending with the IHS system all day, had fallen asleep faster than Jett. Lara watched over the both of them by the light of a small bedside lamp. She dozed off, only to awaken in the middle of the night, not sure of where she was. Once she remembered, she shut down the light and allowed herself to fall into a proper sleep.

When she eventually woke up she saw Frank sitting in a chair that looked as if it might collapse under his weight. He held a small plastic cup in his hands and sat staring at a rain-covered window. Fog on the inside of the window obscured the individual beads of rain that bled down the glass. From where Lara lay it appeared as if something were alive on the other side of the window, struggling to be seen.

"Frank?"

"He's still asleep," Frank said with a hoarse whisper. He offered up a grim smile. "I was able to make coffee but it's not very good."

"I'm okay, thanks." She sat up and looked over at Jett in the other bed. The boy's breathing was rough.

The little chair creaked when Frank stood up. He crossed the small room with just a few steps and sat down beside her. Lara leaned over and put her head against his shoulder.

"I was hoping this would all have been a nightmare and that I'd wake up and none of it had happened."

"No such luck." Frank pulled away from her.

"I hate myself for bringing him here."

"Don't," Frank's harsh voice startled her. "You didn't bring him here. I did."

"I didn't try to stop you."

"I didn't give you a choice."

She took the cup from him, taking a sip of what proved to be cold and very bitter coffee. "You were right, it's not very good."

Frank made no reply. He continued to stare at the rain on the glass. He bit his upper lip, exposing his bottom teeth. She knew that look. He wasn't angry. He wasn't afraid. He was working out a solution. Did he think he could find a way to free Jett?

"What are you thinking?" She put a hand on him. He ignored the hand and the question. He chose, instead, to stand up and cross to the window. He stood against it, examining the view below, despite the rain smearing the glass.

"He slept so well tonight." Lara turned and looked at her boy.

"He was tired."

"It was a long day for him. Too long. And it didn't help, all of the anxiety he must have picked up from us. And then that..." she stopped herself before she mentioned what had happened on the street. She had not told him about losing Jett in the passing parade. She had known it would upset him.

"Then what?" Frank seemed to pick up on her fear of telling him the story. He turned to her and demanded she continue. "What were you about to say?"

"Nothing, Frank. It was nothing."

"What happened? And don't tell me it was nothing."

"It was while you were in talking to the IHS man about the apartment. I lost...Jett. For just a moment.

"Where did you lose him?" Frank asked with sudden alarm.

"When we left that horrible place and you stayed behind to argue with the IHS man, for a very brief moment Jett got away from me. We were separated for a short time. But not very long. There was that parade. All of those ghastly masks and he just slipped away. It was okay, someone helped me find him."

He stepped in close and grabbed her arm. "What do you mean, Lara? Who found him?"

Frank had never been this harsh with her. Did he think she had been careless with Jett? Perhaps she had been a little careless, but he was overreacting.

"Who?" his voice hardened, his grip tightened.

"I don't know," she shook her head in an effort to think more clearly. She tried to pull her arm away but he clamped down harder. "Frank, my arm! Let me go! We found him, that's what matters."

He stared at her arm and quickly let it go. She thought he might apologize but he only backed away from her.

"Tell me about this someone."

"There was a woman there." She hesitated, could see his eyes turn cold. "She was terribly kind. I'd lost Jett, but when the crowd parted, she was standing there with her hands on his shoulders."

"Did you see anyone else? Did they try to keep Jett?" He was scaring her now.

"Frank, what's wrong? It was just a woman. She was very kind. She handed him over to me and left. That was it."

"Why didn't you tell me?"

"Don't do that. Don't make it sound like I did anything wrong. Jett ran off, a woman helped me find him. And everything is okay now. Okay?" The fear of losing Jett had begun to course through her anew and she felt panic threaten to return.

"Think again, was anyone with the woman?"

"No, she was alone."

Frank's harsh response had been both unexpected and upsetting. Lara did her best to understand. Frank had been on edge since the IHS men had knocked on their door. Of course, he should have been on edge. They had basically imprisoned his son in a bleak, miserable world. What father wouldn't be upset and need to vent his rage a little?

Lara rubbed at her arm and just wished that her husband would vent in a less painful manner. She did take some comfort in the fact that Frank was so unbalanced over Jett's fate. A kind and thoughtful husband and father, he was not always the most attentive father. It helped to know he was so upset about Jett.

Lara watched Frank at the window again. He paced back and forth, paused occasionally to look at her or Jett, then turned his attention back to the window.

"Frank—"

"I'm sorry, Lara. I didn't mean to—" he softened his tone. "You're right, you did nothing wrong. I overreacted. I'm just upset about Jett. That's all it is. I shouldn't take it out on you."

"I know, I'm upset too." She met him at the window and slipped her arms around him. This time, he did not pull away.

24

When MacNally woke up, he found his partner sitting at the kitchen table. Neither man spoke as MacNally scowled and poured water into a mineral-stained glass. He swallowed the water but left enough in the glass to wet his hands before running his fingers through his thin hair.

After pulling on pants and a shirt, MacNally snatched up the tie he'd been wearing the night before and looked at it. There were bits of blood on it from the shooting. He looked down, inspecting his shirt, and saw more blood.

"Hell, I don't know if I got a clean shirt anywhere." MacNally yanked off the shirt and rummaged through a pile of clothes. He had to search several more places in the apartment before he found a shirt that satisfied him.

His partner watched but remained silent.

"You got a spare tie in one of your pockets, Fenelli?" MacNally asked as he moved a few things around on top of a dresser looking for a replacement tie. When Fenelli didn't answer, MacNally began to get pissed off. "What the hell you doing here, anyway? Did I give you a key to my apartment that I don't remember?"

Aggravated by Fenelli's silence, MacNally spun around and tried to curse but the words could not form as his mouth snapped shut. Sitting at the table was Bus Number One. The raw damage from the Riot Tamer was extensive.

And then the chairs at the table were empty. MacNally ran more water from the faucet and stuck his face under the flow. He held it there as long as he could stand the cold water. When he came up for air, he checked the table again. No visitors. That was good. Simple grogginess mixed with the trauma of a shooting had knocked him off kilter for just a moment. It was nothing to be worried about.

Without a tie, he grabbed his hat and coat and paused before leaving. He took a deep breath and opened the door. Fenelli now appeared to be standing in the hall facing the door. This time MacNally did curse at him in an attempt to clear the apparition away.

"That's no way to talk to your boss."

MacNally stared at Captain Jenkins a long time before responding.

"I guess you're right." He reached out and touched Jenkins' shoulder. Solid as the moon on which they stood. "You come up here to stand in my way?"

"Yeah, that was my plan." The head of Lazaretto Homicide did not move and would not allow MacNally to pass. "I heard about last night—the shooting. You okay?"

That last question was genuine. MacNally nodded. "They find out names for the buses?"

"Buses?"

"The dead guys on the floor of *The Mad Russian*."

"Yeah, they had names. That's why I'm here. Invite me in."

MacNally backed away from the door.

"Nice place, MacNally. We're obviously paying you too much." He made a quick circuit around the open room, pausing before the table with its one chair. He almost made a comment about it but chose to move on. He stopped a few steps shy of a fogged over window. "One of them was a guy by the name of Graph. Small time guy. Him I wouldn't worry about."

"We should worry about the other guy?"

"Not worry about him. You killed him, remember?"

"Unintentionally."

"Yeah, I know," Jenkins nodded, an odd smile briefly appeared, "the waiter did it intentionally. Damn my eyes I've never seen that before. Put the riot tamer inside his ribs before he fired. Graph was all over that bar. Your guy, that was just self-defense, reflex, you saw him fire and fired back. Boom. That's all it was."

"Cut it out, Jenkins. Who was the other one?"

"You never heard of a kid named Braniff, have you?"

"That animal was no kid. Who's Braniff?" MacNally knew he wasn't going to like the answer.

"Braniff Spaeth." Jenkins cocked his head and eyed MacNally. The two detectives' eyes locked for a heartbeat. "Yeah. That's right. Jonnie Spaeth's kid brother."

"I always knew I was the lucky type." MacNally bit his upper lip, then said: "Spaeth's got no reason to be here. He don't touch the Lazaretto. What's that gangster doing sending his boys in here?"

"Your guess…" Jenkins' voice trailed away. He was staring at the window again despite the fact that he couldn't see through it.

MacNally reached up to loosen his tie that wasn't there. Jonnie Spaeth. Jenkins was right. Don't worry about the dead man. Worry about his brother. A very alive and dangerous criminal.

"Okay," MacNally nodded, thinking through the implications, "we start by getting the waiter into custody. We can protect him. I can protect him. At the same time, we contact Dneprish Security. Maybe Phasian too. They can send in air patrols. Just to be safe. For a start, anyway."

Jenkins swallowed hard. Said nothing.

"More than likely this kid brother was fooling around where he shouldn't be. Jonnie Spaeth is too smart to do anything, anyway. We take precautions, though. Maybe someone on Dnepr talks to him. Off the record. Maybe it blows over."

"Sure." Jenkins turned away from the window. "Maybe so. For now, take a few days off. Last night was a hard thing. You need time to…gather yourself."

MacNally watched Jenkins cross the room and put his hand on the door, stopping only after MacNally spoke.

"Sam. What about the waiter? You have to do something for him. Get him someplace safe. Hell, you can stick him in Alpha." Though the quadrant had closed, travelers could buy their way in during the grace period, and Sam could arrange it without the required fee.

Jenkins' nod was almost imperceptible and too enigmatic to read. The look on his face, however, was plain enough. He wasn't going to stick his neck out for the waiter. MacNally's boss pulled open the door and walked out. He made it to the elevator but MacNally caught up to him as he waited for the doors to open.

"Listen," MacNally spoke slowly, his tone sober, "Russell and I can take the waiter, disappear. Give you time to—"

"Russell's gonna take your caseload. I may give him Chandler, or Lin Kwan." The doors slid apart. "Don't worry about the waiter. And don't tell me what you're gonna do. I don't wanna know."

"Dammit, Sam! What are you—"

"Just a couple days, Ed. You've had a traumatic experience. Take some personal time."

And then Jenkins faced him with an outstretched arm. The two men shook hands. When the two doors slid together MacNally was left standing alone. He glanced down the empty hallway. At that moment, the ghost of Arturo Fenelli would have been a welcome sight.

 25

When Pete let himself into Lilly's apartment, Lilly knew she would never be able to keep the truth from him. Lilly was known for her discipline and practical lifestyle. She never slept late, never lay about wasting the day, and never wasted time feeling sorry for herself. Combating that sort of behavior was more in line with her usual activities. As soon as Pete saw she was still in her robe just an hour before noon, he didn't hesitate to begin his interrogation.

"If I told you I was fine, would you stop asking questions?" She had to make at least one attempt to avoid telling him. If only to spare him the melodrama of her personal problems.

"Only if you demanded that I stop as my employer. But then I'd just look for another angle to pry the truth out of you. So let me ask again, and this time answer honestly. Are you okay?"

"I am not."

He nodded, accepting her answer without comment. He did not need to ask more questions. Lilly was not the sort of woman to be coquettish. They both knew this and so he waited as she decided how much to say.

"You know, I'm not the kind of girl to be led about by her imagination or emotions. So don't think that's what's happening here. But something is wrong, Pete. You remember I mentioned my former husband?'

"You did more than mention him. You nearly panicked when you thought you'd seen him. Did it happen again?"

"Yes. I was out in Center City, and I'm positive I saw him. More unsettling, he saw me before he disappeared, as if he wanted to remain hidden."

"When was this?"

"Yesterday. In the late afternoon."

"Have you told Lepov about this?"

"Yes. I don't know if he understood that it was more than a trick of the light. He was distracted with something else and I didn't press the point. Maybe I wanted to believe that it wasn't real, too. The less said the better. That kind of thing."

"And was it real?"

"I might have said it wasn't this morning. But either I'm now sure Shay is here in the Lazaretto, or I'm losing my mind. Last night, I was sure I heard him. Heard his voice, out loud, here in my room. I wasn't asleep."

"But you didn't see him?"

"Not this time."

Pete smoothed down his mane of hair as he considered her story. His mind was eager to solve puzzles and this was right up his alley. He never avoided a challenge like this.

"I could simply check his status on Conde Sur, but that wouldn't give us any solid evidence. They've been known to keep sloppy records, maybe worse than our own here in the Laz. What we need is to get someone to go and personally put their eyes on him to verify he's there or not. That's pretty simple, really. She's right there on Sinop."

"Now wait a minute, Pete. I don't want you dragging Sun into this. She doesn't need to go anywhere near Conde Sur."

"It's not dangerous, Lilly. And this is exactly the kind of thing she handles well. There's nothing like an Army clerk to untangle the bureaucratic quagmire of the penal system. All we need her to do is go up to the prison barges and verify he's still there. He's either there, or he's not. And if I send a request from here, she'll have a little weight behind her request. At worst, he's escaped, and no one at Conde Sur will want to admit it, but they won't be able to dodge both the Lazaretto Police and the Army."

"I still don't think—"

"Sun will be fine. She's not that delicate, if you remember."

"No, I remember," Lilly couldn't help but remember. The diminutive Sun had nearly been murdered by Chitti Sienté and left both to bleed to death and drown in a rat-trap of a room in one of the oldest districts of the Lazaretto. Somehow she had survived through sheer determination that even now was impossible to imagine. It wasn't Sun's strength that held Lilly in check. It was something more personal.

"Pete, the problem here is that if you ask her to do this, then this becomes more than just an oddball incident. It makes it that much more real. It validates my neurosis. I can't back up and just say I was mistaken. You know?"

"Sun won't talk about this at the next Army picnic, if that's what's worrying you. And we won't have to tell Lepov either. Okay? Let's just say we're doing it to make sure my new boss has the peace of mind I require in order to work for her. Make sense?"

"No, it doesn't make sense. But it is satisfactory. Should I call Sun and explain?"

"No, ma'am." Pete wagged a finger and gave her a mocking scowl. "I've been looking for an excuse to talk to her for a few days now. And this call gets charged to my boss."

He winked at her and Lilly did her best to smile at him. He was doing everything he could to make her feel comfortable, including the comment about the cost of the call. He seemed determined to prove that her visions of Shay had been nothing to worry about.

And that had to be the answer. They had to be nothing more than visions. They would soon learn that Shay was safely locked away on his prison barge and then her only concern would be a slight loss of dignity as they laughed at her paranoia.

26

He took some consolation in the fact that he held off for four full hours. If he were in the mood to be honest, Lepov would have admitted that he had already changed his mind two hours after they'd walked out the door and had only waited the other two hours to see if he'd change it back again. But since this involved Gloria, he wasn't about to start being honest with himself anytime soon. Hell, then he'd end up admitting he knew all along he was going to cave in.

Somewhere Lilly had to be getting a spine-chilling premonition. This was going to tear apart in so many directions Lepov clenched his jaw and swore he'd quit thinking about it. The lies were going to pile up for the rest of the day.

He'd tracked them down to a hotel near the Alpha Quadrant entrance. Alpha was in lockdown which left the hotel at nearly minimum occupancy. This was obvious when the desk clerk eyed him with a fair amount of bewilderment. Lepov didn't approach the clerk; he already knew which room Gloria and Dannen were using. But Lepov wasn't going to their room. He was in no hurry to see them and he wanted to play down the fact that he was recanting his refusal to work for them. His reluctance fortified his resolve to wait for them.

They did not come down to the lobby. She did. Alone. She was halfway across the open red carpet, tugging on a pair of black gloves, when she saw him stand up from a corner chair. It angered him that she displayed no surprise. At least she didn't gloat with a smile. Lepov knew all too well that the absence of the smile did not prove she wasn't gloating, but it made it easier to swallow his pride.

"Tell me he wasn't lying about this deal."

"He was lying, Grey." Lepov questioned her with eyes that had long ago learned to do so without words. "I was coming to find you. I can help you find Jardyn. He didn't stay in Alpha. He's waiting for me. But we need your help."

"We? Is that you and Dannen or you and Jardyn? And before you answer you should know I already regret coming down here."

"Me and Lou. We need your help. Kry is dangerous."

"Tired of Dannen already? Did you last longer with him than you did with me?"

"Don't make jokes, Grey. Not now."

"I wasn't joking. You're taking up with another man and I'm supposed to help you carry the furniture again?"

"No," she put a hand on his arm, her touch so soft he couldn't feel it through his coat, "Lou's not that kind of friend. We just both wanted to get away from Kry. But Kry's not easy to leave. He's aggressive, and jealous, and he doesn't like to lose."

"You've just described the majority of men. What makes him so special?"

"You're not like that, Grey. You've got kindness. Lots of it."

"Yeah? It must take up so much room there isn't any left for brains. You know I actually came down here to accept your job offer? Now listen to you. I must have been out of my mind."

"What a happy coincidence," Dannen's deep voice came from the other end of the lobby. Lepov could see Gloria fight off the impulse to look startled that Dannen had been behind her. She waited and Lepov knew she was wondering if Dannen had heard anything they'd said. Dannen crossed the room. "Gloria was just about to go back to your office and attempt to persuade you to reconsider."

"No coincidence, Dannen." Lepov stared at Gloria long enough to examine her for any signs of deception. He'd been able to read her from top to bottom after they'd been married a while, but he worried that he'd lost his touch during their separation. He wasn't sure one way or the other. She stood with her back to Dannen, her eyes pleading with him to stay.

"It's not too early for a drink, is it?" Dannen held out a hand indicating the entrance to the hotel bar. The room was empty.

"I might have said yes before you two showed up at my office.

But I'm not sure there's going to be a time that's too early anymore."

Lepov slid onto the nearest barstool and watched Dannen do the same. Gloria had followed them but stood off to the side, clearly not sure if she wanted to stay or go. Lepov didn't look directly at her. He needed to keep eye contact with her to a minimum. He had decided to take the job but he was only going to do so while keeping her at arm's length. Her damsel in distress bit was not the kind of scene he'd wanted to get written into.

His most lucid justification for taking the job was the one that said he wanted to help them get what they wanted only to get them out of the Lazaretto. God only knew how bad things might become the longer they lingered in the Laz. Lepov expected things to get bad if he took on Gloria as a client but he wanted to believe he could control the extent of the damage she could do.

"Shall I find a bartender?" Dannen looked over at the empty side of the bar.

"Forget about the drinks, Dannen. Let's get some basic rules laid down."

"Certainly. You are, after all, the professional here. What do you suggest?"

"You can start off by cutting out the condescending indulgence. I haven't been handled like this since Gloria announced she was severing our marriage in half. You've stuck the knife in already, no need to whisper softly in my ear now that I'm bleeding to death."

"You're exaggerating, but I can take a point."

"You pay up front. I decide how to do this. You don't interfere. That's for any client. No exceptions." Lepov didn't have to look at Gloria, she knew who he was addressing. "And when I tell you to forget Jardyn and get out you do it. I won't lie to you. If I can find him, I'll find him. If I can't, then you won't be able to no matter how long you stay and how hard you try. So if I say go, you go. Both of you."

"You aren't suggesting I would leave my wife behind are you?"

"Not at all. As I recall, she's the one with the talent for leaving someone behind. I haven't eaten lunch. That doesn't help the sickening feeling I'm got in my stomach right now. So I'm gonna go eat something—no, before you offer, don't bother. I'll eat alone. When I'm done, I want everything I'll need back at my office. Everything on Jardyn, the Luger, Frobe. That'll be enough to get started on. Oh, and one more thing, I want to know who your buyer was."

Lepov tried to leave as quickly as possible, before they could try and stop him. He needed to get away from them. It was going to take a little time to get used to the idea that he was working for Gloria. He didn't want to have to look at her while his mind tried to wrap itself around the idea.

"Just a moment," Dannen reached out and grabbed Lepov by a coat sleeve, "I have a few ground rules too."

"Kry, don't." Gloria stepped in, alarm showing through where Lepov had expected anger, "let him go."

"I'm a big boy, Gloria, I can handle a few rules." He stared at Dannen, waiting.

"You keep me informed as much as possible. I won't give you my buyer's name. And you show my wife some respect. That last one I'd demand of any man."

"I'm not just any man, Dannen. I'm the first man, the other man, and the last man you need to worry about around your wife." Lepov tipped his hat at the woman he had considered dead for so many years. "Good day, Mrs. Dannen."

It was always a victory when you could leave a meeting with a client and avoid hitting them square in the teeth. Lepov watched the hotel doors roll up and away from him and he enjoyed the feel of the cool rain in his face. It didn't remove the sick feeling from his gut, but it did help him regain control over his temper. It wasn't that he suddenly felt as if he'd made a mistake in taking the job. That had been understood from the beginning. But the fact that he couldn't make it through their first meeting without taking a shot at Gloria and nearly getting into a brawl with her husband underlined just how big this mistake would turn out to be.

Lilly was going to kill him when he told her what was going on. Unless she chose to walk out on him. He might be deserving of either scenario, but he could handle the former better than the latter.

Lepov tried to find a place to eat as he wondered how in the hell he had managed to walk into a day like this one.

27

Jonnie Spaeth.

MacNally's luck could not have been worse.

Two men walk through a door on an average night, in an average bar, and an average cop makes a decision that will change everything he's ever known. Stay in your seat, look away, and the world goes on. Stand up, stick your nose in it, and life, as defined by Edward Patrick MacNally, becomes an alternate world, filled with the shadows of what once was as well as what will inevitably become a violent conclusion.

Jonnie Spaeth.

MacNally had little time to consider his Captain's cowardly

conduct. If he had been afforded the time, he could have spent hours expressing his anger and disappointment with the man who had been his boss for over two decades. He could have pointed out that they had once been detectives together. Green, eager, and both too interested in skirt-chasing to settle down with a good woman the way Fenelli had. He could have spent just as much time reminiscing over the times Jenkins had saved MacNally's skin, or how MacNally and Fenelli had gone that extra mile to solve a case that made Jenkins look like a genius.

But there was not going to be any of that. Time was not just a luxury he could not afford: it was a necessity he would never be allowed. Time had run out before the clock started.

Jonnie Spaeth.

As soon as Jenkins disappeared into the elevator, MacNally was already thinking two steps ahead. He returned to his apartment just long enough to grab his hat, the Riot Tamer standing behind his door, and his service weapon.

He meant to get out as soon as he grabbed these three items, but he stopped at the sink and added a quick cup of water. His throat had gone dry as he moved through his rooms. He filled it a second time and poured more of it down his throat. He would have preferred whiskey but he needed to keep his mind sharp. The chill of the water helped to clear his mind.

He had no time for regrets or recriminations, but he still had time to think; time to plan his next move.

He had to get to the box. That was paramount. Nothing else mattered. Somewhere in the back of his mind he considered whether or not he was going to tell Lepov. It was not an easy decision. But it was one that could be made on his way to the box.

He stood at his open door. Reaching into an inner pocket, he pulled out his data tag. He had considered leaving it in the apartment. But without it he would never get his car moving. And besides, if they were coming for him, they would check his apartment anyway. No point in drawing them into a location they were already going to hit.

He stuffed it back into the pocket and grabbed the Riot Tamer. No reason to take the stairs. Yes, he was going to defend himself. No, he wasn't going to panic. He stood in the center of the elevator and patiently waited for it to drop him to the ground floor and open its doors. He stalked through the small lobby, head held high.

Involving Lepov was a problem. He would willingly help; Lepov wasn't the type to ignore a friend in need. But MacNally wasn't the type to drag a friend into his own trouble lightly. He would only do it if he thought it would make a difference. Involving Lepov was only an option if it increased MacNally's chance to survive. He wasn't going to ask Lepov for help just for companionship. Sure, he didn't want to face this alone. But that wasn't the issue.

He was almost across town before he thought about Jonnie Spaeth again. He didn't want to. But he couldn't avoid it.

Officially, Jonnie Spaeth was the owner of a small transport business that operated out of Bukovina. This modest fleet of strato-tankers kept busy supplying loads of Bukovinan oil to the other planets in the Euxine system. Spaeth's transports were a common sight in cities capable of receiving off-planet transports.

Unofficially, Jonnie Spaeth ran a large portion of Bukovina as if it were his personal kingdom, financed by his ironclad oil monopoly. Backed by an aggressive cartel on Earth, Spaeth gained control of the oil through a ruthless campaign that only started with transportation. The colony worlds were still young and unprepared to resist Spaeth's coordinated takeover of the trade. Those few who attempted to oppose him were easily removed. Before resources on Earth could be mustered to derail him, Spaeth was firmly in control of a commodity that all of the planets desperately needed. His corrupt yet lucrative influence convinced politicians to turn a blind eye to his actions and recognize him as an exclusive supplier.

Spaeth might have been a respectable business man after that. His past could have been overlooked if his past would have remained in the past. But Jonnie Spaeth was an emotional man. He was a greedy man. And he was easily angered by any man who might challenge his role as the sole supplier of Euxine oil. Spaeth earned a reputation as a man who was not just willing to eliminate the competition, but was known to do so with his own hands.

His violent tendencies left a foul taste in the mouths of the politicians, but they had little recourse to oppose him. The colony worlds were too distant from Earth to rely on any sizable military intervention. And while the colonies had one, central military force, it was too dependent on Spaeth's oil to move against him.

The colonies had come to the conclusion that as long as Spaeth made no attempt to enlarge his empire, they would allow him to run his affairs as he saw fit. That they had little choice in the matter was clear, though it was impolite to speak of it at government functions.

MacNally, like most decent men, despised the politicians who allowed Spaeth to operate. But like most decent men, it did not bother him enough to do anything about it. A cynical comment now and then was enough to salve the conscience; Spaeth existed, and the common man did his best to ignore the fact.

For lawmen like MacNally, they were more directly aware of Spaeth and his penchant for breaking the law. But it did not mean there was anything to be done about it. Law enforcement was hired by the government. Government was run by the politicians. It did not pay to stand up to Jonnie Spaeth.

MacNally had been right when he said Spaeth did not operate in the Lazaretto. Yes, his transports passed through the shipping port. However, Spaeth never personally travelled. There were always rumors that he travelled outside the Lazaretto system, bypassing the quarantine, but such rumors could never be confirmed. Cops like MacNally had been happy that they never had to deal with Spaeth. If he were breaking the law and jumping from one planet to the other without the quarantine process, who would dare to speak out?

Who, indeed? That was the real problem. On the rare occasions when Spaeth came out into the real world, no one dared try and stop him. He was inviolate.

And MacNally was being blamed for the death of Jonnie Spaeth's kid brother. There was no way to know how the man would react. But the odds that he ignored MacNally were poor at best. The better money was on Spaeth making a show of his grief and his vengeance. He was not the sort of man to allow an insult to go unpunished.

All MacNally could hope for was that Spaeth's short attention span would allow him to move on to more pressing matters if MacNally could stay ahead of him. Jenkins had already signaled his unwillingness to help. Russell had been removed from the equation — something MacNally couldn't really argue against. It meant MacNally could go to ground on his own. Without the added worry of someone else to protect.

Logically, this left Lepov out of the fight as well. It meant he'd never had much of an option about that in the first place. He couldn't, in good conscience, expose Lepov to whatever was coming.

And no matter what was coming — be it a single assassin, an armed platoon of Spaeth's gunmen, or even Jonnie Spaeth himself — MacNally had to disappear. And that meant he had to ditch his PDT as soon as possible.

The box was near, but MacNally did not get close to it. He drove along a street perpendicular to the box and kept going until he was well beyond that point. He would have to ditch the PDT, his car, and double back to the box. He chose a SubTransit station where he could toss the PDT into an open SubTransit car. It would only take about ten minutes to walk from there to the box.

He would try to make it in eight.

28

They waited for two hours before the overweight woman with

thinning hair led them into a small office. A man with an ill-fitting face pointed at a chair, as if all three of them should sit in it. Lara sat down and pulled Jett onto her lap. Frank stood beside her.

"I'm Jacob Twoley, Assistant to the Placement Director. Your tag?"

The IHS man pointed at a tag reader and Frank placed his tag on top of it.

"Sorry about that. Our machines are a little outdated. We're supposed to get proximity readers very soon." His words trailed off as he tapped rapidly on his deskscreen. To Lara, it looked as if the man were repeatedly hitting the same two letters, reminding Lara of a child playing a game.

"What was the problem?" Twoley asked without looking up.

"With the accommodations?" Frank asked.

"Yes. You did not take possession of the apartment. You made an urgent appointment—that's what my secretary wrote here—*urgent*—so I am under the assumption there was a problem with the apartment."

"We never saw the apartment. The building itself was filthy. Unkempt. The elevator out of service." Frank kept his temper in check. Lara wished he wouldn't.

"Elevator out of service?" Twoley sat back in his chair and very deliberately eyed the Dassins. "That's the first I've heard of that. I'll check it out as soon as we're finished. Was that the extent of your urgent business?"

Lara knew the man was making fun of them, though he tried to hide his mockery behind a well-practiced air of concern.

Frank did no such thing. He crowded the edge of the clerk's desk, clearly angry.

"The elevator is hardly the issue. What we really need is to speak with someone about our son. I am told there is an appeals process, and before you say it, I am aware that it is lengthy and hopeless. I just want to know what our full options are."

"I understand, Mr. Dassin." Twoley gave them an encouraging smile. "I wasn't aware you were interested in filing an appeal. And you're wrong. The process is not hopeless at all. A little expensive, sure, but don't think of it as hopeless."

"Do you mean that, Mr. Twoley?" Lara tightened her hold on Jett as he squirmed on her knee.

"Well, I'm not an expert on the appeal, I'm just a Placement officer. I'm sure someone at the Review Board can explain it to you."

"We were told something about a case officer. One would be assigned."

"Well, Mr. Dassin, I'm sure that must be true, but I don't know who assigns the case officer. That might come from Public Affairs...no that's not right. Excuse a moment of bad memory. Case officers are issued by Patient Affairs. They both start with P, sorry. Patient Affairs can tell you who your case officer is."

"And that's where we start the appeal?" Lara tried to ignore the hope that begged to be recognized in her breast.

"Yes, isn't that what you said?"

Lara looked from Twoley to Frank then back again. She didn't understand what he meant. Frank looked just as unsure.

"Okay, so can you call Patient Affairs and get the name of this case officer?" Frank must have read the worry on Lara's face. He added a measure of urgency to his tone. "We must meet with him right away."

"I can't just call over there and get his name. You have to go see them. But don't worry, they'll make everything right. They're very good at what they do."

"And what are you good at, Mr. Twoley?" asked Frank.

"I'm good at placing people in the homes they need. And to prove it, I'm going to do everything I can for you." He opened up a file on his deskscreen and began repeatedly tapping it again.

"You can find us a better apartment?" Lara's voice rose with her expectations.

"No, Mrs. Dassin. I'm sorry, I don't think you understood. You'll have to use the apartment we assigned to you, unless you want to pay for one of your own. But I will make sure the elevator is working by noon tomorrow. You have my word on that. And again I am sorry for such an inconvenience. If someone had only told me sooner, I could have had it fixed by dinner time. What else can I do for you?"

They fared no better at Patient Affairs.

The woman behind the desk at Patient Affairs spoke with a saccharine, measured tone. Lara hadn't been spoken to like that since she was a child.

"I wasn't expecting a request for a case officer this soon. You understand? Most people don't start this process until there is a real need. We don't assign case officers unless there is a specific need."

"I told you, Miss Bey," Frank's effort at concealing his frustration was fading quickly, "we have a specific need. We want to begin the appeals process."

"You do?" Miss Bey looked genuinely puzzled. "That's not something we can handle here. That takes someone at the Board of Review to sanction. A case officer here has very limited authority."

"We understand the Board makes the final decision. We just want to begin the appeal. File the appeal."

"You don't understand, Mr. Dassin. You cannot file the appeal without Board sanction. I'm sorry, but that's the policy. I don't make the rules."

"Then let's save some time," Frank leaned towards Miss Bey and Lara reached out to hold him back. It would not do Jett any good if Frank were to get thrown out of the office or into jail. "Tell me your supervisor's name and I'll talk with him."

"I can't do that. But you can tell me why you want to meet with my supervisor, and I can do my best to help you."

"Assign us a case officer," Frank insisted.

"I've already told you I will. Was there anything else?"

Lara stood up and put an arm around Frank before he could respond to the woman's maddeningly phony smile. Frank scooped up Jett as they left Miss Bey's office.

29

She stood in her kitchen staring into the empty sink. Lilly wanted to believe that she was only tired. That she was simply not thinking straight due to a lack of sleep. As if sleep would erase the thoughts that crowded her mind.

She had spent the morning bantering with Pete, doing her level best to ignore what had happened the day before. It was, after all, not that remarkable. Her husband, from so many years ago, had begun to appear to her as if he were a ghost. That might have made sense if the man were dead. But for all she knew he was still alive and securely incarcerated at Conde Sur. Or perhaps he had been released and was indeed skulking about the Lazaretto. But if he were, it would mean he was not there to reminisce with her. They had clearly looked into each other's eyes, surrounded by the parade of death, if it had in fact been Shay. The fact that he did not approach her, did not speak with her, could only have meant that he wanted to keep away from her. Unless it meant he *could not* speak to her — if it was physically impossible.

Yet he had spoken to her, in the night.

She shook her head. Filling the sink, she cleaned her lunch dishes, placing each antique plate and companion saucer into a drying carousel. The dishes had been part of a deal that had fallen apart in the early years of her artifacts business. A client had wanted her to purchase authentic dishes from the early 20th century, but Lilly had been fooled by a broker on Dnepr who sold her reproductions. They were still plenty old, just not the kind of old the client had been looking for. Lilly had not been so embarrassed at the fact that she had been taken. She had been more upset that the client had realized it before she had.

She had learned early on that she could never take anything at face value. Her career depended on going to the third and fourth level of authentication before risking her money or her clients' money on whatever piece was being sought, no matter how anxious the client was to get their hands on it.

These sightings of Shay had to be handled in the same manner. So far, she had no proof that what she was seeing was Shay. She had to wait for Sun's report. Then she would do what she could to pursue and verify exactly what she was seeing. Until then, she had no reason to think about, worry about, or even speculate about the few fleeting moments she had thought she'd seen Shay Stewart.

Drying her hands, she crossed the kitchen floor and moved down the hallway until she came into the main living room. Pete had left after they had eaten lunch. He was finalizing his paperwork for entering Alpha Quadrant. Although he was keeping his apartment, he had to arrange for his extended absence. Lilly had enjoyed watching him make his plans. He was giddy at the prospect of travel. Even an optimist like Pete felt the weight of the Lazaretto and knew it was a good thing to get out of it.

Sitting down on her couch, Lilly laid her head back and tried to allow herself the chance to nap. She knew she wouldn't sleep long. But five minutes of sleep could be just the right answer to a mind too overloaded with questions and anxieties.

When she reopened her eyes, her head was turned to one side and she could see the clock. Ten minutes had passed; some of them in sleep. Lilly could not be sure if she had been awakened by a noise or if it had happened randomly. Either way, she turned in time to see a man's form at the window. The glare from the overcast afternoon shrouded the man's image. The only thing Lilly knew for sure was that this form of a man had been at the window with his hands touching the glass. Before she could stand up, his black form dropped out of sight.

Lilly rushed to the window and tried to look below. She could see nothing. The window had a scrim of condensation coating it. In the bright glare she put her hands up and touched the handprints left on the glass. She watched as the condensation bled down in rivulets, obscuring the two images.

Lilly watched her own hands begin to tremble. They did not stop. She pressed against the cold glass. By the time she finally brought them under control the handprints on the outside of the glass had been washed away. Lilly pulled away her hands and hugged herself, warming her long fingers in the synthetic folds of her blouse. Where once she had seen handprints on the outside, she could now see them on the inside. She knew they were her own, but she couldn't help imagining they were made by phantom hands.

It really wouldn't matter what Sun could find out. The fact of the matter was, Shay was here. How that could be didn't matter. Lilly placed one of her still-cold hands over her mouth as she tried not to laugh with madness. She didn't have to be told if Shay was dead or alive. He'd just been watching her again, just outside her room, his hands resting against a window that was staring out from seven floors above the city.

It was more than Lilly could handle. She'd done her best to hold on to a few basic explanations that would allow her pragmatic mind to reconcile with the visions she had been seeing. It was time to admit that she could not handle this on her own. Yes, Pete had offered to help, but that was not who Lilly needed. She needed Gregor. This went beyond a reasonable concern. Real fear was beginning to take over.

She grabbed a TransitCar without daring to look up at the exterior of her building. Perhaps she would have been happy to discover Shay clinging precariously to a ledge just below her windows. She knew very well that she would not see him. He was gone. Just like he had disappeared in that crowd. Just like he had disappeared in the window reflection. Even his voice had disappeared after speaking to her that one, haunting phrase.

Trust me.

She sat very still during the ride to Gregor's office. It had been difficult not to demand that the driver get there as fast as possible. It had been just as difficult not to look back and see if Shay were following them, skimming above the traffic, his hands held out still pressed against imaginary glass, condensation dripping from his fingers.

Lilly conjured up an image of Gregor, if only to banish the image of Shay. He would laugh at her. Tell her she was acting like an excitable woman. Gregor would not like that. He was more attracted to her sense than anything that might smack of sensibility.

Again, when exiting the TransitCar, she swung shut its door without looking back to see if Shay hung above the road, watching her. The possibility of it began to overpower her and she hurried up the steps and into Gregor's building.

The old elevator, creaking as it rose, was safe. It had no glass, nothing in which to cast a reflection. Lilly, despite her shame, was grateful for this chance to take in a deep breath. She needed to collect herself, be as calm as possible before speaking with Gregor. He did not need to see her off balance.

When the doors slid open she kept her eyes on the scarred,

wooden floor, stepping out of the elevator quickly. It was easier to speculate on the age of the floors, and why this insignificant building would have real wood instead of synthetic. She realized for the first time that wood had once been alive. Unlike stone, wood had been a *living* thing, and that under her feet was a layer of something once alive that was now dead.

She should have turned around and gone back home. Gregor would never be fooled into believing she was in control of her mind at this moment. He would see right through any attempts she made to hide her fear and confusion.

As it turned out, she was right to think that going home would have been better than going into Gregor's office. But that had nothing to do with her state of mind.

Opening his door, she stepped in and found Gregor sitting at his desk. A blonde woman stood beside him, her hand resting on Gregor's hand. The woman slowly withdrew her hand and Gregor's face betrayed his anger at Lilly's entrance. All three of them quietly held still for three or four beats.

"Hello, Lilly," Gregor was first to recover. He slipped something small off his desk and put it in his pocket as he stood. "May I introduce Mrs. Dannen? She's my...well, actually, her husband is my new client. Mrs. Dannen, this is a very good friend of mine, Ms. Lilly Stewart."

"It's nice to meet you," the blonde turned and nodded; her smile and visual examination of Lilly quite deliberate.

"I didn't mean to interrupt, Mrs. Dannen." Lilly returned the scrutiny.

"Please, call me..."

"Gloria," Gregor stepped forward, supplying the name before the woman could, "Gloria Dannen. She once had the dubious honor of bearing the name Gloria Lepov."

This time, the beats counted out in silence were much higher than four or five. It was obvious to Lilly that Lepov was not sure how to act. He was clearly irritated even as he displayed embarrassment. Gloria Dannen did not display anything with her smile. Her eyes remained in a holding pattern, not willing to show anything more than just a hint of amusement.

Lilly should have found a way out of this moment. She was always the level-headed one who knew just what to say. But here, now, as she fled from Shay's ghost, she had not been prepared to meet this very real, living ghost from Gregor's past.

The longer the silence, the more Gloria's amusement began to show. Lilly was beginning the think the only way out of this was to take a page out of Gregor's book and make a fist and use it on the woman.

"I'm glad to hear you're a good friend of Grey's," Gloria said, "he's never had too many of them in his life. He needs every one he can get."

"She's the best friend I've ever found." Gregor crossed to Lilly. "If I had any sense I'd marry the woman, but then again, my last proposal left some doubt as to whether I had any sense to begin with."

"Oh, there was never any question about your level of sense, Grey." Gloria began to pull on long gloves as she moved to the door. "Miss Stewart, I can see by the level of embarrassment on Grey's face that he's going to have a lot of trouble explaining my presence here. Let me help a little. Until this morning, Grey had no idea my husband and I were here. We have hired him to help him locate something for us. Once that's done, we'll leave this Lazaretto. It's nothing more than that. I only came here to deliver a data tag he requested. Don't be hard on him."

As if she had done him a favor, Gloria turned and nodded at Gregor with satisfaction. She gave Lilly one last look, though what she was thinking could not be plainly read on her pale, round face. Before Lilly or Gregor could think of a response she slipped out the door.

"Want to ask me today if I believe in ghosts?" Gregor stared at the closed door.

"No," Lilly answered. "I don't have to. If there's a perfectly rational explanation as to why Gloria was here in your office, there might just be one to explain why Shay was outside my window a few minutes ago."

Gregor didn't bother to ask her what she meant. He just opened a drawer and pulled out his bottle of scotch. While he unscrewed the cap, Lilly grabbed a glass from a shelf behind the desk. He poured enough for both of them.

"Lilly..."

"Don't." She left the glass on the desk and pulled him to her. She kissed him then, like she never had before. Gregor wasn't the only one willing to fight for what he wanted.

30

"I really need to hire my ex-wife more often," Lepov still had his arms around Lilly as they both stopped to take a breath, "I'm pretty sure you've never kissed me like that before."

"And I may not again," she said without adding a smile. "You aren't completely off the hook, I just needed to..."

"Let me know what I had to lose?"

"Something like that."

"I look forward to my next, more urgent warning."

He had not expected her to be standing there bantering with him when she had walked through the door. It had been one of those five-star moments when someone walks through the door at the worst possible moment.

Gloria had been in the office for only a short time, sent by Dannen to deliver the data tag with everything he'd asked for. Lepov hadn't been happy to see she'd come alone and he'd done his best to let her know it. She had tried to explain, to continue the conversation they had nearly started in the hotel lobby.

"I told you I could help you find Lou." The words had sounded more rehearsed then than the first time she'd uttered them.

"And you told me you weren't switching lovers," had been Lepov's reply. He had wanted to throw her out but she was fascinating to watch, even if she couldn't be trusted. What would she try next?

"I'll help you find him, but you can't tell Kry where he is."

"I'm not new at this, Gloria. Let me do my job. You tell me what is really going on and I'll decide what to do. I think I can handle that much."

"Don't take this lightly, Grey. He's dangerous to us and he's dangerous to you too." She'd gone too far, too quick. Laying it on that thick had failed to enchant Lepov. When he'd reached out to take the data tag she'd set on the desk, she had put her hand on his and Lepov had been ready to shut her down. Only Lilly's entrance had saved him from slapping his former wife and throwing her out of the office.

Maybe Gloria had known it. Maybe she'd tossed out that little goodwill gesture as she left in an attempt to undo her mistake. Lepov had almost bought the performance, relieved that he would not have to explain everything to Lilly on his own; he had nearly fallen for Gloria's kindness.

Sure, he'd be careful around Dannen. More importantly, he had better be careful around Gloria. He may have just signed on to a deal with two devils, with one of them already working against the other. What really bothered Lepov was not that Gloria had tried to suggest Dannen was dangerous. There was something else that had to be considered: why would the man send her to him alone? If he were already lying to Lepov, why allow Lepov's former wife time alone with him? It made Dannen look like a fool more than a threat.

"You don't hear me, do you?" Lilly put a hand to his face and pulled him around until he could look in her eyes.

"Just something on my mind." Lepov looked at her long enough to consider what she had told him. "You aren't the type to see shadows and cry wolf. So tell me again, is Shay dangerous?"

"I don't know."

"I'll check with Conde Sur. See what his status is."

"We're already doing that." She stopped him from interrupting. "Pete has talked to Sun, and she's going up to the prison barges to try to see him, if he's there. We weren't going to involve you in this. I didn't want to worry you."

"There's a quadrant closing, I wish you could get out of here." It was a thoughtless desire to speak aloud. Cruel, really.

"You could go."

"Now you're just trying to get me away from Gloria."

"It's not a bad idea. Anything to get you away from her."

Lepov wanted to believe she was only joking but he knew better.

"Well, hell. Don't you know you can't run from your ghosts?" Lepov pulled away from her and picked up the glass of scotch. He offered it to her. She declined. "Looks like we both have to face our demons. Might as well do it together."

He drank the double portion and hoped the demons were only metaphorical.

31

As the old saying went: no news is good news. The New Yorker wished he had never heard this latest news. It was as bad as it gets. And it was his job to take it to the Australian. Bad news like this couldn't be handled gently, either. There was no way to soften the blow.

He sat at his desk and wasted a few, short breaths. The longer he put it off, the better the chance his boss would hear it from another source. The only thing worse than delivering news this bad was failing to be the first one to deliver it. At least that was the case when it was your job to keep the boss informed on *everything*.

The Ursuline — he had begun teasing her with this new nickname, in memory of the nuns who used to torture him in school — was expecting him for lunch. She'd better forget it. Foolish theological discussion would do him no good today. Firm resolve and the proper balance of sympathy and anger: that was going to save him more than any prayer or symbolic gesture.

He hurried down the hall and knocked on the Australian's door. After his boss muttered a few words, he entered the office.

His boss, standing by the large, uncovered windows overlooking the Bukovinan plain, did not turn to greet him.

"Is the news any better today?" The Australian's tone conveyed his expectations that the answer to his question would be negative.

"No." The New Yorker took a moment to practice the words he would use. He took too long.

"It must be bad news. I could feel it when you walked in the room. Can you say it without watering it down? I'd rather you get it over with."

"Both of the men I—we sent are dead." He hesitated just enough to see that the Australian was not going to explode immediately; he waited for the rest of it. "They were gunned down in a bar, last night, by a police detective. I'm sorry."

The Australian turned slowly to examine his assistant. He snatched a heavy ornamental lamp from his desk, slamming it against its glass surface. The glass held—it was far too thick to shatter—and he tossed aside what was left of the lamp with another swing of his arm.

"Who is the detective?"

The New Yorker double-checked his memory before he spoke the detective's name. He did so several times to be certain his boss understood him completely.

"An Irishman." The Australian had a sudden, faraway look in his eyes. When he refocused on the New Yorker his eyes had never looked so intense. "My brother was a real idiot. More muscle than brains. But he was all heart. He volunteered to go to the Lazaretto to bring back these thieves. Insisted I let him go. It was supposed to be easy. A simple job."

The New Yorker explained that he had already activated the Slovaks. They could find this hero.

"They might. And if they do, it won't go unappreciated. But that's not how it will play out. Not this time. We don't rely on anyone else from this point on."

"You mean—"

"We are going to go in there, find these guys who stole from me, kill them, and we'll do the same to my brother's killer. This Irishman will die. And so will everyone who had anything to do with this theft. The day they decided to steal from me was the day they murdered my brother."

The New Yorker nodded, unable to generate any genuine sympathy for his employer's brother. He had been a brute, a bully, and he liked to beat up women. There wasn't one reason to mourn his death or avenge it.

But there was no way to say that to his boss. And so he kept his mouth shut and started making a mental list of everything that had to be done before they boarded the *Strike*.

32

Lara Dassin had never wanted more than a simple life with her family. Frank had been a kind man; a quiet, gentle friend of her sister's who had surprised her with his interest. She had not stolen him from Louise. Frank had not been that kind of friend. He'd been a fellow student of Louise's at the University and they had kept in touch once they'd graduated. Passing through San Francisco, Frank had dropped by for a visit. Louise had been out of town and Lara had been forced to play hostess. She hadn't minded in the least. Frank, older by nearly ten years, had a firm resolve about him that immediately appealed to Lara.

Her parents dead—a father who had died while she was an infant, a mother who had died while she was a teenager—Louise had become a mother for Lara. No one had been there to replace her missing father. Lara had never lied to herself when it came to the role that Frank had taken in her life. Yes, she'd agreed to marry him. Yes, she loved him as a husband. But Frank had the sober bearing of a father figure and she knew this had been missing from her early life.

Frank had dark eyes, a square jaw, and blond hair that refused to lie flat at the side part. His wide, flat forehead wrinkled when he worried but smoothed out completely when he smiled. The wrinkles were more likely to be seen than not.

Lara had come to depend on Frank's attention to details. She knew that no matter what happened, Frank would make certain their family could handle whatever came their way. His discipline and clear-thinking formed the basis of Lara's security.

And since Jett had been removed from quarantine, her security had been tested beyond its limits. She had expected Frank to step in and calm her maternal fears. Instead, Frank had been on edge; he grew more unbalanced as each hour passed.

"It isn't as bad as I thought it would be." Lara stood at the entrance to the small kitchen. "Cleaner than I expected."

They had dragged themselves up the seventeen flights of steps to the room supplied to them by the IHS. She had talked Frank into trying the apartment. The IHS man had promised to get the elevator working, after all. Why spend money on a hotel if they didn't need to? There was no telling how tight things might get in the future.

"This was a bad idea." Frank switched on a light and moved down a short hallway, opening the few doors he found.

"Give it time, Frank." Lara fought down her restlessness. She was worrying more about Frank than Jett. "You know that we'll be okay, don't you? That I still love you?"

"Sure," he said, nodding. His smile did not erase the lines across his forehead. He pulled at his tie, slipping the knot. A quick jerk and it snaked around his collar and dropped into his hand.

Lara watched him unbutton the front of his shirt, then the cuffs. She decided to back off. Perhaps he just needed time to accept things. Maybe he just needed a good night's sleep.

She was amazed at her own ability to take in their situation. That her only son was sick and trapped in a world such as the Lazaretto should have left her emotionally incapacitated. But it hadn't. She couldn't say why, but a desire to meet their hard luck head on rose within her even as Frank seemed to unravel. It was probably just instinct; she knew Jett was relying on his parents to maintain hope and foster courage in the face of such troubling changes. That Frank seemed unable to do so only strengthened her resolve to provide that constancy for Jett.

She turned her attention to her son, bathing him, dressing him for bed, humming a tune that was sure to bring a yawn to his young, tiny mouth. She rubbed him dry with a towel.

"Are you tired?"

He shook his head.

"Then I shall read to you."

A knock at the front door threatened to shake the door off its hinges. Lara left the little bathroom and entered the main room, eyeing the door with more than a little alarm. Before she could reach it, Frank rushed past her and blocked her.

"Don't," he ordered. He stopped at the door and touched it carefully with both hands. Leaning forward, he placed an ear against it. The knocking started again.

"Get back in the room with Jett!" His look was enough to make her run for her son.

At the hallway, she stopped, torn between fear and curiosity. What was Frank hiding from her? What was it he couldn't say? She stood at the end of the hall, holding onto the door frame as she leaned around the corner, afraid now to find out what was haunting her husband but unable to look away.

Frank was still at the closed door, talking to someone on the other side. She could not hear what was being said. Frank did not unlock the door. After a few more muffled words were spoken, Frank raised his voice.

"Okay! I heard you. Just let us be." He turned his back to the door and leaned against it. The lines on his forehead were beaded with sweat. He reached into a pocket and pulled out a pack of cigarettes. He was too nervous to light one of them on the first attempt. By the time Lara worked up the courage to approach the door, Frank had calmed down enough to make eye contact with her.

"Can you believe it?" Nervous laugher ended in a harsh cough. "They got the elevator working already. How's that for service?"

"What's the matter, Frank?" She searched his deep-set eyes, placing her hands against his unbuttoned shirt. "Talk to me."

"Not tonight. You go to sleep. It's been a long day." He leaned down and kissed the bridge of her nose. "Go on, I'll be along in a while. Cut off the light, would you?"

He dragged a chair over to the one window in the main room. Dropping into it, he sat forward, his elbows resting on his knees. When Lara switched off the light, she could see the red glow of his cigarette reflected in the window. It grew bright red then faded out as the reflection was blocked by a dark cloud of smoke.

33

There was nothing like a cold, wet night to allow a man the comfort of his own thoughts in total privacy. Lying in bed with nothing more than an undershirt, shorts, and a thin blanket, Lepov lay with his arms folded behind his head. He was staring at the ceiling — a patch of lattice-work shadow created the impression of being imprisoned. When the lights from outside his apartment dimmed in the pouring rain, the prison look was replaced by a solid black that reminded him of being jammed into a coffin. Even the cold air of his bedroom couldn't dispel that dark memory. He could smell the salt water and his own sweat and he brushed the blanket away in the flush of memory.

Pushing up on one elbow, he rolled to his side as he worked a kink out of his neck. If this was the kind of nonsense he was thinking about before he was asleep, he sure as hell didn't want to fall asleep and get a look at the dreams waiting for him. He sat up the rest of the way and let his feet rest on the cold bare floor.

He wanted a cigarette.

Lilly would have pushed him back into bed and insisted he stay there. Gloria, so many years ago, wouldn't have cared if he had left the house in search of a bar. She wouldn't even have asked where he had gone when he came back.

It amused him to think he avoided sleep for fear he'd dream of Gloria again. It was a sure sign he was losing his mind. After all, he had agreed to work for her in the wide-awake world. Why would he not dare to dream of her? She wasn't any more dangerous in his dreams. Yes, his imagination could get the better of him there, but at least there the damage was only illusion. Whatever she was up to in the real world could do him serious and irrevocable harm.

So why had he agreed to it?

Lepov pulled on a pair of pants and tugged the belt tight. He pulled at his blinds enough to be able to see through the slats out into the rain soaked streets. He kept the lights turned off.

He had agreed to work for her because the fact was he had never done anything to oppose her. Not even at the end. When she had announced she was leaving, he had helped her do it. Had never thrown her out. Had never burned that bridge. He'd just stood at his end of it as she crossed over and went her own way, never looking back. Now she was back, standing in the middle of it, beckoning to him, and he had already taken a few steps in her direction.

He had learned to not want her back. That had been easier than he had expected. His co-workers had expected it to be easy but they had never known just how much he cared for Gloria. How he had believed the forever part. How he had watched her announce she was leaving; his heart numb and only able to hold still and wait until she followed through with her inexorable dedication to her goal. Not wanting her back had taken just long enough to remove the tangible strands of her out of his life. He had never spent much time digging around and washing out the intangibles but he had figured it wouldn't matter when he left for the Lazaretto. It was a testimony to the strength of his deeper feelings that he saw the Lazaretto as a fresh place to restart his life.

Lilly had sealed the deal. He had found all he needed with her. There was no going back to Bukovina. No need for it. No angle to it. His business didn't exactly pay the bills, but he had enough saved up to keep him going a while.

Despite the cold room, Lepov half-filled one side of his kitchen sink with cold water and lifted two handfuls of it to his face. He let the water run down into his shirt. It hadn't cleared his head completely but it helped. If he was going to be awake he needed to think more clearly and deliberately.

It wasn't doing him any good bitterly rehashing Gloria's leaving. It would do just as little good to make foolish plans about his future with Lilly. The one was over and done, the other would happen just fine without the uncalled-for speculation.

Lepov needed to get a better grip on Dannen and Gloria. At first he had assumed they were working together to use Lepov and somehow leave him holding the bag or, at the least, leave him as a patsy for whatever scheme they were involved in. With those options in front of him he knew he should have turned them down. But it had seemed wiser to go ahead and stick his head in the noose if only to keep an eye on them as he worked out their game.

But that damsel bit Gloria had pulled off had been convincing enough to add a full dose of doubt to Lepov's head. It should have simply made Lepov more suspicious. It had been too obvious. Too neat. The husband that Lepov hates needs his help and the wife that left Lepov is willing to expose the her husband's plan? She might still have some kind of feelings for Lepov, but not ones that were strong enough to go against the man that brought her into the Laz.

As crazy as it sounded, Gloria was not the disloyal type. Sure, she'd left Lepov, broken her vows, and set herself up with another man. But everything about it had been out in the open. There had been no sneaking around behind his back. She had never lied about her intentions. Once she'd decided to abandon him, she'd done it with the most straightforward manner Lepov could imagine. She had always been able to look him in the eye. It hadn't made Lepov's pain any less, but at least it hadn't added to it.

It was this kind of oddball honesty that made Lepov think there might be something to Gloria's warning. If Dannen were setting him up, Gloria might think nothing of telling Lepov the truth. She might even feel obligated to do it. In her personal world, built on personal ethics that Lepov could never quite understand, maybe she felt as if she owed Lepov the truth.

Maybe. And maybe she really was afraid of Dannen.

Lepov sat down at his desk and powered up the screen. If he was gonna be up all night he might as well get some work done. He was not going to have an epiphany that would settle the question of whether or not Gloria was on the up and up. No, the only way to work that out was to keep both eyes open and keep both Gloria and Dannen within arm's reach as he took one careful step at a time.

He accessed the data tag Gloria had given him. He was going to have to examine it with the patience of a star-counter. He not only had to search through it as a detective hired to help the Dannens, but he also had to look at it from the point of view that either Dannen was lying to him and Gloria was trying to help him, or from the more likely point of view that Dannen *and* Gloria were lying. Hell, maybe Dannen wasn't lying, only Gloria.

"Way to go, Lepov." He stared at the background report on the Luger as he spoke aloud. "You not only take on the clients from hell, but you take on a case that's centered on the gun used in one of the most famous suicides ever. Next thing you know, I'll be letting Satan into the office to discuss the terms of a deal for my soul."

Lepov shuddered. Maybe he already had.

34

The *Strike*, a custom built StarGen Infiltrator, pulled free of Bukovina with its characteristic shudder, which was the only indication of its fight with the planet's gravity. It only lasted long enough to be noticed, left a slight twinge of nausea in the belly, and it was over. The New Yorker looked across the jumpseat bay at the Australian, who was sitting with his eyes closed, not at all interested in the ship's passage through the stratosphere.

The Ursuline was a different story. Strapped into her chair, she had twisted herself to one side in order to catch a glimpse of the rapidly shrinking vista that was the western hemisphere of Bukovina. Already it was difficult to see evidence of the major cities beyond their diamond sparkle lights.

She continued to gaze at the image—it lingered on the screen longer than usual, perhaps the pilot was aware that a first-time flyer was on board—and the look on her face was mesmerizing. The New Yorker had made so many off-planet jumps he no longer paid attention to them. He had never enjoyed them as much as she was enjoying it. Not that he could remember, anyway.

Bringing her had not been his idea. The Australian had suggested it. He couldn't understand why. He had been surprised that the Australian even knew she existed. Maybe he shouldn't have been. The boss always knew what was going on.

When he looked back at his employer, he could see the man's eyes were partially open; he was staring at the Ursuline. The New Yorker felt uneasy. The suggestion to bring her along had been out of place; a friendly gesture he had not been prepared for. There had been little time to consider what it meant.

It might be best to take the time to consider it. The Australian never did anything without a purpose.

"Have you ever seen anything so beautiful?" She turned to him and he could see her eyes glisten. He smiled at her. She was already returning her attention to the screen.

"You should be able to make the call." The Australian shouted across the bay. Raising his voice was unnecessary. The *Strike* was already streaking through the thermosphere, meeting no significant resistance. The noise from its twin rockets was relatively low as they kept moving at speeds far exceeding sound. Still, it was easy to imagine that it was necessary to raise your voice.

The New Yorker opened a link and waited for a reply, nodding at the Australian as he did so. The link would take a few seconds to be completed. But it would be crystal clear once it was locked. More importantly, the shroud could be activated beyond the planet's atmosphere, which would calm the nerves of the man he was calling.

The Source.

"You are clear."

It was always best to begin this type of conversation with that little statement. Their sources were always nervous, never quite trusting the technology. A simple affirmation that it was working went a long way.

"Sending the most recent histories on your man. Reader points with available confirmations. You will see there is an address. It is valid and static." This one was a professional; he had come highly recommended. No stuttering, no hedging. Even better, no audible anxiety. Finding the Swede might be easier than he had expected.

"Second subject?"

"Not yet." The Frenchman was good. It would take luck to locate him.

"And the Irishman?"

"Still working on him. We have a watcher. Just a matter of time."

The New Yorker was not disappointed. They had not expected it to be easy. At least they had a place to start. That the Swede had a static address was interesting. He wasn't running. He should have been in an exit quadrant. Scanning the histories, it was obvious the Swede had indeed been in one of the quadrants but had suddenly left.

Why would the Swede stop running?

35

It had started with a simple discovery: one very old, perfectly preserved, and highly illegal Bushmaster XM-35 Cerakote. MacNally and Fenelli had found it after smashing through a door in a poor housing section on the southwest edge of the city. A murderer by the name of Mot Weeks had been holed up in the house. Weeks had been easy to disarm—he'd only had a malfunctioning shockhammer in his hand when the detectives had come through the door. But the Bushmaster they discovered had been an odd little puzzle.

Weeks had murdered an IHS bureaucrat by the name of Markins in a desperate attempt to put a face to the system that had exiled him in the Lazaretto. Weeks had simply followed Markins from her office to her home, knocked on her door, and hit her in the head with a shockhammer three times. It was a crude murder attempt and the bureaucrat lived long enough to identify her attacker. MacNally and Fenelli broke down his door and made the arrest.

What they could never understand was the assault rifle. Weeks had the Bushmaster in his possession, he wouldn't say how he had acquired it, and he had no explanation why he had chosen not to use it to shoot the woman. He had plenty of ammunition. If he had used it he could have made certain she would never have lived long enough to identify him.

The Bushmaster was rare, a relic from the beginning of the American Troubles. The early, heated debates over gun control had erupted into a shooting war between local militias, teaming up with local law enforcement against Federal agents bent on carrying out the first of the controversial National Weapons Confiscations. The bitter, bloody regional conflicts lasted for more than a decade and led directly to the suspension of Constitutional law in the former United States of America.

The Bushmaster had become a symbol of the resistance. It had also been systematically eradicated from the hands of the populace by a government that promised safety to a population willing to trade their freedom for safety. Over time, the assault rifle became a highly prized collector's piece. It came with an automatic prison term and a fine that was impossible to pay. The few collectors who managed to get their hands on one never boasted of the fact.

How Mot Weeks had come to have one in his house, and how he had been able to get it into the Lazaretto, was more than just an interesting mystery. It was a landmine sure to create a lot of casualties when it exploded. The presence of a Bushmaster inside the Lazaretto would trigger intervention from the military. Heads would roll not only in the halls of Lazaretto law enforcement, but above them, in Lazaretto Administration. It was even possible the Lazaretto would have lost its civilian administrators.

As much as MacNally had disliked those in power, he well understood how much worse life in the Lazaretto would become under military rule. Not that it would have mattered to him or Fenelli. Their role in discovering the rifle would have assured their dismissal. If their own Captain hadn't fired them for bringing the weapon to the attention of the military, someone in Lazaretto Administration certainly would have done it.

And so MacNally and Fenelli never mentioned the rifle in their report. Weeks never said a word about it either. He understood just how dangerous his own position had become. Murder was a rap he could deal with; the prison barges weren't impossible to survive. But to be charged with the possession *and* transport of the Bushmaster could only lead to a lifetime in prison with no parole.

Deciding to cover up the fact of the assault rifle was a simple matter. Deciding what to do with it was something else. MacNally had kept it at his apartment for a nerve-wracking two weeks until he had come up with a solution. He could not store it anywhere associated with his or Fenelli's name that could ever be searched. And he could not hide it in any place where someone might eventually stumble across it.

Packed with a population so afraid of disease they routinely refused to be taken to the hospital, MacNally knew the one place in the Laz every citizen avoided. He stood next to a gate in a stone wall on the far western edge of the city. He tapped a code into a digital lock and the gate swung inward. MacNally stepped through it.

The burial of the dead in the Lazaretto had a troubled past. At first, the dead were buried on this rocky hill overlooking the Lazaretto. It was a traditional solution to the disposal of the dead. Bodies were sealed inside caskets and lowered into graves. But the ever increasing fear of contagion led to unreasonable efforts to overcome paranoia and superstition. Massive, aboveground mausoleums were built to contain the remains while keeping them out of the soil. Most people, dissatisfied with these precautions, turned to cremation as their disposal of choice.

MacNally and Fenelli had been assigned a space in one of the largest mausoleums as a benefit of employment with the police department. Though it was a source for many jokes, it was not an unwelcome benefit. Most men and women working for the police were not highly paid, and most of them never left the Lazaretto. Some by choice. For others, like Fenelli, the decision had been made for them.

MacNally stood in front of Fenelli's grave—a red granite square in the mausoleum wall a little over a meter above the floor. The inscription was simple. *Arturo Vincenzo Fenelli. Husband and Best Friend*. The dates of his birth and death—a span of fifty-six years—and that was all.

"Is this why you showed up in my apartment this morning?" He put a hand on the polished granite, over his partner's name. "I'm in trouble. I guess you know that."

A square to the right of Fenelli was reserved for his wife Lynne. The granite there was blank. MacNally had no idea if Lynne would ever leave the Lazaretto. So far, she had chosen to stay, God only knew why. MacNally could only guess that she wanted to stay near Arturo, though what good that did her in such a lousy place as the Laz he didn't know.

Maybe Arturo appeared to her too.

To the left of Fenelli's square, one space over, was the square reserved for MacNally. Like Lynne's, the square was blank. No name, no date. MacNally wondered why he'd never had his name engraved on it. He would never leave the Laz. It was his home, no matter how rotten it could be. The job and the city had become a part of him. Yes, maybe it had wrapped itself inside him like a tumor that couldn't be removed. But MacNally had come to terms with this truth decades ago.

So whether his name appeared in the granite now or later, there was no denying that this would be the final resting place of one Edward Patrick MacNally, Homicide Detective. If, MacNally wondered, the dead ever find any rest on this rock.

But he wasn't ready to climb inside there just yet.

And this wasn't the box he'd been thinking of.

The square in between. An unpolished chunk of granite, darker than the ones on either side. Flanked by Fenelli's corpse on one side and MacNally's eventual resting place.

Working with only a small handlight, which he set on the floor, MacNally inserted a small, steel key-rod into a hole in the bottom left corner of the middle piece of granite. It took a little effort to engage the mechanism. Once he felt it engage, he pushed on the granite face. It gave slightly, then pulled away from the wall enough that MacNally could fit several fingers under the bottom lip. The granite swung up. It was heavy and MacNally had to use both hands to heft it completely open. Once it reached the fully open position, brackets locked in place.

There was no casket. The Bushmaster was wrapped in cloth, in the far, back corner. MacNally did not reach for it. He ignored it. He wasn't there for the rifle.

Over the years, after they had decided to keep the rifle, the two detectives had occasionally added to their stash. A few times they had made copies of files that were too important to lose in the system. Ones that might have been removed by a corrupt official who the detectives had irritated. These were small insurance policies, which had never been needed. MacNally didn't even remember their details. The files could have been thrown away by now but he'd never bothered to do it. They had placed another weapon in the box after a fatal shooting that had involved a fellow officer. This had been a replica of a Ruger Panther, a polymer composite automatic pistol that had become popular in the late 21st century. While they were illegal to carry, collectors were allowed to own them if the firing mechanism was inoperable. This one was not. A friend on the force had retired, and he'd offered it to MacNally. Service weapons issued by the department were electrically fired, and rarely lethal. Many police officers were not above arming themselves illegally to improve their ability to protect themselves. MacNally had bought the Panther, but had eventually placed it in the box. He had never felt the need to carry it.

The last time he'd visited the box had been shortly after Fenelli's death. At that time, he'd placed an envelope in it with a detailed explanation of the truth surrounding the official death of the Lazaretto's Chief Administrator Claude Reno. If MacNally ever died, someone, one day, would eventually find out that Reno had not been burned to death, but had in fact lived through the fire, and had been hidden away in a clinic in the Lazaretto. MacNally would never reveal the truth while he was alive, but it seemed like a story that should eventually be told. At that same time, he'd stashed a few fake PDTs in the box. These had been taken off a low-life Lazer by the name of Montillo, who'd been a reluctant witness in an investigation. Montillo had been murdered before he'd been of any use, and the PDTs had been destroyed.

All but three of them.

MacNally grabbed the PDTs, two boxes of ammunition and the Panther. Just as he grabbed the granite slab to swing it back into place he considered the rifle. Beside it were a dozen boxes of ammunition. Enough to fight a small war. It was tempting to grab it too.

He'd leave it for now.

The granite slammed shut and MacNally bent to retrieve the light.

"It's easy to sneak up on an old man with a hearing problem."

MacNally swung around and jammed the barrel of the Panther into the neck of the man standing behind him.

"And stupid to sneak up on an armed man with nothing to lose."

"Take it easy, Ed." Russell stood his ground, his hand wrapped around his service weapon. It was pointed at the ceiling. "Did you think I was here to kill you?"

"You really are a dumb kid, aren't you?" MacNally withdrew the Panther and shined his light in Russell's eyes. "Always the smart detective, huh?"

"You know, as soon as I heard, I tried to think what you would do. I was looking for a clue to a safe house, a hole you'd be able to dive into. But when I looked at your records, I came across your paperwork for this place. You know, it's a little obvious, don't you think?"

"No, I didn't think so."

"Well, it is. Fenelli and his wife have a space. And so do you. But you listed the other one as reserved for a spouse. Now, people who don't know you might fall for that. But how could anyone who knows you believe you'd ever seriously think that one day you would marry? I mean, really? You, Ed?"

"Alright, enough of that. You can't be here. You gotta get out of here, and you can't be seen. What did you think you were doing? Rescuing me?"

Russell stepped around MacNally to examine the polished granite of Fenelli's grave. "With all due respect, Arturo Fenelli's dead. And no matter that I've been reassigned, I'm your partner."

"Well that's really brave and loyal of you, Russell." MacNally aimed the light back into Russell's eyes. "But you don't really have any idea what you're talking about. I'm so deep already that you can't make a difference. All you'll do is end up buried with me. So let me say this once. I appreciate your offer. More than you know. But I can't accept it. Is that clear?"

"So I just turn my back and do nothing?" Russell reached out and covered the light with his hand. MacNally aimed it at the floor.

"That's what you do."

"Ed—"

"Don't, Russell. Get out of here." MacNally stuck out his hand. Russell took it.

"If you change—"

"I know. If I do. I will."

Russell shook his head and walked away. His steps echoed in the stone cold chamber like the ticking of an old-fashioned clock. Time was indeed running out, MacNally realized. If Russell could find him this easily, he had little time to prepare for Spaeth.

36

Lilly sat up in bed, stifling a cry. Her hair, let down from its ponytail, covered her bare shoulders. It was not enough to ward off the chill of the night. She pulled on a sweater as she tried to remember what had awakened her.

Someone had called her name. The word had been as clear as if spoken by someone in the next room.

Lilly.

Not another entreaty to trust. Just an insistent call of her name.

"Lilly!"

She stood and slipped through the dark until she reached her front door. The image of a man could be seen on the other side in the low light of the public hallway.

"Lilly?" This time a knock accompanied the calling of her name.

Releasing the main lock, Lilly swung the door inward.

"What are you doing?" she asked Pete Landon. He stood a few paces from the door, his eyes lit with alarm.

"We'd better talk."

He glanced up and down the hall before following her into the room. She watched him reset the lock.

"They let him go, didn't they? Shay's here." She did not feel fear. But there was a measure of relief in knowing what to expect.

Her relief evaporated when she saw the expression on Pete's face.

"Lilly, I don't know how to say this. I guess I'd better start with Sun. She went to Conde Sur."

"Already?" Lilly could feel fear begin to work its way into her being. She focused on the trivial to ward off what could only grow stronger. "She's hardly had time to do it."

"Well, on any normal night, I'd make a quick-witted boast about Sun's abilities. But this isn't a normal night. And I need to be clear about this so you know everything. So that you can process this, okay? No, just wait, don't ask any more questions. Let me tell you everything."

Pete's manner unnerved Lilly. He thrived on mystery, loved to play the magician. Whenever he had solved a puzzle, he loved to reveal what he'd learned with smoke and mirrors in order to amaze his audience. She had never heard him like this. He wasn't putting on a show. He was as low key as he could possibly be. She involuntarily shook, waiting for him to speak.

"When I called Sun, she was already traveling. She'd already left Fort Mai Ling, her RailTransit was just getting into Seagen. Her plans were to take a flight to Carandolet, which I believe is on the other side of Sinop. Which means her flight was going to go exosphere to get there. Even better, her flight was military, which meant she was able to call in a favor and have the flight make a stop at Conde Sur. The deal is, I called her this morning, and she arrived at the barges by the afternoon.

"Now, she had a little trouble convincing the warden to allow her access to Shay's records. Conde Sur is pretty tight. They don't fool around up there with security. Anything out of the ordinary means trouble for them, so they take everything very slow. She wasn't refused access. They were just very slow to authorize it. Calls were made back to Mai Ling, even to the Sinopeese Justice Department. I'm afraid Sun owes more favors than she started out being owed."

"I never should have asked you to do this. There's just no reason..." Lilly tried to apologize but Pete cut her off.

"Don't interrupt, remember? She was finally allowed to speak with one of the controllers there, who was very defensive with her. Sun had first thought her arrival had been treated as unexpected, but she has been around government slobs long enough to recognize when she is being handled. Far from being unexpected, her arrival had been anticipated, and more importantly, prepared for. All of the delay, all of the supposed tight security had really just been a way to allow these guys a chance to defend themselves. To control Sun's investigation."

"Pete, what are you talking about? Sun didn't have an investigation, she was simply checking on Shay."

"Yeah, I thought you'd realize that. But no one there knew this. They thought her casual questions were hiding a more aggressive agenda. That only happens when someone has something to hide."

"So what were they hiding? What happened to Shay?" Lilly felt her skin tighten, as if the temperature in the room had dropped thirty degrees. She grabbed the edge of the table and tried to stop her hand from shaking. She tried to look Pete in the eye, but he was avoiding her.

"Three weeks ago, Shay attempted to escape. He was being transported to Seagen for psychiatric treatment. As the SecureTransit began its docking procedures on its return to Conde Sur, Shay, along with a few other prisoners, overpowered their guards, forced them into the docking lock, and attempted to pilot the SecureTransit out of orbit."

"Oh, God. What do you mean *attempted*?" Lilly really wanted to ask Pete what he meant about psychiatric treatment, but his use of the word *attempted* left a grim possibility that made her sick to her stomach.

Pete finally looked at her, his eyes softening as they met hers. She knew what he was going to say before he spoke the words. "The ship was disabled as it broke orbit. Scans showed that the hull had been breached before it reached freeflight. The scanners lost it before they could determine if anyone was still alive, but there couldn't have been. Officially, they're calling it a malfunction. They were not going to report the escape attempt. The deaths were recorded as accidental."

Lilly had trouble catching her breath, sucking in deep breaths like a sprinter at the end of a run. She fought to stop. There was no reason to mourn Shay's death. He was just a part of her past. He was only a bad memory. She had moved on.

She had betrayed him. She had imprisoned him. She had killed him.

She had loved him.

She loved him still.

It had not even occurred to Lilly that she had thrown the coffee cup until she saw Pete jump up from the table and cross to her, his hands closing over her own as he pulled her up out of her chair. Despite the strength of his hands, hers were still shaking. She struggled against him, determined to throw anything else she could find. He pulled her against his chest and wrapped his arms around her. She gave up then, allowing him to take her weight as she fell into his protective embrace.

She cried, full of anger—more angry at Shay than with herself. But that changed. Then changed back again. She felt Pete effortlessly pick her up and carry her to her couch, where he gingerly put her down. She tried to get up as soon as he let go of her. He stopped her.

"I'm okay, Pete. I just have to clean up the mess I made." She knew how irrational that sounded even as she said it.

"Forget it, okay? I'll take care of it." He stroked her hair, like a father calming his emotionally distraught teenage daughter. Lilly had never thought of Pete Landon like this. He had always seemed too large, shaggy, and full of foolishness.

"Were you ever married, Pete?" He shook his great mane of hair. Lilly pulled away from him, hugging her knees. "Sometimes I wonder if we ever were. We weren't like a typical couple. We were never joined at the hip. Half the time we were on different planets, never had time to get to know each other—to reach deeper than the first few layers. People have so many layers, you might break through two or three of them but you still don't ever meet the real person."

As she spoke, Pete began picking up the pieces of the broken cup. He went in search of a rag. Lilly paused and did not resume speaking until he came back into the room.

"I don't think I had far to go with Shay. There weren't too many layers to him. He was like Gregor. You had to peel back that first, fake layer of shyness, tear away a few insecurities. Brush off a slight wash of cynicism. Beyond, that, Shay is what you expect to find. Decent enough when things are going his way. A fighter when they aren't. Quick to laugh and quick to fight. Wary of strangers but trusting when it comes to his friends."

"Far too trusting."

"And your layers?"

"Hmm," she shook her head softly, a vague smile on her lips. "He tried. I resisted. I've never allowed anyone to pry. Maybe if I had, if Shay had come to know me, he wouldn't have crossed that line. I wouldn't have sent him to jail. I wouldn't have killed my husband."

"I'm really sorry, Lilly." Pete had finished cleaning up her mess. He stood in front of her, hands at his side, unsure of how to act.

"Don't be. Would you thank Sun for me? This sort of news is not easy to hear. Especially when...you know, it's my own fault. When someone dies, and there are old sins still on your slate, you can never erase them. They just hold in place, like your last memory of a person. The living grow older but the image we carry of the dead remains the same. It is no different with sin. If we never correct it in time it just remains. A ghost. A ghost."

Lilly thought of Gregor. Perhaps he'd been right. Maybe ghosts were just replayed images of our sins and mistakes. If so, it was no surprise Shay was haunting her now. Maybe she had better get used to it.

Pete was reluctant to leave her alone. She had to promise him she would call if she needed anything. What he did not understand was that even after he left, she would not be alone. It was very possible she would never be alone again. She just hoped that it was only Shay's voice that had infiltrated her apartment.

Lilly.

37

MacNally walked out of the cemetery gates cautiously. He had activated one of the PDTs. It didn't matter what name it had assigned him. He'd find out what it was the first time he used it. He would have to pick up some supplies. Then he would need a place to sleep.

He couldn't go back to his place. What he needed was a place to think. A place he could defend. There were any number of hotels he could use. It was possible to take a room and remain hidden. If his luck held, he might stay hidden indefinitely. But then what? Hope that Spaeth tired of the search, gave up, and went home?

Would it be better to prepare a defensive location? Could he hope to draw Spaeth into a trap? It would have to be done right. Done in a way that would draw Spaeth in, not just his gorillas. Spaeth, with a few men, MacNally could handle. But he could never hold off a determined assault. Even if he went back for the Bushmaster.

And then he realized he was being selfish. He had completely forgotten about the waiter. The man who'd saved his life. The man who had no way to protect himself.

MacNally had walked several blocks from the cemetery gates before he started looking for a TransitCar. He hated to be dependent on a hired car, but he dared not use his own. His car, and the riot tamer, would have to stay where he'd left them. When he finally waved down a car, he took a seat in the back and eyed the driver carefully. The odds that this driver had already heard that Jonnie Spaeth was looking for MacNally were too low to worry about. MacNally was wary all the same.

"Where you headed?" asked a black man with a thick, western Bukovinan accent.

MacNally gave him an address and sat back in the shadows of his compartment. He felt the Panther pressing into the small of his back. He wished he had pulled it out of his belt and stuck it in the outer pocket of his coat.

As soon as the TransitCar dropped and stopped, MacNally had decided to keep the driver. No reason to keep switching drivers and cars. The more people who saw him the more chances someone might talk to Spaeth.

"Can you wait?" He reached out with the new PDT and watched the reader pick up the signal. *Ty Willems*. It was a safe enough match. At least it hadn't been a female name.

"I got all night. Will you be long?"

"I shouldn't be. Just keep charging me." MacNally pushed his coat out of the way and extracted the Panther. He jammed it into a side pocket.

"Oh, you can be sure I'll do that." The driver flashed a smile but MacNally could see questions behind the man's eyes. Well, he can have questions, MacNally thought, he just won't get any answers.

A short walk down the block and a turn of the corner took MacNally to his destination. *The Mad Russian*. Yes, he was returning to the scene of the crime, but he wasn't going to stay. He needed to find that waiter. Before Spaeth showed up looking for him. The waiter, if he had discovered the identity of the man he'd shot, would not be on the job. Maybe someone there would know how to find him.

He pushed open the door and stepped into the bar. A quick sweep of the booths and bar assured him no one suspicious was waiting for him. No one sat at the bar. One couple sat in a booth. The woman was facing the door, the man sat with his back to it. This was not the position a professional would use to lie in wait for MacNally.

To his agitation he saw the waiter—the man who'd shot Graph— behind the bar, leaning against it. He stood up straight when he saw MacNally.

"What are you doing here?" MacNally made it across the room so fast the waiter backed up in fear.

"Calm down, man. What do you want with me? The cops already talked to me."

"Talked to you? Come here!" MacNally reached over the bar and snagged the man by his arm. He dragged him down the length of the bar and pushed him toward the back of the room, aiming for a low door.

"Hey!" The waiter pushed back but was too light to hold his ground. He almost fell through the door.

"Through here." MacNally guided him with his heavy hand down a short hall and into a kitchen. A man wearing a white apron came around a corner and tried to keep them from entering. MacNally pointed at the man and said "Get out!"

The man didn't argue.

"What are you doing?" The waiter jerked free of MacNally.

"I'm returning the favor. You saved my life, now I'm gonna do the same for you. What's your name?"

"Alan. Why?"

"Alan, when the police talked to you, did they tell you who those two dead gorillas were?" Alan shook his head. "Yeah, that's what I thought. The man you shot was a guy by the name of Graph. He's not too important. But the other guy's name was Spaeth. His big brother's Jonnie Spaeth. I see that means something to you."

Alan's face had turned white.

"Hey, hold on. I didn't shoot him. I didn't do that!"

"Yeah, you shot his friend. I was there, I remember. And I shot his brother. Think we should write Jonnie a letter explaining that?"

"This is insane. I don't believe this." Alan tried to pace in the small kitchen but he couldn't find enough space. He made a fist and pounded on a countertop. "Why'd I do that? Why'd I get involved?"

"I don't know, Alan. But you saved my life. And like I said, I'm gonna save yours. I'll get you out of here, and we'll find a way to stop Spaeth." By then, the Panther was in his right hand.

"Yeah, okay. I like that. Only, why didn't your friends tell me all this sooner? Why didn't they take me into protective custody or something?"

MacNally didn't have an answer for him. The man could see the truth without one.

"Where is everyone? Are you alone?" Alan didn't wait for an answer this time. "Shit, man. Your own people won't help you?"

"We can talk later. Let's get out of here first. Back door?"

"This way."

Alan waited for MacNally to check the hallway. It was clear. He led the detective deeper into the building, pausing finally at a wide steel door with a crash bar on it.

"Leads to?"

"An alley. It's well lit."

"Can you kill the lights?"

"A small one over the door, but there are larger ones on each side that light up most of the area in front of the door." Alan touched a switch on the wall. "That kills the one over the door, for what it's worth."

"We'll be fine. Spaeth couldn't get here this soon. I'm just being overly cautious."

"That's okay by me. I like cautious." Alan stepped back from the door.

"Out and to the right. I've got a TransitCar waiting on the side street. We move fast but don't have to run, okay?"

Alan nodded. He was holding his breath.

As the door opened, the shots came from inside—behind them.

Star pellets hit the door close to MacNally's head. A number of them hit Alan in the back of his head. The pellets, fired from the other end of the hall, though fired electrically, broke through the soft tissue below one of his ears. The waiter screamed in pain as he fell against MacNally.

The body, dead weight as it hit the detective, shoved him to the floor of the alley. He felt blood hemorrhaging from the wounds, soaking him. One of the shots must have sliced his carotid artery. If MacNally didn't act fast, he'd have similar wounds.

He pointed the Panther back down the hallway and fired three times. It didn't do any good. He needed the riot tamer for this work. At least the thunderous noise from the Panther would make their assailant hesitate.

The shooter had made a mess of the waiter's head. But the man had not died quickly. His cries, though mercifully short, were pathetic and difficult to bear. Humane ammunition, indeed.

Who was this shooter? He'd been watching the waiter. That was obvious. Was Spaeth already here? Doubtful. Probably just a watchdog who had been assigned to the waiter to keep an eye out for MacNally. Well, he'd been dumb enough to walk into that one.

No more gunfire came from the hall. MacNally, covered now in Alan's blood, decided to roll the body off him. With no more shots being fired, he didn't need to use it as cover. He fired two more times down the hall and pushed the body one way and rolled the other.

No returning fire. MacNally pushed with his legs and backed up against a trash bin. He checked himself in case he'd been shot unawares. He was fine. He'd been lucky.

Pulling himself up on the trash bin, he tried to wipe his hands on a dry patch of his coat. The Panther was slick with blood. He tried to wipe it down. His service revolver was still in its hip holster. MacNally pulled it free and left the shelter of the bin.

The alley was empty. He could have gone back into the building, to hunt down the gunman. But why? This was a nobody. Probably just an opportunist who was looking to earn some favor from the boss. MacNally's best move was to get back to the TransitCar and disappear.

He looked back at the dead body that had been alive just moments before. A man he'd promised to protect. Hell, he'd done nothing of the kind. Had, in fact, led him into an ambush. It made him wonder what chance he had once Spaeth actually arrived.

He made it to the end of the alley and looked around the corner to his left. The TransitCar was still there. He looked right. Saw no one in the street.

MacNally took two steps out of the alley when he saw the flash of the gun and caught a glimpse of the woman firing it from the far side of the street. The woman from the bar. Half of the couple that had been sitting in the booth. Her companion must have been the one who shot down the waiter.

He heard the distinct whine of the electrically fire gun and knew there was no way she could miss him. Raising the Panther, he saw the spread of star pellets a split second before they ripped into him. He felt them punch through his coat, fired the Panther, and dove at the TransitCar for cover—all in the same breath.

Book Two

Betrayal

38

The driver's name was Bril Abbot. He'd been driving a TransitCar for more than ten years. Before that, he'd been a professional soccer star. Leading New Madrid United to two straight Euxine Cups, he'd been invited to tour Earth, sponsored by the league. It was decided that his celebrity might be able to increase the interest of fans on the home planet. Give the colony teams a bit of respect.

They had not even considered the dangers of his passing through the Lazaretto. Before Bril knew what had happened, he was exiled. Never one to quit or silently accept his circumstances, he fought tooth and nail to appeal the decision. The virus that had been found in his system was mild, and he could find no one who could explain why it was on the Lazaretto's list. Filing appeals and hiring lawyers on Earth as well as back at New Madrid, he ran into one wall after another. The faceless, inevitable roll of IHS policy could not be reversed.

Bril knew it was over when the league ceased to answer his calls. He was a goldmine for them, and if they had given up on him, it was better than even odds that they knew the score better than he. They understood he'd been lost. They cut their losses and moved on. There would be another star to promote. Perhaps this time they would think twice before sending him through the Lazaretto. Maybe a virtual tour would be enough.

But for Bril, his life as a soccer player was over. He left behind a fiancée who refused to join him, a mother who mourned his loss, and a game that had suddenly become meaningless. He'd been able to keep his money, but had spent the majority of it on his fight with IHS. Eventually, he'd ended up with a job as a Transit driver to provide for a place slightly better than the one IHS had offered for free.

For a while people recognized him. They were happy to meet such a popular athlete. At least until they remembered that he had been exiled. Then they asked to be let out wherever his TransitCar happened to be. They did not understand or believe him when he told them he no longer had the virus. Besides, who wanted to take a chance?

He'd switched to driving at night, when he could keep the lights of the car low and his passengers only rarely recognized him. It was better that way. His fares no longer fled the vehicle. He was able to make enough money to get out of the IHS room. He had found a measure of peace.

When the shooting had started, Bril had disengaged his brakes and shuddered the drive into reverse, hoping to get clear of the gunfight. But as his fare—the big man with the bushy mustache—fell to the ground, it was obvious he'd scored his own hits on the woman across the street. As quickly as the firing had started, it had stopped. The woman lay with a pool of light on her back, her legs perfectly still, the soles of her shoes perpendicular to the street. The rest of her body above the waistline struggled spasmodically, hands clawing at the sidewalk. Bril's fare was facedown. Considering the shots Bril had seen slam into the man's coat, he had expected the man to be dead. But to his surprise, the man was moving. Not much. But he could see that both his arms and legs were operating together, crawling in the direction of Bril's car.

Bril wasn't stupid. He'd heard the shots in the alley first. He had not been sure what they meant until his fare appeared covered in blood. But he knew there had to be another shooter somewhere. Was the first shooter down like the woman? If so, it was safe to leave his car and help his fare. But if the other shooter hadn't been brought down?

Bril gave up his debate as he watched the man continue his wounded crawl. The man needed help. He was the victim here. He couldn't prove that, but his instincts told him it was so. The man had been nervous in the back seat. Wary. But he had not looked like the sort to start trouble. He did look like the sort to end trouble.

It was foolish guesswork on Bril's part but once he made his guess he stuck with it. Sliding the car toward the dying man, he locked it down and clambered out. Bril was still athletically strong. He always had been, without much need to work at it. The man on the ground was heavy. A massive weight that was not easy to get into the back seat. All that blood made it harder to move him.

His fare cried in pain. He was conscious. He was also still holding the gun he'd fired. Bril was aware of it, and kept the man's hand pointed away from the both of them. He knew better than to try and take the gun out of the hand.

"Hold on, guy. Don't fight me. I gotta get you in on your back. Let me turn you over. Hospital's not far from here."

The gun swung around and Bril looked into the open barrel.

"Forget the hospital."

"Okay, forget the hospital. Now what?"

The man recited an address that was outside of Center City.

"I hope you know what you're doing." Bril slammed the door shut and ran around to his side of the car. He didn't even bother to look for the other shooter. If someone started shooting, Bril didn't have a chance. Why look for the bullet?

He unlocked the brakes and powered up. The TransitCar slid free of the street and banked around the corner. No one fired at him as he increased his speed. For the moment it looked like he was not going to be shot dead on the street.

No chase cars appeared in his viewscreen. Bril kept his speed up as much as he dared. It was late enough that there was no cross traffic at the intersections, but all it would take was one delivery truck or another TransitCar out looking for late fares to collide with them and it would be all over. Even if Bril lived through a collision like that, the man on the back seat wouldn't make it. He needed medical attention fast.

Far too much time passed before he finally approached the end of their run. Bril risked the last intersection at full speed. He executed a tight turn to ram the TransitCar to a hard stop. They had stopped dead on the address he'd been given.

Out of the TransitCar, Bril dragged the man from the back seat and lifted him in his arms. It was a struggle to make it to the entrance of the building. He was the size of two men smashed together. The man was dead weight now.

At the entrance, he dropped the man beside a pair of glass doors. They allowed entrance to one of the tallest buildings in the Lazaretto. Bril had no idea what he was supposed to do.

"Where am I going?" he asked, kneeling to listen for a reply from the seemingly dead man.

"Twenty-third floor. Number six." The man tried to say a name. Bril could not be sure he understood correctly.

To his surprise, the glass door opened. Bril left the man at the entrance and sprinted across a large lobby. At a double bank of elevators, he pushed a button. The doors did not open. What was he supposed to do? Look for a stairwell and sprint up twenty-three floors?

Then he saw the communications panel. At the far right of the elevator doors he keyed in the apartment number. He had to wait a moment until he finally heard a man's voice respond

"Yes?"

"Mister, I don't have much time to explain. I've got a friend of yours downstairs bleeding all over the street. You know a big guy with a big mustache?"

"Did he give a name?"

"All I could understand was *Arturo*."

There was silence on the other end of the comm. Bril waited, wondering if the man had written him off as a nutter. He couldn't decide if he should just go back and try to take the dying man to a hospital.

One bank of elevator doors slid open. A man in a heavy robe and a stylishly cut beard stepped out of it. He was short, stout, and behind a pair of glasses were eyes that burned intently.

"Where is he?"

Bril led him to the entrance.

"Help me." The newcomer grabbed at the wounded man's shoulders and Bril helped him get the body into the elevator. As the elevator rose, the short man knelt to examine the bloody mess. "What do you know?"

"I believe he was shot twice in the body. Maybe more. I'm not sure what happened at first."

When the elevator opened they dragged the body into the man's apartment. Once inside, it took both men to lift the body up onto a large dining table. From a back room, a dark-haired woman appeared with towels.

"Maria, cut off his coat. And the rest of it. We have to find the damage. This is too much blood. He should be dead."

Bril watched them work and did his best to stay out of their way.

"He said no hospitals. I don't know why." Bril tried to explain. It made no sense to him.

"You are a friend of MacNally's? A policeman?"

"No. I've never met this man before."

"You helped him. You weren't afraid of his blood?" The man, obviously a doctor, asked as he washed the blood from his patient's torso.

"He was my fare. He was in trouble. And I got nothing to worry about. NE." He held up his data tag.

"I am sorry to hear it. But you are a good man to help. Can I count on you a bit longer?"

"Name it."

"He obviously doesn't want to be found. Yet he's trialed blood all over the front of the building and the elevator."

"Have you got a bucket and hot water and soap?"

"Maria will show you."

Bril followed her into the kitchen. What had he gotten himself into?

39

It would take some getting used to. Lara kept expecting the sun to come up in the morning, as it did on every planet. No matter if the planet was close to the sun or far removed, it was still a constant truth on any planet: the sun came up in the morning. The chill of the night would eventually be burned away. Even on the coldest planets like Arcobia where the sun did not warm the air, the psychological effects of its appearance warmed the heart.

But not in the Lazaretto. Here, though the clock tracked the hours of the day just as easily as any other planet, Lara never knew for certain that the day had begun. Yes, the sky changed from black to gray, but that was not enough to trigger the internal clock she needed to feel rejuvenated after a night's sleep.

Jett would never know the warmth of a sun; the blinding brilliance of a sunny day.

Little thoughts like this threatened her sanity. She pushed the thought aside. She could not allow it to gain a foothold on her psyche.

"Breakfast?" She leaned over and touched Frank on his shoulder. It was odd for him not to be up before her. She wondered how late he had stayed up. She could not remember him coming to bed.

"Just coffee." He sat up, eyeing the clock and the room.

"I think we can be down at the offices before they open. Perhaps we'll be first in line. Or at least very close. The weather is not too bad. The rain seems to be holding off. It won't be too cold or wet to take Jett out. Don't you think it is important to be down there as early as possible?"

"I don't know." Frank rolled out of bed.

"Don't do that," Lara spat out her words. She'd been holding back the fear and frustration that had been mounting since that first knock at the door by IHS. She had tried to combat her despair, but Frank wasn't helping and this wasn't a fight she could win on her own. His distraction was growing into indifference.

"Can you give me a reason not to?" he asked, a hint of desperation in his voice, as if he seriously couldn't think of a reason not to give up.

"How could you even ask that? You've got all the reason you need wrapped up in that blanket over there." She turned to look at Jett who had been up early but was now curled back up under the covers; his mussed hair the only bit of him showing.

"It won't do any good. This appeal..."

"You can't know that. You've got to give it a chance. The process wouldn't exist if there were no chance for it to work. And even if there's a one in a million chance—we take that chance!"

"I'm not talking about our chances of winning the appeal." Frank's voice rose and his surety cut off her pleading prematurely. The look in his eye confirmed what she had guessed. Something was wrong. Something beyond the obvious.

"Talk to me, Frank. Whatever it is, tell me now. I asked you last night...you said it was nothing." Lara began to shiver. Her eyes watered.

Frank's eyes softened and he came to her, pulling her close. For a moment, despite everything, she felt safe in his arms. But she knew this would not last. Knew it was only a prelude to something she could not be ready for. Frank had been protecting her from the truth. What truth?

"I didn't mean for any of this to happen. Before I tell you, you have to know this. I did what I thought was right. What I thought was best for us. Remember that!"

Frank was silent, waiting for her to say something. Maybe promise him understanding. Maybe profess her forgiveness before she knew what he had done. Something. Anything. He wanted assurance or maybe absolution. But she couldn't give it. She was too afraid to say a word. She stared at him, waiting for him to continue.

"We can't stay here, Lara. It isn't safe. People are going to be looking for me. For us. I thought that I might be able to get away from them. Get us safely to a remote place. There's no job waiting for us. It was a ruse. A false trail. I just needed to get us some space. Someplace where we could disappear."

"What are you talking about?" Lara searched his eyes for a sign that he was joking. That he was playing some cruel joke on her and the boy. She saw nothing but fear and guilt.

"I don't even know how to begin."

"Please, just start making sense," she begged.

He opened his mouth to speak but no words followed the action. Lara had seen this before. Frank had trouble confessing guilt. It did not matter if the guilt was self-evident, he just could never bring himself to speak of it. His silence grew.

"Is Jett sick because of something you did?"

"No!" He answered without hesitation.

"Then what? Something's wrong. Something awful for all of us, and you have to tell me. I have to know what's happened to us. Don't hold it in!"

"What does it matter? What does it matter if I tell you what I did? It won't change the fact that they're going to kill me."

Lara pulled away from him, pushed away from the bed, stumbled against a chair and stared in horror at her husband. He wasn't joking any more. The look on his face said it all. Her heart began beating so fast she put a hand to it in an attempt to slow it down. It only beat faster.

"Start making sense." She looked down at Jett's sleeping form and drew strength from it. At the moment, she would have to ignore her fears and start taking control of their situation. No longer could she rely on Frank to get them through it. "Frank, if you can't tell me what is happening, I'm going to take Jett and walk out of here. We'll go to IHS alone, and when I'm done, I won't come back here."

"But the more you know the more danger you'll be in."

"You can't leave me out of this. Can you guarantee that we'll be safe if you don't tell us?"

Frank shook his head.

"Then tell me. I've been upset enough over Jett the last twenty-four hours. Protecting me from the truth won't help that right now. You have to tell me."

"You think so?" Frank's sarcasm was laced with confusion. "Is it gonna help you to learn that your husband has been working for a crook all his life? How is that supposed to help you?"

"You're an accountant! What do you mean?"

"I'm an accountant who works for one of the most dangerous men in the Euxine."

Lara waited, afraid to hear the name. She watched Frank light a cigarette, wished he would throw it away and say what he needed to say. Instead, he turned away from her. She pulled him back.

"Who?"

"His name doesn't matter. What matters is that we were supposed to be in quarantine, where we'd be safe, while I thought of some way to disappear once we arrived on Dnepr. But we can't do that, can we? We're stuck here, in this joke of a trap. I can't even think of what I need to do. We can't stay here, we can't run. They'll find us. We might as well call them up and make it easier on them."

What was Lara supposed to say to that?

"The worst part of this," he added, with bitterness in his tone, "I don't even know if I can sacrifice myself for you and Jett. If I turned myself in to these guys, would they leave you alone? Would they let you live? Or would they..."

Up until that point, Lara thought she had known fear. Thought she had faced the terror of a mother who has discovered her son is sick and the world is bent on abandoning him. But then, right then, as Frank's expression filled in the words he could not bring himself to say, Lara experienced fear for the first time. Real, gut-tearing, breath-stealing, heart-splitting fear.

"Jett?" she asked, allowing Frank an absurd chance to alter the truth of what he'd just explained. She gave no thought to herself. Let them do what they would to her—to Frank. But Jett? Frank had to be wrong. Whoever they were, they couldn't want to harm Jett. It was unthinkable!

"Tell me what you did!" She advanced on him, her fear a springboard for anger. He was fiddling with his cigarette again, obsessing over it. She snatched it from his hand, burning her fingers on its tip. "What have you done to Jett?"

"I told you, Lara, I did what I thought was best. I needed a way out. You're right, I'm just an accountant. But I was learning more and more about things I shouldn't. I was getting deeper into things that would have eventually sent me to prison. I had to get out, but they weren't going to let me. I had to get money. I had to find a way to finance a change."

"You stole from this man?"

"There was this old gun. It was worth a lot of money. It was part of a collection. I was sure we could do it and no one would notice. We had it all worked out."

"We? There are others involved?"

"Yes, don't you get it? I didn't steal anything. I just told them about it. They paid me. My part's done. If we'd made it out of here, we would have been free."

"We would have been living in fear. Waiting for them to find us."

"It would have worked."

"Does that matter now? What are we supposed to do now?"

"I have no idea." He tried to take her hand. She wouldn't let him. Instead, she moved to Jett and pulled the boy into her arms and refused to look at her husband.

40

Lepov spent the next morning in a futile effort to find anyone outside the gates of Alpha Quadrant who might have seen Jardyn leave before the gates were locked down. Futile efforts were his specialty. He was pretty talented at wasting time, too. These weren't the sort of skills a man could develop through hard work and careful study. Hell no. These things came with a man in the same way a birthmark did: from day one. And you just couldn't dodge them when they were inconvenient. They dogged you till the day you gave in and died.

But it didn't mean a man had to give in without a fight. Even futile efforts had their place. It was why Lepov occasionally succeeded as an investigator. Searching for a needle in the haystack was the kind of operation where ninety-nine point nine per cent of the time you were destined to fail. But the fact of the matter was, if you grabbed each and every piece of straw, you had to find the needle eventually.

Lepov liked to think it meant he possessed a dogged determination. Gloria had once said it another way, telling Lepov he was perfectly suited for mindless activity.

How nice to have her back in his head.

With an image of Jardyn in his hand, Lepov started with those who worked the gates. This was guaranteed to be a waste of time since the flood of people leaving a quadrant before it closed was at its high-water mark during the last few hours. Anyone not wanting to be stuck in the forty-day quarantine had to be out when the gates were shut. Repairmen left by the droves. They drifted from quadrant to quadrant, working on the plumbing, broken windows, mechanical issues, and anything else that plagued the wet, rotting buildings that housed the quarantine population. Service people like barbers and dentists worked out of shops and offices that they did not keep open during lockdown since most travelers just didn't like to leave their rooms once the gates were closed. The quarantine public, as a whole, tended to hide inside their rooms, collectively holding their breath in hopes of avoiding stray pathogens.

Lepov did his best to talk with as many gate employees as possible, sharing the Jardyn image, asking if anyone remembered the face. As he'd expected, no one could recall seeing it. But it was a starting point. From there he worked his way out to the TransitCar drivers.

"No, don't think so." A lumpy-faced driver squeezed an eye shut and pushed on the side of his neck with the palm of his hand. "I think I'd remember if I'd seen him. What'd he do, steal your wife?"

"That's very funny." Lepov smiled, as if he enjoyed the banter, and moved on to the next driver.

"Good-looking guy." The next driver was a not-so-good-looking woman. "Him, I'd remember. Sorry."

There weren't many drivers to canvas. With the quadrant closed, only a few people were moving to and from its entrance. He would have to move on to Beta Quadrant to find the drivers who had been lined up outside Alpha the day before. He considered doing so after lunch. It depended on how ambitious he felt.

A nagging thought refused to stop pestering him as he worked. Gloria had said she could help him find Jardyn. But Lepov had wanted to avoid that if possible. In the first place, she'd only said she could help him find Jardyn. She hadn't said she knew where he was. He wasn't about to allow her to follow him around, *assisting* him. And then there was that bit thrown in about Dannen. How had she put it? *You can't tell Kry where he is.*

Dannen was his client. Sure, Gloria was too. But he wasn't about to let her manipulate him into taking sides. So she said he was dangerous—said he was the jealous type. Was she naïve enough to think there were men who weren't? All of his years chasing down cheating husbands and wives had taught him that everyone was jealous. Some a little more than others. But it didn't take much to expose people's innate desire to protect what was theirs.

If Gloria thought she could play games with him, she was going to have to work a lot harder at it.

Twice he thought he'd found someone who knew something but both times the someone's turned out to be stringing him along, hoping to make a little money on the side. Lepov didn't like to disperse money during a search like this. It just brought the greedy people to the front and greedy people would say anything for a chance to increase the size of their credit accounts. He had found that almost without exception, people who actually knew something useful wanted to share it. It made them feel important. And that was a feeling that could never be over-valued.

Here in the Lazaretto, where the value of life was as tenuous as the air through which you might contract pneumonia, the general public wasn't about to turn down a chance to feel important.

"Was he sick?" A tiny little woman in a heavy winter coat asked as she pushed a stiff bristle-brush broom along the curb outside the entrance. "This some kind of mistake from IHS? You with them idiots?"

"No, to all of your questions." Lepov stepped out of her way as she continued along the curb, steadily cleaning the concourse. He had the distinct idea that she wouldn't have stopped if he had remained in her way.

"You been here a while," she said, her head swinging back and forth in the same motion as the broom, "this guy steal your wife?"

"You guys should all get together before your shift starts and draw straws to see who gets the good lines and who doesn't. Otherwise, you all just end up repeating the same bad lines."

"You think so?" The woman stopped sweeping long enough to give Lepov a serious once over. "Ain't nobody seen the guy in your little picture?

"Not yet," Lepov said in an attempt to sound care-free. "And I seem to be running out of options."

He turned to look at the few drivers who sat in their TransitCars, a few other men and women working at menial jobs along the street. As large as the entrance area was, it seemed deserted. About the only place left to look was the Transit Station, the steps of which were accessible from either end of the concourse.

Choosing one of them at random, he walked around its thick, stone railing. The wide descent of the steps was well lit, and a garishly painted yellow rail divided them in half. A man wearing the institutional green of the Lazaretto Maintenance Services was working on a small grey box that was affixed to the bottom of the rail, half way down the steps.

"I didn't think they fixed anything around here." Lepov stopped beside the man and made eye contact with him.

"It ain't fixed yet," the man said, returning his attention to the box.

"Proximity reader?" Lepov had no illusions that Jardyn was still traveling under his proper Personal Data Tag.

"It is when it's working. Right now, it's just a hunk of wires. It's also a great source of irritation to me. I was an electrical engineer on a mining platform. Damn good one. We swung through here because our Platform Manager wanted to take some time off on Dnepr. You know, *that* sort of time off. Like he couldn't just hire a few of them to come up to the platform, right?"

"And you thought his idea sounded like a good one?"

"Well, the wife had been dead for—let's just say too long, you know? I went with him. Had the time saved up."

"He got through scot-free and you didn't. That about right?"

"No, though it looked like it at the time. I couldn't get off this rock—bad luck, that—and he went on to his little vacation. When he came back through, well, let's just say he got a little more than he wanted. I may be working on entry level devices like this, but there aren't too many openings for managers in this place. Last I heard, he was driving a garbage truck."

The engineer chuckled as he hooked up a small handheld to the box. Lepov obliged the man with an appropriately similar laugh.

"When you get finished with that, look around. Seems like most of the gadgets in the place don't work." Lepov tipped his hat, though the man was concentrating on the handheld, and moved to go around him.

"Aren't you going to ask me?"

"Ask you what?"

"You been pestering people all morning with that picture in your hand. I was up by the doors earlier, working on a facial reader. You've been at it for hours. Did you give up or find what you were looking for?"

"No, I didn't find him, yet. Haven't given up yet, either. I just assumed you were sent to fix the reader and you aren't based here at the main gate. Was I wrong?"

"No, you were right about that. They don't base maintenance guys like me anymore. Not when they don't have enough qualified personnel, that is. But if I had been dispatched here for a repair yesterday, I might have seen who you're looking for. Let me see."

Lepov held the image up for the man to examine it.

"Yeah, it was a long shot. I don't recognize him. Hang on."

The man unhooked the handheld and wrapped its contact wires around it before stuffing it into a deep pocket in one side of his canvas pants. He stood up, stretched his back, then turned to look down into the Transit Station.

"Chris!" His voice echoed off the stone steps and it sounded to Lepov as if it bounced all the way to the bottom step and kept right on going into the station.

A kid, his red, freckled face appearing at the bottom step, yelled back. "What you want, Zee?"

"Get up here, boy!"

The boy ran as fast as he could up the steps, his little legs pumping hard to lift him up each riser.

"Chris, I want you to meet—" Zee turned to Lepov with a raised brow.

"Lepov. Gregor Lepov. Nice to meet you Chris." Lepov stuck out his hand. The boy eyed the offered hand, made a few quick internal calculations, then firmly shook it before quickly letting go.

"The boy here is more than just a shoe-shiner. He's got the best eyes on the street, isn't that right, boy?"

"I dunno. I guess." The kid watched Lepov warily. "What was I supposed to see?"

"Seen him?" Lepov held out the image. The boy snatched it so quickly Lepov couldn't have stopped him if he had tried.

Chris said nothing as he examined Jardyn's face. He took too long. By the time he'd said no, Lepov did not believe him. But he had to admit he was impressed. The boy wasn't going to give information just to feel important. He was going to wait and see if he could gain anything from what he knew.

"Nah, din't see this guy." The kid made a show of shrugging his shoulders.

"Okay, that's too bad. But it's not your fault. Thanks, anyway."

Lepov snatched the image back and tucked it into his coat pocket. He paid no more attention to the boy, focusing instead on the man called Zee.

"Don't work too hard."

"Oh, I won't. Like you said, there's too much out there waiting for me to fix it. But there's no end to it, so I don't get too excited."

"Thanks for your help." Lepov stuck out his hand. Zee did not take it. Whether or not he was still contagious or he was just accustomed to people avoiding him it was hard to tell.

"I don't think I helped you much."

"Well, that's the way it goes, sometimes." Lepov still hadn't looked at the boy.

He started back up the steps instead of going down into the station. This way, the boy would have to purposely follow Lepov, instead of heading back to his shoe-shine equipment. It would tell him if the boy had kept silent in hopes of increasing his reward, or if he just wasn't going to divulge what he knew at all.

The boy followed him. Lepov hid the smile on his face as he stepped back up on the street, turned away from the concourse and headed into the city.

41

Lilly had never really slept after Pete left. She'd fought off the urge to call Gregor. He was fighting with his own ghosts and she was in no mood to help him. If anything, they would have been a hindrance to each other. Word of Shay's death might have eased Gregor's worries about his return, but he would have seen right off how much it upset her, would have quickly deduced how this could change things for her. Change things for the rest of her life.

So she had forced herself to leave Gregor alone. Even after the gray smudge of the morning illuminated the wet streets outside her apartment, she did not seek him out. Whatever he was doing—for Gloria—it was better if she did not get involved. The sooner he was done and the sooner his former wife was gone, the sooner Gregor could find some peace.

But could he? If she could so easily recognize that she would never be free of Shay, even after his death, did Gregor have a chance at peace as long as Gloria was still out there, always able to step back into his life? She'd seen how that woman affected Gregor. He had appeared so…defeated. No, Gregor hadn't given up, he never would, but even a defiant man can be defeated. He just refuses to lie down, despite the burden of having failed. And that was exactly how Lepov had appeared while Gloria was standing next to him. His self-assurance, the bedrock of what made Lepov a man, was no longer there.

Lilly wondered if she had been wrong about not calling him. Maybe he needed to know she still needed him. Wanted him. Even if it exposed her own highly protected vulnerability, it would be worth it to counteract that woman's presence. Lilly showered, dressed, and left for Gregor's office before she could change her mind again.

She didn't make it to Gregor's office. Outside her building, as she hailed a TransitCar, she watched one pass her by with a man sitting in the back seat. Though she did not want to acknowledge him, she knew it had looked exactly like Shay.

No sooner had the thought crossed her mind when the TransitCar rolled to a sizzling stop on the wet street. The back door opened. She could see a man's hand push it completely open.

Lilly's heart beat painfully in her chest as the cold air of the morning mixed with sudden fear to chill her deep within. She steeled herself, fought off the urge to panic, and closed the distance to the open door.

She climbed inside and the door shut.

"Hello, Lilly."

Lilly couldn't speak. She stared at the man beside her with a mixture of shock and anger and guilt and even a little pity. She had not been this alone with Shay Stewart since before the day she'd betrayed him.

"I'm sorry. I thought you'd be expecting me. I thought you'd seen me already, a few times. I was trying to give you time to adjust to my being here. Are you okay?"

It was Shay. It was really and truly her husband. The man who was supposed to be dead. The man who was never supposed to come back into her life. She started to reach out, to touch him, to make sure he was real, but she held back, afraid to discover he didn't really exist.

"You're — the escape wasn't successful."

"I wondered if they would tell you." He smiled, perhaps relieved that he did not have to explain. "Well, it was more successful than they admitted it was. Who wants to acknowledge the fact that a bunch of prisoners escaped from their facility?"

"What are you thinking?" Lilly was slowly regaining her power of speech. And with it came her power of reason. "Why would you come here? You must be crazy!"

"There's the Lilly I knew. I was beginning to think she'd disappeared while I was away. Oh, how I missed that girl. Hurray for Lilly the Logical!" There was no bitterness in his tone, no cynicism.

His hair was just as black and thick as ever. That sparkle in his eye that had once won her young heart was still there, accompanied as it always was by that sly, impish smile; that playful expression of a kid who knows he's getting away with it was still indelibly stamped from his raised brow to his dimpled chin.

"Driver, up here." Lilly leaned forward, directing the driver to drop them off at the next corner.

"Oh, let's not stop. What say we let him drive around in circles, we'll pretend he's blind. At least pretend he's lost."

Lilly repeated her command and pushed open the door before they'd come to a complete stop.

"Lilly, hold up, girl. I need you to pay the driver. I haven't got a PDT." He grabbed her arm to keep her from fleeing. When she turned to him in exasperation, he let go of her and pulled his pockets inside out. "See? No tag, for obvious reasons."

Lilly reached back inside the TransitCar and swiped her tag on the reader. The driver thanked her and pulled away as soon as she slammed the door.

"Hey, hold on," Shay put out a hand to keep her from running off. He leaned in to get a closer look at her. "What's this about? Why the tears? You think I'm here to fight? That I'm mad? Don't even. Can't you see? I'm not angry. It's just me. Just old Shay."

"Don't you get it?" Lilly pushed him away, angling toward a café in the lower level of an apartment building. The steps leading down to the café's door were slick and Lilly almost lost her footing. She wanted to get inside, where no one would see them. She'd never used this café before and that's why she'd pointed it out to the driver. She needed a place where no one would know them or remember them.

"What should I get?" Reflected in the café window, she could see Shay quick-step down the stairs behind her, his hands in his pocket. He had always been light on his feet. He had the grace of a dancer and the agility of an acrobat — yet more of his charms that had caught her young eye. "Come on, Lilly — hey, this is a nice place, here."

The café was elegantly decorated. Red and gold dominated the design, and Lilly did not wait to be seated. She chose a corner booth near the back. Sliding in on one side of the table, she waited for Shay to take the other bench before she spoke.

"What you don't get is that I just spent the night believing you were dead. I sent you to prison and like you always do, you couldn't just do what you were supposed to. You tried to escape and I was told you had died. Do you know how long a night I've just been through? You could have come to me two days ago. But you had to wait until after I spent a night thinking I had killed you. You wanted to play games. Cat and mouse. Tease me. Then this dramatic appearance in the back seat of a TransitCar. My God, you're still just a dumb kid fooling around. You still won't think of anyone but yourself!"

Shay wasn't the only one at the table surprised by her outburst. She had been completely unaware just how angry she'd been when he opened that TransitCar door until she rattled off her speech. Now that it was out, she didn't regret a word of it. It certainly had, however, startled her.

"Didn't do what I was supposed to, eh?" Shay tilted his head as he decided on a response. "I can't deny that. I was supposed to just sit there in an old ship, watching Sinop drift beneath us, knowing we'd never step foot on any planet ever again. You're right. I didn't do what I was supposed to. But you didn't either.

"But why worry about this sort of thing, eh Lilly? Let's order something to eat. I'm starved!"

"I didn't come in here to eat. And what do you mean, I didn't either? What was I supposed to do?"

"Nothing, Lilly." Shay's smile was surprisingly genuine. "You weren't supposed to wait for me. That would have been asking too much. I never spent time hoping you'd wait."

"Oh, don't try that. You aren't jealous. You didn't come back to win my hand again." Lilly's eyes narrowed. "Did you come back here for money? Was that it? And what did you think you would do even if I gave you money? How did you think you'd get out again?"

"I sure missed you." His playful smile reminded her that his easy charm could easily make a girl forget her troubles. And he could also make a girl forget how untrustworthy he really was. "So, did you want to hear the story of how I made it here?"

"No."

"Really?" He looked terribly disappointed. "It's a good story."

"I'm sure it is. Do you want to hear the story of why I turned you in to the police?"

"No, I guess I wouldn't." His playful smile faltered. He looked away in order to regain his care-free attitude. "I suppose we ought to leave our stories in the past where they belong. That would be best, don't you think?"

"Why are you here, Shay?"

"I really don't know, my dear. I suddenly had all the time in the world and I couldn't think of anyone else I wanted to spend it with. That sounds pretty stupid, I guess. Or I could put it another way and say I just didn't have anything else to do."

For the first time since he arrived, Lilly smiled. What else was she supposed to do? She had suffered through the guilt of betraying Shay for so long she wasn't about to turn him in again. And if she didn't do that, what else was she supposed to do?

He chatted away, talking nonsense as he always had, and she did not try to stop him. For a little while it was as if he had never been in prison; as if she had never sent him there. A little part of her grew angry at fate for allowing this to happen. It was unfair to have this taste of what life had once been like; to experience what life could never be like again. But there was another part of her that was happy and thankful for this moment.

She gave in to the latter emotion, embracing this chance to be free of her guilt. For the next hour, she thought only of Shay and what he had once been to her.

At least this way, she wouldn't have to think about Gregor or the return of his wife.

42

The ship was completely silent now; streaking through the void of space. They were free of their jumpseats. The Ursuline was resting in one of the sleepers, the Australian had joined the pilots—probably telling them about his imaginary years as a deep-space pilot—and the men they had brought with them were scattered across the bay floor, catching what sleep they could. A few of them were still awake, checking their weapons.

The New Yorker was sitting in the galley. He stared at a cup of coffee, the surface of which was completely still; no matter that they were traveling faster than any non-super-spatial ship had a right to. For reasons he would never understand, the ship made not the slightest vibration.

He took the cup in hand and drank what was left.

It wasn't that he disagreed with his boss. The Swede had to be punished. No doubt. After all, the Swede had been a trusted employee. He had been given much. Paid well. Yet despite this, he had conceived of the plan to steal from the Australian. Even worse, he had recruited other men to help him, conspiring against the man who had treated him so well.

Of course the Swede could never have pulled off the theft without the others. The German had done the dirty work. He'd been the one to actually grab the artifact. But it had been the Frenchman who had worked it all out. He'd been the one to devise a way into the Australian's office. He'd been the one to work out the removal of the artifact from its glass housing.

The Englishman had told them everything. And for that, the New Yorker was grateful. Without him, they would have never discovered who was responsible.

Which always left the New Yorker wondering why the Englishman had come to them with his information? His gratitude only lasted so long. After it came suspicion and a feeling that something was wrong.

The Englishman. He was an odd man. He came from money. Good stock. Perhaps a bit too good. His hands had been dirty in the past. And this recent incident proved he would not hesitate to dirty them again when the opportunity seemed right. He could be forgiven a certain *eagerness* to keep his hand in the game. No man, once he's dipped into the world of theft and greed, can ever really walk away from it. That wasn't the issue. What the New Yorker would never understand was why the Englishman decided to join in on a hit against the Australian, only to turn on his friends and throw himself on the mercy of such a merciless man.

And so the Swede would be punished. The German had already met his end—accident or not, it had been an inevitable outcome. The Frenchman would get his in the end. He could never remain hidden.

Surprisingly, none of these punishments were being carried out from a position of anger. Actually, the Australian had been almost amused at the little team of thieves and their brave attempt to cheat him. He had even expressed admiration for the Englishman, who had been gutsy enough to join in the theft, then turn on his partners as he threw himself on the Australian's Mercy Seat.

And that was the real reason the New Yorker was bothered by the orders to find and punish the Swede. It was merely for show. The Australian felt obligated to show the world that he would not allow anyone to take advantage of him. And as much as the New Yorker understood this, he held deep misgivings about the punishments that were to be meted out.

Violence had never been difficult for the New Yorker. He had grown up with it. It had been the basis for his childhood on the streets of St. Saen. You didn't back down from a fight if you wanted to survive. And he hadn't backed down and he had survived. But every step he took as he climbed out of those slums to reach his present position had been for a reason. He'd never struck a boy or a man who hadn't stood in his way. He had taken pride in that. He had become known as a fair, albeit fierce, man.

He had attracted the Australian's attention with his tough, yet just approach. It had marked him as a trustworthy individual in a notoriously untrustworthy world. The Australian's interest in keeping a man dedicated to fair play at his side was no reflection on the Australian's views on fair play. It merely demonstrated the man's desire to surround himself with people he could consider safe.

Rarely had the New Yorker found himself at odds with his employer's goals. For the most part, he had easily followed along with the Australian's ruthless yet controlled ascent to the top of a criminal empire that was run more like a sovereign state than a den of thieves. Though at odds with the colony worlds' rule of law, they held to their own strict set of laws which kept order where chaos was all too eager to rise. Imposing law on the lawless was difficult yet essential.

But in the case of the stolen artifact, the New Yorker was no longer in lockstep with his boss. Yes, the rule of law had to be upheld. But to what extent? Was an iron fist the only possible solution to the preservation of the law? Or was it possible, was there any way that mercy could be incorporated into the preservation of order? After all, the theft of the artifact, a trinket of little significance, in no way threatened the stability of the Australian's empire. The very fact that the Englishman had voluntarily come to them was evidence that law and order was not in danger of crumbling to pieces. Why not, then, dispense a little judicious goodwill?

The New Yorker's thoughts switched to the Ursuline. She was having a bad influence on him. Her admiration for the religious notion of forgiveness was obviously to blame for his present line of thought. He'd have to be careful about that. There was no point in allowing her to corrupt him to the point that he ended up in trouble with the Australian. That would be disastrous.

He poured more coffee and headed for the cockpit. It would be wise to make sure the boss was not unduly terrorizing the pilots.

43

The shoeshine boy had provided information that had sounded fairly promising. Lepov had spent the rest of the day rediscovering a truth he'd learned many years ago: not everything that's promising delivers. In this case, the boy had been able to tell him where Jardyn had been heading when he'd left Alpha. But when Lepov arrived at the Hotel Malibu, no one there had heard of Jardyn, and they'd certainly never seen him.

At least the kid had given him something else he hadn't expected: a description of Jardyn and his companion.

Lepov had hung around for awhile, just in case he got lucky. He never did. Jardyn did not show up.

A long, crowded trip on a SubTransit brought him back to his apartment. He climbed the steps, tired and ready to quit thinking about his work. Missing persons cases he hated more than any other type. The last time he'd poked his nose into a case that was centered around missing people he'd almost become a permanent fixture at the bottom of the Aegean sea.

Yet another reason to despise Gloria for bringing him this job.

He rounded the last flight of steps and stopped dead. His luck couldn't be this bad. But then again, why would he think it would be anything but?

She was there, sitting on the top step, huddled against the wall, difficult to see in the stairwell's poor lighting. A shadow hid her face, but he could see her eyes, big and scared and he knew it was an act before she said the first word.

He climbed the last steps, brushing past her without saying a word. He pushed through the door and let it swing shut without waiting for her.

Gripping the door handle of his apartment door, he heard the door lock disengage. She hadn't followed him yet. He stepped into his front room and left the door open.

Maybe she really hadn't been there. Maybe she was just the

product of an unbalanced nervous system. Maybe it really was just a lack of vitamins as Lilly had insisted. How nice to think that Gloria would go away if he diligently took his supplements.

He heard the door beside the elevator finally swing open, its rusty hinges seemingly louder than usual. Her heels tapped lightly on the wooden floor; her pace too measured to suggest she was upset. She was, as she always had been, firmly in control.

He pulled off his coat and stood a few steps inside the door, waiting for her. When she finally appeared, she stopped at the door, partially hiding herself behind the frame. She leaned against it, her head tilted so that half of her face was illuminated from the lamp in his front room.

"If you're waiting for an invitation you'll have to stand there a very long time. I never invite clients into my home. It's not professional."

"Grey..." her voice was almost too soft to be heard.

"You'll have to speak up," he said, tossing his coat on a hook behind the door. He turned his back on her and walked away. "I don't hear as well as I use to."

"Grey, wait!"

"I'm not gonna wait!" He spun around and fought the urge to strike out at her. "I waited plenty when you left. Gave you time to make as big a mistake as any husband was willing to put up with. I was willing to wait then. I waited too long. You didn't know that, did you? You moved on and never looked back. I'll bet it never dawned on you that your husband was standing still, letting life flow by him as he waited for you to return. You can ask me to work for you and what's-his-name, but you don't get to ask me to wait anymore!"

He retreated deeper into the apartment, hoping she would leave. He jerked open his refrigerator, its single bulb shining bright in the dark kitchen. There was nothing there he wanted. He'd opened it just so his hands would have something to do. Just so his hands wouldn't ball into fists.

The glow of the light bulb shone on the counter and he saw his half empty bottle of bourbon. He slammed the door and grabbed the bottle.

"Grey." She'd followed him. She was just inside the kitchen now. "You're angry at me."

"Angry at you?" He reached next to the sink and switched on a light. It's harsh blue-white glare caught her by surprise and she winced. He grabbed two empty glasses and tossed them on the counter. One of them fell over. Righting it, he poured out drinks for both of them. "Why would I be angry with you? You left me because

I bored you. Now you show up here with husband number…three, isn't it? Or was there another one crammed in there between this guy and the one I carried the furniture for?

"Well, anyway, it doesn't matter. This present husband of yours walks into my office with you in tail and you announce that you're not only involved in a criminal undertaking but you're also going to emotionally blackmail me into helping you. You've got me tracking down your new lover and now you show up because you want to remind me that your husband is a danger to you and me and your missing lover.

"I'm not angry with you, Gloria. I actually think I'm more amused than angry. You really ought to see what this looks like from my side of the rubber room."

He gave her one of the glasses and lifted his with a nod of his head.

"Here's to foolish people doing foolish things."

"You aren't foolish," she said, grabbing his hand to prevent him from taking the drink. "Maybe I am, but you're anything but foolish. It's why I came to you. Why I convinced Kry that we should hire you. I knew that once you were involved, you'd know the best way to deal with this."

He pulled away from her and finally took that drink. She took a sip of hers before speaking again.

"At least you aren't angry, Grey. That's important to me."

"I never said I wasn't angry, Gloria. You're missing the point. I said I wasn't angry at you. But that doesn't mean I'm not angry at me. And I can assure you that I'm plenty angry with me. I hate watching a man stick his head into a noose for no logical reason."

"You can quit if that's what you want. I would walk away and I wouldn't come back. If it's what you really want."

"Oh, don't be a hero." He poured a second drink—he was well aware how bad an idea that was—and carried it into the front room. He set it on a side table and began unrolling his sleeves. The room was becoming unexpectedly hot. "You really don't get it, do you? If I thought I could just quit this job whenever I decided you and Dannen had lied to me one too many times, I wouldn't be angry with myself. But I knew full well the moment I said I'd listen to your story I was in this thing all the way. I knew you'd get hold of me and I wouldn't be able to get free. And don't stand there with those big eyes and your innocent look of surprise! You knew it too. You probably even knew it before the first day you rode the elevator to my office. You counted on it."

"Grey—"

"And cut out that *Grey* nonsense, Mrs. Dannen. Cut out all of it and tell me why you're here—the truth—or so help me God I'm gonna throw you down those stairs." He tossed down the second drink and wanted badly to throw the glass at her. Instead, he dropped it on the table and dropped himself into the corner of his sofa.

Lepov's head was spinning. The drinks weren't to blame, but they weren't helping either. He knew he was overreacting to her but he couldn't find a way to turn it off. Her scared eyes and shaky voice had not only failed to elicit his compassion, they had awakened a dormant anger he had not realized still existed. He took several deep breaths and stared at her, willing her to either explain herself or exit the apartment. He didn't care which one she chose.

"I told you I can help you find him. But you have to promise me—you have be sure you don't tell Kry when you've found him. Tell me. Only me. Kry would kill him."

She had slowly been moving toward him. Now, she stood beside him. The light was behind her and he could only see her silhouette.

"And you too, I suppose?" His tone had softened. He recognized that it had and though he didn't want it to, he couldn't hold on to his earlier fury.

"I don't know." Her words a mere whisper.

"So tell me where he is."

"Promise first." She put a hand on his.

"Not to tell your husband where your lover's hiding?"

She pulled her hand back. "I told you he's not my lover. You're being just as jealous as Kry."

"It's an inherent fault with all past and present husbands. We don't like our wives running around with future husbands."

"He's not a future husband. And the only man Kry really needs to worry about is—" she slowly sank onto the edge of the sofa. Before he could stop her, she'd leaned against him and her lips brushed his. He turned away at the last moment. Her kiss wet his cheek.

"You just called me your wife." Her breath was hot. The drinks were souring his stomach. He pushed her away but she resisted.

"So now you're gonna tell me where to find Jardyn, and I tell you where he is, and you two slip off into the night and Dannen gets drunk and waits for you long enough to realize you're never coming back. Is that the picture you were hoping to draw?"

"It isn't my first choice. There are other possible outcomes."

"Yeah, I guess there are." He turned to look in her eyes. He had to know just how far gone he was. He needed to know if he had any chance of surviving her game. He shifted so that he could put an arm around her, pulled her tight, and kissed her. She was no longer resisting him.

Despite the years, despite the bitterness, in that moment they were young lovers again, saturated with the familiarity that overtakes two people who have managed to become one: the taste of her mouth, the feel of her tongue on his, the knowledge that her hands would slide up between his shoulders even as his slid down the curve of her legs. The feel, the smell, her transformation from scared girl to a hungry woman, it was a moment that Lepov had feared and desired and known he would have to conquer.

He pulled back and looked into her eyes again. She waited, her ragged breathing yet one more distraction. He waited too. Long enough to allow the fog to lift.

"You're gonna have to remember something, my dear."

"Okay, I will." She put her head against his shoulder.

"I'm an investigator. I may not be a damned good one, but I'm competent enough. Enough that I've already found a witness who saw Louis Jardyn leave Alpha quadrant shortly after his pal Frobe was killed. A witness who has a very good memory. Good enough that his description of Jardyn's traveling companion was very detailed."

She sat up, wide eyes sparkling in the lamplight.

"You see, I would have known he was describing you even if I hadn't known you were in the Lazaretto."

She drew back and he was sure she was going to hit him. Instead, she simply pushed away from him and stood to her feet.

"You're trying too hard, Gloria. And for no reason. I told you I was going to find Jardyn. I already agreed to the job. Stop treating me like I'm made of glass. I'm not gonna fall to pieces. I'll do what you want. Because I want you out of here more than you want to get out of here."

"He called me the night Frobe was killed. He was scared—"

"I don't want to hear your story. I really don't care. I told you to tell me the truth. You didn't do it. That was stupid." He could taste her lipstick on his lips and he wiped it away with two fingers. "Now tell me the truth this time. Do you know where he is?"

"The Malibu Hotel."

"I already know about the Malibu. He wasn't there. Something—someone spooked him. Where was he supposed to go if that happened?"

"He said he would leave a message."

"Where?"

"With a bartender, at a little place called *The Maple Leaf.*"

There were any number of reasons to kick her out and quit the case. But the fact remained he wanted to do whatever it took to get her out of the Lazaretto. The only real good news had been his victory over their past. At least for that one moment he had proven that he could keep his head no matter how much she worked at confusing him.

Now he just had to figure out a way to take all of her lies and reshape them into the truth. If he could do that, he'd be a miracle worker.

44

They had spent the afternoon in the café: Shay talking, Lilly listening. She had decided at some point to allow him to ramble on. She had not been able to detect any trace of an ulterior motive, a disguised bitterness, or anything else beyond his boyish happiness at spending the afternoon with her. As incredible as it seemed, Shay held no animosity toward her.

She did not want to believe it. That he would forgive her so easily was yet another reason to feel guilty for her sins.

"You're looking troubled again." He leaned forward over the table, examining her eyes. "What's bothering you this time?"

"I never could hide anything from you." She paused, afraid that he would point out she'd been able to hide her betrayal from him. She was relieved to simply see him smile and nod.

"So, don't hide it. And don't brood. What's the matter now?"

"I just don't know what to do with you. We can't sit here all day. I'm not sure you should come back with me to my apartment. There's a lot to consider. Where have you been staying?"

"No place." He obviously wasn't going to explain.

"Gregor would know what to do."

"Lepov?" Shay's face clouded over and his tone hardened.

"You know him?"

"I've seen you with him. I've learned enough."

"I won't ask you to understand." She felt the room grow cold and suddenly wanted to get away from the café. She pulled out her PDT and signaled for the waitress.

They said nothing more until they were out on the street. Wind blew hard on them as they passed in and out of shadows along the street. The streetlights were on, as they always were, but it was already getting dark enough to be able to see dark patches between each cone of light.

"You're already lying to me, Shay, I can tell. You said you didn't expect me to wait for you, but you're angry about Gregor."

"Am I? Yeah, I guess you're right. No matter how gracious a man wants to be, it's hard to see another man take his place."

"He hasn't taken your place." Lilly pulled tightly at her coat in an attempt to ward off the chill of the coming night. She noticed that Shay was not wearing a coat, just a thin, cheap suit; he showed no sign that the cold bothered him. "No one will ever take your place."

"That's a comforting thought, my dear. But if you don't mind my asking, what exactly does it mean?"

"Just what it says. There won't be another husband for me. You were the one and only."

"What about this Lepov? Does he know that?"

"Maybe. I doubt it. Probably." Any one of those answers might be accurate. She had no way of knowing. Until that moment she hadn't really known that she would never have another husband. But right then, there on that cold street, she knew it to be true.

"I don't know too much about this guy, but..." Shay clucked his tongue with disapproval, "I wouldn't bet he'll be happy to hear it."

"Gregor Lepov is a hard man to understand. You have to trust me on that. Whatever it is he's thinking, you can be sure it won't be what you expected. There's always the chance he'd be relieved to hear I don't want to remarry."

"And yet here he is, on this crazy moon, staying...to be with you."

"What?" Lilly stopped and turned to look at Shay.

"That's why he's here. For you."

"No," she said, a soft chuckle escaping her cold lips. "I don't mean to laugh at you, but you've got it backwards. I'm here because he wouldn't leave. And I wasn't about to let him stay behind again and sink into another one of his depressions. He nearly drove me crazy the last time I left him here. When he refused to go, I decided I wouldn't either."

Shay was smiling crookedly at her again. He seemed to be looking straight into her soul.

"And yet you have no intentions of marrying him. But you'll hang around here, in this God-forsaken place, so you can what...keep him from despair?"

"Yes, I think that's a fair way to say it."

"Makes me want to wring his neck," Shay concluded without shame or anger. He almost seemed tickled at the idea.

"Why do you say that?"

"Well, you're here for his sake, and he's off *working* for his ex-wife. That's not very honorable, if you ask me."

"You've been busy, Shay." Lilly tried not to acknowledge the wisdom in what he'd said. "I knew you'd been watching me, but I didn't realize you'd been watching Gregor. What are you up to?"

"Me?" Shay put a hand to his chest and gave her his best innocent expression. "I'm just trying to look out for my girl, that's all."

Lilly made no reply to that. Instead, she tucked her chin into the collar of her coat to try and ward off the chill wind. She didn't like the turn their conversation had taken. What right had Shay to spy on her or Lepov? And more importantly, what right had he to be so damned right about Lepov's behavior?

45

Dimmed lights in the room made it difficult for him to identify his location. He tried to turn over, to see more of the room, and the heavy dull pressure on his stomach was too much. He nearly passed out.

"Hold still. You'll be okay." Her voice was sweeter than his mother's. He had no idea who she was.

"Where?" He had no idea if she had heard him—if his lips had actually formed the word.

"You're somewhere safe, that's all you need to know."

He suddenly realized this woman should not be talking to him. After all, he'd shot her. Two or three times. She should be dead in a pool of her own blood.

"Don't struggle, detective." She spoke soothingly, but he wasn't fooled. He wouldn't listen to her.

"Edward, please. You've got to trust me. You don't need to worry. My husband Georges, Dr. Duvalls, has stabilized you. We understood that no one should know where you are. We've not told anyone. Now stop that and relax."

He did, if only because he could not continue to put forth more effort. Exhausted, he lay still and tried to speak.

"Maria?"

"Yes, it's me, Maria. Now stop worrying and relax."

Arturo's sister. He was beginning to remember. The TransitCar driver had made good. MacNally did as he was told and tried to relax.

But there were too many questions and he could not wait for answers.

"Where am I?" He managed to ask the full question this time.

"We have you at the clinic. You had lost too much blood. Georges could not treat you without moving you here."

"Who knows?" He tried to sit up and was overcome again with abdominal pain. His head was also beginning to spin.

"Really, Edward. You can't keep talking like this. This is my last answer. Then you will have to rest. No one but the Transit driver, Georges and Karl knows you're here. Karl works here, he's in security. And he will make sure no one else knows you're here. We needed him to help get you inside. Bril, that's the driver, he couldn't move you on his own, not with you bandaged as you were. And he also couldn't move you fast enough. You were in need of blood, and the two of them were strong enough to move you without causing additional damage."

She faded from his view. He did not know if she stopped talking or if he ceased hearing. His world collapsed into a tiny void where no one could ever find him.

She was smiling the next time he focused on her.

"Welcome back." She wiped his face with a cool washcloth. "How are you feeling, Edward?"

Instead of answering her he tried to push her away. She did not seem to notice. She faded from view again.

"He'll be coming around soon." A man's voice. With a heavy accent. "I'll stay. Go home, Maria."

He couldn't see the man. The room was black.

"Detective?" A light hit his closed eye. MacNally tried to close it more.

"I'm awake." He reached out to push away the light and pain shot through him. He dropped his arm and fought off nausea.

"Yes, okay. Keep your arm down. That will hurt, I imagine."

MacNally's ability to understand his environment was growing by each passing moment. He wrinkled his brow and sampled the light without the filter of his closed lids. It was painful at first but that helped clear his mind even more.

Within an hour he was sitting up, drinking from a plastic cup and trying to make sense of what had happened to him. After listening to Dr. Duvalls explain everything that had happened since Bril Abbot had delivered MacNally to their apartment, MacNally had come to a decision. He had changed his mind.

Another hour passed before the man he had sent for finally arrived.

"I knew you'd change your mind." Russell approached MacNally's bed and carefully examined his partner. "You look terrible. Does this have anything to do with the two corpses we found last night? One man shot dead in the back of *The Mad Russian*, one woman shot dead on the street outside it. Both of them shot several times by a very large caliber handgun. The woman, in fact, was shot through the spine—her damned spinal cord was cut."

"Don't sound so sorry for her. Why didn't you mention the waiter? He lived?"

Russell shook his head.

"Poor bastard. To answer your question, yes this has everything to do with those bodies. But for the record, I didn't exactly change my mind. It was changed for me. I can't do what needs to be done. So you get your wish. God help you."

"I'll manage." Russell pulled up a chair. He leaned forward and looked MacNally in the eye. "What needs to be done?"

"I need you to get a few things for me."

"Sure."

"First things first. Are you sure you want to do this? Have you really thought about this?" MacNally knew the kid's heart was in the right place, but he needed him thinking with his head, not his heart.

"Did you really think I was too young to figure out that if I help you I'll end up on Spaeth's list? Honestly Pops, sometimes you're damned insulting."

The smile Russell gave him was all bravado. But despite the attempt at levity, MacNally could feel the weight of the moment. Perhaps it was time to stop thinking of Russell as a kid.

"Listen, Braniff Spaeth gave me a name before he died. I asked him who he was looking for. He gave me a name, but I didn't know if it was legitimate or if he was just throwing me a bone. He said the name Dasson, or Dazen. I don't know. It was hard to be sure. I didn't think much of it at the time. It wasn't a lot to work with. But maybe you could do something with it, since you can still work out of the Precinct."

"What else?" Russell pulled out a notebook and wrote down the name with several different possible spellings.

"Hold on. Slow down. If it really is who they were looking for, we gotta get to him first." MacNally stopped talking long enough to put a hand to his side and curse. It suddenly hurt to breath.

Russell watched him with his usual pinched expression. He looked back at the door. "You want me to call the doctor?"

"I'm fine," MacNally lied, painfully waving away the suggestion. "It's mostly superficial damage across the stomach and chest, you know? Damned star pistols. But it's a *lot* of superficial damage."

"Death by a thousand cuts, huh?"

"What?" Now was not the time for Russell to start mumbling. The close-fired shots of the Panther had done nothing to improve MacNally's hearing.

"Nothing. And don't worry, I get it. If I can, I'll find this Dasson. What else did you want?"

"You gotta find me a place to hole up. I can't stay here. Too many good people are gonna get hurt if I do. It's gotta be somewhere even Jenkins can't find me. Which reminds me, did you get the message about your PDT?"

"MacNally, I told you not to treat me like a kid. It's safely back at my place. Your TransitCar driver picked me up. He's a good guy. From what the Doctor tells me, you wouldn't be alive if he hadn't stuck his neck out for you. You're lucky someone helped you. I guess you weren't able to refuse his help, huh?"

"Don't be sore, Russell. I was trying to keep you from getting hurt."

"You should've tried to keep yourself from getting hurt."

"There's one more thing I need you to get." MacNally winced with the pain and knew he needed to rest again. Duvalls had told him it would take several days for him to get his energy back. His blood pressure was back to acceptable levels and the pain from the skin damage could be managed. But for now, he needed to sleep as much as possible.

"You want a younger man's body?"

"You make jokes, but it isn't a bad idea." MacNally tried to smile. He could see Russell beginning to worry about him. He made an effort to sit up straight. "I need you to go back to my spouses final resting place."

Russell nodded. It was time MacNally started taking Johnnie Spaeth and his associates seriously.

46

Frank's stunning confession had left Lara at a complete loss for words. She had wanted to scream at him, curse him, even beg him to retract his story. But she had felt so unbalanced by this stupefying reversal of their circumstances that she had been unable to focus on any one thought. Even worse, it had stolen from her the belief that there was something they could do for Jett.

Now, it seemed, exile was the least of his problems.

There did not appear to be any good reason to follow through with an appeal. Even it if were successful, it would never even come up to the committee in time to keep them out of danger. This man, this gangster, would find them long before the wheels of justice started to move.

This realization had cut the legs out from under Lara. She spent the day in shock, listlessly lying around the room unable to think of a response to Frank's news.

At one point she'd even pondered the right and wrong of trying to make a deal for Jett's life. But no matter how angry she'd become toward Frank she finally decided she could not use his life as a bargaining chip.

Their best hope lay in disappearing. But neither one of them had any idea how to go about it. They were dependent on their PDTs to buy food, and while they could afford to pay for a place to stay, there was no way to do so without a data tag.

The desaturated sunlight, washed out by the day's cloud cover, had already come and gone. Several times during the day rain had lashed at the windows. They had never really seen the city below them. And even as day turned to night and darkness swallowed their view from the seventeenth floor, they could not easily make out the lights of the streets below. They could, however, occasionally see pale little scenes of night life in the building opposite them.

She could hear the elevator rattling in its cage. It was just across the hall from them and it became audible a few floors below. Each time it did, she watched Frank tense, listening for when it stopped at their floor. Whenever it did, Frank would stand up, stare in dread at the door and hold perfectly still.

This constant tension was wearing Lara to a frazzle. She tried at times to break the mood. She would play little games with Jett. Or try to sing to him, holding him all the while. It did not work. There was no way to lessen the pressure.

Adding to the pressure was her inability to talk to Frank. She could feel a growing resentment that left her mute. There was nothing she could say to Frank simply because there was nothing he could possibly say in response. Nothing, anyway, that would make up for the enormity of his grievous actions.

He had betrayed them. He had promised to provide a secure home for her and their son and he had failed to do it. He had allowed something brutal and sinister to threaten their world—had in fact been the cause of it. She could not understand how he had let—how he had made that happen.

For his part, he had not spent the day trying to explain his actions. He could obviously see that she was not about to accept his paltry excuses. After his initial entreaties for understanding, he had retreated to his chair where he spent most of the day sulking.

Jett had quickly sensed that his parents were troubled and it set him on edge. He was full of anxious energy, grouchy, and food only made him more so. Lara had even considered taking him outside for fresh air, or whatever it was that shrouded the streets of the Lazaretto. Frank had immediately ordered her to remain indoors. She didn't fight him. She did not like the idea of Jett out in such bad weather. It had only been a desperate attempt to alleviate the frustration of the lengthy day.

Without a word, Frank undressed and took to one of the beds. He turned away from her, pulling the sheet over him.

"I won't do this tomorrow," she said to him.

He did not move or speak.

"I know you hear me, Frank. I'm not going to sit here all day again waiting for someone to come through that door and kill you or our son. Even if it is inevitable that they will find us, we can't just sit here and wait for them. It was stupid to sit here all day. We wasted all this time. I could have been down at the IHS, doing something to change this situation. Doing something to save our son."

Frank twisted around. "And what is it you think you're gonna do to save our son? Go on, tell me. What do you think IHS is going to do for him? They're the ones who suggested we just leave him here. A sick kid. Leave him and move on to our new lives somewhere else. These people don't give a damn about that boy."

"Well, don't judge them so harshly. You didn't either. If you had, you wouldn't have endangered us all."

She didn't want to fight any more. There was no point. She would go to IHS in the morning and see what could be done. Maybe she would even go to the police. They would at least be able to keep Jett safe. And her. She didn't even care, at that point, if they did anything for Frank. He had hardly earned protection of any kind.

47

"I love it." She lay on her back, her hands reaching up to touch the screen. "It's so delicate. Like a swirling soap bubble. Don't you think so?"

The New Yorker lay beside her, in the cramped confines of the sleeper, watching the image of the moon on the screen. He had crawled in beside her in hopes that she might be in a friendly mood. Her mood had not turned out to be the issue. The damned sleeper was too small for sport. He felt the heat of her body against his and he decided it was for the best. The sleeper was too hot as well.

"Well? Don't tell me you're gonna avoid answering this question too."

"Sure, I guess it does. A big damned soap bubble. Made by the Lazaretto Soap Company." He pushed her a little to make more room. He pushed again to get her to turn on her side. She ignored him.

"Why do they call it that? What's a Lazaretto?"

"Are you kidding me? You don't know? Where did I ever find you, huh? A nut house?"

"It looks so peaceful."

"Sure, from here. But that's just an illusion. See, everyone who wants to take a trip from one planet to another stops right there." Now he was reaching up, pointing to the center of the image of the moon. "That's Aegean. It's a moon that orbits Sinop. We can't see it right now, from this distance and angle. Most of it is covered in water except this one island. It rains most of the time, it's always cold. You never get to see the sun. It's really a lousy little place. But anyway, all these people come here, and no one's allowed to go anywhere until they land on this moon and wait for forty days."

"What are they waiting for?" With her finger she drew a circle around the edge of the moon.

"Nothing. They just have to wait. But if anyone gets sick during that time, then they don't have to wait anymore because they'll never be allowed to leave. They get this stamp on their PDT that says *nullus exidus* — no go — and that's it."

"It says what?"

"Those are just fancy Latin words. But it mean *no exit*. If you're sick, you stay. That way diseases won't spread from planet to planet."

"And then what?"

"There's no *then what*. The people who can, leave. The people who can't, stay."

"Until they die?" She lifted her head and looked at him in alarm.

"Actually, I don't think they can even leave after they die. It's kind of an eternal thing, you know?" The New Yorker chuckled at his own observation.

She reached over and smacked his arm. "How can you laugh at that? That's a terrible thing. All those people stuck there, even after they've died. It's just like I was reading."

"What is?" He leaned in close and could see the conversation had upset her.

"Your Lazaretto. A place where no can ever leave, full of the sick, the damned who are forever caught in a dead world, cold, miserable, dark. I was just reading about a place like that the other day. They called it *Hell*."

"Hell, huh? Yeah, I guess you could call the Lazaretto that. But you know, my dear, hell doesn't really exist. That's just old superstitious stuff."

"How do you know? Maybe we ended up making hell a real place. Maybe that's what this is." She reached up yet again, only this time she dared not touch the screen. Instead, she held her hand open in such a way as to hold back that malignant moon from falling down on top of them.

"What if we get stuck in this Lazaretto?" Her voice had become very small.

"We won't. The *Strike* here is designed to get us in without being seen. We go in, we do what we have to , and we get back out. Quick and easy. Nothing to worry about." He pushed at her again and this time she rolled over so that her back was against him. He draped an arm over her and stroked the silk fabric that covered her soft belly. "You'll be perfectly safe."

"Says the man who's taking me to hell," she whispered.

"Go back to sleep." He raised his hand and shut down the overhead screen. An afterimage of the wispy, turbulent Lazaretto was still visible in the darkness of the hot sleeper for just a moment. He inhaled the sweet perfume of the Ursuline's hair and waited for the afterimage to fade away.

But even after it did, her words remained in his dreams.

48

He'd put Gloria in a TransitCar outside his building. She was going to have to tell Dannen a convincing story to keep him from wondering where she'd been. Lepov didn't worry about her. If she were ever forced to fight a duel, lies would be her weapon of choice: right *or* left-handed.

Lepov had never heard of *The Maple Leaf*. He grabbed the next TransitCar and asked the driver if he'd heard of it. The man shook his head but he was able to locate it on a scrolling map. It was across the street from Terran Park, surrounded by trinket shops along Bosporus Avenue.

Terran Park had been designed by the Lazaretto Administrators to be a tribute to Earth. It was meant to provide the confined crowds of travelers a last chance to enjoy the grass between their toes before a quadrant locked down. But Lazaretto travelers had their own ideas, and meeting in the pastoral setting of a lush park was not one of them. Most people facing forty days of quarantine embraced a *carpe diem* posture and reveled their nights away in the Center City clubs. Terran Park was largely uninhabited.

Along the northern edge of the park, Bosporus Avenue was crowded with tax-free shops where travelers could buy nearly everything from the Euxine System. A majority of the items were tacky replicas of Phasian Living Jewels, Dneprish perfumes, Bukovinan knives, and many other items that Lazaretto travelers discovered — much too late, of course — were not only worthless, but had no practical value during their extended layover. A few of the shops did in fact handle quality items, including a wine shop that sold authentic Sinopese wine. Such wines had great value during the forty-day quarantine for those who could afford it.

The Maple Leaf was tucked in behind the shops, just off Bosporus. If Lepov had to guess, it was used by the shop owners and their employees, not their customers. There was no large sign signifying the existence of the bar. Its front was discreetly painted to match the surrounding buildings and only a small light perched immediately above the door.

"You want I should wait?" asked the Transit driver.

"Yeah, give me a few minutes. I won't be long."

"Take your time." The man locked down the TransitCar and left his hire light switched off. Before Lepov could climb out of it the driver had already leaned his head against his door and it looked like he had immediately fallen asleep.

He hoped the driver would have little time to nap. He pushed his way into the bar and liked what he saw. It wasn't empty, but it wasn't jammed packed either. This gave him a chance to get in and out without drawing attention to himself, as he would have in an empty joint, while the bartender wouldn't be too busy or spooked by the chance that someone was watching him without his knowing it.

Lepov took his time as he walked down the short flight of steps. He carefully looked at each person there. This was hard to do if you didn't want to attract attention. And Lepov preferred to remain anonymous. He only took the chance to examine each and every one there just in case Jardyn was foolish enough to be watching for Gloria.

If he was, Lepov couldn't see him.

The bartender looked terribly out of place. He looked powerful enough to be the main event at a Euxine Championship bout. Lepov stuck his tough-guy persona in the pocket of his coat and did his best impression of a humble, friendly Joe.

"Nice place you got." Lepov slid onto a stool and looked around. Gloria had said the bartender's name would be Fred. He was disappointed to see no name tag on the man's vest. "It's kind of out of the way but I've heard good things about it. I was told to ask for Fred."

"Why?" The bartender did not offer his name, offer to find Fred, or look very amused.

"Uhh...my friend tells me Fred makes a mean—" he had no idea what sort of drinks they made there, and there was no menu visible, "—drink. Yep, he makes a mean drink."

"He makes a lousy fighter, that's for sure."

"He does?" That did not sound good. "Then you can't be Fred. You look like you'd be a very talented fighter."

"I'm good. You have good judgment. But Fred didn't. He listened to me tell my tales of battling the best boxers on Dnepr. Which is saying something. If you've ever been to Dnepr, especially to the western provinces, you'd know what I mean. And Fred knew. He knew I was good. But he thought it was something he could learn. Like playing the damn-fool accordion. He doesn't understand it takes a lifetime of instinct, a real talent for wanting to bloody your opponent. You gotta be a sonofabitch killer before you step in that ring."

"And you're..." Lepov nodded with a wink.

"Yeah, I am. Not so much anymore. My joints, you know." He threw a slow, mock right at Lepov's jaw, coming just short of fully extending his arm. "Elbow can't take the impact. I still got it here, in the hand. But the support's gone."

Lepov waited for the retired boxer to add more. He didn't.

"I'm Gregor." He held out his hand.

"Tom." Tom didn't hesitate to shake hands. It felt like Lepov had grabbed the landing gear of a transport ship.

"So what happened to Fred?"

"He's laying on a bed in the flophouse upstairs. He can't sit up, he can't eat, he can't do nothing but swell up like a balloon."

"Jaw broken?"

"You've done some boxing, haven't you, Gregor?"

"No, I've never had the kind of brains it takes to box. So it is broken?"

"Nearly in half."

"Damn." Lepov smacked the bar.

"What's the matter?"

"Tom, I got a problem. I got this lady-friend."

"Yeah, then you got a problem." Tom looked down at the empty bar in front of Lepov. "You never ordered a drink. You gotta order a drink to sit here."

"Yeah? I guess that makes sense. Make me a mean drink. I don't care what it is."

"So this lady-friend?" Tom turned around and started making the drink.

"She sent me over here to get a message that was left with Fred. Now, I did worry that he would hesitate to give it to me since he was supposed to give it to her, not me. But she's asked me to get the message. And if I could talk to Fred and explain that, I think he'd listen and then tell me the message. But if he's hurt like you say, first of all, he can't tell me the message, and secondly, he's liable to be sore about what happened to him and he might just decide not to tell me the message, even if his jaw wasn't broken."

"And you want me to—"

"Tell Fred that Gloria would like him to tell me, Gregor Lepov, the message."

"You should have told me your full name to start. Fred was expecting you. And he gave me the message to give you."

"No kidding." Lepov bit his lip and considered that.

"What's the matter? Isn't that good news?"

"Not really, Tom. But go ahead and tell me the message."

Tom told him the message. He said it twice. Fred had obviously made him memorize it word for word. Tom made sure he did not make any mistakes.

It was the sort of message he had expected. Jardyn had picked out a hotel at random and he had left a few cryptic clues as to which one it was. Making them cryptic clues had been a waste of time. They weren't terribly cryptic.

It also wasn't terribly far away. Jardyn was staying just a few blocks down on Bosporus. He wasn't being particularly clever.

And neither was Gloria. Ever since she'd told him where to find Jardyn, Lepov had been bothered by one simple thought. If she had known where to find Jardyn, why hadn't she simply gone to him instead of going to Lepov's place and doing her best to seduce him? It was damned suspicious looking. Did she think he was really that stupid?

He thanked Tom, paid for the untouched drink on the bar and went outside to signal the Transit driver. As they turned east on Bosporus, passing late-night crowds of trinket-shoppers, Lepov wondered if maybe she'd have been right. After all, despite the fact that he knew she was not dealing straight with him, there he was approaching Jardyn's hiding place alone, with no idea of what was awaiting him there.

For all he knew, Jardyn would shoot him when he knocked on the door. Or maybe Kry Dannen would. When Lepov realized it was even possible that Gloria could be waiting there to shoot him, he concluded he was definitely stupid.

He entered the small hotel, climbed the stairs to the third floor, and banged on Jardyn's door with the back of his hand.

"Jardyn! Gloria sent me. Open the door."

To his surprise, the door opened immediately. A tall man with a full head of dark and shiny hair stood just inside. His pleasant smile, formed below a set of high cheekbones, fit his relaxed, handsome appearance.

"Can I help you?" His accent was unfamiliar to Lepov. It sounded as if the man had once lived on Earth.

"I'm a friend of Gloria's."

"Who's Gloria?"

Yeah, Lepov hadn't figured this was going to be easy.

Russell stood in the shadow of the iron gate, watching the empty street. Rain hit the pavement like pebbles poured from the sky. The sudden heavy shower didn't bother the young detective. It was good cover. He saw headlights approaching and kept out of sight until they stopped just a few meters from him.

He bent to retrieve the bundle he'd tucked up under a stone sill in the wall and stepped into the rain. The rear door of the TransitCar swung open and he tossed the bundle inside. He made two trips back to the wall and was thoroughly soaked before he finally climbed in the front seat.

"You're getting my car wet," said Bril.

"Considering what I just threw in the back of your car, water's the least of your problems." Russell ran a hand through his wet, curly hair.

"Do I want to know?"

"I don't think so."

"Okay. You want to get your man first or ditch this stuff before we get him?"

"We'll get him first. He's on the way. Just don't draw attention to us while you're driving. This would be a bad time to have your car searched."

"I take it you never worked traffic detail, is that right Detective?" Bril looked over at Russell with a lop-sided smile. "Not too many officers are interested in pulling me over in this kind of rain. Hold tight, now."

The TransitCar rose quickly, the sound of rain on the roof increased to a powerful roar. Bril laughed as he spun the nose of the vehicle around and engaged the drive.

They sped across the emergency lanes which ran between the upper floors of buildings in that section of the city. Some of the buildings did not reach that elevation and Bril took advantage of them to cut across their rooftops.

"If you're trying to impress me, don't. I was serious when I said you don't want to get searched right now." Russell tried to keep an eye out for police cruisers in the heavy rain.

"Relax, Russell. There's no one up here. Trust me. It's late, it's raining, and there ain't no patrols in this neighborhood. Besides, I'm dropping down right over here."

"Don't bother," Russell pointed to their right. "Keep her up. We'll land this thing on the roof of the clinic."

"I like that idea." Bril cut in between two massive buildings and out the other side of them. The clinic was just ahead of them. "You want me to go in with you?"

"No, I'll manage. Just be ready to move when we come out."

Russell slipped out the door before the TransitCar came to a complete stop. He was beginning to get worried about the time they had left. There was no way to know how soon Spaeth would be a threat. It was quite possible there were already more teams out there looking for MacNally.

He had to wait for the big security man Karl to open the rooftop door. Together they rode the elevator down to MacNally's floor. Dr. Duvalls was in the room, along with his wife. They were prepping MacNally for the move.

"The repair-screen needs time to heal." The doctor was talking to both detectives as he handed Russell a small bottle. "He takes these every four hours. They support the repair. The scrim is already thick enough to prevent bleeding, but it can't take much strain. Don't let it get wet. As it heals, it will tighten across his chest and he'll be uncomfortable. But he'll have no problems breathing as long as he's on his back and resting."

"Okay," Russell nodded. He turned to address MacNally. "So you be a good boy and stay in bed. You heard the doctor."

"All joking aside, it is important, detective." Duvalls gave MacNally one last disapproving stare. "You do not have to leave. I'm sure we've been able to keep your presence here a secret."

"But are you willing to bet the life of your wife, your staff, and your patients on that?" MacNally coughed.

"No more of that, Edward." Maria wiped his forehead with a cool cloth and firmly pushed him back against his pillow. "If you can't stay down, I'll insist that Detective Russell takes me with you. And that, I believe, would defeat the purpose of this move."

"Yes, ma'am." MacNally closed his eyes and allowed Russell and Karl to take over.

"Don't worry, Mrs. Duvalls. I'll make sure he gets loaded safely." Karl disengaged the locks on the wheels of the bed and gave it a push.

"No you won't," Russell guided the front of it through the door. "None of you are going to the roof. You won't see us leave. You won't know what we loaded MacNally into."

"You sure you don't want me to stay with you?" Karl asked. "From the sound of things, you could use another trained man."

"I'm sure we could use you, but I want you here. You need to get the Duvalls out of here. Is there anyone else who knew MacNally was here?" Russell looked from Karl to Duvalls. They both shook their heads.

"But Detective," Duvalls countered, "we will bring suspicion upon ourselves if we leave the clinic. We need to follow our usual routine. We will leave when it is appropriate. But not before."

Russell didn't like it, but the doctor was probably right. One last push and MacNally was in the elevator. Russell thanked the Duvalls then backed into the elevator as the doors closed.

"Where you taking me?" MacNally asked.

"It's a surprise. And no peeking, Pops."

50

"So do I stand out here and wait for the rain to fall harder or do I get to step inside?"

Jardyn had made a few more laconic attempts at convincing Lepov he'd never heard of Gloria, had never heard the name Jardyn, and had never heard of a plot to steal an old gun. Perhaps he expected Lepov to just turn and walk away.

"Why would you come inside?" Jardyn leaned forward to completely block the entrance.

"Look, I get it. You're being careful. You're worried about Spaeth. You don't want what happened to Frobe to happen to you. So you think you need to play this out like I got the wrong guy. But you're overlooking two things. One is the fact that I know what you look like."

"What's the other one?"

"You aren't being careful, you're being stupid. If I was with Spaeth, I would have shot you through the door as you were turning the handle."

"Maybe I've been careless. But that's no reason to call me stupid." Jardyn stepped aside and pulled the door open so that Lepov could squeeze by.

"I disagree." Lepov pushed Jardyn out of the way and shut the door. He pointed toward a set of chairs and Jardyn led the way.

"So I was right about Frobe? Spaeth got to him?" Jardyn dropped in a chair and tried not to look scared. He wasn't doing a good job of it.

"I don't really know. I was hoping you could shed some light on that. Officially your partner had an accident. The way you're playing hide-n-seek made me think you must know otherwise."

"I was just guessing. When Frobe disappeared, I was sure he had just found a bar where he could pass out after a night of drinking. But I knew almost right away that didn't make sense. He was as nervous as I am now. I was more complacent, not him. There was no way he would have been careless enough to fool around in a public bar." He was able to smile at his use of the word *careless* despite his unease.

"Well we can talk about this later. I'm taking you out of here, someplace I can control. I have a few ideas." Lepov crossed to a window and examined the street. He could see the front bumper of the TransitCar he'd left waiting by the curb. The rest of the street was empty. The rain was behaving, falling lightly on the puddles under the street lights.

"I'm not going anywhere." Jardyn's practiced, measured tone could not hide his irritation at being ordered around.

"And why's that?"

"I suppose you were going to say that you wanted to take me to Gloria. As if bringing us together would be a noble and touching feat. But you are overlooking something that should be painfully obvious."

Lepov shrugged his shoulders in reply.

"We were already together. We separated for a specific reason. We have no desire to…put all of our eggs in the same basket…you understand the meaning of that, Mr. Lepov?"

"I think I get the gist."

What Lepov didn't say was that he had never intended to put Jardyn and Gloria in the same room. There was still too much that didn't add up. And Jardyn's present attitude was something to add to his list.

"I don't want to be near Gloria right now. There would be no point. After what happened to Frobe, I'm don't think even she could fault me for changing my mind."

"I sort of got the idea that Gloria saw a point in meeting with you. Only I was under the impression you wanted to meet her too. If you didn't, why the cloak-and-dagger message? Why not just stay hidden?" Jardyn tried to reply but Lepov immediately tossed out a few more questions. "And why would Frobe's death change your mind? Even if we discover that Spaeth was responsible for the accident, you had to have known Spaeth was coming for you. You didn't think you were all going to get away spotless. Why let Frobe's death change your mind?"

"We did get away spotless." Jardyn held a finger to his lips; something was bothering him.

"Maybe. Maybe Frobe is accident prone. I wouldn't know. But when something as valuable as that gun becomes a basis for partnership, the probability of accidents drops quickly."

"Now you're suggesting I had something to do with Frobe's death. That's tacky," Jardyn said absentmindedly. It looked like something was still bothering him. "Tell me Mr. Lepov, what did you mean when you said *cloak-and-dagger* message?"

"The note you left at the bar. For Gloria. You could have simply left a straight-forward address. There was no point in trying to mask it. Maybe you didn't trust Fred. But I doubt he would have had much trouble figuring it out if he had wanted to. It wouldn't have slowed down Spaeth, though. Take a little friendly advice and don't complicate things, Jardyn. I understand what happened to Frobe has you rattled, but you need to start thinking more clearly."

"That's very good advice." Jardyn suddenly rose and disappeared into a small room in the back. He came back almost immediately, a locked case in his hands.

"Look, I'm not gonna drag you out of here," Lepov said.

"You're very generous." Jardyn set the case on a table and inserted a key into it.

"You don't want to go, that's up to you. I'm not gonna stand here and discuss it all day."

"Yes, you've clearly done your duty."

"Yes, I have." Lepov watched him open the case. It was as he had suspected: the stolen pistol was encased in protective foam. "Anything you want me to say to Gloria?"

"Just a moment, Mr. Lepov. If you don't mind..." Jardyn had bent over the case, carefully examining it. "Would you mind answering a question for me?"

"If I can."

"Gloria hired you to find me, and she told you that there would be a message from me at this bar."

"That's not a question, but yes, she did. And before you say it, I know what you're going to ask."

"You do?" Jardyn had closed the case and turned it over, peering closely at the hard, synthetic seams.

"You're about to ask me if I thought it was strange that she wanted me to find you instead of just coming herself."

"And if I had, your answer would have been...?"

"Yes, I did think it was strange. But according to her she didn't want her husband finding out where you were. She seems to think he'll be a bit jealous. Temper problem, from what I understood. Did you lose something?"

Jardyn had opened up the case again and had removed the foam packing. He stopped to look at Lepov. "Are you a jealous man, Mr. Lepov?"

"Not really. I give up easily—where women are concerned. A woman taught me a long time ago that men don't have proprietary rights over a woman like they think. They reserve the right to back out of a promise on the slightest whim. There's no point fighting a truth like that."

"Gloria." Jardyn nodded. "Oh, yes. I know who you are, Lepov. You're no private detective she found in the classifieds. I once heard her say that you were the only man who ever trusted her. It doesn't say much for you."

"Which one of us are you trying to insult? And in case you thought I was naïve, you should know I'm aware you two walked out of Alpha quadrant together. Seems I'm not the only one with a soft spot for untrustworthy blondes."

Jardyn said nothing as he went back to his examination of the case and its contents. Lepov watched as he abruptly ceased his inspection and returned the pistol to the case.

"I hope you realize this stays with me." Jardyn snapped the case shut.

"I want nothing to do with that." Lepov decided to go. Jardyn did not want or need Lepov's help. And his clients weren't paying him enough to kidnap a fully grown man. "I'll tell the Dannen's you weren't interested in their invitation. Should I tell them you'll be in touch?"

"I have a feeling it won't matter what you tell them, Lepov."

Lepov walked out. The TransitCar was still waiting and Lepov sat in the shadow of the back seat as it sped down Bosporus. He was angry. Not at that crack about trusting Gloria. He deserved that. He wasn't mad at Jardyn for refusing to go with Lepov either. Hell, if he had been in Jardyn's shoes, he wouldn't have opened the door for anyone, including someone claiming to be Gloria's ex-husband. He wasn't even mad at Gloria for getting him mixed up in this mess.

He was mad at himself. Mad that he still couldn't see what Gloria was up to. The only thing he knew for sure was that she was leading him down a path that she'd chosen and so far he'd taken every step. It was time to do something she wouldn't expect. Yes, she'd told him where to find Jardyn. And now he was supposed to raise the alarm and tell her that Jardyn wouldn't play fair.

For starters, Lepov decided he wouldn't raise any alarm. He told the Transit driver to take him home. He would get a good night's rest. Then, in the light of day, he'd decide what to do next.

That was the idea, anyway. But when he reached his apartment, it was clear he was going to get anything *but* rest for the remainder of the night.

51

Someone was talking above them. The muffled voices should have helped Lara sleep, so rhythmic was the conversation. Yet, instead of it lulling her sleep, she spent the darkest hours of the night bending her will to the words she could not understand. She needed to know what they were; needed to know for Jett's sake. No matter how absurd it was, she held an unshakeable belief that someone was trying to tell her the answer to her dilemma. That voice had the answer. It knew what she should do. And if she only paid close enough attention, she would eventually decipher the words and she too, would know what to do.

And then footsteps pounded down the hall outside their door. She felt Frank tense, knew he too was awake in the darkness. She wanted to reach out to him, let him know he wasn't alone. But she didn't. It was too soon. She could not bring herself to commit such an act of kindness. One day, perhaps. But this wasn't it.

The footsteps had faded away. There were no others. The only sounds left were the rain on the window and the voices in the room above.

She felt Frank sit up. On her back, her head turned away from him, she closed her eyes nonetheless. She had no desire to talk. There was nothing that could be said well at such a dreadful hour. One of the rare bits of marital advice her sister had ever given her centered on this fact: a wife should never allow her husband to discuss anything important late at night. No one ever behaved rationally when tired. No one ever spoke with kind resolve in the hours before dawn.

"If I had any nerve I would go down to the lobby and wait for them. Just to keep you and Jett safe."

He knew she was awake. Knew it as she had known he was. One of the advantages—or was it a disadvantage?—of being married. Still, she said nothing in reply, hoping that he would decide he had been wrong to think her awake.

"Is that what you want? You want me to leave?" He put a hand on her. He wasn't fooled.

Eyes still closed, head still turned away, she said, "Don't be stupid. I told you what I want. I want to go down to IHS. I want to fight for our son. Why can't you understand that? Is it so hard?"

He let out a long, hard breath. His way of letting her know he was irritated. "You can't go. You can't be in public. None of us can."

"And this is better?" She sat up, pulling away from him, her knees drawn to her chest. "Sitting here? Don't you realize that we'll be easy to find? IHS put us here. There's a record of it."

"But who's to say they have access to records like that?"

"You are!" Lara was not just angry with Frank. She was angry with herself for allowing him to draw her into this argument. "Didn't you start all of this by telling me you've learned how this man operates? That you were fully aware of the breadth of his reach? Were you making that up?"

"No."

"Then we cannot stay here. We've got to go somewhere else. How could you have sat here all day? It's not enough you put us all in danger, now you want to just sit there and let them come. Maybe you should go down to that lobby. Maybe you should offer yourself up like a ritual sacrifice!"

She'd said it. And she hated herself for it. But that wasn't enough for her to retract it. The talking in the room above them had stopped. The rain had ceased hitting the windows. The distance between them seemed to multiply as the bed expanded to the size of the apartment and more.

"I didn't mean that," she finally said. By then, he had left the bed and was sitting in the chair near the window.

"I've been sitting here all day for the simple fact that I honestly don't have the slightest idea what I should do." His back was to her. She saw him fish a cigarette out of a packet but he did not light it. "We don't have any way of disappearing. Everything we do is tracked. We've got nothing to trade. To use to get us off the board. And if we did, where would we go? We're on a damned island, on a little moon that we can never leave. Jonnie Spaeth doesn't have to find me. He doesn't need to do anything to me. Our life is already ruined. We have nothing."

"Which is why we have to try, no matter how futile it seems. Don't you understand that, Frank? Don't you see that we can't allow ourselves to give in to the despair that stains every street in this city? God, I can feel it. It gets in your clothes, in your pores. There's no sun! We haven't been here but a few days and I can feel it. I feel like I need to wash my hands, again and again.

"And that's why we can't stop. It doesn't matter if one of them comes through that door. Until they do, we have to try to get Jett out of here. He can't stay here. He'll die before he ever becomes a man. And if he doesn't, I can't imagine what sort of man he would become."

"Then go," he said, an exasperated laugh escaping with his words. "I won't stop you. But I won't help you. We would do better to get out of this apartment. I just don't know how to do it."

"Frank," she leaned over and switched on a light. "You said you meant for us to disappear once we landed on Dnepr. Right? You had a plan. We would have had to dispose of our data tags. Get new identities. You had a plan for that, didn't you? You must have an idea of how we can do that here."

"No, no that doesn't work. We were supposed to receive our share of the job after it was sold. They were going to contact us there, on the planet. But now, here, we'll never see a bit of that money. They won't come back here looking for us. And even if they did, it would take too long. Spaeth will find us long before then."

"So, I'm going then, in the morning. I'll go early and I'll be back as soon as possible."

"Wasting your time," he mumbled. She had barely been able to catch his words. But she'd heard enough.

"And I'll keep wasting it. That's my son, and he's worth every minute I waste! Worth far more than you and the time I waste arguing with you. As his father, you ought to know that!"

She nearly broke the lamp as she groped at it to kill the light. She was finished talking. Her sister had been right, of course. Late-night discussions were not healthy. She should have kept her eyes closed along with her mouth.

52

Lilly had avoided it as long as possible. But no matter how many times she hinted it was getting late, Shay had shown no intention of leaving. They had ultimately ended up at her apartment. She had not been able to find a way to make him leave.

They talked long into the night. Most of the conversation had been carried by Shay. He wasn't just acting like a man who'd been locked away in prison; it was as if he'd been in solitary confinement, and he was talking for the first time in years. Of course, Lilly had to admit to herself that this was nothing new for Shay. He had always loved the sound of his own voice.

"You know, Lilly, I spent a lot of time knockin' my head around on account of how I treated you. We had a good thing going and I tossed it out like I thought it was something common, something I'd find again easily enough when I wanted another one. You know, I tried to blame that on you for a while. You always made it seem so natural, so right between us—so right it was simple, sustained without the slightest effort. But don't think I blamed you long. No, I knew you weren't to blame."

"I'm glad," Lilly said, amused at the idea that she did indeed deserve some of the blame. They were both sitting on her sofa, and Lilly had kept to her side of it, her legs folded up beneath her.

"I know, I know. Old Shay as chivalrous as ever! But I'm serious. Don't let me off the hook so easy. And don't think I have either. Don't let my smiles and charms fool you. A man hits some rough stretches in confined orbit. I never knew which was worse. Staring out at that damned planet beneath us, with its promise of life and freedom and—*normalcy*. Or staring into the vastness of space, where the only visible signs of life were the fires of stars. Stars so far away you couldn't know if you were looking at one that was still burning or one that had died out thousands of years ago.

"They were both hell. Enough to drive a man to his...well, to escape."

"Shay, I really had no idea..." she reached out and put a hand on his shoulder. She had never given any thought to what would happen to Shay after his arrest. She'd been angry, and that was all that mattered. "I don't know how to—"

"Hey," Shay covered her hand with his, "don't start that kind of talk. I didn't come here for that. We've lost too much time to waste it on regrets and finger-pointing and explanations. There's no need for that, is there?"

"How can we not?" Lilly had begun to lean into Shay but she pulled back as she considered his words. "You expect me to believe you've shown up here with nothing but goodwill and love?"

"Is that so far-fetched?"

"Yes, to be honest. It is. It certainly isn't natural."

"Who says?" His crooked smile was interfering with her attempts to think clearly.

"Shay, don't you get it? I've given up my work. The traveling, anyway, to be here, with Gregor. I haven't been sitting around waiting for your return. What we were…it ended."

Shay continued to smile. She had missed that about him, the way he could always keep a smile on his face no matter what was happening around her. Of course, there had been plenty of times that it had irritated her. Nothing ever seemed to bother him.

"There's no ring on your finger, is there?" He turned her hand over to inspect it. Once he'd proven his point, his fingers tightened over hers and he lifted them to his lips.

"You keep acting like nothing has happened, Shay. Have you forgotten that you're an escaped convict?"

"Not an escaped convict. Did you forget I'm dead?"

Lilly tried to pull away her hand but Shay held tight. She wanted to be angry with him but she couldn't do it.

"I should take you away from this awful place." Shay's eyes gleamed in the lamplight. "You shouldn't live here. No man has the right to ask you to stay here. Let me get you out of here."

"I can't leave with you." She was astonished to realize how much she wanted to go with him. She was disturbed to realize the truth of her own words.

"All you have to do is say you want to."

"Shay, you aren't listening to me. Stop playacting like a little boy and listen to me. I can't leave! And I hardly think an escaped convict could get out through quarantine. For once in your life, be serious."

"I got me and my friends off a prison barge. Don't think I couldn't get us out of this rotten city."

Lilly was finally getting angry. Not at Shay for anything he'd done in the past. But she was angry with him nonetheless. Angry that he had showed up uninvited, to highlight her foolishness in thinking she could be happy in a deathtrap like the Lazaretto. It didn't matter that she would be with Gregor. It wasn't enough. She wasn't made to sit by and allow the weight of life to slowly smother her. She needed to travel, needed to move on, to know that she wasn't confined to one place, or even one man.

Had that been true all those years ago? Had that been why she'd so easily turned Shay over to the police? Had she, even then, been looking for a way out of the confinement of marriage?

She left Shay on the sofa, moving to the window where she could look out over the lights of the Lazaretto. How had she thought she could live here? What imprudence had led her to this point?

She cursed Shay for his arrogance. It was nothing new. He'd always been this way. Had always carried with him a confidence that he could mold Lilly to whichever crazy idea he would devise next. The hell of it was, he was usually right.

"Why did you wait until now? What took you so long? Why did you wait until I thought I was happy?"

For once, Shay had no answers.

53

"You know, my brother was younger than me."

The Australian stood facing the viewscreen; Aegean spun within its swirl of clouds. The New Yorker thought it looked like it was boiling. He tried not to smile when he thought about the woman's *soap bubble* image and refocused on his employer.

"Much younger?"

"Not very. He was only a half-brother. Different fathers, you know? That's why he was so much bigger. Built like a orbit tanker, wasn't he?"

The New Yorker had not known the brothers had different fathers. It explained the size difference. It did not explain the similarity in their violent natures.

"So where do we stand? Any news yet on our intrepid thieves?"

"We know where one of them is. The other one hasn't been found yet, but I'm confident that will change. They couldn't have fled to a smaller trap than this Lazaretto."

"I agree. That was the reason we were so damned sure it would be easy to grab them. It is the same reason my brother took few precautions. This Lazaretto is indeed a trap. A deadly one. Don't talk to me of confidence. Talk to me with specifics. You understand?"

The Australian's rapid transformation from reverie to anger did not worry the New Yorker. He was used to it. He physically backed up a few steps to show the proper respect for his employer's ire. It was enough to mollify him.

"The Swede had moved into an exit quadrant. However, he has since left it, and now sits in one location. He seems to be waiting. Most importantly, he is not running. He will probably not have the stolen item. The missing man will likely have it. My source has little hope of locating him. He hasn't said that, of course. He'll be hesitant to admit this. However, it is in someone else's best interest to see that this man is found."

The Englishman. He had to be making an effort to find the Frenchman. If the Frenchman slipped away with the artifact, then the Englishman would be left in a dangerous position. And he would have the best chance of finding his partner.

"So when we arrive, do we take one of them right away?" The Australian was not one to usually ask for advice. The New Yorker did not reply without giving the answer serious thought.

"If we do, and the other one hears of it, this might make him impossible to find. Of course, we don't want to let him disappear on us." His answer was in no way decisive. But it was honest. Grabbing the Swede could be the wrong move. "I advise we move slowly when we arrive. I wouldn't think it could hurt to wait a day or two. Watch him. Wait to see if the other appears."

"And the Irishman? I want to deal with him as soon as we land."

"I've heard nothing yet. However, we have alternate sources if this one does not produce."

"Use them. Don't wait." The Australian's voice rose, waking several of the men in the bay. "I'm not rushing off to sit in that garbage dump to wait until someone spots this hero. I want to know where he is when we land. Got it?"

"I'll make some calls." The New Yorker prepared to leave, but the Australian grabbed his arm.

"I know what you're thinking. My brother wasn't high on your list. But don't take this lightly. He was my brother. There's nothing more to say. Do whatever it takes to find that Irishman."

"You're the boss."

54

Lepov had known something was wrong the moment he saw the big black man sitting against his door.

"You Lepov?" he asked as soon as Lepov stepped out of the stairwell.

"If you're not mad at Lepov, then yes I am. If you are mad at him, then I've never heard of him."

"I've been waitin' for you."

"Well, you really should have waited at my office. I open in about eight hours. Is this something that can't wait?"

"I'm not a client. I'm a Transit driver. MacNally sent me."

"Is something wrong?" Lepov had known the answer before the man spoke.

"It's not good." The driver had headed straight for the elevator. "I'll take you to him. I'll explain on the way."

And that's what he did. Lepov sat in the front seat as Bril Abbot gave him as many details as possible. From the moment MacNally stepped into that bar, through the shootings, the news about Spaeth, and the ambush.

"So where are you taking me?"

"Not far now. We're close."

Lepov looked around and a funny feeling hit his gut. They were in a deserted neighborhood. Not many people liked to live there. It was too close to the shipping port.

A wall separated the West End district of the city from the Shipping Port, a completely automated zone that was routinely soaked in a biocide known as Shipper's Formula. This highly toxic spray allowed for non-living cargo to pass through quarantine at an accelerated rate. Crews for the cargo ships remained in orbit and had no contact with the cargo once it left the Lazaretto. Though IHS denied any possibility that the formula could spread beyond the walls of the port, most city-dwellers believed that the West End was unhealthy, and only the poorest individuals took shelter in the shadows of the port walls.

"One of these abandoned apartments?"

"No." Abbot, though he had slowed down, was still moving through the streets, even as the walls of the shipping port drew nearer.

"You heading where it looks like you're heading?"

"You're the detective." Abbot smiled as he came to the last street that ran parallel with the wall. He turned left and drove beside the imposing structure until he came to a bay door. It was closed. Abbot jumped out of the TransitCar and jogged over to the door. He tugged at it until is slid up and away. He hurried back and drove through the dark opening.

"You gotta be kidding me." Lepov stared into the darkness surrounding them. Abbot left him again, this time to close the big door.

The darkness was complete.

Lepov heard Abbot's footsteps fading away to his right. For a brief moment he thought the man was leaving him. But the footsteps suddenly stopped and a mechanical switch was thrown. A naked light bulb lit a corner of the bay.

They were in a large, brick warehouse. A storage house for Lazaretto supplies that were ready to be distributed throughout the city. Having just come through the shipping port, supplies were left isolated in these storage houses for five days as a precaution.

To Lepov's relief, the great concrete bay was empty. Large docking bay doors, filling the entirety of the port wall, stood silently closed. Lepov saw warning icons strewn about the bay and he didn't need a training manual to understand what they all meant. This was not the kind of place you wanted to bring the family. It wasn't the kind of place you wanted to bring yourself.

"Over here," Abbot gestured with his hand. A steel door with a flat bar barricade lock stood behind him.

Lepov crossed the empty space. He watched as Abbot inserted a key into the center of the barricade lock. With a twist, it shifted all four flat bars out of their slots.

"I guess it wouldn't help for me to point out that going through that door is a bad idea. I suppose you already know that."

Lepov didn't want to sound paranoid but there was no reason to leave this point unspoken.

"I like all you detectives. Nothing gets by you guys." Abbot put two hands on the door's handle and strained to pull it open. "There's nothing dangerous on the other side of this door. It doesn't even have a seal on it."

Once he had the door open enough, they entered a dark, short hallway. Abbot shut the door, locking it again with the key. The only light in the passage came from a sign at the other end. It read: DANGER, NO ENTRY.

"Now who would put a door where no entry is allowed?" Lepov looked from the sign to Abbot, both of which were awash in red light. "Somebody's got a funny sense of humor."

"Maybe it's like my old grandmother used to do. She'd put a jar of cookies on the table and tell us not to eat them. Then she'd leave us alone in the house."

"And?"

"We'd eat 'em. I always figured if she didn't want us eating 'em, she would've hid them in the pantry." Abbot's hand grabbed the door handle.

"No key this time?" Lepov had figured out there was no immediate danger and Abbot was only trying to worry him.

"No key." Abbot opened the door.

There was no rush of hot, poisonous air. No sirens wailed. The red light was immediately replaced by a dull, pale white shimmer. A small, simple room with only a few furnishings was all that could be seen. In one corner, a small sink stood alone. Along the opposite wall, a bare metal desk and chair kept company with a matching pair of waist-high bookshelves. A table was shoved into the corner behind the door. On the wall opposite the door they had just entered were two more doors.

"How much is this a month?" asked Lepov. "This should be cheaper than my apartment, which would be a first."

"If you want, I could ask."

"No thanks, I'm sure there's a waiting list. We keep going?" He headed for the other doors.

"Not yet." Abbot stopped him just as Lepov had reached out for the handle on the left door. "Don't do that."

"Let me guess, that's the door that's dangerous to open. No sign, no lock. I should have known. This is the Lazaretto, after all."

Abbot turned and opened the door on the right to reveal a closet. From here he pulled out two old and stained decon suits.

"Oh, hell." Lepov eyed them with dread. "This just gets better and better."

"Put it on. Seal it. I check you. You check me. This you can't joke around about."

"Oh, not a chance." Lepov put one leg into the fully encapsulating suit and fought to keep his balance. "I once joked around in a decon suit when I was a rookie cop and died on the spot. No one laughed. Decon suits have killed lots of lousy comics."

Lepov struggled with his suit. Abbot was more graceful with his. After they engaged their atmospheric harnesses, they closed up their suits.

"Hold still." Abbot reached out and grabbed Lepov from behind. "And pay attention. You're gonna do this to me. And you're gonna do it right."

"You sound like my wife on our wedding night. I know, I know…I'm paying attention."

Once they were done, Abbot led him through the door on the left. They descended a staircase into a series of passages lined with sagging pipes. Lepov pointed out the many leaks where liquid dripped into puddles. Abbot just smiled behind his faceplate.

"Steam condensate. That's not the bad stuff." His voice, while audible, sounded like it was coming from another room.

As they moved along, Abbot continued to explain their surroundings. Although the shipping port was fully automated, like all such things, they did require maintenance, which required maintenance workers. The entrance they were using was rarely used. A larger, more modern decon room had been built further down the line.

They still were not in the hot zone of the shipping port. These tunnels allowed workers to move about without coming into contact with the deadly toxin that saturated the port. The decon suits were only a precaution. If they did cross into the hot zone, they would not be able to exit through the small room where they had entered. They would need to use a decon room to purge their suits before removing them. Otherwise, there was a chance of the Shippers' Formula contacting them while they removed the suits.

"So how did Russell end up taking MacNally down here?" asked Lepov.

"That was my idea. He said he was looking for a place where he could keep MacNally out of the way. One of my first jobs was working down here. I figured out really quick that it wasn't a great career choice. But they paid pretty good. So I made it about a year before I grabbed a Transit job. I figured that even gangsters might be leery about crossing into the shipping port. Even tough guys are afraid of bio-toxins."

"Well, sure, you'd have to be stupid to be doing this." Lepov eyed a fairly substantial leak. He hoped Abbot knew what he was doing.

"That door on your left, Lepov. Open it."

This one led to a much smaller room than the first one they'd encountered. It was almost too small for the two men. But once the door shut, Lepov understood. Abbot smashed a large, flat disk and the room was engulfed in a deluge of water. Its buffeting force shoved Lepov into his guide, who pushed back.

"Keep on your feet. It gets worse."

It did. But it did not last long.

Once the water drained from the catch basin, Abbot opened a second door.

"We're here," Abbot said needlessly.

Lepov was staring into the barrel of a large caliber pistol. Menya Russell was behind it. He lowered the weapon and pointed to his right. "Suits go there. And thanks for coming."

"Any time." Lepov allowed Russell to break the seal on his suit, then accepted his help so that he could get out of the suit without falling down. Once he and Abbot were finished, they followed Russell across the room. It was similar in size to the entry room.

MacNally was lying on a bed in one corner.

"You don't look any worse than you usually do."

"You do," MacNally shot back.

"Well, I've had a run-in with a devil." Lepov didn't elaborate.

They shook hands. The contact lasted a heartbeat longer than usual. It was Lepov's way of letting his friend know he was worried for him. He could see by the look in MacNally's eyes that it was more than sufficient.

"Any particular reason you dragged me down into this rat hole?"

"Misery loves company, don't you know?" MacNally rolled over awkwardly, as if he were made of wood, then pushed up into a sitting position. "No, it's alright. I'm getting better all the time."

Lepov frowned as he watched the detective grimace in pain. "Oh yeah, you're looking good."

"Oh, don't start. My chest is gonna have more scars than hair, but it doesn't go deeper than that. Of course, I hurt everywhere, *a lot*. But I'll live."

"Okay, then. So why am I here?"

"Abbot filled you in, didn't he?"

"Sure. You stuck your nose into a nest of needle-whips. And you can't get it out. It's the price you pay to be a hero. But that still doesn't tell me why I'm here. You want the four of us to shoot down Spaeth when he shows up? I sort of doubt he'll be alone."

"It might come to that. But right now, anyone associated with me is a target. Russell was supposed to stay out of this but he's too young and stupid to do so. All he had to do was follow orders but he couldn't do something simple like that. Abbot here has the same problem I got. He had to be a hero."

"A man hires my TransitCar gets top-notch service." Abbot smiled. "We go that extra kilometer for the man who gets shot down before he can climb in the back seat."

"So that makes three of you who are more stupid than the average man. I'm still waiting to hear why I'm being stupid."

"I wanted to leave you out of it, Lepov, but that wouldn't have been fair." MacNally stood up slowly, grabbing Lepov's arm for support. "Lots of guys down at the precinct know we're friends. It won't take Spaeth long to find out about you. I didn't want you out there without fair warning."

He was right. From here on out, he would have to watch his back. And now that he knew where MacNally was hiding…

"That's very noble of you, MacNally. But if you think that telling me where you're hiding gives me a chance to bargain for my life if Spaeth grabs me, you're not thinking right. Even if I told him, he'd probably just kill me anyway."

"That isn't why I did it, you idiot. I know full well you'd love to go to your death protecting me, just so I'd have something to feel guilty about. I told you because there's Lilly to be considered. Anyone who wants to get to you might try to use Lilly. I don't know what you should do about it, but at least you get the chance to think it over now, instead of being surprised if something happens to her."

Lepov felt his gut turn on him again. MacNally was right.

"I know," MacNally said, "I make a fool out of myself in that bar and now Lilly's in trouble. If I could undo it—"

"It's not your fault, Mac."

"What I don't understand," Russell turned to Lepov, "was why you and Lilly are still here. Why didn't you just leave when you had the chance?"

"Shut up, Russell," MacNally waved him away.

"It just never made sense to me. They were both in Alpha quadrant, their exit was paid up."

"What did I just say?" MacNally's sharp tone silenced his partner. He gingerly sat down at a table. "It's none of your business."

"It's okay, MacNally." Lepov was already going over his options. "I don't see any sense in bringing her down here. There's no telling how long she'd have to stay here. What is this place, anyway?"

"An emergency shelter. These were designed to be a place for workers to dive into in the case of a catastrophic failure of containment. The exits are too far from here." Abbot held up a hand to keep Lepov from speaking. "I know, it looks like a trap. But there isn't a more defensible place in the city."

"Like I said, I can't bring Lilly here. My best chance would be to find a random room to rent."

"You need a new PDT. I've got one you can use," said MacNally.

"They'd be looking for any place with a new occupant." Abbot reached into his pocket, then tossed a set of keys to Lepov. "Use my place. No one can connect me to any of this."

"You didn't log MacNally into your route log?"

"I was using this PDT, not my own." MacNally gave it to Lepov.

"I called in once after the shooting," Abbot explained. "They think I'm taking a few days off. And yes, that's normal for me. I'm a bit lazy. I don't drive every day. You can use my car. And take my PDT. It will look less suspicious if I'm showing up on the grid where I'm supposed to."

"You go with them." MacNally shook his head when Abbot tried to argue. "Non-negotiable, my new friend. You've gone far and above the call of duty. You stick around and you're liable to end up dead. Lepov, you rent a place with that PDT I gave you. It's clean. And Spaeth isn't a wizard. He can't connect it with you, with me, or anybody.

"Besides, Abbot, you've got the only key to that door. And Russell here has to leave with you guys, because he's got to track down the guy Spaeth's men was looking for. And if he finds him, he's gonna bring him back here. So the key has to be on the outside."

All of the men looked around to see if anyone had any objections. At least at that point, no one had any that was worth mentioning.

"I should have brought you a book, or a toy." Russell looked down at his seated partner.

"Russell, if you'd brought me a woman I wouldn't even be able to annoy her. When you clowns leave, I'm gonna go back to sleep. I can't sit up like this much longer."

"Remember what the doctor said."

"I know, I know. Four times a day. I got food, water, and a bed. That's all I want. Get out of here."

"You want me try to find you a woman in case you get to feeling better?" Lepov helped MacNally get back on his feet.

"I think I'd rather you brought me a bottle of whiskey."

"You nasty old drunk." Lepov put a hand on the detective's shoulder. "It's good to know one of us is gonna get a good night's sleep."

MacNally watched the three men begin the graceless process of donning their decon suits.

55

Lilly rolled over and wished she had stayed asleep. She knew without looking that it was still the middle of the night. She didn't want to see the clock. Didn't want to know just how little she had slept. It was best to assume that most of the night was gone. If only she could keep her eyes closed and fall back asleep as easily as she had awakened.

Why had she awakened? The question was more than idle curiosity. Something had disturbed her sleep. Someone.

She switched on her bedside light and looked directly at Shay. He was standing at the window.

"I thought you were going to stay on the couch."

"I did. It just felt all wrong. Like I was a misbehaving husband who'd been banished from the *boudoir*."

"That's exactly what happened, Shay. Don't you remember?"

"You know, you've got a point? I guess that is what happened." Shay gave her a cautious smile. "I don't guess I'm pardoned?"

"Don't Shay. Neither one of us is ready. We're too far apart to even joke about it."

"Sure, I guess so." She knew he wasn't actually agreeing with her. When he spoke again, she knew she'd been right. "I'll bet you a dinner a day we're farther apart than, say, you and Gregor Lepov."

"Don't start," Lilly ordered him. "Go on, go back to the sofa. Neither one of us should be talking right now."

"Why did you say you can't leave with me?"

"Good night, Shay."

"Good night, my eye. I know as well as you why you can't leave with me." His voice had turned hard.

She reached for the light, to shut it off, and shut him out. But he wouldn't let her. He grabbed it and moved it out of her reach.

"Come on, tell old Shay why you can't leave. You think I'm stupid? Think I can't put two and two together? You get awfully defensive when I add Gregor Lepov to the conversation."

"Is that suppose to be an accusation? Because if it is, I'm not going to deny it. I told you quite simply that you and I were done. Long ago. And yes, Gregor Lepov and I mean something to each other. What that is, I'm not really sure. But it doesn't give you the right to badger me about it."

She had no intention of letting him hold this over her head. There were no more obligations between them. No more promises to keep. They'd all been broken, by both parties.

"At least you're honest about it, my dear. I might even say you sound proud of it." Shay's face, darkened by shadows, was suddenly alarming to her. "I wonder why that is? Maybe we're supposed to believe it's because Mr. Lepov was there for you in your time of troubles. You know, that miserable time you experienced right after you sent your husband off to prison. I'm sure that was a rough patch. Just how long ago did you meet the good Mr. Lepov?"

"Shay, turn around and go back in the other room."

"Direct questions bother you? Did you meet him after or before you called the cops in on me? Run into him during your many trips off planet? Why won't you leave, Lilly? Too painful to leave your lover behind?"

"Turn around and get out!" Lilly could not believe what was happening. She'd almost allowed Shay to convince her that it would have been a good thing to leave the Lazaretto with him. He'd done it again. He'd taken his charm and her inexplicable blindness toward him and turned her inside out.

"You think I'm gonna leave you? You think I *can* leave you? Lilly, you don't get it, do you?"

"You're the one who's never understood. I don't regret turning you in, Shay. The only thing that's ever bothered me is the fact that I never hesitated to do it. It didn't bother me in the least to give them your name. But when I think about it, even that shouldn't have been a problem, since I'd married the kind of man who deserved to be betrayed."

Before Shay could say anything, someone pounded on Lilly's front door. She could hear Gregor calling her name. Shay heard him too. He stared at her, slightly triumphant.

"I'd rather you didn't introduce us." Shay turned his back to her and studied the darkness beyond the windows.

Lilly nearly ran into the other room, so urgently did she need Gregor at that moment. If anyone could make Shay back down it would be Gregor. She unlocked the door and jerked it open.

"Get dressed. You've got to get out of here." Gregor brushed by her and strode quickly to her windows overlooking the street. He scanned what little he could see in the early morning darkness. "Well?"

"What are you talking about?" she asked.

"You want an explanation. I'll give you one after we've gone. Just get some clothes on and grab a few more. You may be gone a week or more."

"I can't just do that. I've got—"

"Ed MacNally's been shot. Some very violent men want him dead. And you and I are potential targets. Anyone who is a possible source of information will be targets. I'm getting you out of here, now. If you won't pack, I will."

He started toward her bedroom but she stopped him.

"I'll get it. I have to dress first. Wait out here." She pushed him away and hurried into her room, completely shutting the door. She stood for a moment, leaning against it, listening to the solitary sound of her beating heart.

56

Lara debated whether or not to take Jett with her as she prepared to leave. It might have been better to give those people at IHS a visual stimulus to remind them of what was at stake: the life of a vibrant young boy. But in the end she decided to leave him with his father. The risk of taking him out in the cold, wet Lazaretto was too much. He already seemed weakened by his condition, though Lara could not be sure if that was actually the case or it was only a result of her imagination.

Still, it was better that he stay indoors. It would also be better that Frank was forced to care for him. If he would not help her talk to IHS, then he could at least take care of the child.

Lara left the apartment quietly, as both Jett and Frank were still asleep. She wore the best ensemble she had with her. She intended to give no one any chance to look down upon her and her family. She might be the mother of an exiled young boy, but it did not mean she was inferior to anyone at IHS.

She left early enough that the grey light of day had not yet disturbed the black of night. The streets were not deserted; Lara was surprised to see so many people moving about. She had assumed that the cold, rainy weather would keep people tucked away in their beds. She realized that this would not be the case in the Lazaretto. If it were, no one would ever want to get out of bed.

Yet another reason to fight this exile.

She walked two blocks to the nearest SubTransit station. It would be cheaper than using a TransitCar. And Lara was already determined to save their money whenever possible. She was anticipating that their efforts to save Jett would be costly. She did not want to learn they could not use an avenue open to them for lack of a little currency.

The nearly full SubTransit car swayed along as it twisted through dark tunnels that occasionally broke out into brightly lit stations. It did not stop at every station. But every time it did more commuters filed in. By the time they neared IHS headquarters, Lara was disturbed at the size of the crowd. She had hoped to be ahead of such a crowd, now, she was in the middle of one. Her hopes for a quick interview were quickly fading.

A flood of SubTransit riders flowed out of the car and up the steps of the station with her. As she had feared, nearly everyone on that car was headed for IHS. She tried to walk without allowing panic to overtake her. She felt the instinctual tug to push a little, to speed up and try to gain position in the thick of the mob. It was not just a tug within her. The swarm surrounding her seemed to murmur in her ear. To spur her on in her need to get ahead. Still, she resisted. Knowing that the more she pushed, the more those around her would begin to rush as well. It felt as if the slightest disturbance would set this mass into a chaotic sprint for the entrance of IHS.

But as they emerged out of the station and into a wide open plaza fronting the massive IHS headquarters, Lara could feel the crowd begin to thin. She saw that a large number of their group was sliding off to the left, as if drawn by an inaudible summons. She wondered if she should follow them. Far more people were going in that direction than those who were aiming for the main entrance.

"Don't worry about them," a woman with soft, friendly eyes caught Lara's attention. "Those are all employees. They don't use this entrance. They all scurry to their little holes for a dull, mind-numbing day of IHS employment. Be glad you aren't one of them. It is a terrible sort of punishment."

"Oh, I'm sure." Lara said, to show her appreciation. In truth, she had no sympathy for anyone who might work for such a heartless organization.

"You seem on edge. And you are very early. You know the offices don't open for another hour and a half."

"Yes, I am on edge. And I do know I'm early. I just want to make sure I get in to see my case officer." The two women continued to walk toward the entrance. A little ways ahead, a set of wide, concrete steps rose up to meet the glass entryway.

"Case officer? Were you thinking of filing an appeal?"

"Yes, how did you know?"

"There is very little reason to speak to your case officer otherwise. I hope you aren't putting too much hope in this appeal. I would like to save you the wasted time and hope."

"You're very thoughtful," Lara said, increasing her speed. She did so not in an effort to beat the woman to the entrance, but to get away from her saccharine kindness, which was just another attempt to defeat her belief that she could do something positive for her son. She would not allow a stranger to break down her faith. What, after all, would she have if she allowed it to be broken? What would Jett have left?

She was so pleased to be only the fifth person in line at the entrance that she was able to ignore the cold wind that blew hard around the corner of the building. At least they were out of the drizzling rain. A narrow stone portico shielded those in the front of the line. If she had been just a few minutes later, she would have been standing in the rain.

This had to be a good sign. And as the doors were unlocked, she felt certain that their case officer would encourage her desire to file Jett's appeal. Those who had disparaged the idea were merely influenced by their own pessimistic attitudes. She understood. The Lazaretto fostered such pitiable outlooks. But she would stand firm against it. The Lazaretto was not going to take away her faith that there was a better future for her son than the one dictated by IHS.

57

By the time Lepov had Lilly settled in Abbot's home, a small house on the far southern edges of the city, he had given up on thinking about sleep. He dozed a little as Abbot drove them across town, but it wasn't enough rest for any practical purposes. But once he was sure Lilly was in a secure location he saw the sky turn gray and he was too aware of the dawning day to be able to sleep.

He wouldn't have been able to if he tried. The excitement of MacNally's news had worn off but he still had not been able to shake the misgiving that had unsettled him after his meeting with Jardyn. He kept thinking of Jardyn's assertion:

We did get away spotless.

At first blush Lepov had simply thought Jardyn had misspoke. That he'd meant to say they *did not get away spotless*. That he had left that one word out from a simple slip of the tongue. But there was no reason to believe that. He had said it quite deliberately. His tone had been firm, nothing mumbled, nothing slurred.

What if they had? What if Spaeth had no idea who had stolen the pistol? Why then, would Frobe have been killed? Or why would Spaeth's brother and that other flunkey be here in the Lazaretto looking for someone, all the while armed and willing to pull the trigger on the first man to stand up and challenge them?

How did most people learn about something they hadn't witnessed? The obvious answer was that somebody told them. Somebody told. Someone wasn't playing fair.

The lack of sleep was making it hard for Lepov to gather the pieces of the puzzle into anything that resembled a logical picture. Abbot offered him coffee and he was grateful to feel it warming his gut. It cleared his head enough to remember more of Jardyn's words. He remembered that Jardyn said he was going to ask a question that turned out to be only a statement. It hadn't been a question:

Gloria hired you to find me, and she told you that there would be a message from me at this bar.

Could it have actually been a question?

Gloria hired you to find me, and she told you that there would be a message from me at this bar?

Earlier, Jardyn had asked Lepov what he had meant about a message. Was it possible that the message had not been from Jardyn? There had been one point on which Jardyn had actually been willing to agree with Lepov: untrustworthy blondes.

And then the coffee hit him hard enough to remind him of the resolution he'd come to just before he met Bril Abbot outside his door. He was tired of Gloria dictating his steps, and he wasn't going to allow her to manipulate him anymore.

Using Abbot's TransitCar, Lepov made it back into Center City in less than an hour and parked in the back of Gloria's hotel. He knew exactly what had to be done, which was exactly the opposite of what she'd begged him to do.

At the front desk, he asked that a call be made to her room. As he had hoped, Kry Dannen answered.

"You awake, Dannen?" Lepov asked without preamble.

"Where the hell have you been? You were supposed to keep me informed of what you were—"

"Listen, Mr. Dannen. As my client you have a little room to make demands on me. But at this point of my investigation, you've lost that privilege. No, don't talk. Just listen. And don't get so impatient. I want to see you down in the bar, now. Just you. Leave *her*. If she walks in that bar I'm leaving and you'll never find Jardyn. If you understand me, don't even bother to nod, just hang up."

The line went dead.

Dannen must have been dressed already. He made it to the bar in less than two minutes. Lepov was sitting at the end closest to the door. Dannen stopped as soon as their eyes met.

"You had better have a very good reason for your bad manners, Lepov. And a damned good reason for insisting my wife not come with me. I told you I wouldn't allow you to disrespect her."

"You did, I remember it like it was two days ago. Or was it three? Maybe I don't remember it as well as I first thought."

Dannen approached Lepov, his air of sophistication losing its battle with his base nature. "What are you up to?"

"I think you have an idea, anyway. Otherwise I think you would have gone ahead and brought your bride along with you. You didn't, which suggests I'm on the right track. And before you start turning red, let me kill the suspense for you. I found Jardyn. Talked to him last night. He's still got the gun, and he's sitting in a hotel room down by the northern edge of Terran Park."

"Just like that?" Dannen allowed a hesitant smile to crease his stony façade. "You found him? I'm quite impressed. She was right about you."

"Well, she has an instinct about these things, I guess." Lepov couldn't decide if he'd tell Dannen about Gloria's part in finding Jardyn. It seemed best to tell the man where to find his partner and not to get involved in a marriage that was tangled up with another man. Whatever Gloria's game had been, he didn't want to play the role she'd chosen for him.

"You have the address?" Dannen asked, his face plainly suffused with relief.

"It's all right here." Lepov handed Dannen a data tag. "My fee will be drawn off your account..." he looked at his watch..." actually, it already transferred. The banks opened five minutes ago."

"It's been a pleasure doing business with you, Mr. Lepov." Dannen was eager to go. He paused. There was something else on his mind. "About my wife—"

"Let's agree on one thing, Dannen. She's your wife and my ex-wife. You treat her like you think she should be treated and I'll do the same. We'll leave it at that."

"If you insist." Dannen slipped the data tag into an inside pocket of his suit coat. "Goodbye, Mr. Lepov. You've been invaluable."

"Lot of people say that." Lepov waited till Dannen was gone before he made his way to the back door. The coffee rush was fading fast. He needed to get back to Lilly. He needed to get to a bed. He wasn't even sure he'd be able to make the drive back to Abbot's house.

But at least he hadn't let Gloria pull his strings. And once they were out of the Lazaretto, he could sleep for a week. He would even try to take Lilly's vitamins. For once, his near future was looking pretty damned good.

It was a bad sign when you were so tired that you forgot a close friend was being hunted by a notorious gangster. A bad sign, indeed.

58

Dassin.

It had taken Russell no time at all to find the name. He had hit on it almost immediately. The name was on a list of recently labeled exiles. Usually, when a traveler was removed from a quadrant and listed as *nullus exitus*, their names were flagged for law enforcement. That was a precaution against a recent exile causing a disturbance. It wasn't uncommon for this to happen once they began to understand how desperate their situation had become.

Frankly, Russell could see why many of them ended up causing a disturbance. The exile system was harsh, cold, and generally illogical. A reasonably educated traveler would always be quick to rebel against such an unfair and poorly designed system.

IHS did not care. The police had to care, it was their job. But their only concern was that no one touched off any unrest that might spread to the thousands of exiles trapped in the Lazaretto.

And so when Menya Russell typed in the name Dassin, with its many possible spellings, he was immediately alerted to the fact that a Jett Dassin had been exiled just three days before. One day before those two killers ran into MacNally at the *Mad Russian* looking for a Dassin.

"Russell!" Captain Jenkins pointed at Russell and then jerked his hand towards his office. "I want to talk to you."

Russell nodded at his boss and quickly typed in a few commands. The information on Dassin disappeared from his deskscreen. He entered Jenkins' office with a yawn that nearly injured his jaw.

"Kwan says you haven't been playing nice with her. You got a problem working with a woman?"

"No. If I can learn to work with MacNally I can learn to work with a woman."

"You got a point." Jenkins was distracted by Russell's observation. He sipped from a cup of coffee and it put him back on track. "Where have you been all night?"

"I was home." He was glad they'd been paranoid about his PDT.

It had stayed in his apartment for the entire night.

"Kwan says you weren't answering your calls. Why not?"

"Can I be honest?" asked Russell.

"I hope so." Jenkins leaned forward to better hear his answer.

"It was MacNally, he's why I didn't answer."

Jenkins' eyebrows rose as he did his best not to jump up and demand to know what his young detective meant. He made a great show of patiently waiting for Russell to continue.

"I'm not gonna lie to you, Captain. I don't like what's happened. MacNally's in trouble, and you're asking me to turn my back on him. And if the reports are right about that second shooting at the Mad Russian, then I'm worried Mac's been injured, or worse…"

"So you didn't answer your calls?"

"I couldn't sleep. So I took a sleeping tablet." He looked away from Jenkins then added: "And I had about three beers. I woke up this morning in the kitchen."

"You're lucky you woke up. Didn't they tell you those department sleep aids shouldn't be mixed with alcohol?"

"No one warned me I'd end up in the kitchen." Russell could see his story would work. Bosses were quick to believe their subordinates were mostly ignorant people who needed to be looked after.

"Kwan's waiting on you. We got a man's body found early this morning. You two take a look."

Russell met Detective Pearl Lin Kwan on the far side of the office. Russell had met her before but had never worked with her. She was a little older than him, a little taller than him, and was built like a middleweight prize fighter. No one ever called her Pearl.

"I was beginning to wonder if you'd gone on vacation." Kwan had a habit of staring directly at whomever she was addressing. Staring too hard. It made most people uncomfortable. Russell, well versed in MacNally's often offensive behavior, was not bothered in the least by her over-the-top communication skills.

"I did. I'm back. It was a mini-vacation."

Kwan smiled politely at his attempt to be funny. "Look, I realize our little team will only be temporary. And I know that a lot of the other detectives here don't like your partner. But you should know I respect MacNally. He's a good detective. He's an ass, which I'm sure you've figured out. But so's my brother, and so were half of the guys back in my neighborhood. It doesn't mean there wasn't any good in them, you know? And after what MacNally just went through—that was a rough shooting from what I heard—I completely understand his need to take some time off."

That was the official line at the precinct. If any of the detectives knew that there was more to the story, they weren't saying. Kwan wasn't. She grabbed a coat after downing what was left of a coffee on her deskscreen.

"Now, I believe there's a corpse waiting for us with our name on it."

Russell liked Kwan. She was smart, confident, and always professional. He did not like the fact that he would have to lie to her, leave her on her own, and probably anger her for a very long time. But he had no choice. He certainly didn't know her enough to trust her.

She drove and Russell wished that he could catch some sleep as she did. He decided, however, that this would be the wrong way to start their partnership, regardless of how little he intended to work with her.

They arrived at a shopping district along Bosporus Avenue and found their body—male, about forty years old—in a cheap hotel room. A uniformed officer gave them the basics: the body had been found face down on the bed with one gunshot wound in its chest, no signs of a struggle, no signs of a gun.

IHS had already checked the body and Visuals had already been taken. Kwan and Russell watched MedTechs prep the body to remove it.

"Sure has been a lot of gunplay lately." Kwan examined the chest wound before the MedTechs sealed up the body. "Those three down at the Mad Russian. One of them took a hit from a star pistol, but those other two—like this one—were put down by a very large handgun that actually used gunpowder."

"You think this is more of the same?" Russell already knew the answer to that. MacNally had only told him about shots fired at the Mad Russian. He'd said nothing about this guy or the hotel.

"Related? That's possible. But it wasn't the same gun. Whoever fired those shots at the Mad Russian is carrying a hand cannon. This is not from the same gun."

"So who is he?"

"The reader gave us what was obviously an altered PDT. Kids stuff. Not professionally done. They're rebuilding it. Should have his name soon."

A young officer had approached them and coughed to attract their attention. "Sir?"

"Yes?" Kwan turned and gave him her usual direct stare.

"Oh, sorry, ma'am. I just thought you'd want to know we got a hit. We ran this location through the Transit records and we got lucky. There were a few TransitCar's hired for this address in the last twelve hours. But one in particular brought a passenger here, then stayed for about ten minutes, waiting for the same passenger, who then was taken to a second location. It seemed out of place."

"Someone dropped in for a visit?" Kwan shrugged. "It's not a smoking gun, but we'll check it out. What was the name of the fare?"

"Gregor Lepov."

"Isn't that your partner's friend? The Investigator?"

Russell nodded. He was quickly trying to remember if Lepov had said anything about his current case. If he had, Russell couldn't remember it.

"You know him, don't you?" she asked. Russell nodded again. "So is he a suspect or a witness?"

"A witness." Lepov was no murderer.

"Okay, for now, he's a witness. Can we find him?"

"I'd rather it just be me. He can be difficult."

"After we finish up here, I'm willing to let you go find him. Despite his rough edges, as I said before, I respect MacNally. So go and see his friend and see what he says. There's just one thing." Kwan stepped in close and Russell was surprised to learn that she smelled faintly of jasmine. She looked too tough to consider cloaking herself in the aroma of flowers. "If he doesn't cooperate, or you think he's not being straight with you, will it be a problem for you to bring him in?"

"He's MacNally's friend, not mine. I'll do what I need to do."

"So let's try to get a name to match up with this body. Shall we?"

Russell nodded yet again. He had to admit that working with Kwan might actually be more enjoyable than working with MacNally: she wasn't insulting, she wasn't quick to judge, and she was a far more attractive sight than the old man.

And she smelled of jasmine.

There was a certain irony — as well as a distinct lack of logic — in the fact that Pete Landon was engaged in field work now that he had officially retired from the police force. It was the kind of thing that he would never have done in the past. But friends had a way of breaking each other out of their comfort zones. And for Pete, who had never found too many people worthy of the label *friend,* he was suddenly awash in them.

Menya Russell was hardly a good enough friend to force him out of his comfort zone. However, Russell's request had been something that was for MacNally's benefit, and MacNally had been the long-time partner of Arturo Fenelli, a truly good friend of Pete's who had died in the line of duty. So there was a certain kind of logic to helping Russell.

And Russell's terse, urgent message had been simple. He needed to get to Jett Dassin and make him disappear. There had been no address for Dassin. Just his basic profile data. Although he no longer worked for the police, Pete still had access to most of their networks. He hadn't exactly removed all of the trapdoors he'd installed in their systems. He had briefly considered it when he resigned, and of course he had assured his boss he'd removed them all, but he just hadn't been able to resist the temptation to keep a few hidden access points to all of that data. And he was absolutely positive his boss was well aware of the fact.

Russell's message was not only brief, it contained this unequivocal final note: *do not contact me.* At first Pete had thought it was all a joke. The message was sent with only a basic encryption that would not prevent anyone from breaking it. However, the tone of the message suggested that Russell had little time to write and send it. Taking the message on faith, he'd used a little of his magic to backtrack the message and scrub it from the precinct records. It would not be impossible to retrieve, but it would take a puzzle genius to figure it out. And the police had just lost the only one they had ever had.

When he saw the address and which floor Dassin was on, Pete had little faith he'd find a working elevator. He was pleased to discover he had been wrong. It was slow, and smelled of things he did not want to identify, but it was working. And he was happy not to have to climb seventeen floors.

It had taken a bit of convincing to make someone open the door. He knew they had to be inside. If he understood the situation correctly, these people were in danger, and it was natural for them not to answer a knock from a stranger.

"Mr. Dassin? You'll need to trust me. I'm a friend. I'm with the police, and need to get you to a safe location." Pete had to admit to himself that even he wouldn't believe such a story.

"Look, I don't know too much about what is going on. But I'm going to tell you all I know. A police detective I know to be completely trustworthy has told me that Jonnie Spaeth is looking for you, Dassin. I am supposed to move you from here, and keep you hidden. That's all I know. Now if I was with Jonnie Spaeth, I doubt I'd be knocking on your door. I'd have already come through it."

Nothing.

"Come on, Jett. Don't let me down. I don't want to be responsible for letting Jonnie—"

The door lock disengaged and the door flew open.

"Why is Jonnie Spaeth looking for Jett?" A haggard man with red-rimmed eyes towered over Pete. He was scared, shaking, and angry enough to make Pete nervous.

"Jett Dassin?"

"I'm his father! Spaeth's looking for me, not Jett. Why do you think he's looking for Jett?"

"Look, let's talk about this inside. And before you ask, I don't have a badge. I just left the force a few days ago. I know that might be hard for you to —"

"A badge wouldn't help, right now. Did you think I trusted the police?"

"I wouldn't, if I were you, and I was one of them. May I?"

Dassin stepped back, still too wary to show any signs of welcome. But he did not stop Pete from stepping inside.

"Answer my question." The man slammed the door. "Why would you think Spaeth is after Jett?"

"I don't have an answer. I wish I did. What I do know is that a Jett Dassin is in danger, and needs to be moved somewhere other than this apartment."

"And this was from a cop?"

"Yeah, but like I said, he's a good cop. Now I understand you have a few options here. But think them through. If you don't trust me, then you can stay here. If I'm lying, or just plain wrong, then you would have been right to stay. But if Spaeth is really coming for you, staying here is very bad. It took me no time or effort to find you. I was just given your name." That part was not entirely true, but Pete knew that it would be just that simple for Spaeth to find an address. "Now whether your son Jett is in trouble or it's you, I don't know. Does it matter at this point? As I said, if I'm a danger to you, you're already dead. I found you. You don't appear to have any way to defend yourself. Do you?"

"I'm just about desperate enough to believe you. But I don't like it. I just don't have a choice, do I?"

"You always have choices. There just are not many better ones right now. I'm Pete Landon."

"Frank Dassin. Jett's in the back room. I hate to tell you this, but I can't leave."

"Look, Mr. Dassin, you're gonna have to."

"I can't!" Dassin ran his hands through his thick hair, as if he were fighting off a migraine. "The boy's mother is gone. But she's coming back. We leave, she won't find us."

"Where'd she go?"

"IHS. She's trying to file an appeal for the boy. I told her it was a waste of time."

"No, no that's perfect. She'll be there forever. We can go there, pick her up."

"What if she's already gone when we get there?"

"You'll have to trust me on this: you're looking at the one man in the Lazaretto who knows how to find anybody, anywhere, on this lousy rock."

"Come in and meet my son. If you can look him and me in the eyes and tell me you can find his mother, I'll trust you. But you need to know it's only because I don't have any other ideas. You'll have my family in your hands."

Pete swallowed hard as he followed Dassin into the back room. When he saw the young boy, he felt his pulse quicken. Whatever Russell had just thrown in his lap, Pete hoped it wasn't as bad as it was beginning to look. Once, a failure on the job had nearly cost the life of the woman he was now hoping to marry. He thought he had been finished with that sort of responsibility. Now, in the space of an hour, he had been given the lives of three people to hold in his hands.

It was always a bad idea to make promises when you didn't even know what was going on. But it didn't stop Pete from making one.

60

The Irishman had vanished. That was the only way to say it. Presumably, the Slovaks had been shot dead by the Irishman. They had been watching for him at the bar, and one of them ended up dead in the back of the bar while the other one was shot to pieces on the street outside. The report he'd read said her spine had been severed by a direct hit from a high-caliber bullet, while a second one destroyed most of the chest cavity on her left side. Someone was either a damned good shot or lucky as hell.

The Irishman. It had to have been him. The report also said that a lot of blood in the alley indicated that someone—again, most likely the Irishman—had been shot up too. But since then, no trace of him had been found.

It was time to increase the pressure on his source.

"You are clear." They'd already landed, and the shroud wasn't operable. But the New Yorker didn't hesitate to lie to his source.

"Nothing yet on your missing man." The Source sounded far too at ease. That would have to change.

"Focus on the Irishman." He knew this was a subject that made the Source uncomfortable. To give up a fellow detective was completely different that supplying the location of a known felon.

"He's no rookie. He knows what he's doing. I'm not promising anything." A little anxiety came through with that response.

"Does he have help?"

"It's possible."

"If he isn't alone, then someone can be tapped. If you can't do it, give me a name." The New Yorker wondered if the Source was actually playing both sides. It would be a stupid, and fatal error.

"I'll try and—"

"You'll what?" The New Yorker smiled when he heard the source stutter before responding.

"I'll, I'll do what I need to."

The New Yorker cut off the connection without another word. It was best not to recognize the source's willingness to comply. Better to leave the source wondering if the New Yorker still thought there was a problem.

He had hoped that when the call came through, it would be the Source with immediate news. Instead, it was the watchers who had been assigned to keep an eye on the Swede.

"He's moving. And someone is with him."

"Do you recognize this *someone*?" He'd sent out images of the Frenchman and the Irishman. Maybe they had just gotten lucky.

"No, never seen him before."

"You're following them?" They had better be.

"Yes. They've taken a TransitCar. We're staying with them."

"Give us your route. And then stay back. Don't let them see you. But don't lose them. You do not want to know what happens if you do."

It was hard relying on men he didn't know. He decided to tell the Australian that they should go ahead and grab the Swede now. There was no reason to risk losing him. The fact that someone new was with the Swede was something that should not be taken lightly.

The route came through and he loaded three men into a box truck that had been waiting for them when they landed. The Australian and Ursuline would stay behind. There was little time to sets things up properly. They would have to make a quick grab at the Swede.

His men were armed with Para-Lazars. After all the shootings, they knew there would be pressure from the media and the politicians to push back. The Australian had influence enough to conduct his business but he lost too much of it if he allowed the streets to get bloody. Besides, grabbing the Swede should be relatively simple. He did not think that the Australian's brother's death meant it would be difficult. It just meant the Australian's brother was inept.

The Australian stood by the entrance ramp to the *Strike* as rain fell on the darkened landing pad. He was holding an umbrella for the Ursuline, who was huddled beneath it. She was cold, shivering. From the New Yorker's perspective, she looked afraid. Maybe she was. The Australian had put his arm around her, as if to warm her in the cold wind. Instead, it looked as if he were holding her at his side in an attempt to keep her from breaking loose.

Was this his way of ensuring that his right hand man completed his assignment with alacrity? Had she become a part of the equation? It would be just like the Australian. The New Yorker should have fought to leave her behind.

"Don't let him slip away. And after you've got him, find me that Irish bastard! Now!" He shook when he yelled, and the Ursuline shook, though whether it was from her own fear or it was the Australian shaking her the New Yorker could not decide.

His man behind the controls shuddered the engine and the truck whined as it rose off the tarmac. They needed to reach the Swede before he managed to slip his watchers. Losing him would be the kind of news that, when delivered, might just get him or the Ursuline killed. The Australian was losing patience.

61

In just a few hours Lara had been ignored, pacified, hustled, abandoned and pushed around by a system that had no interest in her, her son, or anything that smacked of humanity.

She had never come up against anything so cruel and soulless.

First, the building itself had seemed designed to defeat her. There were no directories to aid her in finding the proper offices. There were no IHS guides to move you along in the right direction. She had spent precious time backtracking and wandering the halls until she had finally met an unexpectedly kind older gentleman who was willing to explain where she needed to go.

But getting there did not mean she had accomplished anything. In the entry office where she was supposed to meet Jett's case officer, she was left sitting on a hard plastic bench for hours without one explanation as to why she was not being attended to. Two other people were waiting with her. One of them gave up and left, which was a tempting idea until the other person, a woman similar to Lara in age and even appearance, finally spoke.

"That's what they're hoping for. They just want you to give up and leave. And most people do." Her confident tone had convinced Lara that she knew what she was talking about. Lara had stayed, and she was finally ushered into the case officer's office just a few minutes after that.

But dealing with the case officer had been the worst experience of her morning. With no trace of irony the case officer asked her why she would want to risk the health of the entire Euxine system by allowing Jett to leave the Lazaretto. Didn't she, as a mother, understand how precious life was? That people needed to be protected from the sick so that they, in turn, could remain healthy and productive? Did she not understand how vital this was to people? Didn't everyone have the right to be healthy?

No matter how she responded, the case officer was able to turn her words against her. She made her sound as if she were putting her son's life above every other citizen's.

Though she had not said it out loud, she had wanted to tell that self-righteous fool that as the boy's mother, she would most certainly put her son's health above anybody else's.

She hadn't needed to say it. The case officer, a woman of advanced years with skin the color of the Lazaretto sky, had probably already filed her report on the distraught and dangerous woman who had been raving about her son.

The appeal had not been filed. She had been asked—no, the proper term was *ordered*—to take a week to consider her decision before the paperwork would be filed.

Lara had refused to rush out of the office. No matter how much she felt the desire to flee that horrid, awful place, she would not let them see her lose her composure. She had kept her head high and her pace measured as she walked the long corridors until she finally left the building through its grandiose entrance.

It helped that the rain had actually stopped for once. The clouds had backed away; there was a feeling of open space, no matter that the clouds still covered the sun. The cold morning wind had been replaced by a more gentle, even warmer wind from the south.

The plaza before her was nearly empty. She stood on the edge of the top step, looking out over that view, wondering if this really would be the only city that Jett ever knew. She marveled that even now, during what must be the best weather they had seen so far, the entire city still gave off a spirit of despair.

But just then, she saw him. There, across the plaza, standing on a stone bench, Jett was walking along its edge, his arms spread wide as a way to keep his balance. When he reached the end, he bent his knees, then jumped off the end. His little body did not go far, but he jumped up and down after he landed as if he had just jumped over a great river or canyon.

Frank was beside him. They had come. She couldn't believe it. No matter that Frank had been right and she had been wrong about the case officer. Frank couldn't know that. Yet there he was, he had come to support her after all.

As she started down the steps she saw that another man, with a great mane of red hair, was standing with them. He was talking with Frank. They were not looking her way and so she could not catch their attention by waving. Jett was back up on the bench, and did not see her either. She waved anyway, hoping they might catch sight of her.

By the time she made it to the bottom step she could no longer see her family. A small truck had dropped down onto the plaza, blocking her view. She watched as its back door rolled open and several men jumped down from the opening. They were very large men. Lara was overcome with fear as she realized what was happening.

The men began to run in the direction of Jett and Frank. Lara shouted in frustration. She too, broke into a run. The truck did not allow her to see what Frank was doing. She tried to say something, anything, that might save her family.

"Get out of here," she murmured, knowing full well that no one could hear her across the plaza. As she drew near the truck, its engine drowned out her repeated entreaties, no matter how much louder she became.

"GO! Run, Frank! Don't you let them take my son!" She had to angle her run to pass by the truck. By the time she broke around the far side of it, she was shouting Jett's name. Her voice still could not overpower the truck's engine.

She couldn't see Jett or Frank anywhere. The red-headed man was gone too. Even the men who had jumped out of the truck were nowhere in sight. She didn't understand. She was crying now, still repeating Jett's name.

"Jett! Jett...*Jett.*"

"Is that the boy's name?" A voice came from behind her, just audible in the wash of the engine noise. "You must be Dassin's wife."

Lara spun to face the man who was standing less than a meter away. His eyes were bright blue, his hair blond, and his face carried a wide, disarming smile. A short, compact man, she knew right away this man was dangerous despite the smile. The eyes were blue, but they carried more than a hint of madness behind them.

"God, please, don't." She tried to back away, wanted to run, but he had already grabbed her by the arm. His iron grip was excruciating.

"God?" His smile faded. "Don't tell me you're gonna start talking about God, too. I already got a girl that does that. Why don't you come sit in the truck while we wait for my boys to bring your husband and boy—Jett, was that his name?—back to me. It's warm in the cab. This whole place is always too damned cold."

He looked up at the clouded sky and shook his head. Then he pulled her toward the truck.

"You're the one, the one he told me about? You're Jonnie?"

"Am I Jonnie Spaeth?" His smile reappeared as he laughed at her question. "No, darling. I'm just a guy who works for him. Like your husband used to. Only I didn't steal from Jonnie. So far, I'm still considered a good employee. My name's Towers. Tommy to my friends. Now go on and get in there. It's cold out here."

Lara stumbled as she tried to climb into the cab. A dark, bearded man was on the far end of the bench seat. While he looked dangerous, as least there was no madness in his eyes. As the man who called himself Tommy Towers climbed in beside her, she realized it really didn't make much difference.

62

Lilly sat in a corner of Bril Abbot's front room and stared out at his front yard. It was small, not even big enough to hold a proper picnic. She hadn't thought about picnics in a long time.

At one time, while growing up on Sinop, when she'd just been a little girl named Lilly West, her parents had loved to take her on trips into the foothills that surrounded her home. At the time, she'd thought they were mountains, and the fact that her father could carry her on his shoulders to the top of a mountain made him the grandest man she'd ever known. In the cool glare of the sun, they would eat whatever wonders her mother had packed for them as her father would tell them all tales of his early years as a space scout.

His stories only added to her assurance that Edward West was the most amazing man alive. A little girl's dream that faded away with time and was completely erased when she met Shay Stewart. A little girl's dream that she wished she could recapture. But unless she learned how to forget Shay and the mess he had brought to her life, she would never be able to return to that simpler time in life where a father's love was all a girl ever needed from a man.

She looked away from the window and looked toward the room where Gregor Lepov was now sleeping. She wondered if he could have ever been a father like hers. Perhaps, long ago, he had held within him the promise of a great father. But he too had found someone who had stolen the chance for that promise to come to fruition. He too, must regret his choices.

She had been alarmed when he had shown up at her place — alarmed that he and Shay would meet and quarrel. But Shay had refused to come out and meet Gregor. Had even refused to allow her to mention to Gregor that Shay was in the bedroom. She did not know if Shay had been right to demand she keep him hidden but at the time she'd been unbalanced by Gregor's story about Ed and the danger to which they had all been exposed.

But why had Shay been so insistent? Did he think Gregor would turn him in? She could understand his concern, but she knew that Gregor would do nothing unless she asked it of him. She knew, as Shay ought to have known, that Gregor was less likely to turn in Shay than Lilly.

She stood up and paced the room, agitated as she thought about Shay. She knew why, of course. He had confused her with his talk of old times and his nonsense about her running off with him.

She couldn't leave Gregor. All it took was a little time away from Shay to realize how crazy his words had sounded. And that's what she needed: to be away from Shay, to not allow him to confuse her with his nonsense.

That was the real reason he didn't want her to see Gregor. He knew she wouldn't be vulnerable to him with Gregor there to keep her clear.

As soon as he woke up, she would tell him. It would be the best way to convince Shay that she couldn't go with him. Then he would go. He wouldn't want to stay. Not in the Lazaretto. It wasn't the kind of place a man chose to live in for a woman he didn't really love. Not the Lazaretto. It was the ultimate test of anyone's love. People were routinely abandoned here. To stay behind was not a decision that could be made lightly.

She'd once heard someone say that love was something that demanded nothing. It wasn't true in the Lazaretto. Here, when a loved one was sick and unable to flee the darkness of this moon, love demanded a decision. You either had to accept the fact that life beyond this rock was no longer an option if you wanted to be with the one you loved, or you had to denounce your love and walk away.

Lilly knew this was not a difficult decision for mothers. It wasn't even difficult for wives to make such a sacrifice. But she wondered: was it harder for men to do this? Harder for them to give of themselves? What man would be willing to accept exile in the Lazaretto with her?

She did not notice she was still pacing in the room until she came to the end of it and found Gregor watching her from the doorway.

"You look nice in a house. I could get used to this." He fought off a yawn. "I could get used to coffee too. Got any?"

"In here," Bril Abbot called from the kitchen.

"I want to go in there," Gregor said, pointing toward the kitchen.

"Wait, Gregor, not yet," she put a hand up to his chest, holding him back. "Before you go in there, before you do anything else, I need to tell you—"

"Okay," he said after she hesitated. "Don't be shy, there's coffee in the other room waiting for me."

"I didn't tell you last night, but Shay was there, at my place."

"Maybe you'd better wait until I drink some coffee. It sounded like you said Shay was at your place last night."

"I did," she nodded. "He wasn't killed in the escape. He's been here, watching me. And now, he has this crazy idea that I should go with him, leave the Lazaretto. Go with him to—I don't know where—Dnepr, maybe, or—"

"Okay, slow down, Lilly. You gotta let me drink some coffee. I only slept a few hours. Not enough for a normal day, and certainly not enough to have a conversation like this. Let me drink some coffee, wake up, and then we can talk about Shay."

"Just tell me you'll come with me and talk to him, please!" She was shocked at the intensity of her own demand.

"Okay, okay. You can take me to him." He leaned forward and kissed her forehead. "It's gonna be okay, everything's gonna be fine."

She was embarrassed at her unchecked emotions. Yet another reason to get Shay out of her life. And if anyone could do it, Gregor would be that one.

63

"In here," Pete pointed to a door and looked around to make sure he could see none of the men who had been pursuing them. There were still plenty of people on the street, but Pete was tall enough to get a full view of the area. Their pursuers had shown no signs of stealth in their headlong rush to get to Dassin. It was unlikely they had suddenly melted into the crowd.

Dassin, still carrying the boy, pushed through the door and Pete followed close behind. Between two shops—a shoe store on one side, a window repair shop on the other—a narrow, long corridor led them to a staircase. It too was narrow. It's steep risers made sharp twists around a thick wooden rail. Pete kept them moving, ignoring each door they passed.

After about three flights, he put out a hand and held Dassin back.

"This will do." He sat down and took in a long, deep breath. Dassin lowered the boy and set him on the steps between both men.

"We wait for a little while. See if anyone comes through the door down there."

"And what if they do?"

"We make a lot of noise. These rooms are full of people."

"In the middle of the day?"

"Oh yeah, don't think of this place as your home town where everyone is off to work. These are people with no place to go. Exiles who are living in an IHS room, fed by IHS. Many of them have been here longer than you might believe. Most of them too sick to be mobile."

"Like us," Dassin look up at the railing that spiraled out of view. "Like we would have ended up."

"Not really. No offence, but your family is far better off than these people. For one, you can work, your wife can take care of the boy. This opens up all sorts of options for you. I know this place must look like Hell to you folks, but people have found ways to be happy here."

"So how are a bunch of sick, bedridden exiles supposed to help us if Spaeth's men come up those stairs?"

"These people live in great fear. It comes with their isolated, helpless situation. So they are quick to ring the alarm. I was a cop down in these streets. We were quite used to rushing down here for whatever little panic had spread among these poor people. There are blocks of these little passages."

"You guys came rushing in for every false alarm?"

"Well, if you didn't, the panic would spread. Mostly we came to calm everyone down. There was usually no reason for the alarm, but it was something that had to be dealt with. And there's a precinct just around the corner from here. They would be here in no time."

"But we don't want the cops," Dassin's voice rose.

"Which is why we haven't gone to the precinct." Pete spoke softly, doing his best to keep Dassin from the same type of panic that easily infected the exiles around them. "Neither of us could keep running much longer. And if we hadn't shaken them by now we weren't going to change things much by continuing to move through the city. So we just wait a bit, hope that we're clear."

"Then we go back and look for Lara?"

Pete turned to look down the steps, as if he'd heard something. It was just a safe way to ignore Dassin's question. It wasn't that he had no answer for him. He just didn't like to be the bearer of bad news.

When the box truck had dropped in front of them, Pete had been the first one to notice the men scrambling out of it. He might have resigned from the force, but he still had a beat cop's instincts for trouble. Sweeping Jett up into his arms, he yelled at Dassin to follow him as he sprinted for the SubTransit entrance. Not even sure if the boy's father was following him, he charged down the steps with no intention of jumping on the SubTransit car that was just sliding into the station. Instead, he dashed across the tiled floor of the station and double-stepped halfway up the other set of stairs.

Only then had he stopped and only then had he seen that Dassin had stuck with him. From there, he had waited until he saw the feet of the men chasing them rushing down the steps they had just descended. Taking a chance that none of their pursuers had stayed topside, Pete had clambered out of the station and handed Jett to his father as he'd urged them to keep moving. For just a heartbeat he had turned to look out across the plaza.

And he had seen what could only have been Dassin's wife being manhandled back to the truck by a tough looking man in a short jacket. The woman had jerked her arm in an attempt to break free of his grip, all the while her head twisted around as she tried desperately to see something near the street. Pete had known right away she had been looking for her son and her husband.

How was he supposed to say that to Dassin?

"Listen, Frank, we can't..." Pete decided they had too many problems to worry about the man's feelings. He just hoped the man would understand the uselessness of going back for her. A desperate man was rarely logical. "We can't go back for her."

"We've got to. She's probably already headed back to the apartment. She could be walking into a trap. You said you were the man who could find her. If you were lying—" Dassin reached down and grabbed Pete's shoulder.

"Take it easy, Frank. Listen to me. You told me that you are the one Spaeth is looking for, right?"

"Don't change the subject. Did you lie to us?" He still had a grip on Pete's shoulder.

"No, I did not. And I wasn't changing the subject. They're looking for you. And you need to keep that in mind when I tell you what happened to Lara."

"What do you mean?" His grip tightened.

Pete stared at Dassin's hand on his shoulder until the big man let go. "What I mean is that when we came out of the SubTransit station, I saw a man taking Lara to the truck. Hold on, just take a second to listen. She's okay. She has to be. They won't do anything to her. They'll use her to get to you. But she's safe, for now."

"God help us," Dassin whispered, absentmindedly putting a hand on Jett, who'd tried to climb the rail. "It's over. They got her, it means they got me."

"Not necessarily," Pete said with little conviction.

"And you had us running away from them? What the hell were you thinking?" Dassin turned toward Pete, eyes lit with rage. "They don't want her, they want me! They'll be looking for me, to make a deal. And you had us running away!"

"Just hold on, hold on." Pete stood up, backing down a few steps, hands held up to keep Dassin from advancing. "First of all, if they had grabbed all three of you, no one would have been allowed to go. This way, we're gonna be able to negotiate with them. Secondly, we need time to get some help on this. We aren't going to do this alone."

"And all of that wastes time. That's more time that Lara is in their hands."

"They won't touch her. She'll be scared, but she'll be safe. But if she's the kind of mother you say she is, she would be mad as hell if you allowed Spaeth to get this boy." Pete watched the fire burn out of Dassin's eyes.

"What do we do? I don't know what we're supposed to do."

Pete gave the man time to breathe. He needed it. It was going to be tough to get through the next day or two. It was going to be hard on all of them. But Pete had an idea.

When they finally left the narrow corridor and returned to the street, they could not see anyone who might have been working for Spaeth. Pete flagged down a TransitCar and gave the driver an address. He needed to get Frank and Jett to a safe place, then he needed to call in some help.

Pete was great at solving puzzles but this was gonna take more muscles than brains. He was suddenly glad he'd been making new friends.

The streets around Bril Abbot's house had very little traffic on them. And what vehicles Lepov did see were in no hurry. It was as if the unusually bright, rainless day were actually a sunny day, with no clouds to prevent golden sunlight from filling everyone's spirit with goodwill and cheer. Of course, there were still clouds, and the sun was not really visible beyond a brilliant white disc among high, gray clouds.

Even Lepov was tempted to roll down the window of Abbot's TransitCar and let the wind wash over his head as he whistled a tune. He didn't. The temptation was fleeting. In fact, even back on Bukovina, when he had been young and in love with his new bride, he'd never whistled a tune in the sunshine of a country drive. Not that he could remember, anyway.

But there was little he ever allowed himself to remember from those days. He'd have been happier if he never again remembered he had once had a young bride. If he never saw or heard from Gloria again, maybe one day he would truly forget. Now that he'd finished the job Gloria and her husband had hired him to do, it was a real possibility that he could begin the process of forgetting.

Now, if only he could help Lilly to take a few steps down that same road.

She was beside him, watching the houses glide by the window.

She did not look as if she would give in to any temptations put to her by the nearly unfettered sun. For her, it still seemed she was being battered by a storm.

"We aren't going to be able to stay long." Lepov reminded her. He'd already said it once. But she hadn't acknowledged him. "The risk we're taking is not just a risk of our own safety. There's MacNally to consider."

"I heard you the first time."

"I just didn't want you to be angry when I tell you we have to leave. If he's there, and we talk, we'll have to keep it short." What Lepov didn't add was his confidence that Shay would not be there when they arrived.

"There won't be much to say," she told him. "You can tell him why he needs to go. And then he will. He doesn't believe I'm really through with him. He won't listen to me. But I think if you say it, while I'm standing right there, he'll listen."

He could see she meant every word of what she'd just said. He wished then that Shay really would be there. That it could end as easily as she imagined that it could.

"Why is it you think he'd still be there? You say he knew I was taking you away, that he understood I wasn't bringing you back for several days. He even understood why. So what makes you think he'd still be there, where he'd be a target for Spaeth?"

She kept watching the houses, which were soon replaced with closely stacked townhomes. Not long after they appeared, they began to also see larger, modern apartment buildings. Nothing like the brick and mortar buildings that Lepov lived in near Center City. These were more expensive, and certainly more elegant. Close by were the Terran Towers, which overlooked Terran Park.

Lepov tried not to think about Jardyn, who had been hiding out just on the other side of the park. It was no longer his concern. Whatever Kry and Gloria Dannen did about Jardyn and that stolen gun was their own affair.

Lilly remained silent. Perhaps she too doubted that Shay would be waiting for her and so she did not wish to speak the words aloud. In much the same way, a part of him was reluctant to believe that his dealings with the Dannen's had actually come to an end and they would simply disappear from Lepov's life without as much as a wave goodbye. He too, did not wish to speak of his fears. Better to allow them to remain unbidden in the back of his mind.

"I am through with him," she said softly. Lepov had only just been able to hear her. "I want you to know that. It's not my fault he's here."

"That's not anything you need to worry about, Lilly."

"But you've got to believe it, so that when you tell him, he'll believe it."

"And so I tell him his former wife is finished with him, he'll say 'sorry to hear it, but I understand' and then he just flies away?"

"You're making fun of me." She turned around with a sharp look.

"No, I'd never do that, not you. To be honest, I suppose I do believe you. I suppose I must. Otherwise how would you explain what I'm doing here?" He could see a cloud pass over her eyes. "Now what's the matter?"

"I was just thinking about what we're doing here. Shay thought I was being a fool, to stay here for you. He was wrong."

Lepov turned his full attention back to the road. He didn't want to have this discussion. Not then. Yes, they needed to talk about why they were in the Lazaretto, but this wasn't the time. He hoped that if he concentrated on driving, she would change the subject on her own.

"He thought I was being naïve, staying here for you while you were off working with Gloria. But you weren't kidding, were you? You said that when you were finished she'd be gone, and she is. I don't think I really believed that."

"I was pretty low on faith, myself. Guess we both got worked up over nothing." Changing the subject to Gloria wasn't his idea of a good idea, but at least it was something different. "I keep thinking I'm gonna hear a knock on the door and she's gonna come right back into my life."

"Why did you do it, Gregor?"

"Why'd I take the job from her?"

"No, I mean, why'd you stay in the Lazaretto? Why'd you make me stay? You knew I'd stay if you did. Why couldn't you just enter a quadrant like everyone else?"

He *had* entered a quadrant. Could she have really forgotten that? Or maybe she just didn't want to think about it. Well, that was okay with him. It was best if neither one of them thought about it. He used their arrival at her place as an excuse to talk about something else.

"Now just wait a minute, Lilly. I'm not gonna stop here. I want to make sure no one is hanging around who shouldn't be. There's still a chance you're a target."

They kept driving as Lepov examined the street. No one was visible. If they were watching, they were well hidden. Lepov circled again before he finally dropped the TransitCar near her building's main entrance.

"Do we wait again?" she asked.

"No, come on. Now, we move fast. I warned you we wouldn't have much time. Come on." He jumped out of his seat and they both hurried up the steps and through the doors. He'd taken one quick look as they passed through and he felt pretty sure no one was watching. But he would not take long. They couldn't take that chance.

He made her wait in the hall until he checked the apartment. He went in slow and searched it carefully. When he came back to the door he only allowed one lamp in the front room. He closed the drapes as she made her own search of the rooms. As he had said, Shay was not there.

Lilly was on edge, disturbed that Shay was gone. Lepov had expected it and so he was already thinking ahead.

"We're gonna have to go, Lilly. You understand, don't you? He's not here."

"Don't treat me like a child, Gregor. I can see he isn't here. But that doesn't mean he's gone. What if he just went out for food, or maybe he changed his mind and he does want to talk to you, and he's out looking for us."

"Even if you could prove any of those theories, it wouldn't change the fact that we can't stay here any longer. Now you said you would listen to me. I came here, I gave him a chance to appear. He hasn't. We're going."

"Don't talk about him like he's a ghost." She was getting angry, but she never said another word. At that moment, a footfall outside the door caught their attention. Lepov put up a hand and moved quickly to the front door. He waved Lilly away and she retreated into her bedroom.

Whoever was on the other side of that door was doing his best not to make noise. Lepov had his Shockhammer in his coat pocket and his fingers tightened around its handle. He waited.

A knock on the door. It was nearly impossible to hear, so soft was it. But regardless of how soft it was, it was improbable that any of Spaeth's men would have knocked. Lepov was curious but not about to be careless.

He waited longer. When he heard a second knock, no louder than the first one, he couldn't wait any longer. He stood to one side of the door, disengaged the lock, and held the Shockhammer at the ready. Whoever came through that door had better be quick if they didn't want to take the impact of a fully charged hammer blow.

As soon as he disengaged the lock, the unknown person on the other side began to turn the door handle. Lepov lifted the Shockhammer to chest level with his elbow bent. The door swung open slowly.

"Lepov?" The voice was Russell's.

"You alone?" Lepov didn't drop the hammer.

"I thought you were going to get Lilly out of here. What are you two doing here?" Russell came through the door slowly. He saw and noted the raised Shockhammer but said nothing as he shut the door.

"I did get her out of here. We came back. But we're going. I see you got MacNally's bad habit of tracking my PDT."

"I guess you can't get around without it. No fake's in your bag of tricks?" Russell watched Lepov put the illegal Shockhammer back into his pocket. "Why do you carry that around, Lepov? If you're gonna carry an illegal weapon, at least carry a star pistol. I'm sure MacNally or I could even get you an old service weapon. That Shockhammer's just gonna make somebody mad."

"Spoken like a man who's never been hit by one before." Lepov walked over to Lilly's bedroom door and knocked on it twice. "It's alright, dear, the good detective Menya Russell is here to...why are you here, Russell?"

"I looked you up because you've got a real problem."

"All of my problem's are real, kid. I don't get the luxury of dealing with phony problems."

"That's good, because that means you're used to dealing with them. So deal with this. My new partner and I are investigating a murder of a man down near Terran Park. In a little hotel off of Bosporus. You look like you know what I'm gonna say next."

Lepov would have paid a stiff fee to be wrong, but he knew good and well what Russell was about to say. He should have known it was going to happen the night before. He should have known it was going to happen three days ago.

Being right was no good when you were too late to do anything about it.

"Were you going to say that you'd found Louis Jardyn's body? If you were, just tell me one thing. Am I a witness or a suspect?"

"Both," Russell said without hesitation. "I know you didn't do it, and my new partner knows enough about you to cut you some slack. So if you're willing to tell me what you know, I won't have to bring you down to the precinct."

"Did you find a black case there, about this big?" Lepov knew the answer before Russell shook his head. "Stupid, stupid me."

"Does that mean you can tell me what this is about?"

It was Lepov's turn to shake his head.

"Come on, you're gonna have to. Or you're gonna meet the very able, and very hard-headed Pearl Lin Kwan. I doubt that's gonna go very well."

"Tell her you didn't find me."

"That will work for only so long. Now I know you didn't kill this man. He was shot with an old-fashioned handgun. That means something to you, I can see it in your eyes. Talk to me, Lepov."

"He was with me all night, Detective." Lilly stepped in and stared down the young man, daring him to question her.

"That's enough, Lilly. I'm not gonna tell him and he's not gonna take me in. Now like I said, Russell, we have to get out of here. We've been here too long already. If you don't want to allow us to leave—"

This time, the footsteps were loud, to the point that they could all hear them coming up the stairwell. There had to be several men, if not more. They were not making any attempts to be quiet.

"Lilly, go on," Lepov gestured toward her door yet again, and he had the Shockhammer back in his hand. Russell drew his service weapon. "Let me take them at the door with this gut-buster. I may be able to get a couple of them. After I do, I'll drop to the ground and you can hit anyone who's left standing."

"What's the matter, you don't think I can shoot them as they come through the door?"

Lepov never answered. Outside, in the hall, someone was calling Lilly's name even before they heard a knock on the door.

"That's a voice I recognize." Russell moved to the door and opened it. Pete Landon entered with a tall, blond man trailing behind him. The man was carrying a child in his arms.

"What is this, poker night?" asked Pete, looking from Lepov to Russell.

By the time everyone finished telling their stories, Lepov realized they should have left the stories for after they'd arrived at Abbot's. They had been at Lilly's too long. And the odds were that the next footsteps they heard wouldn't belong to anyone friendly. Nearly everyone Lepov knew was already with him. And it was unlikely that MacNally would have dug himself out of his hole to make a visit to Lilly's.

He sure as hell didn't want to wait around and see if Gloria would appear again. In fact, that was the first thing he had to do. He was going to have to confront her. Jardyn was dead, and if Lepov wasn't careful, he might get caught in between the Dannen's and the police. And now, with Frank Dassin standing in Lilly's kitchen, it was even money that they were all diving into serious trouble.

Pete drove Lilly back to Abbot's. After a heated debate, it was decided that the boy should go with Lilly. It was agreed that Frank Dassin needed to be safely hidden away. Russell agreed to take him to MacNally. With both men impossible to find, Spaeth would have few options. And Russell and Lepov could try to track down Spaeth in order to see if anything could be done about getting Lara back.

It was the best they could do with so little time to think. Lepov waited until they all left, then walked down to the nearest SubTransit station. He had never been more unsure about what was going on with Gloria and Kry Dannen. But since he'd told Dannen where to find Jardyn, and Jardyn had turned up dead, he was beginning to think that Gloria had been telling him the truth all along.

65

Nothing had happened as she had expected it to. After the men had returned to the truck—without Frank and Jett—the truck had taken them through a twisting tour of the streets of the Lazaretto until it disappeared down a ramp under a massive building of which Lara saw very little before they were surrounded by darkness.

She had expected them to take her to a bare room, maybe something without windows, just a chair; they would lock her in and she would be left in total darkness. But after removing her from the truck, they'd put her in an elevator and when its doors slid open she'd been surprised to see a large suite that overlooked the city.

She'd been left alone and the elevator was locked down. She waited for several hours. She examined the entire suite, excluding two rooms whose doors were locked, looking for a way to escape. She found none. She had eventually sat down on a luxurious chaise lounge and tried to sleep.

The sound of the elevator doors whisking open woke her.

A stocky man, probably over sixty years of age, with a silver beard and short, thin hair on the crown of his head came into the suite. He came straight to her, stopping just before he was close enough to touch her and stared uncomfortably at her, as if he were trying to memorize her face.

"You've been behaving yourself in here. I like that. I don't like misbehavior." His voice, low and cultured, was soothing to her. She knew it was deceptive and would need to take care not to allow it to put her off her guard.

"I don't like being kidnapped."

"I'll mention it to my assistant. It was purely his choice to do it. I think he believed you'd be of some value to me. Will you—be of value to me?"

"Do the people who work for you have a habit of doing things on their own, or do they do what they know you want?"

"Oh, I think that's a pretty fair question."

Though he had been staring at her, the man had a strange habit of never actually making eye contact. She briefly wondered if he was blind. She finally concluded he wasn't. He just seemed to avoid making eye contact wherever possible.

"I often ask a similar question. Mine is phrased something like this: do my people do the things I ask them because they want to, or do they do it because of the many times I've taken the life of those who did not do what I ask them. Now, don't come to your own conclusions on that lightly. There isn't much difference between the two motivations. And what differences there are would have to be classified as...subtle."

"Mr. Spaeth," Lara said.

"Oh, that's very good. I don't think Mr. Towers told you my name, did he? I'm sorry, that doesn't really matter, does it? I can obsess over trifles."

Lara sat perfectly still as he spoke. As he circled her, his indirect attention kept her off balance. She could never tell if he was looking at her or not.

"Lately, I've been obsessing over the fact that your husband had so little respect for me that he stole from me. To be more precise, he hired outsiders to steal from me. Now this was a breach of trust. It was really very shocking. I'm sure you must feel the same, or did he tell you about what he was planning? Did he mention to you that he would be putting you and your son in danger?

"I didn't think so. You don't have to answer, I can see it clearly in your eyes." He seemed to be sincere in his comment, despite the fact that he never once looked directly into her eyes. "So now that we can agree that your husband did not act in good faith to either one of us, I think you'll see the wisdom in helping me find him. And that, Mrs. Dassin, is the extent of what I am asking you to do. Which is already a subject we have discussed; what happens to people who don't do what I ask them to do? You remember that, don't you?"

She nodded.

"That's good, so that means you can help me, and I can try to help you. It's only fair. And it's good business."

"I can't help you." Lara finally spoke.

"Oh, but you'll have to." Spaeth stopped circling her and sat beside her. "And since you don't know me very well, I'll give you the benefit of the doubt. See, I've already warned you what will happen if you don't do what I ask. But instead of acting as I usually do, I'm going to give you a second chance. See, if I do, you'd can't say I've mistreated you. I should have killed you. Already. But I didn't do it. And in a way, this makes me your messiah, right? It makes me your savior."

Was he being serious? Or did he think she was so feeble-minded that she would simply give up her husband from sheer gratitude? Was she supposed to clasp her hands together and swoon at his merciful generosity? She hated this man with his silky, deep voice, talking to her as if he were a snake charmer and she a simple, stupid creature that could be forced to do whatever he asked.

But she knew what he couldn't know. She did not know where Frank would have taken Jett. She drew strength from this one, concrete fact.

"I'm going to do better than just save you, Mrs. Dassin. I'm going to save your son. All you need to do is tell me where they went."

She had been reluctant to allow him to look into her eyes, no matter how indirectly. But now, she faced him, unafraid. And she allowed a smile to appear on her lips. This man could not make her talk. He could not make her lead them to Frank. If they couldn't find him, it meant Frank had abandoned the apartment, and she did not know anything that would be of value to them.

"Okay, then." Jonnie Spaeth put his hand on her knee then patted it twice. "We'll do this another way. It wasn't that we needed you to find them, it just would have made it happen with less delay. But don't think you've done anything to help him. You see, we won't even have to look for him—once he understands that we have you—he'll want to give himself up, for your sake. He won't be able to remain in hiding. He'll come looking for us. And we'll have you to thank. So you see, I don't need your cooperation. All you have to do is sit right there, and that will be cooperation enough."

She tried hard to remain expressionless as he hovered over her a few moments more. She tried so hard to deny him what he wanted. To deny him that chance of seeing her break down under the realization that her husband's capture was already a *fait accompli*. She wanted so badly to hide her despair and wretchedness. But she could see by the look on his face that he had read it all despite his inability to look straight at her.

That he was laughing about it as he stepped onto the elevator was only that much more maddening. Yes, perhaps she was angry at Frank for what he'd done to her and Jett, but she wasn't going to sit there and allow Frank to give himself up for her. Not if she could do something about it. She sure wasn't going to do what this man expected of her. How had he put it? *All you have to do is sit right there, and that will be cooperation enough.*

Lara wasn't about to sit still and cooperate.

Not a full minute passed from the time Jonnie Spaeth left on the elevator when one of the locked doors at the far end of the room opened up. A young woman joined her. She had deep green eyes, and a round, glowing face. Her hair was cut short, and she walked with short, quick steps.

"Is he gone? I really don't like that man. He's just terrible." Her laugh was so free and easy, Lara wondered if this girl were mentally incompetent. Then she saw the girl's face switch to a sudden, deadly earnestness. "Tommy tells me Jonnie is dangerous. You're going to have to stay away from him."

Lara sat in silence, unsure of how she should respond to this woman's sudden appearance.

"I'm Shirl." She smiled wide. "I heard what he was saying to you. I can't believe Tommy works for such a creep."

Lara tried to think quickly. Was this a carefully laid trap? Or had she just found an ally? She had no time to figure it out. And nothing upon which she could base a decision. All she could see was this woman's sincerity in her eyes. Lara knew that even sincerity could be faked.

"Listen, honey," Shirl sat next to her, "don't listen to all that talk about him being your savior. I've been reading about those. And you can take my word for it. Jonnie Spaeth is no savior. He's what is called a devil. Now, what's your name, honey?"

"I'm Lara."

"I like how that sounds: Lara. It's a good name." Shirl had no trouble looking her in the eye. "Have a little faith, Lara. You aren't alone. It'll make Tommy mad, but I want to help you if I can. So tell me everything that's happened and why you're here. Then we'll put our heads together and see if we can't figure out a way to get you away from here."

Lara wanted to believe her. She needed to believe that something good had just happened. For Jett's sake, she would have to take a chance.

66

In the space of a few hours, they had lost the Swede and the Australian had become impatient to find the Irishman. It was the kind of day the New Yorker expected in the Lazaretto. He couldn't remember a time he'd come to the quarantine moon when he hadn't been miserable. At least he hadn't been disappointed.

He was being forced to speed things up. He never liked doing that. It was always an invitation to disaster. But this was the trouble with not being the man on top. Only the man calling the shots chose the tempo. Everyone else had to keep up. It wasn't the first time the New Yorker longed to change his position in life. The Australian had been a solid employer, but he had never been a fair or superior manager. This recent desire for revenge coupled with his impatience was just another reason to hope that one day something would change.

But it wasn't going to happen today. The New Yorker knew it, and so he made the call to the Source, demanding a meeting.

"Are you crazy? I can't meet you in the middle of the day. You must have lost your mind." The Source was as angry as the New Yorker had expected.

"You don't seem to understand that I am not giving you an option. Meet me in an hour."

"Or what?" The petulance in those words could not be ignored.

"There's no *or what*. You still keep thinking there's an option. He demands results and you are not producing them."

"I've got results. You just haven't asked for them. If you'll listen for a minute I'll tell you what we've found."

More than likely this was just an attempt by the Source to stall, to prove that some measure of control was still held by the Source. The New Yorker left no room for evasion. "Unless you've found one of the men we're looking for, you haven't found anything of value."

"We found one of them." The Source explained how the Frenchman had been discovered dead in a hotel room. "At first I thought it had been one of your men who did it. But your insistence on a meeting tells me it was someone else. Who, I wonder, might it have been?"

The New Yorker did not answer that question. It was best not to speculate in front of the Source.

"You will still meet with me. But this news buys you a little time. Find the Irishman. You don't have much time left. Tonight, no later. If you can't provide us information, there's no reason for you to remain in your present employment."

"I'm doing what I can!" The Source knew better than to challenge the New Yorker's threat. The Australian could make one call and the Source would be out of a job. It really was that simple.

"That's what I was trying to say. You can either find information or you can't. Which is it?"

As soon as the call was terminated the New Yorker stopped to consider the question raised by the Source. Who might have been the one to get to the Frenchman? The Swede hadn't done it. He wasn't that bold. If he had been, he never would have brought in the other men. No, he wasn't one to stick a gun in a man's ribs. It had to be the Englishman. Had he done it to curry favor with the Australian? If so, they'd be hearing from him soon. And he would have the artifact with him.

If only that would satisfy the Australian they could load up the *Strike* and be back in Bukovina in no time. It would be the right thing to do. Forget the Swede, forget the Irishman. Any chance they had of getting out of the Lazaretto without further trouble was the best possible fortune.

They could leave the Swede's wife behind. She'd be no trouble at all. No point in killing her.

The Ursuline would be happy for her. He was aware that they had already become friends. And that was fine with the New Yorker, as long as they did not have to do anything drastic to her.

He prepared to go to the Australian. He would advise him to wait for the Englishman to call, then get the hell out of the Lazaretto. It was the best option they had.

67

The sun was setting. It wasn't visible, but on some days the people of the Lazaretto were more aware of its setting than others. The unusually bright, rainless day was drawing to a close. As if in payment for the fair weather, a cold wind was chilling those in the city who were still moving around. A massive thunderhead was rolling in under the high clouds that had been hovering over the city. Soon, the city would be soaked.

Lepov was standing on a street corner watching the entrance to Gloria's hotel. He did not know if they had checked out yet. He was betting that they hadn't. Beta was not closing down for a few days and there was no reason to rush to their new rooms in quarantine.

He recognized the fact that there could be other suspects in the Jardyn killing. Just because he had told Dannen where to find the murdered man didn't mean Dannen was guilty. However, it certainly put Dannen in a tough spot. There was always the chance that Spaeth had been able to kill him. And judging by the story of Frank Dassin's wife, it appeared that Spaeth had already arrived in the city.

But the fact that Lepov had just been to see Jardyn could not be ignored. As an investigator he had learned that coincidences did indeed occur in the natural turn of events. There was, however, a reduced probability of coincidence relative to the significance of the event. And Jardyn's death, and the disappearance of the stolen pistol, in conjunction with Lepov tracking him down, were significant events, to be sure.

So it would have been plain foolish to disregard Kry Dannen as a suspect in the murder. It would also have been a slap in the face of common sense.

Armed with this perspective, Lepov stepped off the curb and approached the hotel. He glanced up in the direction of their room. He knew which floor it was and where it was in relation to the street. If someone up there was watching him he wasn't about to hide his face. Let Dannen know he was coming. Lepov even tilted back his hat to allow Dannen a better look.

He nearly bulled into the door as it rolled up and away from him.

A thin little man behind the front desk jerked his head up when Lepov passed near the desk. The little man called his name.

"Mr. Lepov!"

He had considered passing by without acknowledging the desk man but changed his mind.

"Your PDT reader is working, I see. What can I do for you?"

"Yes, I'm sorry, but I was watching for you. Mrs. Dannen asked that I give you this." He held out a paper envelope that was sealed.

"Thanks," Lepov put the note in his pocket without reading it. "Is she in?"

"Yes," the man looked as if he could not decide how much he should tell Lepov.

"It's alright, you know. They're my clients. Is Mr. Dannen in as well?"

"No," he said quickly. The look on his face clearly said that he suddenly regretted answering.

"It's not like that, now. In fact, if Mr. Dannen arrives while I'm upstairs, feel free to let him know I'm up there. We'll behave."

Gloria was just as nervous to see him as the desk clerk had been. That had caught him by surprise.

"What are you doing here?" She backed away from the door. She was wearing a long silken nightgown with a lace peignoir over it.

"You look on edge, Lori." The familiar name had slipped out before he could hold it back.

"Grey, you always did know me well. But didn't you read my letter? Didn't that little man give it to you?"

"It's here. I just don't like to read before bedtime. What's going on?"

"Who says there's anything—"

"Gloria, listen to me." Lepov spoke clearly, raising his voice just enough to command her attention. "Tonight, of any night, you've got to be honest with me. And no games. You understand? There's too much at stake now."

"What's happened Grey?"

"This morning I did what you asked me not to do. Dannen hired me to give him the information on Jardyn. Yeah, I'd found him, over by the park. He was holed up in a hotel—just a little place—and he was plenty scared. We talked a good bit, much of it was about you."

"What do you mean you did what I asked me not to do?"

"I told my client about it this morning. Before you were awake."

"Oh, Grey, you didn't!" She reached out both arms to him and he thought for a moment she was going to embrace him. Instead, she grabbed his arms and pulled on him as if she meant to pull him down to the ground. "You don't know what he's capable of. I told you that!"

"I know, I know what he's capable of. I just heard from a friend in Homicide. Jardyn's dead. He was shot earlier this morning."

She clung to him and he braced himself as her weight pressed against him. She sobbed once, bit her lower lip to regain her control, then suddenly slapped Lepov hard across the face.

"You bastard. You've killed me. He's been gone all day. I didn't know where he was. But now I understand. He's got the pistol. He's going to the fence. To sell it. But if he murdered Lou, he'll know about my involvement. He'll be coming back for me. To kill me. Why didn't you listen to me—"

"How was I supposed to know? How was I supposed to trust you?" He'd had his reasons for going to Dannen instead of her, but in that moment he could no longer remember them. And no matter what they were he knew they would sound weak and foolish in light of Jardyn's death.

"Trust me? Grey, I've not always treated you well, I know that. But I've never lied to you. Even when I left you, I didn't lie. You know that."

She must not have been counting her vows. By now, Lepov had his arms around her, in an attempt to keep her from slapping him again. He held her tight against his coat. She had struggled at first but now was content to be still in his arms. The smell of her hair, her perfume, her breath, it confused him all over again.

"Jardyn, he told me, that you.." What had Jardyn actually said? He could no longer remember.

"There's nothing he could have said that would have made you distrust me. Maybe it was your own cruelty that convinced you not to trust me. You were always one to imagine troubles that weren't real. To pursue suspicions that should have been left to die out on their own. You mope and you dwell and allow your own petty little thoughts to fester until you eventually convince yourself that I'm no good, or I can't be trusted, or anything else that occurs to you. And now, you've done it again, only instead of pushing me, your wife, away and toward a new life, you've killed a man by your foolishness.

"You've killed a truly good man." Her tears started again. Her head was lying against the breast pocket of his coat. He put a hand up to her and pressed it against her hair. He should have defended himself. He should have asked her to explain why she'd ever needed him to find Jardyn when she knew where to find him all along.

No. He wasn't going to start suspecting her again.

"Where's Kry?" he pulled her away and looked down into her eyes.

"I don't know. He's been gone since this morning." Now free of his arms, she looked down at her gown and she seemed startled at her appearance. "Oh, God. Look at me. What am I doing? All dressed up, for Kry. When he was out there killing Lou. I look like a fool."

"You look nice, Lori."

"It's sweet of you to say so, but I've got to change. I can't go anywhere like this."

"Go?" Lepov followed her into the bedroom.

"You've got to get me out of here. Grey, he'll kill me. If he's sold the pistol, he'll be done with me. He was just keeping me around to make sure he could find Lou. And I was right. I led him right to him. I told him to hire you, and he did, and you did it for me, and you led him right to Lou. And now, he'll have no more use for me."

She'd sloughed off her peignoir and pulled open a closet door. Inside, she sifted through hanging clothes until she found a blouse and a pair of slacks.

"And what am I'm supposed to do with you?" He watched her drop the gown to the floor. It had been a long time since he had shared a bedroom with her and watched her undress. Back then, it had been something he'd grown accustomed to. That had been a long time ago.

"Take me with you," she said matter-of-factly. When he didn't reply, she turned and at that moment she too felt the awkwardness in the room. She quickly threw the blouse over her and neither one of them spoke until she'd finished dressing.

"Gloria, we can turn Kry in to the police. There's a detective I know."

"No, don't do that, Grey." She grabbed a pair of simple, flat shoes from the bottom of the closet. "I mean, do you have to? If they arrest him, they'll arrest me too. He'll say I helped him do it. They'll never believe me."

"Even if I took you away from here, then what? I wait for him to show up with that gun in my face, demanding to know where you are?"

"Maybe he'd just go. Besides, he probably doesn't even have the gun anymore. This okay?"

The last question was said in a little girl's voice, vulnerable and eager for approbation. She stood straight, the shoes now on her feet, her arms briefly out to her side so that he could see she was finished dressing. A nervous smile on her lips.

"Sure. I don't know what it's okay for, but it'll do."

"We'll worry about what to do in the morning. For tonight, let's just get out of here."

Lepov watched her walk to the door. Her little performance had been perfectly played. Even in a time of crisis, afraid for her life, she'd managed to manipulate him. Had managed to steal his focus so that she could convince him to do as she wanted.

The hell of it was, after all these years, she'd never looked better, in or out of her gown.

68

Russell couldn't believe his bad luck. That he'd been dragged into working with Pearl Lin Kwan—something good at any other time—just before he'd gone to grab Dassin and his family still bothered him. The woman, Mrs. Dassin, might not have been taken. If Russell had been there, he might have been able to prevent her disappearance.

He was being unfair to Pete. Pete was an experienced street cop. He had done the best he could considering how little he had been prepared to jump in and help. It was even possible Pete had done better than Russell might have. His quick thinking had saved the lives of Frank and his little boy.

But now, after having safely taken Dassin into the Shipping Port and introduced him to MacNally, Russell wished he still had Pete back at the precinct to help him try and locate Mrs. Dassin. Pete's skills were just what was needed for this type of work.

The first thing he'd tried was her PDT, which he knew was a lost cause. Spaeth's men had simply crushed it, or something similar, so that it no longer showed up on any of the larger readers. All he had was her last location, which had been outside IHS headquarters. That hadn't been helpful.

Next he tried to match any PDTs that might have been coming from the men in the truck, but it was easy to see that none of them had been using one. There had been no video feeds that allowed him to see the faces of anyone in the plaza. And the box truck had been wiped clean of identifying tags.

He made a quick check with Lazaretto Air Security. They worked double duty at securing the airspace above the city as well as keeping the moon locked down from non-sanctioned flights coming in and—more importantly—non-sanctioned flights leaving the moon. Theirs was one of the more essential missions to maintain quarantine. And for that reason, Russell discovered that they paid little attention to the airspace above the city as long as no one violated the upper layers of the stratosphere.

This last point made by Air Security left Russell wondering how Spaeth would have arrived on Aegean without coming through official entry sites.

Not wanting to waste time playing *What Would Pete Do?*, he called Pete for advice. The puzzle wizard was flattered.

"Let me get back to you on that, Russell. I still have a few tricks up my sleeve, and if I try a few of them, I might hit something. You thinking he's got a ship somewhere, I guess?"

"Yeah, that's what I meant. But you don't have to do it. Just point me in the right direction. How would he get it through Air Security? I don't know much about space flight capabilities. Are there ships that can defeat LAS tracking? Can they masquerade as officially sanctioned ships?"

"I would think Spaeth does something simpler than that."

"Which would be?" Russell prompted.

"Someone is paid to look the other way. Maybe even cover the tracks after they come in. Good grief, he could have landed along with the latest transport and someone simply removed it from the landing report. Spaeth doesn't like to skulk around too much. Unlike some people with great influence, he doesn't shy away from using it."

"So point."

"I just did, Russell. Think it through. If a tracker logged his flight and it was erased—"

"There will be a missing track in the sequence of tracks reported for a given time period. Okay. And if it wasn't erased, and he landed in broad daylight—or the equivalent of daylight in the Laz—he's either listed under a different name, or he's not reported and there's an anomaly in the number of tracks and the number of ships that docked."

"Yeah, well, there's variations in there, but that's the right direction. You sure I can't help? This woman's life is at stake, you know."

"I got it, Pete. I'll—hold on. Change of plans. I can't believe this is happening again. Yeah, you see what you can find. I'll try to look too, but my new partner just walked in the office, took one look at me and is heading this way fast. I gotta go."

More bad luck.

"So what happened with Gregor Lepov?" Kwan asked before she'd even reached Russell's desk.

"I'm working on him. He may have information that will help, but I can say for sure he didn't kill that man."

"Russell, I thought we agreed that you would bring him in if he wasn't cooperating." Kwan sat on the edge of his desk and gave him a long stare. "You playing games with me? Just because I'm not MacNally doesn't mean I'm not smart enough to keep up with you."

"You're right. And yes, I'm playing games with you. How much do you really want to know right now?" He decided to see just how smart she really was.

"Maybe not too much. Bring me something by tomorrow. I'll have to put in a report of some kind to the Captain by then. Don't stick me with this, boy."

Russell nodded respectfully. Maybe she really was as smart as MacNally. Actually, Russell decided, she was probably being smarter than MacNally in this situation. He'd have threatened to beat the information out of Russell.

"There's my new team." Captain Jenkins came out of his office and smiled apprehensively at them. "You two getting along?"

"We're just fine," Kwan said, smiling back at him.

"Yeah, we're just fine." Russell didn't smile as he added: "Working with Detective Kwan is just as rewarding as working with Detective MacNally. It makes me proud to be a part of this department."

Jenkins thought over Russell's remark and seemed unsure of how to respond. He finally just nodded. "Glad to hear that, son. That's good to know."

He turned to reenter his office but stopped short of it. "Oh, and Russell, will you step inside for a moment?"

Russell followed him and waited for his boss to speak. Kwan, recognizing that the younger detective had been asked to follow the Captain alone, did not follow them. Russell did notice, however, that she drifted closer to the office door. She hovered just out of sight of Captain Jenkins.

"Russell, I'm getting worried about Ed. He's disappeared."

Jenkins started fiddling with a box of cigars. He didn't light one, but he picked through the box, examining each one until he found one he liked.

"Is someone looking for him?" Russell asked.

"Yeah, I am. I didn't tell you, but his car was found way the hell out by a cemetery on the western edge of town. It was empty. No sign of Ed. No blood."

"Blood?"

"Well, frankly, after that scene we found over at the Maple Leaf, I can only assume that was Ed doing the shooting from the alley, though God knows where he got a gun like that. If that was him, though, he was bleeding heavily. And he never showed up at any hospital. I'm worried."

"Sir?" Russell couldn't understand how Jenkins, the man who had abandoned MacNally to Spaeth, could say he was now worried. "It seems funny, you worried about MacNally now."

"Listen, boy, don't take that tone with me! Do you think you're funny? I knew Ed MacNally before the first time you spit up on your daddy's lap. That man's my friend. And for all I know he's lying in a hole somewhere deader than King Harry."

"Which explains why you left him alone out there."

"I left him alone out there because I know Ed MacNally. He was better off on his own. He could stay out of sight. Disappear. If we had put him under guard he wouldn't have been as safe as he would have been on his own. Look, I understand you're worried about him too. I can see how you'd think I wasn't doing my job. That I wasn't handling this right. But realize that I'm telling you the truth. Ed MacNally is my *friend*."

"So what do you want from me?" Russell could think of all sorts of counterpoints to everything Jenkins had just said, but he held his peace. Jenkins was in no mood for a debate.

"I'm not stupid, kid. No one has caught one whiff of MacNally since the night of all the shooting. But last night, no one could get a hold of you. I don't buy that story about your sleeping pills. You know where MacNally is. I want you to tell me what you know."

The room had become warm and Russell felt sweat trickle down his back. There were numerous reasons he should distrust Jenkins. Spaeth had influence everywhere. There was no telling what sort of pressure was coming down on Jenkins. He might even be as honest as Abe Lincoln but if someone on the Commission was pressuring him for MacNally's whereabouts, Jenkins' honesty wouldn't keep MacNally safe.

Out of the corner of his eye he saw Kwan still hanging around the door. Unless he was mistaken, she'd inched closer since he'd last glanced in her direction.

"Menya, for God's sake, just tell me if Ed's still alive."

Russell nodded. Just once.

Relief washed over Jenkins. He walked over to his open door, discovered Kwan loitering there, and closed it. He had finally chosen a cigar and he held it in his hand, examining it one more time.

"I lied to you, Menya. I'm a no good bastard. I *did* leave him out there alone. And it wasn't because I thought he was better off alone. If I'd thought that, I wouldn't be worried about him now. Listen, I've heard that a Stargen Infiltrator may have broken Air Security corridor codes. If it's true, that'll be Spaeth. He's here.

"I was told to back off. Sure, you won't be surprised to hear that. Hell, there's probably at least two, if not three commissioners who owe their positions to Spaeth. They're powerful. They get what they want. And I admit I was scared. For me. I cut Ed loose, and it was wrong. If he's hurt, it's because of me. Is he?"

Russell didn't answer.

"Damn it, I can't do this any better than I am. I'm admitting I screwed up. I'm sorry. Now tell me if my friend is okay or not."

"He's pretty shot up." Russell hadn't decided if he was going to trust Jenkins or not.

"Will he make it?" He bit off the end of the cigar and spit it out into a waste basket.

"I think so." Did he really think his boss couldn't be trusted?

"I hope Ed can forgive me." He lit the cigar.

"Why did you want to know where he is? What would you do for him now?" Russell wished he could talk to Pete about this. He already knew what MacNally would say.

"Not all of the commissioners are compromised. I think we could get him to meet with two of them I know who hate Spaeth. They'll be able to get him safely away. Their places are heavily guarded. And I can run interference. Unless you really think he's better off where he's hiding. Do you think he can take care of himself there? For an extended period?"

It was time to give Jenkins what he wanted.

"No, I don't. And for the record, even if MacNally forgives you, I won't. He's in the Shipping Port."

"He's what?" Jenkins pulled the cigar from his mouth and pointed it over his shoulder. "As in *the* Shipping Port?"

Jenkins' lips curled into a smile. "That clever sonofagun."

Sometime during the drive back to Bril Abbot's, Lilly had managed to get the little boy to finally smile at her. Until that point, he had been deadly serious, his face a mask of stone. She had simply put her arm around, said nothing, and stroked his hair. It had been difficult for him to relax. But by the time they'd arrived at the house, he was nearly limp as she carried him inside.

He had never said a word.

She watched him sleep in a spare bedroom in the back of Bril's house: his small chest rising and falling quickly, his mouth slightly open, one arm up around his head.

All that she knew of him was his name, Jett, and that his parents were in trouble. His father Frank had a gentle face, despite the worry and despair that covered it.

"He's been exiled." Pete came up to the door and stood behind her. His shadow covered her own silhouette that darkened the bed where the boy lay.

"Oh, Pete," she tried to imagine the anguish Jett's mother must be going through. "Is he—?"

"It's a blood disorder. Nothing that can't be managed. It has a mild chance of spreading by pathogen, hence its being on the list."

"You shouldn't be here. Sun would never forgive me if you ended up—"

"I'll be fine," Pete stopped her. "Like I said, it can spread, but the odds of that are awfully slim."

They both backpedalled from the room and Lilly gently closed the door. They made their way to the kitchen. Bril was in his own bedroom, sleeping. Rain was coming down on the roof, muffling all others sounds with its dull roar.

"Are you going to stay here tonight?" she asked him.

"No, I don't think so. But I don't want to wake this guy up and ask him to drive me back to town. Do you have any idea where the nearest SubTransit station is around here?"

"I could drive you back," Lilly suggested.

"I'm sure you could. And Lepov would have my head if I let you. He wanted me to get you here safely, and if you took me back, then you'd be out alone and—I know, I know—you're perfectly capable of taking care of yourself. But Lepov doesn't seem to know that."

"He doesn't want to. He likes his women to be a little helpless."

"You're a good match. I think you like your men to be a little helpless too." Pete looked as if he regretted the comment.

"It's okay, you're more right than you know. And Gregor can be a little needy at times. Maybe that's okay, though, you know? He needs me, I need him. Nothing wrong with that."

They had both sat at the small table in the center of the kitchen, though neither one felt the need to take advantage of the full pot of coffee Bril had left on the stove for them.

She had been tempted to tell Pete about Shay, but the way Shay had disappeared made her hesitate. He was a fugitive, after all, and the more people she told, the more there was a chance that the wrong person might find out. Besides, Pete had enough to worry about without getting involved in her problems.

"Sun is excited that I'll be on my way soon."

"I'm sure, although the forty-day quarantine sort of delays the excitement a little."

"Or is increases the anticipation," countered Pete.

"Oh, a silver lining. A good try." They both looked up as the sound of rain suddenly dropped off.

She envied Pete and Sun. Both of them seemed able to see the sunny side of life, even in the Lazaretto. She wondered what that sort of relationship would be like. It was certainly one she would never experience. Not as long as she was one of the two people involved.

"How do you stay so optimistic, Pete?"

"I stay optimistic?" He frowned for a moment, considering her words. "I never really thought about it. I guess I just know that things will tend to work out. After all, if math has taught me anything it is that even when we think things don't make sense, they do, or they will, eventually. There's a pattern to everything. And if you can find it, and learn to anticipate it, then you won't be too disappointed with the world."

"What about the patterns that aren't so good? Like that little boy in there. There is definitely a pattern of misery in the Lazaretto. I'll bet you could have predicted this boy's exile with your numbers. Would that have lessened the pain any for his parents?"

Pete shrugged his shoulders. Maybe he knew she was not expecting an answer.

"I didn't mean to belittle your perspective, Pete. I'm sorry."

"It's okay. You have a right to a little bitterness right now. Life hasn't been fair to you—"

The sound of a vehicle outside the house stole their attention. They heard doors slamming shut, and the sounds of an engine moving away. Pete motioned for Lilly to stay at the table as he moved toward the front room. Lilly wasn't going to just sit there. She followed him and saw Bril standing in the hallway. He'd heard the noises too.

A knock at the door. Bril advanced to it and used a side panel to view the other side of the door. He punched a button on the panel and the door swung open. Lilly saw Gregor and she was about to greet him when he stepped aside to allow his ex-wife to enter first.

They were wet from their walk up the driveway. Though the rain had slacked off it hadn't stopped completely. As a few drops of rain rolled off the brim of Gregor's hat, no one said a word. The silence continued while those in the room tried to decide who should speak first.

Gloria looked around at those in the room with a nervous glance. She had backed into Gregor, as if sheltering beneath his broad frame. Gregor did not seem to notice. He wasn't looking at anyone but Lilly. She could see by the look on his face that he was expecting trouble. She could also see he was asking her to wait until he explained.

She stepped forward. Someone had to break the spell.

"Gregor, give me your coat and hat. They're wet. And hello again, Gloria. You look cold. Give me that coat and let's get you something hot to drink. Bril, do you have any towels?"

Bril nodded and disappeared down the hall. Pete took the coats from Lilly and went in search of a place to hang them. By the time Bril returned with the towels Lilly had ushered the new arrivals into the kitchen where she was pouring coffee for Gregor and she started a pot of water on the stove for Gloria's tea.

"I guess I just look awful," Gloria said as she pressed the towel to her hair.

"Hardly," Lilly said, prepping a cup with a tea bag.

"Is the boy asleep?" Gregor asked.

"In the back room." Pete said as he stood framed by the kitchen doorway.

"I haven't had this many people in my house since I bought it." Bril leaned against a countertop, amused at the full room.

"Look, I'm sorry about that. I just wasn't sure where I could take Gloria." Lilly gave Gregor a sharp look as he spoke. "She's in trouble. I suppose I'd better explain it. This hasn't been a good night."

Lilly handed out tea to Gloria and Pete, as well as one for herself once the water was ready. Before long they had all returned to the front room and found a place to sit. Gloria took a chair, while Gregor and Lilly sat beside each other on a small sofa. There was little room between them but it felt to Lilly as if they were on opposite sides of the room.

Gloria said nothing as Gregor explained that they suspected her husband had just killed a man and might, in fact, be planning to do the same to Gloria. Gregor left out most of the details. Lilly sensed right away that there was much about her story that couldn't be true. She had a feeling Gregor knew this. She could also see that he was unwilling to say it aloud.

When Gloria finally did speak, to add a few details that Gregor had left out, Lilly saw a combination of anger and admiration on his face. His conflict was readily evident from her own perspective. She glanced at Pete and his raised brows told her he could see the same thing.

Lilly found an excuse to leave the room, taking empty cups with her. She didn't want to hear anymore. It was evident Gregor intended to leave Gloria there at the house. Lilly wouldn't make a scene. She wouldn't order Gloria out of the house—it wasn't Lilly's house, after all—but she didn't have to pretend to be happy about it.

She stood at the sink watching rain fall on the back yard. The sound of footsteps warned her that she was not alone.

"Lilly, I didn't want any of this."

"Of course you didn't, Gregor." She kept her eyes on the rain.

"I'm going to take Pete back into Center City. And then I'm going to deal with this guy Dannen. Right now. I'm not gonna let this drag out any longer than it has to. I want her out of here as much as you do." He was close enough to touch her shoulder.

"Gregor," she allowed him to turn her around, "tell me you mean that."

"I don't have to. You know it's true." He touched her chin with the tip of his finger and gently raised her face until she was looking into his eyes. "Now stop this. Lilly Stewart's too tough a girl to let someone like Gloria make her nervous. I didn't fall for you because you were fragile."

He was just trying to cheer her up but his words stung. He was right. She was acting like a wilting flower. It wasn't like her at all. But then again, she'd rarely found competition with someone as formidable as this woman who had once been named Gloria Lepov.

Determined to be the woman Gregor had first known, Lilly walked back into the front room with her head held high. She showed no visible concern when Gregor left with Pete. And she kept her composure after Bril made arrangements for her and Gloria to share the second spare room.

She even managed to smile as Bril tripped over himself in an effort make sure the women were comfortable. He asked them more than twice if there was anything else they needed. They both said they had everything they needed and Bril discreetly retired to his room.

The real test of her poise came when she was alone with Gloria. She had been able to feel Gloria's eyes on her the whole time Bril had set up the two beds. No matter that she had not been looking in Gloria's direction, she had been able to feel her scrutiny. Lilly had come close to losing her equanimity.

But as the two women stood in the little room, each of them close enough to be able hear the other woman breath, it was Gloria who seemed to have lost her poise. She sank onto one of the beds and turned away from Lilly. Her shoulders trembled.

"I can see how you look at Grey and how you look at me." Gloria's voice shook. She paused and put a hand to her mouth. "You should know Grey didn't want any of this. I knew he wouldn't be able to say no to me. Even after what I did to him. He's a good man. I took advantage of him. And he helped me. But because of that, he's in trouble. And now I need your help. I didn't mean for any of this to happen. Don't be angry with me."

Gloria spun around with her last words, pleading with Lilly.

"What do you mean?" Lilly asked. "Why is Gregor in trouble?"

"He's going back to find my husband. I've tried to tell him Kry is a dangerous man. But he doesn't believe me. I think he's going back there to make a deal with him. But Kry's not going to make a deal. He just killed a man. He's not going to let me or Grey get out of this alive."

"What sort of help do you think I could give you?"

"Just look the other way. I can't stay here. I've got to get back to

Kry. Maybe convince him to leave Grey alone. It's me he's after. I can't let Grey go back to that hotel alone. I've got to get there before him. But if Grey contacts you, don't tell him. Just promise me that. I'll go quietly. The man in the other room won't know I've gone. Will you let me go?"

Lilly wasn't sure what she should say. Gloria was rambling. It seemed as if she'd lost her mind. But at the same time, much of what she said was logical. If there was the slightest chance that Gregor was walking into a situation too dangerous for him to handle, she wouldn't hesitate to allow this woman to risk her own life for Gregor.

And that's when the irony of Gloria's manic pleadings hit her. Gloria was asking permission to put herself in danger from the one person in the Lazaretto who was least likely to care if she were injured or killed. Did this woman, this former lover of Gregor's really think Lilly would try to prevent her from going back to the violent man she had chosen over Gregor?

It was all Lilly could do not to laugh as she nodded soberly.

"You do what you have to, Gloria. I'm going to sleep. As far as I know, you're going to sleep too." Lilly turned her back and added: "Good luck, Mrs. Dannen."

70

"It's late and we should call it a night." Kwan had been waiting for Russell when he'd come out of Jenkins' office. When Russell had agreed with her she'd followed him to the elevator and waited till the doors were closed before saying: "Let me take you to the corner café for a late snack."

Russell would have enjoyed the offer if he hadn't been distracted by his conversation with Jenkins.

Now, as they sat in a corner booth, idly picking at their pie crusts, he realized Kwan had made no casual offer. She had an agenda.

"Let me make a statement, and if it's right you can let me continue, if it isn't, you can get up and leave." Kwan pushed her pie away and wiped the corners of her mouth with her hand.

"Okay."

"Jenkins called you in there tonight to ask you where MacNally is hiding." She watched him for a response. "That was statement number one."

Russell picked up his fork and took a bite of his pie.

"Okay, number two. MacNally's hurt, he was in that shootout the other night, and you've got him safely tucked away somewhere."

"That was two statements." Russell kept chewing his pie.

"You need my help, because you don't know if Jenkins is

trustworthy or not. You may have just told Spaeth where MacNally's hiding."

Russell put down the fork and stood up. He swiped his PDT on the table's reader and thanked Kwan for the pie. She put a hand on him to keep him from leaving.

"Come on, I told you I respect MacNally. And I don't like to think of him in trouble without help. Maybe it's because you and I are now partners, it makes me feel responsible for your old partner. At any rate, you should know that if you did tell Jenkins where MacNally is, it was the wrong thing to do. I've been involved in a few cases involving men who were loosely connected to Spaeth. I can tell you I have some real doubts about Captain Jenkins."

"Can you prove this?" Russell asked.

"There's never proof with this kind of thing. He's not taking money, anything like that. But someone has his number. And they know how to call it up when they need it. Now I don't want to lecture you but you should know I've worked in this department far longer than you have. I've known MacNally and I knew Fenelli for many years. If Mac is out there hurt somewhere, and he needs help, then I'm not gonna let you tell me I can't help him."

Russell was impressed to find out that so many people were friends with MacNally. He knew the old man would find all of this sentiment touching.

"And how can you help him?"

"I don't want to see this go on any longer. I want to go get him, bring him back here, and there are more than a few of us willing to stand up with him and face down whatever is headed his way. That's the way it should be done."

"MacNally prefers it this way," Russell said. He tried to leave a second time but Kwan stood up and held him back yet again.

"Let me talk to him. If, after I'm done, he tells me he'd rather be on his own, I'll take him at his word." Kwan, as tall as Russell, did not shrink from looking him in the eye. "Come on, Menya. We're partners."

"That's true, we are." He gave her a weak smile. "I'm too tired to go tonight. Let's go in the morning. You pick me up early. I'll take you to him."

"That sounds good, Menya. Really good. Where exactly is he?"

"He's in the Shipping Port."

Kwan's eyes lit up. "Are you serious?"

Russell nodded, and began to explain. When he was done, she shook her head in admiration.

"I would never have thought of that," she said.

71

He'd been lying in the dark long enough for his eyes to adjust. He could see the walls of the large bedroom suite and the great uncovered windows that looked out over the city. A slight shift of his head allowed him to see the Ursuline lying beside him, covered with a sheet. One leg ran out from under it almost touching his own. Her pale skin easily contrasted against the dark sheets.

He had expected a call from the Englishman all night but it had never come. What that meant he wasn't sure. Perhaps the Australian's impatience was rubbing off on him. Maybe the Englishman would walk through the door as soon as the Lazaretto sun weakened the darkness of the night. It was possible he would simply walk in and hand them the artifact.

The New Yorker didn't believe it would happen. And when the Englishman failed to show up, the Australian would start raising hell. It would be the New Yorker's job, at that moment, to have a plan in place that would keep the Australian satisfied. But as yet, no matter how long he lay in the dark, he had yet to develop a plan that would be of any value.

"You're awake, aren't you?" The Ursuline peeked out from under the sheet, her eyes shining like distant stars. "I could tell."

"Go back to sleep," he said, gently pushing her head back down. "Let me think."

"What are you thinking about?"

"Nothing you need to worry about."

"That's why you can't sleep? Is something bad gonna happen?"

He chuckled at her childlike instinct. She was closer to the truth than she knew. "Nothing bad's gonna happen."

"You aren't gonna hurt her, are you?" Her eyes were looking up at him again.

"Who?"

"His wife."

"What did I say? Go to sleep, let me think."

The signal from the call was loud enough to startle the girl. She pressed against him and he had to reach around her in order to receive the call.

"What?"

"Is it clear?" asked the Source.

"Yes, it's clear," he lied. At this point, he just didn't care who was listening in. The Source was no longer worth protecting.

"I have it." There was an unexpected pride behind those words.

"Have what?" He sat up in the bed; so did the girl.

"I've found both of them."

"Can you send me the location?" It was about time some good news came in. He was happy enough to smile at the Ursuline.

"I'm finished, now." The Source added this with forced confidence. He could still detect a hint of fear behind that bold statement. "No more meetings, no more calls. I've done what you asked."

"Sure, no more calls. At least for now." He broke the transmission. He really couldn't believe the Source had come through. The pleased surprise must have shown clearly on his face, even in the dark.

"It's good news, I'm glad." The girl's eyes sparkled even more than they had before. "Does this mean you can let her go now?"

The Swede's wife. Always she was asking about that woman. Why did he have to tell her something that should have been obvious from the beginning.

"Look, she's gonna be fine. With her, we can do this real easy now. We send in a man who tells them to give up or we kill the woman. They'll come right to us. Simple. Easy. No mess."

"But you wouldn't!" The Ursuline came to her knees, off balance on the soft mattress. "You know it wouldn't be right. You wouldn't kill her. Not really! "

"No, not really, because he won't let it happen. He'll give up."

"But if he didn't. If he didn't give up—"

"Don't worry about that. It just won't happen." Why was she worrying about something that wouldn't happen?

"Don't you ever worry what this does to you?" She took his hand in hers and squeezed it tight.

"What are you talking about? What does it do to me?"

"In here," she pressed his hand to his chest. "You've got a soul, and every time you do this kind of thing—the *wrong* thing—it gets darker in here, and the light it just don't shine like it oughta. You get blacker and blacker and pretty soon you're just like *him*, your boss. And that's just no good."

He should have known this would happen. He just couldn't have good news hit him without something like this. It was a bad time for her to start preaching.

"Listen, you're telling me things I don't need to hear. Got it? You do all the worrying for me and my soul, that's a good job for you. Hell, light a candle for me or pray for me. Whatever it is you do for a lost soul. Maybe it'll stick someday. Can't hurt, right?"

He switched on a light and started pulling on a sweater.

"But you won't hurt her?" she asked again. "I really like her, she's a mother, you know. She has a little boy."

"What did I say?" he growled. He'd spun back around to smack her but the earnest, open look in her eyes stayed his hand. She winced, waiting for the hand to complete its arc. "Stop worrying about that woman. Her sorry, troublesome husband doesn't have a choice. He and the hero will have to come to us, and then *he'll* deal with them. It'll be over. And yes, if it will shut you up, we'll let her go."

She was crying now. She shook with each attempt to stop the tears. He didn't care. For once he had good news to bring the Australian and he wasn't going to let her ruin it.

He was tired of her fool ideas. He sure didn't want to hear any more of them that night. He left the suite and determined that he wouldn't go back. He could sleep in one of the other rooms on the floor below them. As soon as he delivered his good news to the Australian he would find a bed and get some sleep.

By noon they'd be boarding the *Strike* and leaving the Lazaretto.

Later, he briefly wondered if he could keep his promise to the Ursuline regarding the woman. He couldn't be completely certain the Australian would allow her to go free. But the New Yorker felt she had a better chance than either the Swede or the Irishman of getting through the next day alive.

Even if he was forced to kill her, he could at least lie to the Ursuline and tell her the woman had been set free. After all, how would she know the difference?

72

As soon as he dropped Pete off at his place, Lepov turned the TransitCar toward Dannen's hotel. Maybe, just maybe he had come back to his room. And if he had, Lepov would confront him right then and there. No point in delaying the inevitable.

Dannen had played him for a sucker, hiring him to find a man he wanted to murder. Lepov had been so blindsided by Gloria that he hadn't been able to see clearly enough what Dannen had been up to. That couldn't be helped. It was time to change the game in his favor. Time to show Dannen that he, Gregor Lepov, knew how to make a man pay for underestimating him.

The rain was coming down as hard as Lepov had ever seen it fall in the Lazaretto. Colder too. Though temperatures never dropped below freezing, he was sure it was close to that. He parked near the hotel but was still far enough away that he felt like he was freezing by the time he found the shelter of an overhang. His coat was made to keep him dry, it wasn't made to keep him warm.

As he entered the hotel, he thought about those cigarettes in his pocket. The combination of the cold and his lack of sleep left him wanting to break open his pack. His wet hand dug into his pocket and traced the outline of the sealed box.

He pulled out the hand. It was empty. Pulling off his hat, he shook the rain off it then set it back on his head. As he passed the front desk he saw the same little guy from earlier in the day. He didn't say a word to him and the little guy just stared at him.

If the desk man called ahead, Dannen would be waiting for him. It would be better if he wasn't but short of breaking the desk clerk's phone, there was no way to make sure he didn't sound the alarm. If Dannen was prepared for him, Lepov might just be walking into a bullet.

He still had the Shockhammer, but it wouldn't get him close if Dannen opened fire. His only hope was that Dannen would want to know where Gloria was and he wouldn't kill Lepov before he found out.

Only one way to know for sure.

He hammered the door with his fist. He should have stood off to one side but he was feeling reckless. What was the point in being careful now? He'd let his ex-wife's husband play him for a fool. He might as well have pulled the trigger on Jardyn. His own stupidity had been the death of a man. Whether or not that man deserved the bullet in his chest was something else entirely.

Dannen had no right using Lepov to put it there.

A minute passed. No bullet crashed through the door. Neither did the door open. Lepov didn't bother knocking a second time. He worked open the lock with little trouble — sometimes he wondered why hotels bothered to put locks on their doors at all when they were so easy to bypass — and pushed open the door.

He quick-stepped inside and slipped out of the light, pressing himself against the wall. The light from the hall illuminated the room.

Dannen was nowhere to be seen. Shutting the door, he hit a wall switch and searched both rooms. He was alone. Dannen hadn't been back yet. Or if he had, he hadn't stuck around for long.

Near the closet he could see Gloria's nightgown still lying on the floor. He forced down the image of her standing over it. For too many years she'd just been a bad memory, something to forget, something to despise. He didn't need this new memory of her. He hadn't thought of her as a woman in ages. What would be the point in starting that again?

He kicked the gown out of his way and took one step into the closet. A light came on automatically. He stared at the clothes hanging close together, put his hand in between two hangers and pushed half of the clothes aside. He could see nothing out of the ordinary. Could feel nothing as he frisked each set of clothes on the right and the left. The shelf above was empty. He ran a hand along its full length just to be sure. Aside from a few pairs of shoes, there was nothing on the floor.

He wasn't sure what he had hoped to find, but being in that hotel room alone was the first time he had the advantage over the Dannens. It was the first time he could get a look at them without their knowing it. He didn't intend to look away discreetly.

There was nothing important in the dresser drawers. All he found there were memories of a wife he thought no longer existed. After all these years, after two other husbands, her clothes still smelled the same. He hated her for that. She'd switched husbands without any trouble. Why the hell couldn't she have switched perfumes?

There were empty, hard-shell suitcases stacked in one corner of the front room. He broke the locks on them—no point in being careful—and searched them thoroughly. Nothing.

He stood in the center of the bedroom and turned slowly in a circle, eyeing every detail. The bed, wide enough to sleep four—a wife and her *three* husbands?—he pushed aside to make sure nothing was hidden below it. He didn't bother putting it back.

A chair was tucked partially into the center of a desk near the front door and Lepov pulled it out to sit on while he went through each drawer. He searched the center drawer first. Before he could start on the other drawer he saw it. Dannen had been in a hurry but it had still taken Lepov all this time to find it.

The chair had only been partially tucked in because under the desk a black case had been jammed against the wall. The same case he'd seen in Jardyn's room.

Dannen must have been feeling cocky not to have put more effort into hiding it. Or he felt confident no one would be looking for it. Maybe he had expected to kill Gloria by now, maybe that ex-husband of hers too. He was beginning to wonder if Dannen had killed Frobe as well. Had it been Dannen's goal to knock off every one of his partners from the beginning? So far, the only one Dannen hadn't gone after was the guy with the family: Dassin. Maybe he intended to get around to him too.

Placing the case on the desk, he examined the locks. Yes, he would be able to open it without a key if he had a little time. He grabbed the case with two hands and hefted it, shaking it gently. No way to tell if the pistol was still inside.

He pushed it aside and swiped his hand over the deskscreen. It was a small screen, but big enough for his purposes. He cleared the hotel's icon that appeared and on the black, blank screen he started writing. The note was short, to the point. He set the screen to display the note until it was acknowledged. It would not shut down until Dannen came back into the room.

He snatched the black case and paused before he opened the door. He was carrying a time bomb now. And he had no idea how much was left on the timer. At any moment, whether or not the gun was actually in the case or not, one of Spaeth's men could run into him and think he had Spaeth's stolen gun. And if that happened, he wouldn't live long enough to explain his side of the story.

How ironic it would be if he were finally carrying a gun when he needed one—a gun he couldn't put his hands on.

73

As soon as Lara heard the elevator doors close she sat up in her bed. She'd been put in the room next to Shirl's. She had been hoping for this. It was obvious from the muffled voices she'd heard that Tommy and Shirl had been talking, maybe even quarreled. The heavy tread she'd heard moving to the elevator had to be Tommy.

Listening at the door, she waited patiently. After what seemed like much too long, she heard the door of the other room open, then a keycode being entered. Her door snapped open and Lara pulled it wide enough to slip through.

"I had a feeling you'd be up." Shirl looked at Lara, who was fully dressed, and nodded her approval. "I was gonna wake you up if you were weren't. We've got to get you out of here. And it has to be now."

"What's happening?" asked Lara.

They had become fast friends earlier in the day. Once Lara had relaxed her guard enough she'd learned that Shirl was just as she appeared: a free-spirited girl who had hooked up with the wrong guy during an impetuous moment.

Lara had explained her situation and Shirl had been angered by what she heard. She knew that Tommy thought she was stupid and incapable of thinking on her own. But Shirl thought that would work to her and Lara's advantage. It had certainly enabled her to get Tommy to reveal what plans he had for Lara.

"Okay, we aren't going to be able to wait until tomorrow. They've found a way to locate your husband, and they intend to make him turn himself in for you. No, no, it's not your fault. They couldn't even find him. Someone just called them and told them where he is."

"But I can't—can't just let Frank turn himself in for my sake. What if they're lying and won't let me go? What if he brings Jett, and they don't let any of us go?" Lara took Shirl's hand, gripping it tightly.

"That's why I think you should take this chance. Tommy just went to grovel to his boss and tell him about the news he just heard. They'll be talking for a long time—Tommy says his boss never shuts up. So that means we have time to find a way to get you out of here. This isn't a prison. They just thought you wouldn't make much of an effort to get out. You know, just because you're a woman."

"I don't know where to start." Lara looked at Shirl anxiously.

"I've been working on that. It's not as easy as I thought it would be. But we have a few things to consider:

"First of all, if we can't get you out, that won't leave us without options. We can hide you. Even if you can't get to your husband, at least they can't prove they have you. Maybe your husband would then refuse to give himself up. So let's remember the goal is to get you out of reach or at least out of sight."

"But how?"

"Well, I won't brag, but I'm not as stupid as I act. Just because I like to read about angels and God and all that strange stuff don't mean I'm crazy. But," here Shirl scowled as she thought for a moment, "you could probably say I was crazy for getting mixed up with Tommy and Jonnie. But that's not because I'm crazy. I'm just lazy and I was hoping to latch on to a rich guy who'd be good to me, you see what I mean?"

Lara wanted to answer honestly but she knew this girl was risking her own safety by helping her find a way out. She didn't want to say what she really thought of Shirl's choice in men.

"So anyway, here's what I figured. I can hear a motor running. Behind the wall of my bedroom. Now, the only time it runs is when the elevator's moving. So that's gotta be the deal that lifts it up and lets it go down. My mother's husband—not a good guy, I'll admit—he worked in buildings like this. Not here, you know, but back on Bukovina. Well, he would talk about this sort of stuff. We must be at the top of the building because I can hear that motor. So if we can get into that room, there will be some way for guys like my mother's husband to get in there to fix it."

Shirl started walking toward the kitchen. When Lara had examined the kitchen, none of the cabinets would open. To her surprise, when Shirl approached them, she was able to open them.

"Keycode that works on my door opens all the cabinets too. I'll bet they didn't want you getting into these."

Shirl pulled out a drawer revealing a wide array of cooking knives. She chose a large, fat blade with a solid sharp edge as well as a long, narrower knife with serrated edge.

"And with those we do what?" Lara eyed the blades with

desperate curiosity.

"I'll show you." Shirl walked off with the two knives hanging loosely in her hands. She led Lara to the room she'd just been sharing with Tommy.

Lara wondered if it would be possible to just kill Tommy with the knife and use his keys to ride the elevator to the ground level. She hesitantly suggested it to Shirl.

"Kill Tommy? Now, Lara, I like you. I do. But I didn't think you were that kind of girl. And I know I'm not. So if you wanted to kill Tommy you'll have to find someone else to help you. I'm still Tommy's girl and I wouldn't let you do that. I said I'd help you escape, I didn't say I'd help you kill my man. Now stop thinking up crazy ideas and help me. We're gonna have to hurry."

Shirl took her into the room and with Lara's help pulled the bed away from the wall.

"Right here, I think we can cut our way in here."

"Cut?" Lara asked incredulously.

"It won't be that hard. We can get it started with the point of the butcher blade. Watch."

And before Lara knew it, Shirl had scored a small square in the wall by repeatedly running the tip of the blade into the paint layer of the wall. Lara watched the woman struggle to get the blade to penetrate what turned out to be material that was fairly soft.

"Why are you doing this? I mean, you know, why are you helping me?"

"Because I like Tommy a lot. He's a good guy sometimes, which is more than what I used to have in a man. But I know the man he works for is not a good guy. And even though Tommy promised not to let anything happen to you, I'm not sure he can protect you from his boss. And I couldn't stand to think of anything happening to you. We've only just met. You see what I mean? Now hand me the serrated knife."

Lara nodded, wiped a tear from her eye, and leaned forward to wrap her arms around the lovely girl who was willing to risk her life for a stranger. She held her in a hug for a short time then just as quickly she released her.

"Thank you," she whispered as she pulled back. She then handed the wicked looking knife to Shirl.

"This just makes it go faster. And easier." She sunk the tip of the knife into the break she'd made with the first knife and began to saw through the wall."

She worked at the wall for a time, sweating in her satin robe. She stopped several times to allow Lara to take a turn. They cut all four sides and found that a heavy insulation was in the way, after cutting through it, they had to repeat the cuts they'd made on the backside of the wall.

"Once we can pull this piece out, you can slip through. I'll put the pieces back in the best I can, then with the bed back in place he won't be able to see what we did right away. Now in that room you're gonna find a way out of here. I doubt they've guarded that door. You'll still have to be careful. If you can, take the stairs down. And take off your shoes first. Don't use the service elevator if there is one. It will draw attention to you."

"You should come with me, Shirl." Lara said as she handed the knife back to Shirl in order to take a break. "He'll know you helped me."

"Yeah, he'll know. But it will be too late then. And I can handle him, don't worry about me. He likes me. I can tell." Shirl worked the knife with a steady rhythm, patiently allowing the cut to lengthen. They had three of the four final cuts finished despite their aching arms.

"Shirl," Lara spoke after a lengthy silence, "it would be crazy to leave you here. I insist you come with me."

"We don't know what will happen to you when you go through that hole. Maybe I'll be facing better odds on this side." Her little smile filled her cherubic face.

Lara didn't like it. As the last cut was completed, she tried to think of a way to force the girl to join her. Shirl rejected any and all entreaties to leave.

"It just doesn't make sense. I buy you time by staying here. With the bed back in position, and me in it, he won't even notice you're gone. He'll think you're still asleep. In the morning, you'll have had plenty of time to find a way out. And listen, before you give up out there, remember that you gotta find a way. There's no coming back. You promise me you'll find a way. Will you?"

"Okay, I'll try."

"Don't try. My mother always said 'Shirl, don't try, honey. Just do it.' This is one of those things. You just do it."

Lara looked at the hole. The room beyond was dark and cold.

"Don't think about it. Just go. Besides, he could come back at any time. This took longer than I thought it would. And take that big knife with you."

Lara and Shirl both squatted near the hole, peering into its mysterious depths. At the same time they looked at each other. It was Shirl's turn to hug her new friend. She held on long enough to know the girl was more afraid than she had let on.

"Kiss that little boy for me. And God go with you. I'd say a prayer but I haven't learned them right yet."

Lara had to go head first through the hole. She reached out into the darkness with one hand, balancing on the other. It took her several attempts to get situated right so that she could extend enough to reach something to grab onto.

She finally felt a cold pipe and wrapped her fingers around it. Supporting some of her weight on her ribs, she was unable to say goodbye as she pulled herself into the black void.

74

Lepov tried to enter the house through the back door as quietly as possible. He eased the door closed in the darkened kitchen and stopped to listen for evidence that he had awakened anyone.

"You can turn on the light."

Lepov hit the light and saw Bril Abbot sitting at the little table with a cup of coffee sitting in front of him.

"You ever sleep, Lepov?" He pointed at the coffee then pointed at Lepov.

"No, not much. And no coffee, thanks. I actually came back for a little sleep. I could ask you the same question."

"Oh, I've been sleeping. Earlier, before all the rain and thunder hit." Lepov knew Abbot wasn't just talking about the weather. "I did try to go back to sleep but I couldn't."

"Yeah, a lot of that going around. What keeps you up at night?"

"Knock-out blondes who like to cause trouble."

"You got one of those too?" asked Lepov.

"No, I got the same one you have." When Lepov gave Abbot a quizzical look, Abbot explained. "Your blonde isn't as quiet as she thinks she it."

"What'd she do now?" Lepov wasn't in the mood for games. Whatever it was Gloria was up to he meant to shut it down immediately.

"She's gone. That's right. Walked out the front door not long after you left. I'm not so sure your other friend knows it. She's still in her room, asleep. I checked on her. She's just fine."

"She's a…" he couldn't think of an appropriate label for Gloria to use in front of a man he hardly knew.

"Yeah, she is." Abbot hadn't needed to hear a specific label.

Lepov stared at the kitchen floor, unable to properly guess at Gloria's intentions. He'd had so little sleep that he couldn't hardly remember what he had hoped to gain by coming back to Abbot's. Fortunately, Abbot had an inquisitive streak that was just what Lepov needed.

"What's in the case?" Abbot pointed at the black case sitting on the floor beside Lepov.

"Got a screwdriver and a hammer?"

They stood the case on its end and poked at the lock with the screwdriver. Lepov took his time thinking it over before he finally jammed the screwdriver under the clasp and simply smashed the lock by driving the screwdriver with a heavy blow from the hammer.

"You're a pro," Abbot chuckled. The clasp had snapped open.

"They don't teach you that kind of thing in school," Lepov winked at the one-time soccer great.

"They did at my school."

Lepov had rolled the case forward onto its side and gently lifted the lid. Inside its foam packing was the Luger.

"What the hell is that?" Abbot whistled softly.

"That, my friend, is the gun that Adolph Hitler used to shoot himself. The gun that ended World War II, the war to end all wars."

"They called World War II the *Big One*. World War I was the war to end all wars," a voice behind Lepov corrected him. "And Adolph Hitler did not shoot himself with a German Luger."

Both men watched Lilly step into the kitchen. She had wrapped herself in one of Abbot's large sweaters, which hung down to her knees. She came to the table and took the gun in her hand.

"Is this beautiful woman you brought to my house an expert in guns, Lepov?"

"She's an expert in things that are *old*. And that extends to more than just objects like me. If he didn't shoot himself with a Luger, what did he shoot himself with?"

"A Walther PPK."

"I love it that you know that. Do you have a sister?" Abbot pointed at his coffee then pointed at Lilly. She nodded.

"I'd like to say I knew it off the top of my head, but the fact is, when I heard that story this morning about the gun stolen from Jonnie Spaeth I couldn't just take it on faith. That's my job, you know, tracking down historical objects and judging their value. I hope you don't mind, Mr. Abbot, but I borrowed your desksystem this afternoon, while Gregor was asleep. It wasn't hard to find out the truth."

"Is this really a German gun?"

Lilly turned it over and looked closely at it. She handed it to Gregor. "It looks authentic. Early Twentieth Century. It is in very good condition."

"It still fires. And it has been recently. It may not have been used to shoot Hitler, but it was used to shoot a man named Louis Jardyn last night." He peered at the base of the grip then extracted a clip from the pommel. "Loaded, too."

"May I?" Abbot handed Lilly her coffee and then held out a hand toward Lepov.

Lepov handed him the Luger. The man's eyes shone with excitement. "This is a fine handgun. I've seen them before, in books. Never held one. Thank you."

He reverently handed it back to Lepov, who gingerly placed it back in the case.

"Gregor," Lilly nearly whispered, "Gloria's—"

"—gone. I know. She woke the man of the house."

"She says her husband's dangerous. She went back to him, to try and talk to him."

"Back to Dannen? What are you talking about?"

"She thinks she can keep him from coming after you." Lilly sipped her coffee. Lepov knew she was afraid and didn't want to admit it. "Would he? Come after you?"

"He will now." He had wanted to lie to her but she was too smart to allow it. "I've got the case, and he knows it. I left him a little note he won't like reading. Now I wish I hadn't. If Gloria walks in there, he'll use her to get the case back from me. He'll know I won't let him hurt her. He'll know I'd give up the case for her safety."

What had Gloria been thinking? Lepov cursed her valiant idiocy.

"What was in the note?" Lilly asked.

"What?" Lepov looked up at her and for a moment he was too angry with Gloria to understand what Lilly was asking. "The note? Oh, it was supposed to make him desperate. I told him I knew he'd killed Jardyn. Knew he was coming for me and Gloria. I told him I had the case and if he wanted it he could meet me in Terran Park at noon.

"I had all the cards. I had the case, I had Gloria. He was going to have to come after me. And I was going to be ready for him. Now, if Gloria doesn't show up here by morning, you can guess what that means."

He sat down at the table and pressed his hands to his head. He finally looked up at the others in the room and shrugged.

"I'm open to any ideas."

"I'd say you should go to sleep," Lilly said without hesitation. "There's no point in worrying over that woman tonight."

"That woman's my—" Lepov almost said it. He'd seen the look on Lilly's face and knew he'd made a mistake. "—used to be my wife."

As always, Lilly had been right. He should have gone to bed. If only Abbot had gagged him as soon as he'd entered the kitchen so he couldn't say anything stupid. But he hadn't, and Lepov did say something stupid. As tired as he was he could see how much it had hurt Lilly.

It was too late for Abbot to gag him, but the big soccer player did the next best thing. He put a hand on Lilly's shoulder and coaxed her out of the room.

75

MacNally wasn't very happy with his new roommate. The former Spaeth employee was quick to whine about their near-prison conditions. For MacNally's part, he didn't mind the windowless room. Sure, it was cold and damp. But he'd been on the receiving end of several shootings and he liked the fact that they were extremely secure in their pseudo-prison cell.

"How long will we have to be in here?" Frank Dassin held up yet another can and read the label. "Where did all of this food come from, the Arcobian Rebellion?"

"Dassin, go sit on your cot and shut up. This may not be a five-star hotel, but it's just what we need."

"It's not a three-star hotel. In fact, it isn't even a hotel."

"Yeah, well it was your fool idea to steal from Jonnie Spaeth. And for that I'm sitting in here with my gut covered in plastic." MacNally sat up and slid a hand under his shirt to probe the scrim. He slowly withdrew the hand and held it up to see it in the dim light. "Now that's an improvement. No blood."

"What are we doing here?" Dassin stretched out on the bed and lay staring at the ceiling. "My wife was kidnapped for God's sake!"

"How many times do you need to tell me that? I know it. My partner knows it. We're working on it."

"What do you mean you're working on it?" Dassin lifted his head and stared at MacNally. "You aren't—"

The first noise was too distant to pay it any mind but the second one was loud enough to cut Dassin's words short. A sharp ring of iron on iron held their attention. After some time, there were several more, and they were getting louder.

"Dassin, listen to me. You're gonna have to help me." MacNally grabbed a nearby water jug and took a few swigs. He washed his mouth out and swallowed. Next, he inched along the edge of the bed until he was leaning against the wall.

Outside, beyond the large iron containment door, they could hear a loud scraping noise. Followed by a heavy clang. After that came the rushing of water.

"Help you how?" Dassin watched the door with rapt attention.

"You see that rifle leaning in the corner? Yeah, the big one. Hand it to me right now."

Dassin, spurred on by MacNally's deadly earnestness, scrambled off his cot and grabbed the rifle. He handed it to MacNally then returned his attention to the door.

"Frank, you ever shoot a large caliber pistol?" When Dassin shook his head, MacNally pushed him away. "Get over in that corner and get down."

MacNally palmed the Panther from a small table by the bed and put it on the bed beside him. As he heard the water cease to run in the decon room, he pulled the table over just enough so that he could rest the Bushmaster on it. He winced a little as he wrapped his arms around the stock and settled in to wait.

After several more loud hammerings of iron on iron, the containment door began to unlock. MacNally reached over with his trigger finger and cut off the lights on their end of the room.

Under the glow of two white lights, the door swung open. There was the slimmest of chances that he'd see Russell and Lepov in their decon suits. However, at first he saw no one. Then, from the extreme edges of the decon room, he saw the first figure. A man with his decon jacket already off, hands wrapped around a weapon.

MacNally ignored the pain in his stomach and opened fire.

The figure tried to sprint into the room when MacNally missed him with his first rounds but as he ran forward the second burst of fire ripped into his chest and MacNally caught a fleeting glance of the man as he was jerked off his feet.

With no time to lose MacNally panned the muzzle of the Bushmaster from left to right, firing a fully automatic spread. He saw a yellow decon suit wave in the air as if someone were shaking it repeatedly.

Though he had stopped firing his hearing was completely gone. He looked in Dassin's direction and saw the man was lying on the floor. Had he been hit? He had no time to consider it. The Bushmaster was empty and instead of loading another clip he tossed it aside and grabbed the Panther.

He waited for several minutes. He was in no condition to stand up and move in on whoever was left in that decon room. It was obvious Dassin was in no condition to do it either.

He never saw any movement but the containment door began to close. MacNally was tempted to fire a few shots into the room just on principle but he had taken too many chances with ricochets already and he didn't want to press his luck as the opening narrowed then finally shut.

As soon as the door closed and the lock-rods rolled into place MacNally called to Dassin.

"You hit Dassin? Come on, get up!"

Dassin sat up, wild eyes staring at the containment door.

"What is going on?" Dassin was yelling but MacNally could barely hear him. Neither one of them would be able to hear properly any time soon.

"I told you there was a plan. It just started a little early. Come on, get me off the bed."

Dassin came to MacNally and helped him to his feet. Despite how bad he looked MacNally was able to remain upright as he pointed at a set of panels on a wall opposite the containment door.

"While I jam the door controls, you get those panels pulled down."

The two men worked in silence. MacNally pausing now and then to catch his breath. Dassin needed some visual prompting on what MacNally wanted him to do. As MacNally short-circuited the door panel, Dassin pried off three large sound-proofing panels that had been installed as a means of deadening the sounds in that all metal room.

Under the panels a red rectangle outlined a sealed emergency exit. Completely encircling the red border were numerous warnings in both large and small stenciled letters. Several languages were used as well. Dassin read several of them before he pointed them out to MacNally.

"Hey, don't jam that door, detective. This looks like a bad idea."

"What?" MacNally had heard him but he didn't feel like getting into an argument. He had one last technical step to complete and the door would be inoperable. He grabbed one of the metal chairs that sat around the table and rammed one of its legs into the panel, shattering the glass controls.

"Hey!" Dassin crossed the room and yanked the chair out of MacNally's hands. "Listen to me! You thought we could get out by that exit, but we can't. It has all these warnings. Come look at this."

MacNally followed him and looked to where Dassin was pointing.

ACCESS TO SHIPPING PROPER PROHIBITED
DECON ACCESS ONLY IN CASE OF ACTIVE BREACH
DECON PROTECTION INSUFFICIENT IN DIRECT CONTACT

"Would it help if I told you Abbot swore these warnings were just exaggeration?"

"This is an access to the main shipping bays. So what this is saying, down here, in the smaller print, is that our decon suits can't handle direct contact with the chemicals being sprayed over the cargo. Decon protection begins to fail after a given time frame based on the type of decon suit and the concentration of the chemicals contacting the suit. This chart, over here, breaks it all down so you can see—"

"Listen, Dassin. I know you're a numbers guy. So I'll give you some more numbers. Those were Spaeth's men out there. I'd guess three of them, and I got two of them. My guess is they didn't have enough suits to get more than three of them down here. But by now, the guy I didn't kill is on his way back to bring more men. Or he's still waiting out there and the other men were already going to join him once they got their hands on more decon suits. While it is possible to hold them off with that cannon I have, all they need are a few hand-poppers to toss through that door. We won't make it through another assault."

"I thought you said this had been some sort of plan." Dassin watched as MacNally fed a full clip into the Bushmaster and placed the Panther by the emergency exit.

"We knew someone would eventually pressure Russell into telling them where I was. And I wanted him to. We needed to find out who we could and couldn't trust. I wasn't about to sit here for the next year hiding from Jonnie Spaeth. I felt pretty confident they would come in here soft, not expecting me to be so heavily armed. The fact that I couldn't get that third man means he'll tell them to bring down more firepower than I can handle. So we go this way."

MacNally, winded from his efforts, told Dassin to fetch their decon suits. It took MacNally longer to get into his than Dassin. He continued to explain when he could.

"Abbot says the this exit takes us straight up two levels to the open port. We're still on the edge of the main bays, so our chances of getting caught in a direct chemical application are practically zero. We stay along the perimeter, and get to the next access ladder which will take us down to another safe room like this one. From there we can get out through one of the gates."

"This guy Abbot's reliable?" Dassin was ready to put on his hardshell faceplate. He held it out before snapping it in place, waiting for MacNally's answer.

"I don't know, Frank. I just met the guy a couple of nights ago. But he's already saved my life once." MacNally strapped the Bushmaster over Dassin's head and shoulder. The Panther was in a holster under MacNally's suit.

Faceplates on, they broke the seal on the exit hatch and had to work the heavy door free from its closed position. It felt like the hinges had never been used. They probably hadn't. There had been multiple coats of paint over them.

Behind the door they found a narrow vertical shaft with ladder rungs embedded in the back wall. As he started to climb, MacNally stubbornly ignored the pain that laced across his wounds. Dr. Duvalls was going to be angry at the damage MacNally was doing to all of his repair work. The only thing MacNally couldn't ignore was his sudden desire to scratch his nose.

76

The darkness had been overwhelming. Lara had spent far too much time on her hands and knees, just moving slowly, her fingers running along the floor until she would hit something. Twice she had hit her head on something protruding in the dark. This led her to move even slower, and reach ahead of her as far as possible while she kept her head down.

Unable to track time, she had no idea how many hours she had wasted. Twice she heard the guttural sound of a motor spin to life. It had been accompanied by a number of noises she could not comprehend. Some of them had to be the cables drawing the elevator cars. This terrified her, not knowing where the cables were. As soon as she heard the motor begin to churn she would drop to the floor and cover her head.

If only she could have found a light.

The first light she finally saw appeared when the motor kicked on for a third time. Something must have been blocking her view the first two times. This time, she could see a red light illuminating a panel some five or ten meters away. It was impossible to be sure of distances with all of the black shapes criss-crossing her field of vision.

Still frightened of any cables that might be spinning above her, she forced herself to use the red light as a guide and she moved as swiftly as she dared towards it. When the motor shut down, the eerie light cut off and Lara froze, trying to hold onto the image of what lay in front of her.

With no way of knowing how long it took her, she crept along until she hit a wire mesh barrier. She worked her way along the length of it, still wary of any protrusions that might endanger her head.

The motor growled to life and Lara nearly fell over from the shock. She must have been close enough to touch it. She saw, once the red light came back on, that it was just on the other side of the wire mesh.

The light was bright enough at this distance for her to stand up and circle around the motor to the panel with the red indicator light. Knowing she had precious few seconds before it cut off, she examined the panel for anything that might be a light switch. She began to panic, sure her red guide would soon shut off again. She began to feel along the edge of the panel, sliding her fingers along the grooves and beveled borders. She felt one finger catch against a sharp metal burr but she did not stop.

The toggle switch was on the bottom of the panel, on the underside. She felt the distinct shape of it and pushed it from left to right. A soft white light came on above her. She nearly cried with relief.

This light was far brighter than the smaller red light. With it illuminating its side of the room, Lara was able to move around without fear. She could easily see where she had been crawling. She was shocked to see she had only crossed about thirty meters of mostly open floor. At no time had she been in danger of hitting or catching her hair in any overhead cables. In fact, if she had walked upright, she would not even have hit her head on anything.

Still on edge from her imagined fears, she wanted to cry when she thought of all the time she had wasted.

The motor she'd been hearing did attach to a series of cable spools. The cables ran up into the darkness. Following them as best she could, she saw where they threaded through a hole high up on a wall. This was on the extreme edge of the light provided by her lamp.

Below this point she saw a short door, only about a meter tall. She pulled out a ring that could be twisted to unlatch the door. Once it was open, she saw that it was the access to an elevator shaft. Even with the door wide open, hardly any of the light penetrated this shaft beyond the first meter or so.

She could see a ladder on the far side of the shaft. A narrow grating no wider than one of her shoes ran around the edge of the shaft. To reach the ladder she would have to step out onto that lip. The far side of the shaft was too far to reach straight across. It must have been two meters deep.

Lara, operating on her basic need to survive, had not stopped to consider anything beyond that survival. But now, as she stared at the pitch black void below her, she did stop and try to decide if she should continue on.

Shirl had seemed to be making sense when she said Lara had to disappear, even if she couldn't escape. The idea that Frank would give himself up and jeopardize Jett sickened her stomach. Though it was Frank's fault for setting this nightmare in motion, it was her own fault for ignoring Frank and going to IHS alone. Maybe, if she hadn't gone, they would all have safely escaped Jonnie Spaeth. But now, as a result of her own, stubborn behavior, she had led them all straight into a disaster.

Shirl had been right. She couldn't go back. No matter how impossible it seemed, she would have to try and get through that shaft. That she should have searched the rest of the motor room occurred to her but she was firmly convinced she'd wasted too much time. They would be looking for her as soon as they checked her bedroom. And she had no idea how long she would need to traverse the shaft.

Judging by the size of the elevator she'd ridden to reach the suite, she felt sure there was plenty of room for her on the ladder if one rose up from below. It wouldn't make sense to install a ladder that would have put workers in the way of the moving cars.

One step on the narrow shelf would be enough for her to reach the ladder. Just a confident step to one side, a strong push with the foot, and she could reach out and grab a rung with both hands.

She had to try it.

Don't try, honey.

Lara thought of Jett. She knew he was just one step away. One quick step.

No going back. No time left. No cooperating with Jonnie Spaeth.

She squeezed through the small door, holding to the top of the opening as she stood straight, her back against the wall. A sliver of light hit the shelf where she needed to put that one step. Her body was blocking the rest of the light. She couldn't see the ladder rungs but she knew they would be there.

Don't try, honey. Just...

Lara let go of the opening, took a step to her right and pushed off for the ladder. She knew before she did it that it would be too far. Switching directions, she tried to grab at anything on the wall to her right. She felt the edge of a steel girder and her fingers clamped down on it. It was, in fact, a track for the elevator car. The groove was slick with grease and Lara had no chance of holding on to it.

Like Shirl, she'd never learned to pray. If she had, she would have tried to say a prayer for Jett before the first time she hit her head.

Book Three

Vengeance

77

When only one of the three men returned, the New Yorker knew they had been set up. It sounded like the Irishman had been waiting for them. Had maybe even lured them into that decon room.

The New Yorker watched dispassionately as the survivor stood on the edge of the decon room, his suit now slick with water and neutralizers. He started to take a step out of the room but a voice stopped him.

"Don't move. Not yet. Put your arms straight out and turn slowly around."

That was the shipper they'd brought with them. A local who knew the procedures. He had come willingly after taking a sizable payment. This had been an acceptable expense. No need to coerce a man to work for you when your health was at risk. Better that he should be working of his own free will.

"Stop!" The shipper stepped forward—not too closely—and visually examined the decon suit. "It's torn. Just under the arm, left side."

The survivor put his head down while lifting his arm high, trying to see the tear. When he lifted his arm he growled in pain. "I think I took a hit!"

He started unfastening the faceplate and jacket harness. The shipper did not stop him. He did, however, take two steps backwards. Once he shrugged off the jacket, the man could see his shirt was soaked in blood below his armpit.

"Are you serious?" He was more indignant than afraid. "I never even felt it!"

"Is he toxic?" The Right hand backed up a few steps. "I mean, with that hole in his suit, did he pick up—"

"No, I doubt it. He would have to have had the formula on him in liquid form."

Once the suit was fully removed he stepped out of the room and another man, a former medic, came forward to treat the wound. As he worked, the New Yorker questioned the survivor.

"Did you get a shot at him? Did you hit him?"

"No, I didn't get a shot at him." The man's tone bordered on petulance, but his heightened sense of alarm at the sight of the blood soaking into his pants was most likely the cause. "Like I said, he had a stutter gun that scared the hell out of me. I was the only one he didn't shoot to pieces—well I thought I made it out okay—because I was on the ground. It took everything I had just to move and hit the button to close the door."

"So after that?"

"After the door closed? I looked to see if my partner was alive—which he was not—and I couldn't check on the other one. But I'd seen him get cut in half as he rushed the target. It took me a few minutes to decide what I should do. I was wondering if I should try to get back in there but then I saw the access panel go dead. He killed the controls. That door won't open. So I came back here."

"I thought that room was a trap, no place to go." The New Yorker turned to stare accusingly at the shipper. "I thought you said he couldn't get out of there except through that door?"

"I don't think he can." The shipper pulled out a key and inserted it into a blank panel by the entrance. A menu appeared and he pulled up a schematic of the shipping port. He expanded the section they were in and began to trace the thin blue lines. "If he's in this safe room, which is just a place to use for any big time line breaches, he can't—"

The shipper leaned in close to the diagram and shook his head. "No, he wouldn't do that."

"Do what?"

"This one has an emergency ladder to the surface. Leads right up to the port proper. But he wouldn't do that. Too dangerous. One mistake with their suits and they're dead."

"More dangerous than waiting for us to come back with more firepower?"

"Well, in that case, if they really do this, they have to come out at one of the main access gates. Unless they find another ladder access back down...hmmm. They could, theoretically, go just about anywhere."

"Don't tell me that." The New Yorker put a hand on the shipper's shoulder and made sure he had his full attention. "If I could get you past that jammed door, and I made you climb that ladder, where would you go?"

"Okay, okay. I get it. Just let me think. I guess if he's clever—"

"Forget clever. He's on the run. He needs to move fast. How does he get out of here fast?"

"Well, that's not too hard to guess. He'd do this." He started to explain.

Russell knew they had taken a grave risk. He did not mind taking a risk if it was for the right reasons. It galled him, however, to know that in this situation, MacNally had actually taken all the risk. Russell had only been the one to set the trap.

Even before he'd sought out his transfer to the Lazaretto from

Arcobia, he had always imagined that the life of a police officer consisted of patrolling the streets in search of the nearest bad guy; there would always be a crook hanging around causing trouble and it would be Russell's job as a police officer—a good guy by his title alone—to stop them if possible, or catch them for the purposes of punishment. It had been his goal since he joined the force to always be in the middle of this exciting game.

But as he began to learn the life of the detective, he had found that there was much more to combating crooks than just walking the beat and knocking guys over the head with a baton. No longer were the crooks simple to spot—traditionally the guy running down the street was guilty of *something*, and chasing him was not only exhilarating but it was almost always rewarding once you caught him. Russell was learning that sometimes everyone was a suspect and none of them were foolish enough to run when the police started looking in their direction. Intimidation played no role in such cases. A detective's most effective tools were often half-truths, manipulation, and deception; to be more blunt, lies.

The most effective way to lie was to mix the lie with the truth. And Russell—with MacNally's approval—had done this with Jenkins and his new partner Kwan. He had not been surprised that MacNally's guess had been right. Someone, soon, would be asking where to find MacNally. MacNally had even added the detail that whoever asked about him would swear it was out of loyalty to MacNally that they were asking. He had been surprised, however, when both Jenkins and Kwan tried to pin down MacNally's hiding place.

He'd been forced to act quickly. Giving them a location for MacNally had been part of the original plan. Russell had to hope that MacNally had been ready. There was little doubt that either Jenkins or Kwan was going to give MacNally's location to Spaeth. For one thing, it was impossible to believe two detectives respected and cared enough about MacNally to stick out their neck for him.

And now, in the early morning, it was time to find out which one of them he could trust and which one of them had betrayed MacNally. To get things started, he stood at the entrance to his building and dashed through the rain once Kwan arrived to pick him up.

"You're on time," Russell said, wiping rain from his wet, curly bangs.

"Is that so remarkable?"

"It is to someone who's worked with MacNally."

"You're with me now, kid. Get used to it." She shuddered the engine and they began to rise rapidly. "Buckle up, I'm in a reckless mood. At this time of the morning, the police lanes should be empty.

I figured we'd take Masthead up to First Avenue before we cut over to Colony. From there we can enter the Shipping Port—I still can't believe that's what we're doing—at the central hub."

"No, don't do that. Just head straight out here. We'll swing around to the port from the West End."

"Why?" She cocked her head and gave him a funny look.

"Just trust me." Russell watched the street drop ever lower as she continued to ascend.

"You're the navigator. Off we go." She engaged the drive and Russell could tell she wanted to ask more questions. She chose, however, to channel her curiosity into her driving. It made for a very fast, very less than safe trip.

He tried to keep an eye on her without staring directly at her. By now she had to realize he was taking her to a different location than he'd told her the night before. If she had given away MacNally's position, she was showing no signs of distress at the thought that she'd passed on bad intel.

Either she was very cool under pressure, or she was one of the good guys. Russell hoped for the second option. Though he was reminded that she would never be a good *guy* as he caught yet another hint of her jasmine scent.

By the time he directed her to park in the warehouse bay he felt the first slick hint of fear. Had MacNally been able to handle himself? If he had been one hundred per cent healthy Russell would not have worried. As it was, he could not know if the old detective could hold his own against Spaeth.

Opening the door to the shipping port antechamber, Russell considered letting Kwan go ahead of him. If she was working for Spaeth, and she realized he had given her a bad address for MacNally, she might put a gun to his head and demand to know where MacNally really was. If she did, and she realized that she was now about to meet MacNally, she might go ahead and kill Russell before donning the decon suit. Once she made it to the safe room, she'd be able to keep MacNally off his guard long enough to extract the gun from her suit and put a bullet in his brain.

But it would look too suspicious to allow her in first. He was there to show her the way. He took the chance and stepped in ahead of her. His hand was inside his coat, his fingers wrapped around the grip. He would have very little time to react if she pulled her weapon.

As soon as they entered the room he knew Kwan was not the one to worry about. The room had obviously had visitors. The once Spartan room was now a mess and included a great deal of blood near the table where a discarded decon suit lay crumpled on the floor.

"Jenkins." Russell stood over the bloody suit and wondered if

MacNally was still alive. He removed his hand from his gun. Kwan saw the empty hand emerge from his coat.

"I guess that means I passed, huh?" She offered up a quick smile.

"Yep." Russell immediately began digging through the closet for clean decon suits.

"You suspected Jenkins, but you gave him the real location. You gave me the fake one. Why?"

"I didn't know there would be two of you who would push so hard to find MacNally."

"I wouldn't say I pushed so hard. I just asked where he was."

"Well, we had a feeling someone like Jenkins would insist on knowing where he was. And we were hoping we'd be right. We wanted Spaeth to come after him." He tossed a clean suit her way. "Get this on."

"We're going in?" She tore off the protective plastic and began to suit up. "MacNally didn't want to stay in hiding. That makes sense. Who knows how long he'd have had to keep his head down."

"Something like that. And yes, we're going in. From what I can see here, someone's been inside, and they came out wounded. If it had been MacNally, he would have left me a sign. But this has to be one of Spaeth's men. Did they kill MacNally, grab him, or miss him? Only one way to know."

"Tell me something before we go in there," she said, holding her faceplate in her hand. "If it had looked like no one had come, that MacNally was safe inside and no one had bothered him, would you have assumed that I'd sent them to the wrong address?"

"Yep." He pulled out his service weapon before he sealed his suit. He didn't want to wander around in there without a gun in his hand.

"And you would have done what, then, shot me?" She watched his hand with the gun with amusement.

"Yep. I would have if you had made a move for your own gun."

"That's good to know, partner." She started to put her faceplate in place when he stopped her with a question.

"Would you tell me one thing before we go in there?" When she nodded, he asked: "Why do you smell like jasmine?"

She stepped in close. "Don't start getting ideas, youngster. I've already slept with one cop. He was enough."

"What cop was that?" When Kwan just smiled in return, Russell didn't want to believe what she was suggesting. "You didn't. Not *him*."

"He was an attractive man. Still is, in fact."

"Still—now you're just trying to make me sick."

"Just try not to think about it, youngster."

"Believe me, I'm not," Russell said, shaking his head.

"And Russell," she tapped his gun hand, "you just be careful with that thing. Don't puncture my suit."

She snapped on the faceplate and entered the decon chamber. He followed her, still thinking about the sweet smell of jasmine even as he tried not to wonder how she could think MacNally was attractive. She had to be twenty years younger than the old man. MacNally should have been ashamed of himself. Russell saw no irony in the fact that he found Kwan attractive, even though she was at least ten years his senior.

Wanting to rush, to get to MacNally as quickly as possible, he forced them to go slow, in case any of Spaeth's men were still in the tunnels. But they saw no one, and reached the outer door to the decon chamber of MacNally's safe room.

His gun hand was now up, and he moved toward the outer door slowly. It was open. He signaled for Kwan to stay back but she ignored him as he had expected her to. She had her own gun at the ready and if he hadn't kept moving toward the open door she would have elbowed him out of the way.

The chamber was a mess. A man lay in the center of it, his decon suit, though still on him, was torn up as if it had been caught in a grinder. Most of it was covered in the man's blood. The faceplate was splintered—it had taken a direct hit. What they could see of the man was not much. But he was far too small to be MacNally.

"Try the door," she said to him. Her voice carried easily through the comm unit. Russell shook his head.

"We'd have to close the outer door then run the decon wash before we could see if the door would work. And I can see that the inner door panel has no power. MacNally's plan had been to see who showed up then shut them out and kill the door so it couldn't be opened again."

"Well, that sounds reasonable. There is another way out, I suppose?"

"Yeah, he's taken Dassin—if they're both alive—out a back exit. It would take him up into the shipping proper, but they'll be okay. We just need to find them and get them safely out of here."

"And we grab Jenkins."

"I don't grab Jenkins, I don't know about you. But I hardly have the evidence to grab my boss. He's not the imminent threat now anyway. If Spaeth was no longer out there in the anteroom, then that means they have an idea on how to find MacNally down here, or they'd be here, trying to break through this door."

"So we go back out the way we came in? I'm hoping you have an idea where MacNally is headed."

"Yep."

"You know, Russell, I'm glad you didn't try to shoot me. You're a lot of fun. It would have been a shame if I'd have had to kill you."

She headed back down the tunnel, and Russell did the same. As they walked, two things weighed on his mind. He wondered what his odds would have been of shooting her before she had been able to shoot him. Watching her walk with strength and grace in the ungainly decon suit, he had a feeling the odds wouldn't have been in his favor. The other thing on his mind was more troubling:

He just couldn't get a handle on her stunning assertion: MacNally *attractive*?

79

She was awake before Gregor. She had hoped to slip away before Gregor or Bril could see her but the big, kind-faced Transit driver was in the kitchen. As always, he had coffee available and poured her a cup.

"You're all dressed and ready to go somewhere, aren't you?" he asked casually. She had expected him to be anything but casual when he realized she had intended to leave.

"I have something I need to do. I won't be long." She knew that sounded weak.

"I could drive you." He wasn't insistent but she could see the concern in his eyes.

"I'll be okay. You may need to drive Gregor, or he'll need your car. Which leads me to a question, if you don't mind my asking one."

"I can guess," he said after chuckling. Lilly decided it was a wonderful laugh. "*Why* am I helping out?"

"You do sort of seem…well, too good to be true," she said.

"You know, I've been asking myself the same question all night. It's why I heard that Gloria leave and why I was up when Lepov came in. I might have been in my room early, but I couldn't sleep. I kept saying, 'Bril, what are you doing with these people? They're gonna get you killed.' And no matter how I look at it, no matter what I say in response, I keep coming to one conclusion: I probably will get killed, and I just don't care anymore, as long as I can do something good for someone. Just once."

"I have a feeling you're being overly modest."

"No, I'm sorry to say it, but I'm not. You see, when you're a big sports celebrity like I was, then you learn quickly that the world loves you, they'll throw money and women, and anything else your way, and you don't ever have to think or care about anyone else again unless you just want to. And to tell you the truth, Miss Lilly, I didn't want to. I was just happy being happy. It's a pretty good gig. A very satisfying one. Don't let people fool you. They'll tell you that money doesn't make you happy. Well, if you can say that, you're one easily dissatisfied customer, let me tell you. No, money and celebrity makes you pretty happy. Anyone who tells you different is just trying to head off other people's envy.

"Now I never said money was fulfilling. Don't mistake the difference. Happiness can be pretty empty. But still, it's happiness. And you can keep happy enough to stay distracted. That's not hard. And that's what I did. Right up until the day I was sitting there in Delta quadrant, planning my triumphant arrival on Earth. I had a girl with me who couldn't get enough of me—which was only true until she heard I was sick—and I had enough drugs to get me through quarantine without the need to spend one day clean and sober. And then it all just evaporated.

"The girl left me—or rather, when IHS escorted me out she chose to stay in Delta. The drugs were confiscated by IHS—and I doubt any officials at IHS ever knew about them—and I spent my money trying to remove my exile status."

He'd kept his casual tone right up until that last statement.

"I didn't have the sense enough to save what money I had to take care of myself here. And I certainly never considered how bad off other people had it here. I just knew that I—Bril Abbot, the best leg in the Euxine League—got a raw deal and deserved better."

"But you learned quickly that you weren't alone?"

"Hell, no. Pardon my language, but it took me a long time to figure it out. It wasn't until I started driving TransitCars that I began to listen to my fares, began to hear the stories of all the people trapped on this crazy moon. I was amazed to discover not just that other people had problems like my own—I found that most people had far bigger problems than I had. I had this crazy notion that since I had so much to lose—money, celebrity, almost the whole Euxine system in my palm—that I experienced the pain of loss far more than common people who had nothing to lose.

"I knew what it was like to have fortune smile on me for a while. But I listened to people who had never seen fortune's smiling face, no matter how fickle it could be. They'd never felt the warm love of another human being, never known the assurance of financial security. They'd never spent a lifetime, a year, or even a day chasing their dreams. They'd been too busy fleeing their nightmares. Ever afraid that their families might starve, or their few friends would desert them. This was all they knew."

Bril tapped his fingers on the rim of his empty coffee cup. Lilly's silence was encouragement enough to keep him talking.

"So I've tried to change that. Though I no longer have the money I once did, I look for ways to help people out. Just being friendly to them is a treat on this world. It's just something I can do for people who are in need.

"And then one day, an old cop is shot down in front of me, and he doesn't give up, he crawls toward my car with his chest cut to ribbons. And I have to jump out of my car and nearly pull my back out of joint throwing him in the back seat. So now I'm in it. And I'm in it till it's over. Today the job is to watch over you and that boy and let Lepov sleep. And he'd be pretty mad if I let you walk out that door."

Lilly leaned forward and put her hand on top of Bril's much larger hand.

"Please, don't stop me. You could, easily enough, but I'm asking you not to. I won't be in any danger. There's just something I have to do. Please?"

She refused to take her eyes away from his. She felt as if she could force him to agree to look the other way as long as she kept his eyes and her eyes locked together.

"I could see he was mad at that other woman when he heard she walked out of here. But I get the feeling he wouldn't be mad at you, dear, if I let you walk out. He'll be mad at me. And he doesn't seem like I'd want to be around him when he's mad. Especially when he's mad at me."

"He's all bluff." Lilly squeezed his hand. "And you're wrong, he'll be mad at me, not you."

"Well, I don't know if Lepov is all bluff or not, but I suppose you're gonna find out that when it comes to saying no to beautiful women, all I've ever been was an old bluffer."

When she tried to thank him with a hug he pulled away from her.

"You forget I'm...one of the untouchables. You shouldn't have even been touching my hands."

"I'm not afraid," Lilly said.

She slipped quietly out the door and began to walk in the direction of the SubTransit station. Only light rain fell on her black umbrella. She walked quickly, irrationally worried that Gregor would have time to run down the street and stop her.

She wasn't surprised at all when she saw Shay waiting for her at the top of the station steps. He ducked under her umbrella and put an arm around her as they dropped out of sight into the station.

80

"Grey!"

He looked up from his desk, put out a hand to interrupt his partner's boring anecdote, and grinned when he saw Gloria gliding across the office floor.

"Hello, glorious!" He dropped his feet from his desk in time as she dropped into his lap. "You know what? I had a feeling this would be my lucky day."

"You haven't gotten lucky yet, but stick around." She kissed him as she tossed an impish look toward his partner.

"I should arrest you two for making a public nuisance—and I could throw in a charge of making everyone here sick." Shojen Weig, the interrupted partner, jumped up from his chair and swiped his hat off his desk. "But instead I think I'll go get some lunch and then maybe disappear for, oh, say, two or three hours. I have a feeling my partner won't be available until then. You think maybe by then you'll be interested in returning to work for some...*work*, maybe?"

"Now you see that," Lepov said to Gloria after catching his breath, "the man hasn't officially been promoted to Captain yet and he's already nagging me about work. I may just have to shoot him his first day on the job. But then, come to think of it, they'd probably give the job to me, and I'm not made for all that prestige and responsibility. No, I guess I can't shoot this poor old man. Not until he gives me a solid reason."

"I won't keep him longer than two hours, will that be okay, Mr. Officer?" Gloria held out her hand and Weig pulled her to her feet. She wrapped her arms around him and whispered in his ear.

"No, don't call him Officer, that's too low in the pecking order now—hey, watch what you're doing with my woman, there Weig. I get kind of jealous when I see my wife nibbling on another man's ear."

"What's that?" Weig pushed her an arm's length away. "I couldn't hear you, partner, I had a Gloria in my ear."

"Would this help?" Lepov unholstered his revolver and slowly swung the barrel until it was pointing at Weig.

"Grey! That isn't funny! You shouldn't point a loaded gun. Don't you always tell me that?"

"Oh, don't worry about that, Lori. This is Wednesday. We cops only load our guns on Tuesdays and Thursdays. Or is that we cops only get loaded on Fridays and Saturdays?"

He shoved the gun back into its holster and this time it was Gloria who was pulling Lepov to his feet. Weig left with a flourish and Lepov and Gloria wandered out into the Bukovinan sunshine for a walk through the park across the street.

"Will they give you a new partner, when Shojen gets promoted?" Her arm was tucked inside the arm he'd offered. She had a habit of walking slightly off-balance, as if she'd been drinking, and she often fell into him. He would simply lift her back to her feet.

"First of all, the promotion's not official, and they could always give it to Toste. But no one really thinks that'll happen. And yes, when he takes that great step up into the heavenly realms, I'll be stuck down here with a new partner. Why, you applying for the job?"

"That's an interesting thought, of course." Her arm tightened on him as she nearly fell over. "You think you might get a female partner?"

"What's this, jealousy?"

"No, I was just curious."

"Lori, I've been a cop a long time now. And I've never found one that could even remotely compare to you. Now what's really on your mind? You didn't come down here to tell me you were worried about me getting a female partner."

"I was just—" she shrugged, unable to look at him.

"Well?"

"Well, you're the detective, you should be able to guess."

"If I had to guess I'd say you were bored."

She laid her head on his shoulder and he knew he'd been right. He couldn't understand that. He provided her with a comfortable home and just about anything she could reasonably ask for. He had even encouraged her to return to school to earn a degree in anything she'd like. The department would pay for it and he just wanted her to be happy.

But that was Gloria. No matter what was going on in her life she was still always just on the edge of dissatisfaction and restlessness. He'd once thought it was his fault, but he was slowly learning it had nothing to do with him.

"I was just going to tell you that you've got to stop him."

"What?" Lepov grabbed her arm and spun her so that they were face to face. "What did you just say?"

"He's going to kill me, Grey. Stop him!" She jerked away from Lepov and broke out into a run. It was then that he saw the great hulking figure of Kry Dannen rushing after her. By the time Lepov began to chase him he was already too late. He began to run, knowing he would never get there in time. He reached for the gun in his shoulder holster and began patting inside his coat frantically. His gun was gone.

And then he could see that Gloria had his gun, and as she ran, she reached back and tried to shoot Dannen. One shot crackled as she continued to run. A second shot followed. Then, in desperation, she stopped, turned quickly, and pulled the trigger. Dannen kept running, unaffected by her errant shot.

Lepov looked down and saw the blood soak through the center of his shirt. The blood was so bright red he at first thought someone had splashed paint over him. He ran for three more steps before he had to stop.

"Grey!" Gloria threw down the gun. "Grey!"

Her scream pierced the veil of sleep under which he'd been hiding. With a determined heave he sat up in bed and looked down at his chest. It had not been an accurate memory. It had not entirely been a dream. It was certainly fair to say that Gloria had been bored. It had also been relatively accurate to suggest she'd shot him through the heart when she'd broken it.

She might as well have.

He was on the sofa in the front room. He stood up and began to search the house. After checking the back bedrooms he ended up in the kitchen. Abbot was serving lunch to Jett.

"Hungry?" Abbot asked.

"She never showed up?" Abbot shook his head and Lepov swore. He saw the look on the big man's face and he immediately looked at the boy. "Sorry."

"Maybe she's at your office?"

"No, the door system would have sent me a message." Lepov suddenly looked around the room. "Did I actually catch you without any coffee ready?"

"No, I filled the warmer up, over there. It'll still be hot." He pointed out a white carafe. "Stays hot enough for me all day in that thing."

Lepov took some and sat down next to Jett.

"How's this one holding up?"

"I'm five." The boy stared at Lepov.

"Yes, well that's pretty good. Married yet?"

Jett shook his head, a puzzled expression clouding his childish face.

"Good for you. Stay away from women, they'll stunt your growth."

"They never did for me," Abbot offered.

"Did you ever marry one?" When Abbot shook his head Lepov nodded, sure that he'd made his point without the need for further words.

"You don't look like you slept enough." Abbot poured more coffee for him.

"I haven't slept enough since...well since Gloria left."

"That was just yesterday."

"No, I meant when she left...you know." Lepov poured the whole cup of coffee down his throat. When he saw Jett staring at him he leaned over and muttered: "don't try that at home. Especially when it's still hot."

"You want me to drive you somewhere?" Abbot asked as Lepov began to pull on his coat. Once he was ready he bent down and picked up the black case.

"I'd rather use your car again if you're willing to let me."

"I'm willing, I guess. But a man who's had as little sleep as you shouldn't be driving. I'm worried about you." Abbot waited until Lepov's hand was on the door knob before he spoke again. "Aren't you even going to ask about her?"

"I thought I already did. Don't worry, I have an idea on how to find her."

"I wasn't talking about Gloria. I was talking about Lilly."

Lepov had the door open now, and the sound of rain and distant thunder helped to cover the awkward silence in the room. Until Abbot said her name he had forgotten Lilly should have been in the house.

"Where is she?" He couldn't honestly say he wanted to know right then.

"She left a few hours ago, walked to the SubTransit station alone. She asked me not to stop her so I didn't. She said she just had something to do and then she'd be back. I don't think she means to come back."

"So you're an expert now, on women?" Lepov regretted his tone and tried to soften it. "Hell, you probably know more than I do. As for Lilly, she'll be alright. She's not going anywhere. And thanks. For telling me about her."

He kept his back toward Abbot and the boy as he spoke. There was no reason to try and explain himself. No reason to make excuses. Lilly was a worry for another day. He had to keep focused on Gloria. He still wasn't sure what he would have to do to get Gloria free of Kry Dannen. But Lepov was willing to do whatever it took.

81

They had tried to follow Abbot's plan once they left the ladder shaft. Startled by the massive size of the shipping bays and the ominous automated sprayers that hung over their heads—dormant at that time, fortunately—they hurried as much as possible in the decon suits in the direction of the next shaft. Frank had not been surprised to see that the shaft was sealed shut.

He had not had any confidence in the plan that MacNally had

boasted of. They had been relying too much on the black man's outdated information. They should have known it would eventually foil their attempts to escape.

But the cop had been unflappable. He hadn't even paused to complain about the sealed shaft. It hadn't been until hours later when Frank realized that MacNally had known they were on borrowed time. Their decon atmospherics, while capable of re-scrubbing air, were always slowly falling behind. Eventually they would have run out of air.

And that had been the deciding factor in MacNally's decision to simply find the nearest manned access gate and walk right out.

The most harrowing part of their walk through the port had been the one shipping bay that had been active. Though they had not been forced to enter it, the overspray from it fogged their faceplates. This had been the last straw. They'd abandoned all pretense of stealth and made straight for a brightly lit access gate.

Banging on the outer door of a decon room, they had to wait about two minutes before it finally opened up for them. Once inside, and the outer door closed, they were happy enough to allow the purging water to abuse and assault them. The process went far too quickly, and despite their knowledge that their air was beginning to taste more than just stale, they were hesitant to break the seals on their suits.

"Are you sure?" Frank asked the technicians who stood just outside the decon room looking in. "Shouldn't you run some tests or something?"

The technicians, obviously confused that two men would suddenly appear from out of the shipping port, nodded, though his own uncertainty was readily apparent.

MacNally muttered one of his usual curses and finally reached up and snapped off his faceplate. As soon as he yanked off his coat, which included fully encapsulated gloves, he reached up and scratched his nose.

"Oh, God, that's fantastic." His extended groans of pleasure were nearly obscene. "I will shoot the next man that tries to make me wear another decon suit."

The technician backed up four or five steps. He was eyeing the big rifle that Frank had been carrying. MacNally had it now, as he'd taken it from Frank just about an hour before they made it into decon.

"Where did you guys come from?" The man finally found his voice.

"We can't tell you that," MacNally began to search his pockets. "I'm with the police department—oh, come on, where's my badge? Are you telling me I dropped it somewhere out there?" He stared accusingly at the technician as he pointed back toward the decon room.

"I don't think you could have dropped it out there. Your suit's fully encapsulated. Wouldn't it still be in your suit somewhere?"

"Yeah, I guess it would. You sure brought me some peace of mind, son. Keep up what you're doing. I can't tell you what we're doing or who we are, but I can tell you that your job is a bastion of great importance. Keep on the job. And if anyone asks, you didn't see us."

"Excuse me?" the man asked with a hefty dose of incredulity.

"No, excuse me. We're in your way, just go on with what you were doing, we'll get out of your way."

MacNally grabbed Frank by the arm and dragged him through the access gate.

MacNally estimated they had about five to ten minutes before the alarm sounded.

"You can always count on people's inability to make a quick decision. That guy will tell his boss, who'll wonder if IHS or the LPD was supposed to be running a drill today. He won't want to report this but it'll slowly work its way up the chain since no one will have the sense to simply ignore us and let us walk away."

"Then what?" Frank asked.

"Then," MacNally had reached a door and he reached out and tapped it with his finger, "we'd better be on the other side of this door. And we'd better hope Jonnie Spaeth isn't standing on the other side of it waiting for us."

Frank held back as the big cop eased the door open and led with that massive handgun he liked to carry. Frank was carrying the rifle again. His shoulder had rubbed raw during their trek through the shipping port. But he knew that MacNally was having his own problems. He was gradually losing height, slumping more as he walked. It was obvious the man's chest was bothering him.

"Have you got a plan once we're out of here?" Frank glanced around at the trucks and smaller vehicles that were lined up haphazardly along the wall near the door they'd just come through.

"Technically, we're out of *here*. But we're far from where I want to be. Come on."

MacNally pulled himself up a little straighter and looked to Frank like he was about to pass out. Then he headed across a street that ran parallel to the wall, a light rain falling on them as they moved in the gloom of the shrouded noontime sun.

"We aim for that." He pointed at a street that ran up a gentle incline toward the crest of a hill. "I'll explain when we reach the top."

Reaching the top had not been as easy as MacNally had made it sound. Then again, the gentle incline had not been as gentle as Frank had first thought it would be.

They were near the top when they heard the vehicles back at the base of the hill. Two box trucks much like the one they'd seen when Lara was taken stopped near the gate they'd passed through. It was tempting to stop and watch the activity below them but MacNally hurried Frank along. They needed to get over the crest of the hill.

As soon as they did, MacNally grabbed Frank and pulled him off the street. A low wall separated two driveways that led to two old rolling garage doors in what looked to be an abandoned row of storehouses. He pulled them to the far side of the wall and sank down against it.

"Give me that rifle and then catch your breath." MacNally reached over and tried to pull the rifle off Frank's shoulder.

"Just hold on. You don't look like you can fire this thing anymore. You think both trucks will come up the hill?"

"No," MacNally shook his head and Frank wasn't sure if it was a way of confirming his negative statement or if he was just trying to clear his head. "Just one of them. They'll split up to see if they can find us faster. It's why I had to get on this side. Don't want the other truck hearing us too easily. And I'm fine. Give me that damned gun."

"I'll do it." Frank unslung the Bushmaster, turning to kneel so that he could rest the barrel of the rifle on top of the wall.

"You don't know what you're doing."

"So tell me. And you'd better hurry. I hear an engine."

"Dammit, Dassin! Okay, look, pull it in tight, come on. This thing will knock your head off if you don't get it right. That's it. Here, let me see. Okay, it's gonna fire three rounds at a time. Don't just hold down the trigger. It'll walk all over on you. Get your elbows up on the wall, here, like this. Come on, I can hear them too. Don't screw this up."

"Okay, okay." Dassin leaned into the wall, he was too tall to keep his back straight. "What am I aiming for?"

"You aren't. Just point it there, about ten meters past the crest of the hill. Once they're over the crest, you just want to hit them. Anywhere. You aren't trying to kill every man on that truck. Just scare the hell out of them and make them drive it off the road. And whatever you do, don't track them so long that you end up shooting at me as they go past. You got it?"

Dassin didn't answer. He was nervous, he could feel his hands shaking. He tried to block it out. The truck was loud now. He knew it would come into sight at any moment. Trying to visualize ten meters ahead of the crest, he felt his mouth go dry.

They'd had nothing to drink since the shooting in the safe room.

The wash of headlights jumped up and over the crest of the hill and the truck overshot the crest, rising a good fifteen meters into the air. The driver allowed it to rise, not fighting the forces of momentum that set them airborne. For one frozen moment Frank thought the truck would just go ahead and ascend to one of the lower driving/flying lanes. If so, their chance to hit the truck would vanish. Perhaps they would never get another chance to find Lara.

And in that same frozen moment Frank suddenly wondered why they were risking Lara's life by firing on the people who held her? But it was too late. They'd already killed those men back in the decon room. Frank pulled the Bushmaster in tight and fired.

At first he thought he'd missed completely. It even looked as if those in the truck had not even noticed he was firing. But then he no longer had a frozen moment to examine what was happening. And he was never quite sure what actually did happen next.

The truck seemed to list to one side before dropping its nose and staring straight at Frank with its brilliantly white eyes. One of them winked out. Something exploded next to Frank. MacNally was shouting *Fire! Frank!* and then something slammed Frank in his shoulder about the same time that the front of the truck exploded into a shower of glass and terrifying thunder.

Then MacNally shoved Frank to the ground, or Frank dove to the ground or the ground reached up and jerked Frank by his collar. He never could be sure which of those three things happened. Perhaps all three of them did. But when he rolled over on the rifle, burning himself on the hot barrel, he heard MacNally curse as the wall seemed to explode around them.

When he finally opened his eyes, the only sound he heard was the thrum of the falling rain. He still felt the pain of the burn on his hand from the hot rifle. The rain on his lips was a welcome relief. He tried to leave his mouth open enough to catch whatever water he could.

"Frank," MacNally's voice was low but desperate. "I dropped the Panther. Where's the Bushmaster?"

He felt around in the debris from the wall until he realized he was still clutching it with his other hand.

"Someone's moving on the other side of that wall. Hand it to me, quick."

There wasn't enough time to hand him the gun. Frank lifted it, got his finger on the trigger, and tried to see through the falling rain. A shadow loomed over him and he never even wondered if he was endangering Lara as he fired two short bursts. The shadow disappeared.

"Give me that," MacNally jerked the gun out of his hands and peered up and over the remains of the wall. When Frank did the same he saw the truck against the wall. It was a busted mess. The driver was now just a dead part of the truck, fused with the glass and steel frame. Lying just a meter from Frank was what was left of the shadow he had hit at close range. Frank should have thrown up at the sight but he was too shaken to respond with sensibilities that were no longer functioning.

"That made a bigger mess than I meant to make. More importantly," MacNally said, scanning his side of the truck for movement, "it was nosier. That other truck might have heard us. We have to move. And the bad news is, I don't know if I can."

"You can." Frank shouldered the rifle again, and gingerly took one of MacNally's arms, draping it over his neck. "Where to now?"

"You still gonna ask me that after I nearly got us killed?"

"We're still alive, which is a miracle. And I'm the one that insisted I could shoot this damned thing. I'm giving you the benefit of the doubt. And next time, you do the shooting."

"Don't sell yourself short, Dassin." MacNally grunted as Dassin adjusted his hold on the detective. "Hell, I've never seen a man shoot a truck out of the sky before."

"Well, I've done a little hunting in my day. But it's been awhile."

"I didn't know you could hunt trucks, Dassin."

Frank didn't say it but he was pretty sure that if MacNally couldn't get moving any faster, they were not only sure to be hunted, but they were going to end up as dead as that truck.

82

"You've lost your mind, Shay." Lilly stood just inside the tree line of Terran Park. The trees sheltered her from the falling rain, allowing only errant drips to hit her uncovered head. Shay was beside her, leaning against the tree. "I can't believe you would suggest that."

"But why not? Why not leave with me? You've had time to think about it since I first suggested it. Don't tell me you haven't been considering it. I know you, Lilly. You like to act cold and distant with everyone you meet but you forget I found out your secret. I know what's behind that proud façade. Lilly the Logical? Hmm, hardly. Lilly the Sentimental. That's the girl I discovered under there."

"Sentimental fool, maybe. But that doesn't mean I'm completely stupid." She scanned the park entrance watching for Gregor. She had no way of knowing which entrance he would use or where in the park he intended to meet with Kry Dannen but she was trusting to luck. She had precious few options.

"I just don't see how leaving this rock with me would make you completely stupid." He sounded hurt but she knew Shay Stewart was never really as hurt as he liked to let on. "You want to talk about stupid you might look at what you're doing out here: standing bare-headed in the rain waiting for your dull-minded private detective to arrive and save his ex-wife from a fate no worse than she deserves."

"And you're standing bare-headed in the rain waiting for your dull-minded ex-wife to decide to run off with the man who just escaped from the jail she put him in."

"Well, I'll agree with you on that one, Lilly. I really should have put on a hat." He rubbed his hair with an open hand. "This never happened on the prison barge."

"Why weren't you there when I brought Gregor to talk to you? Why wouldn't you talk to him?"

"I would have thought that was self-evident, dear." She could see his frustration as he reached up to snatch a twig from the branches above him. He tore the little twig to pieces and tossed it into the wind. "Don't you think I have enough sense to know that with him by your side he'll keep you from listening to me? A man knows when he's lost the respect of his wife. Knows when she's begun to listen to another man and no longer sees her husband as someone with an opinion that matters."

"Shay, for God's sake, I'm not your wife anymore! And if you know I'm no longer listening to you, then why are you here?"

"Can't a fella believe in second chances? Would you deny me this one chance to talk you into coming away with me? To start over? To try again? A little wiser, a little older, and maybe even a little more humble?"

She had wanted to say yes, she wanted to deny him all of that, but right then she saw Gloria and a tall, older man enter the park. The man must be her husband. He walked with a grand bearing, ignoring the rain. Gloria hurried along beside him, her arm in his. She too walked with a measured grace.

No, Lilly realized, she couldn't shut out Shay completely. Ever since she'd seen Gloria in Gregor's office she had known that woman had been up to no good. It was equally obvious that Gregor could not see it. She had an idea that if Gloria had her way—and that seemed quite likely—then she, Lilly, would never get a chance to find some peace and happiness with Gregor.

And if that happened, then Shay was right; why shouldn't she go away with him? After all, he had escaped from Conde Sur. Who's to say he couldn't get the two of them out of the Lazaretto?

She watched Gloria and her husband disappear into the trees as they followed a walking path. Lilly, watching briefly to make sure

Gregor did not immediately appear, began moving through the trees in an attempt to follow the Dannens. Sighing with exaggeration, Shay pushed off from the tree and followed.

83

"You'd better tell me about it." The New Yorker stood in the doorway of the bedroom, staring at the Ursuline who was still curled up in bed, despite the fact that half of the day was gone. "Get up and start talking."

"You never came back to bed last night. I was getting worried." She tried to giggle but he could hear the fear in her voice.

After they'd lost the Irishman and the Swede in the Shipping Port he had decided to come back and get the Swede's wife. With her they might have had a chance to force the Swede—and maybe even that troublemaking Irishman—to give themselves up. But when he'd arrived the Australian had called him into his office to tell him that the woman had been found dead at the bottom of an elevator shaft. After examining the shaft and the motor room from which she must have fallen, they found the hole in the wall that led to his bedroom. *His* bedroom.

The Australian had not interrogated the Ursuline yet. He had left that for the New Yorker. He had not wanted to step on the New Yorker's toes. This was, the Australian insisted, the New Yorker's problem. In truth, the New Yorker was sure this was a test of his loyalty. There was no way he could show the Ursuline any leniency in this situation.

"Did you know these friends of yours locked me in here this morning?" She sat up and tried to display indignation at the two men standing behind him. "That's why I'm still in bed. Thank God I had clothes in here or I—"

He jerked a corner of the bed, spinning it away from the wall, partially exposing the imperfectly covered hole in the wall. He kicked the bed further. The girl lost her balance and cried out as she tumbled sideways and rolled off the bed. Now the scar in the wall was plainly visible.

He bent down, grabbed the back of her neck, picked her up and threw her back onto a corner of the bed. She rolled across it and hit the floor again, this time landing just a hand's width from the hole in the wall.

"Get out of here." He turned around, ordering his men back to the elevator. "When I'm done with her I'm gonna find out which one of you Arcobian *tookrahs* allowed two women to engineer an escape."

"The lady didn't escape!" One of the men thought this was a

debate.

"She's dead! She's of no use to us now, and that's as bad as her escaping. Probably worse!" He would have smacked both of them if the elevator doors hadn't started to close.

Spinning back around he charged into the bedroom and saw that the Ursuline hadn't moved. She was curled up in a ball, her hands clasped around her drawn up knees, and he was sure she was whispering a mile a minute. To who he had no idea.

He sat down on the bed near her, reached down and picked her up with both arms. He could feel her curl even tighter.

"You dumb broad." He set her carefully on the bed, allowing her to roll away from him, still curled in her protective shell. She was still whispering though he still could not make out a word she was saying. "What were you thinking?"

He leaned over her and she tucked her chin in an effort to hide her face as he ran a finger over the curls of hair that covered her forehead.

"Did she really die?" The words were almost impossible to decipher. She'd nearly shouted them.

"Yeah, she really did." There wasn't much more to say. She started sobbing, her body wracked by the effort.

"You've got a good heart, I get it. And you did what you thought was gonna help her. Don't punish yourself. You couldn't know that fool of a woman would die."

"You're wrong!" Her hands broke free and she looked up into his eyes. Her own eyes glistened with tears, highlighting her torment. "I did know. I told her—told it was better to die than not escape. She wasn't going to let you use her to catch her son and her husband. Have you ever loved anyone enough to do what she did? Could you? I know I couldn't. I would want to. But I couldn't! So go ahead, call me a dumb broad. I don't care. I am. I'm a cowardly one too. But don't you call that woman a fool. She was more noble and more—*anything* than you'll ever be.

"So if you're gonna beat me, get it over with. I know you don't have a choice. You got to do it because if you don't *he's* gonna do it. And when he does, he won't stop until I'm dead. So go ahead. You make it look good. And you won't even have to be careful around my jaw since you're not even doing this to make me talk. You're just doing it make me sorry. But even there you're gonna fail. And I won't even hate you. See, I learned this prayer, I wish I'd learned it yesterday to say for Lara. But I learned it today. And I been saying it all day. And the good news for you is that the prayer is for your benefit too. Cause I'm asking for God to help me forgive those who hurt me."

The New Yorker listened to her talk and knew that no matter how crazy she sounded she was right about one thing. He didn't have a choice. He'd considered just leaving her there, in the bed, and going back out in search of the Irishman. But before he did he was gonna have to do exactly as she said.

She really was a bright young girl. She really was shrewder than he had ever given her credit. Because she couldn't have been more right when she said that if he didn't hurt her now, the Australian will hurt her until he killed her.

She rolled away from him, and this time, he could understand her.

"My Father, who is in the heavens…"

The New Yorker stood up, kicked at an oak, bedside table until it snapped apart, and wrapped his fingers around a broken table leg.

##

MacNally wasn't coming. Russell had finally concluded that either MacNally was dead, he'd been taken by Spaeth, or he was lost in the Shipping Port. There was just no way of finding out which scenario was the right one. He hoped there was a fourth one: maybe the old man had found another way out of there. But if he had, Russell couldn't think of what it would be.

"Ideas?" He looked down at Kwan, who was sitting in the driver's seat of her car. It had looked like she was sleeping but he knew better.

"I don't like to be obvious but I have to ask. You are sure this is where he would come out?"

They were parked across the street from the port, near an access door much like the one they'd used to first enter that underground labyrinth. Russell had climbed out to stretch his legs.

"Yep."

"Could he have come out much earlier, and already left?"

"It's possible. But he knew I was going to come looking for him. He'd have left a sign."

"Scratch mark on the wall, secret society kind of thing?"

"Something like that." He didn't take offense at her mockery. He knew she was nervous, worried about MacNally.

"We assume he's alive. And still mobile. Otherwise we'd just give up." She joined him outside the car. Her anxiety was easy to spot by her edgy behavior. "So that means he didn't come this way because something prevented that. So where does he go next?"

"I don't know enough about the port to make a guess." Russell thought a moment. "It's just too big. There are too many access points to cover."

"What would you say to bringing more officers in on this. They can't all be Spaeth men."

"I'm sure they aren't, but if you don't know which ones are, it doesn't really matter how many there are. We talk to the wrong guy—"

"—or woman. Don't be sexist. Women can be corrupt too."

"I'll try to remember that. What I meant was, it would be best to talk to the right guy. And I know who that is. And he doesn't work for the force anymore."

"Pete Landon?"

"Yep," Russell nodded. "He might be able to get us a schematic of the port, or anything else that's useful."

They did not want to use any communications that could be compromised so they went looking for the puzzle man. They found him at his place. He was in a bad mood.

"We come at a bad time, Pete?" Russell followed Kwan through the door.

"In time to see me fail. I've been working like mad to find that woman. Frank Dassin's wife. She's gone. Off the grid and nowhere to be found. I've tried everything to track that truck. No luck. When it left IHS plaza it dropped into some crowded little streets on the West End. But it isn't there. They used some old but very effective deceptions to keep it from being tracked. And that includes the use of several other trucks with the same ID."

"Look, you have to stop taking this personally. We can hope the woman will be fine. They won't hurt her, she's just bait to get to Dassin. These aren't street thugs. Spaeth might be a crook but he's one who knows how to work an angle." Russell could see the guilt on Pete's face. "You did your best, you kept Dassin and his son safe. And you might catch a break finding the woman. But right now we need you to see what you can find on MacNally. We've lost him."

Pete scowled at the news. "What do you mean you lost him?"

"Spaeth's men hit the safe room. But MacNally and Dassin must have escaped. But instead of taking the route I expected, they went a different way. I don't know why. But I need to find them. They're gonna need help."

"MacNally's on the run?"

"Yes," Kwan stepped forward to join the conversation. "We could run around looking for him all day but we need to find him fast. Think you can find him quickly?"

"I don't have to. I can tell you where he was just a few minutes ago." Both detectives waited for his explanation. "A report came in not long ago about a truck accident not far from the shipping zone.

There were initial reports of gunfire but that was immediately changed to a simple report on an accident. Just before that a report of an armed man trying to breach the shipping zone surfaced, only to be pulled with the improbable explanation that it had only been a prank."

"He wasn't trying to breach it—to get into the port—he was trying to get out. It was MacNally." Kwan nodded, approving her own analysis of the report.

"I didn't pay attention to it too much," Pete said, "but that was before I knew MacNally was on the move. He's got to be close to here."

He pulled up a map on his deskscreen and enlarged a segment of it. Drawing a circle around one section with his finger, the highlighted circle doubled in size.

"He came out here," Russell plotted the action, "and had to fight here. He'll move off in this direction."

"Does he have a PDT I can track?" Pete asked.

"I doubt it. He was assuming that if he had to run, they might have been able to pick up his PDT—no matter if it was fake or not—and then they'd be able to track him. I was supposed to be there to get him. And with me he wouldn't need the data tag."

"So I go to visual tracking. You two get down there while I see what I can find. If I can locate them I'll let you know. Otherwise, look for Spaeth's men and follow them. They're obviously not being discreet."

Pete's black mood was passing. He was always exhilarated by a challenge. Having been stumped by the disappearance of the Dassin woman, he seemed revived by a chance to help save MacNally.

"Let's go find him," Kwan said as she pushed Russell out the door.

85

The noise of the rain made it easy for Lilly to remain hidden as she followed the man and woman through the park. They kept to the walking path, Lilly to the trees.

From what she could see, the woman did not appear to be in distress. Lilly could find no sympathy for her. She could not help but think of her as an evil thing that had come to destroy Gregor. She felt no regret at this harsh judgment. Even Gregor seemed to know she was toxic, though he could not seem to stay away from her.

And what did that say about Gregor? Lilly had always admired him for his shrewd ability to size up a man or woman with just one introduction, one quick conversation. Yet this woman, who carried around such an obvious aura of manipulation, defied Lepov's instincts. How was that possible?

"She's cute." Shay said. "I can see why Lepov likes her."

"Shay!" Lilly hushed him, straining to keep her voice low. He put his hands up by way of apologizing. She glared at him. He would think she was angry that he had made so much noise. She knew it was because of what he'd said.

"How long were they married?" Shay asked, his voice no quieter than the first time.

Lilly felt anger threatening to boil over. She watched the Dannens but neither one showed any signs of having heard Shay. Lilly held back to allow space to develop between them.

Glancing at Shay to make sure he was keeping still, his mischievous grin told her he knew she was getting angry and he was enjoying himself. She realized that she was nearly as illogical as Gregor. Shay would always be trouble for her, especially after his escape, and yet she had not found a way to get rid of him. She was actually considering his suggestion that she run off with him.

It clearly meant that she was losing her mind.

Another glance in his direction forced her to stop and stare at him. He too was staring at her and she suddenly felt certain that he knew exactly what she was thinking. Knew just how close she was to accepting his proposal. He confirmed her suspicions when he spoke.

"Just you and me, Lilly. It can be good again. It can be *right* again. You're considering it because you know it is what should happen. Lepov has nothing to do with us."

She turned away, wondering if the Dannens could hear his ramblings. Even if he were right, he was still rambling. He just kept talking, like thoughts in the head of a man sick with fever. It seemed like Shay just wouldn't shut up.

The Dannens had stopped walking. They had entered a clearing that fronted a small lake. The walking path met the lake and meandered along its curved shoreline. Benches and trees dotted this path. The water of the lake was much the color of lead. A cold, molten surface that rippled slowly in the light breeze. Raindrops hit it continually, the tiny splashes appearing as bubbles breaching a boiling surface.

They walked to the edge of the lake, both of them checking the time on their watches. Neither one of them had much to say to the other. They seemed to be two strangers waiting for a bus.

Lilly wondered how long they would have to wait. She was getting cold. As always, Shay had been right, she was standing in the rain with nothing on her head. And now, after that walk through the trees and grass, even her toes were wet and cold. She did not dare to allow Shay to see her shiver.

Lilly saw Gloria check her watch again. This time, however, she immediately turned to her husband and spoke to him in an angry tone that carried across the glade. Lilly could not make out the words but she could hear the belligerence in that voice. The husband reacted sharply to her assault. With his own raised voice he volleyed back at her. Quickly this short exchange heated up. Lilly was caught off guard by Gloria's sudden hand slap across her husband's face. He had been caught off guard as well. He didn't respond. He just stood there staring at her, one hand rubbing the area of the face she'd struck.

There was something wrong about the whole scene. Gloria's indignation or fury lacked impetus. And the husband's reaction was equally out of place.

Perhaps, Lilly thought, the spat would end as easily as it had begun.

But it did not end. Gloria continue to berate him, her voice rising enough for Lilly to understand some of the words. More important than the words, she could hear the distinct tone of bitterness. She could not hear fear. Gloria's attack on a husband she knew to be a killer was bold. Lilly had no doubt about that.

When it finally happened, Lilly knew she should have understood it was as inevitable as the setting of the sun. Gloria screamed an unintelligible word, struck the husband with enough force to knock him off balance, and began to stumble along the banks of the lake.

She screamed as if she'd been stabbed with a knife.

"I was wondering when your boyfriend would show up." Shay tapped her on the shoulder and pointed away from the drama unfolding beside the lake.

Gregor had arrived. He was carrying the black case in one hand. As he came running into view, Lilly realized she'd never seen him move so fast.

Lilly looked to see what he was running toward. Gloria was stumbling backwards, screaming at her husband. He was walking toward her, hands outstretched.

Gregor tossed the case aside as he closed the gap. Then Lilly realized that he was holding something else in his other hand. At full sprint he raised the hand, steadying it with the other. Then, to Lilly's shock, she watched as he slid to a halt.

Gloria was still yelling, kicking now at her husband who had reached down as if to grab her.

She heard Gregor yell the man's name. She also finally recognized that Gregor must have been holding a gun since three explosive bursts from it rocked the small glade and echoed out across the lake.

The man was no longer standing over Gregor's sobbing ex-wife.

"What goes on?" Shay asked.

Lilly had no idea.

86

Gloria was still crying, though her sobs had mostly subsided. Lepov approached her, the Luger still held out in front of him with both hands, his eyes locked on the still form of Dannen. It lay on the shore of the lake, on its back, the head just under the surface of the water. Rain obscured Lepov's vision; he'd lost his hat while running. But he could see enough to know that Dannen was dead. Two of his shots had struck him in the ribs. The muddy water grew even darker with blood.

"Are you okay?" he asked her. She was too upset to speak but made an effort to nod. Lepov was out of breath as well.

"What the hell was he doing?" Lepov stood over Dannen and kicked one of his shoes in frustration. "I was bringing you the damn gun. Why'd you start after her like that?"

He was confused and angry and nothing would have pleased him more if Dannen could have sat up out of the water and given Lepov a simple explanation.

"He was going to kill you. He kept saying it. That when you showed up he was just going to kill you." Gloria tried to stand but she fell over in the soft marshy ground. Lepov knelt down and pulled her back up. She was still crying.

"Okay, now that's enough." He shushed her, picking her up like a child would a doll.

"I couldn't let him do it. I tried to fight him. To get away. I had to warn you."

"And you did, you did good, girl." Lepov took her to the closest bench and gently set her down. "Come on, Lori. He's not gonna hurt you or me. Never again."

"Grey," she whispered his name. He bent low, put his ear to her lips. "Grey, thank you."

Her voice, no stronger than a little girl's, conveyed the full force of her fear and exhaustion and gratitude. That her husband had filled her so full of dread and terror disgusted him. At least he had been the one to stop the man. He'd been the one to put an end to her suffering. In the end, he'd been the one she could trust and rely on. No matter how much Gloria changed, Lepov had remained the same. As solid and dependable as a rock.

He looked at the Luger in his hand and was glad he had been

careful enough to remove it from its case before he approached the park. He had never intended on using it. He'd only meant to keep it out of sight, to deceive Dannen, just to give him a slight edge as he made the trade for Gloria.

But in the heat of the moment, as he'd run to the sound of Gloria's distress, he'd felt the gun in his coat pocket and knew fate had allowed him this chance to take down Jardyn's killer and Gloria's tormentor. He had been well aware of the irony of it all as he shot Dannen with the gun that had started this whole mess.

"What are we going to do?" Gloria asked, sitting up enough to look over his shoulder at the body.

"About what? The police will want to know what happened. We tell them about Jardyn, about the theft of the gun, we just tell them you had nothing to do with it. They'll straighten this all out."

"We can't. No, we've got to get out of here."

"What are you talking about?" He grabbed her shoulders and pulled upright. "Gloria, what do you mean?"

"You've got to hide his body."

"I'm not hiding that body. Have you lost your mind? I get it, you know? This has been traumatic for you. You need some time to let all of this sink in. But you have to realize the police aren't going to implicate you in any of this."

"I'm not worried about the police!" She reached out, stroking his chin as she spoke. "Listen to me, Grey. Kry lied to you. He was playing this thing from both sides. As soon as the gun was stolen he went to Jonnie."

"Spaeth?" He had started to worry that Gloria was lying to him yet again but her story actually made sense. What was it Jardyn had said? He'd been adamant that they had made it off the planet clean. No one knew they had done it. Yet Spaeth came looking for them right off the bat.

"Yes! Jonnie Spaeth. And he told him everything. He was supposed to meet Frobe and Jardyn here, get the gun from them and Kry was supposed to meet with the man who was going to buy it. But he figured that Jonnie would reward him for turning on the rest of the guys. Reward him more than he would have earned selling it. And not just in money. That's what he told Jonnie, anyway."

"What he *told* him? He was lying to Spaeth? He was—" Gloria nodded at him and Lepov suddenly understood. "He wanted Spaeth to kill off his partners so he could end up with it all. But Jardyn slipped the knot. He got away."

Lepov grabbed Gloria by her wrist and pulled on it hard enough to make her squeal. She tried to break free but couldn't.

"Jardyn got away because you were there, walking out of Alpha with him. Dannen was playing both sides but so were you."

"Grey, stop it! I only tried to help Lou after I found out what Kry was up to. I even tried to convince him to give up the gun so that maybe Kry would leave him alive."

"Don't you lie to me now, Gloria. There's a dead man back there and I made him that way because you told me he was dangerous, violent, he'd killed Jardyn and was going to kill you. Now your stories are starting to replicate like a virus. So you be careful and make sure to tell me the one I need to hear. The one that starts with that old-fashioned phrase *I swear to tell the truth and nothing but the truth so help me God!*"

She jerked her wrist free, rubbing it as she answered him. "I was trying to tell you the truth. That's what I was doing. Kry double-crossed Spaeth, he killed Jardyn for the gun and was planning on keeping it himself, without even me."

"So Spaeth has nothing to complain about. Jardyn's dead, the gun can be returned, and maybe we can talk him into sparing Dassin's life. We trade the gun for the man's wife. Why wouldn't he do that?"

"Kry was smart. He had already called Spaeth, told him that you and I killed Jardyn, and we had the gun and were going to try and run with it. Now that Kry's dead, Spaeth will believe it. He'll think we did this on purpose!"

Lepov dropped to the bench and allowed his eyes to drift until he saw Dannen's body lying head down in the water.

"Grey, I'm so sorry." Gloria hung her arms over Lepov and cried. Pulling her close, he did not try to stop her.

Dannen must have been clinically insane. He'd stolen from a crime lord, then betrayed his partners to that same crime lord, all for the sole purpose of manipulating the crime lord to kill the partners so he could double-cross the man he'd stolen from in the first place. It was just icing on the cake that he'd implicated Lepov and Gloria in his plot. And now, though Lepov did not regret killing the man, he and Gloria were trapped in Dannen's outrageous scheme.

"Give me a minute." He pushed her off and stood. Things had spiraled out of control and he knew he had little choice but to keep spinning with it until he could find a way to make it stop.

There wasn't any time to dispose of the body properly. Lepov grabbed Dannen—what had been Dannen—and pushed the body out into the lake. As long as Spaeth didn't know Dannen was dead, they could use that to their advantage. But they had to act quickly.

He watched the dark form of Gloria's husband—now, like Lepov, just a former husband—float out into the lake. It was time to go. He went back to the bench, took Gloria by the hand, and left the lake behind them, retrieving his hat from where it had fallen.

87

Frank was too exhausted to keep going. Judging by the coming darkness, he figured they had been moving for nearly twelve hours or more—ever since the shooting in the safe room—never having stopped for a proper rest. He could no longer stand up straight. His feet were in pain and his shoulder was bleeding; beneath his shirt he could feel the blood running down his back. The worst of it was, they'd had nothing to eat the whole day.

Frank was in much better shape than MacNally.

The old detective had not moved under his own power for most of the afternoon. Frank had shouldered most of the man's weight as they kept to the alleys and entryways of the neighborhoods through which they passed. Twice they'd stopped and sheltered in the shadows of basement steps that dropped down below the street surface. But each time they had not been able to stay long.

MacNally's shirt and coat were stained with blood. Frank had checked many times and they could not see any sustained points where he was bleeding but the scrim across his wounds was torn in several places and blood did weep out of these tears depending on the amount of exertion required as they kept moving.

MacNally's grey skin told Frank all he needed to know. The man was getting worse and would not last the night. They were going to have to make a decision about seeking help.

They had not stopped to ask for help up to this point for several very good reasons. The first reason was simple enough. Spaeth's men never gave up searching for them and they were frequently close to finding their quarry. They never seemed to know how close they were to finding Frank and MacNally, but they also never made any attempt to leave the area in order to broaden their search.

They also didn't want to put other people in danger. Spaeth's men were close and they did not want them to discover anyone had been helping them escape. It was best to stay away from people.

MacNally was unyielding in his contention that Russell was out there looking for them and that if they just kept moving he knew Russell would find them.

But moving was no longer an option. Frank wasn't physically able to keep the both of them going. He found a small block enclosure meant to hold a number of trash cans and he dragged the cans out of it. A rusted sheet of tin covered half of this three-sided corral. It was only about a meter deep and two meters long. The walls were only as tall as the garbage cans.

He dragged MacNally within the walls and helped him get up

under the sheet of tin. It kept the rain off him and he was not visible to anyone who might come down the alley.

"God help me, this place stinks." MacNally looked around and Frank could see the man did not understand where he was.

"I'm sorry, detective. I can't keep this up." It was hard to say any more. He didn't want to say what needed saying.

"I'm not blaming you. You're a helluva cop. A good kid." MacNally patted Frank on the leg. "Come on. Sit down. It's my turn to—" he tried to cough but the pain was so severe Frank could see that MacNally preferred to gag. He didn't begin to breathe again until after he swallowed hard.

"You know what's the worst part of this? You were right about those damn cigarettes. If I'd had a cigarette for every time you told me to quit smoking I'd be dead today, Russell."

The big man, looking small and deflated in his soaked raincoat, began to run his hands over his chest and belly. Frank put his hand out to stop him.

"Don't, detective. It makes it worse."

"I just can't find 'em." He patted his pockets until he finally located the pack of cigarettes. "Would you believe that? Two left? You mind if I take one of them?"

"No, I don't mind." Frank helped him get it out of the packet. He saw that there was really only one but he didn't correct the count. Instead, he guided the cigarette into his mouth and, taking the lighter from MacNally, lit the man's last cigarette.

"Russell?" He blew smoke out in a long, ragged puff. "You hear me Russell? Don't ever let me lie to you. These things taste like shit. Forty years I been smokin' these things. They never tasted good the first time and now, right here in this…"

The cigarette fell from his mouth and landed in rainwater. MacNally whimpered a little when he put his hand to his mouth and realized it was gone.

Saying what needed saying wasn't going to be easy. But waiting around was only letting things get worse.

"MacNally, I gotta go find you some help. I have to leave you. You understand that?"

"Russell, stop talking like a rookie kid who's never chased down his first bad guy and listen to me. You gotta leave me here. You gotta get to a SubTransit and get your face on a recorder. You hear me? You get one of them soulless black eyes, the first one you find, and you just stare into it. You do that you'll be okay."

"Maybe I should leave this with you." It would have been nice to be able to shed the weight of the Bushmaster but MacNally waved him off.

"No, you keep that. I got mine and it's all I need. Now tell me you'll do what I said. Stare into that black dot and you'll be good. Say it, Russell!"

"Sure, MacNally, stare into the black dot and I'll be good."

He put a hand on MacNally's shoulder and was surprised when MacNally's hand grabbed his. He had not thought the man had that kind of strength left in him.

"Goodbye, detective."

"Move your ass, Russell," he growled.

Frank stood up, replacing a few trash cans so that MacNally was partially covered. He began to walk away when he heard MacNally start to speak.

"Hey, I knew you'd show up again. I knew when I saw you in the kitchen it wouldn't be the last time you showed up...Yeah? I guess it makes sense, sure...oh please, when you needed me I wasn't there. I never came. You were on your own and I just let you die. But not you...no, I mean it. You were always the best one of us. And look at me. What a mess...yeah, that's real funny, you don't look that good either...come on, I knew you'd show up. You're too good a man to let me sit here alone...but hey, why haven't you been to see Lynne? You gotta do that. When we're done here...hey, if you don't I'm gonna tell her you came to me and not to her...oh yes I would."

Frank couldn't listen any longer. He held the rifle with both hands and started to move as fast as he could. He knew it wouldn't be fast enough.

88

The Australian couldn't hold the New Yorker responsible for what had happened with the men in the truck. He'd been back at the suite, taking care of the Ursuline when those clowns had let themselves get ambushed. The only good news to come out of it was that the men in the second truck had picked up the trail. By the time the New Yorker had made it back out to the scene of the ambush, his men had been able to point him in the right direction.

But that had been hours ago and there was every chance that the Australian would hold him responsible for what had followed. They wasted the rest of the day combing the neighborhoods around that site, unable to find two obviously wounded men who had very few resources (the street cannon they carried being a palpable exception.)

If the New Yorker had been honest, and there was no chance he was going to be honest with anyone on this subject, he would have had to confess that he lacked much interest in the outcome of the hunt. No, he hadn't felt remorse at the loss of the men. They were mercenaries that no one would mourn. Their own mothers probably wouldn't mourn them. It was the Ursuline that was eating away at him.

He'd left her on the bed. She'd stopped crying, stopped sobbing, stopped sniffling. He'd been afraid to find that she had stopped breathing but his medic, the Spaniard, assured him she would live. It had been the first time in his life that the New Yorker had ever been afraid for someone he had injured. The fear had clung to him like a dead zone where no other emotion could take hold. He hated it, yet even as he did he wished it would never go away. It wouldn't cleanse him of what he had done but it wouldn't allow room for guilt and shame, two emotions he had banished from his life when he had been only a child.

He wasn't ready to deal with those terrifying demons just yet.

"Do we keep searching?"

The New Yorker looked at the man who had asked the question. He was a mean-looking bastard, face full of scars and his body a bundle of muscles and sinew made for hurting other men. Looks could be deceiving. As mean as he looked he doubted this man could ever do what the New Yorker had just done to the Ursuline.

She had been able to keep up her prayer for a short time. The mantra had bothered him. That she had been praying to forgive him had disturbed him. And then she'd asked to be delivered from evil. From *evil*. He couldn't deny that one. Though he always had some kind of an excuse for his behavior and goals he'd never once really thought of himself as evil.

But the evidence was chillingly clear: the evidence of a girl's battered body on the finest of silk sheets.

"Yeah, let's get out of here." He nodded to the man with the face full of scars. "Call your people back. Somehow we gotta convince the boss to let us get out of this hellhole."

Two sharp whistles sounded from a nearby alley. One of his men appeared around the corner and signaled with his light.

"They got something." Scarface jogged across the street. The New Yorker followed.

The alley ran perpendicular from the street for about twenty meters before it made a ninety-degree turn. About forty meters beyond that was a low block wall covered by a piece of rusted tin.

Scarface approached the small trash bin and, using the barrel of his star rifle, flipped away the tin covering. He raised the rifle, sighting on the man he had uncovered.

The man didn't move. The New Yorker moved forward and grabbed a light from one of the nearby men. He shone it on the body. The face first, then across the rest of what had to be the Irishman.

271

"Get a medic over here, now!" The New Yorker sat down on the top of the wall and touched the man's neck with the back of his hand.

He was cold. Very cold.

89

"We missed something, so we start over." Kwan circled back to where the truck had nearly demolished the wall. "They're on foot, so they couldn't have gone far. If they aren't wounded, they are at least exhausted."

"And technically, MacNally was already wounded to start with." Russell kicked at the broken bits of cement block. "That means they can't be far. Or they were caught and taken by Spaeth."

"No, we know they weren't because Pete says he keeps seeing their trucks moving around like they're being driven by blind guys. They're doing what we're doing. They just had a better jump on the chase.

"I don't see how we could have missed anything. I mean, it's dark, we don't have more than small hand lights, and we have no idea what direction they went."

"But we got Pete." Kwan smiled, her teeth shining in the light of a distant streetlight. "They don't have Pete."

"I never should have let him talk me into this. I should have stayed with him."

"Oh, stop." Kwan shined her light in his eyes long enough to make him reach out and push it away. "You're the only one who's been doing something for him from the beginning. And he was calling the shots, like he always does. You know how he is. He would never have allowed you to come up with your own plan. Even if you came up with one that was foolproof he'd veto it. The man was a control nut. He just couldn't let someone else pick the restaurant."

"We still talking about his habits as a homicide detective?"

"Maybe," she nodded, "and maybe not. My point is you can't mope about this. He needs us to be sharp right now, to do what we can to find him."

"I think we've already proven we can't do that."

"You think so?" She smiled again, her white teeth only eclipsed by the flashing green screen on her belt. "Somebody might have just found the last piece of his puzzle."

"You won't believe this," Pete said as soon as their connection was clear.

"Is he alive?" Kwan asked. Both detectives held their breath.

"Yeah, I mean, well yeah. But—"

"Pete, no theatrics, come one, where do we go?" Russell pointed at her vehicle and they both started moving.

"Okay, look, I've sent you the coordinates, but I have to tell you—"

"I know, Pete, you're a genius. Tell me about it later. We're on the way."

"It's Frank Dassin! Not MacNally." Pete's voice rang loud and clear on the deserted street. The detectives hesitated, staring at each other, waiting for Pete to clarify what he'd just said.

"And I didn't find him. I mean, I did. But he just showed up on a Transit screen. He's over on Thirty-Fifth Street, in the SubTransit station. Just staring into a recorder."

"Thirty-Fifth Street? How the hell they'd get way over there?"

"Like I said, I don't think *they* got over there. From what I can see of the station from other angles, he's alone."

Kwan gestured at Russell to get in the vehicle. She had it up and over the street faster than he'd thought was possible. Silence ruled the interior as they sped high over the rooftops. Russell wanted to ask so many questions. What had happened? What had gone wrong? And more than any other question, all he really wanted to know was *where was Ed MacNally?*

They began to drop as soon as Kwan cleared out traffic below them with an emergency radar. They were coming in fast. For them, the short jump over to Thirty-Fifth Street was just a matter of two or three minutes. But if Dassin and MacNally had walked such a distance—it had to be somewhere in the range of fifty kilometers—it would have been a miracle if MacNally had been able to make it.

There was no proof MacNally had made it. Russell tried to prepare himself for what was becoming an awful possibility. He looked at Kwan and saw that she was fighting her own feelings over the fact that MacNally was missing.

"Hey," he said, risking a distraction as she landed near the open stairs of the station, "he wouldn't let you choose the restaurant either, huh?"

"Not a chance." She laughed a little at the memory. "He could be a real jerk. A *real* jerk. But don't get me wrong. There were other things he did that would surprise you. Stuff you wouldn't believe."

"Let's go get Dassin. And please, please don't tell me that stuff. I'm begging you."

She left the engine running as they both dashed down the steps. There, at the base of the stairs, Frank Dassin was still staring into the recorder.

"Frank?" Russell slowed down as he approached. Dassin turned to look at him. He was cradling the Bushmaster in his arms. "You alright Frank?"

"He said to stare into the black eye. He said, *Russell, stare into the black eye and you'll be okay*."

"Where is he, Frank? Come on, we gotta move you, now. Where's MacNally, Frank?"

"I'm sorry, I have no idea where I left him." Frank began to shake as Russell helped him into the back seat of Kwan's car. Russell gently took the rifle and locked it down in the trunk and climbed in beside him. He had to work to keep the man awake.

"Come on Frank, talk to me. MacNally's out there and you know where he is. Don't you pass out. Not yet. Come on!"

Though he'd insisted he didn't know, Frank was able to direct them to an alley three blocks away from the SubTransit station. He knew he was being rough on the man, who was suffering from exhaustion, if not actual trauma — it was hard to tell with all of the blood on his shirt — but Russell needed Frank to go into that alleyway with him. He needed Frank to be sure it was the right place.

Once they found the trash cans Frank was sure. And though he seemed confused by the absence of MacNally, he stuck with his story. It was the place he'd left him. The place that MacNally had been left to die.

Russell wanted to put a bullet through Dassin's head. He couldn't believe this man would walk away from a wounded man. What did it matter that Dassin said MacNally told him to leave?

"What's that?" Kwan shined her light against the base of the interior wall and bent down to look closely. She picked up a small glass vial.

"Let me see that." Russell held out his hand and she dropped it there for him to examine. He finished looking it over and looked up at her.

"Stimulant. Combat medics carry these."

"Military?"

"No, this one isn't. This is the kind of thing special ops guys carry." She shrugged. "What it means, I'm not sure."

"Could it be one of Spaeth's men? Are they those kind of professionals?"

"It would make sense. If the police had found him, Pete would have called us. If these paramilitary types found him, they could be with Spaeth. You think MacNally could be alive?"

"I'd like to," Russell admitted. "I know one way to find out."

"You thinking about Jenkins?" she asked.

"Damn right, I am. I could use your help."

"What do think I've been doing all day? Did you think I wanted to quit now?" She dropped the vial in an outside pocket and helped support Frank as they headed back to the mouth of the alley.

"Maybe we ought to get this guy to a doctor." Kwan watched him as Russell helped him back into the car. "Who was the doc you took MacNally to?"

"I'm okay," Dassin said, out of breath and unable to keep his head up straight. "If you think you can find MacNally, then do what you have to. I'm good here."

By the time they were airborne, Dassin was asleep, slumped against a door. Russell leaned forward to talk to Kwan and was hit again with the scent of jasmine.

"Are you objectifying me?" Russell was close enough to her that she had been able to feel his breath on her neck.

"No, I'm trying to keep my balance as you drive. I was going to ask you if you know where to go."

"Do you?" she asked.

"Do I know where Captain Jenkins lives? No, I don't."

"Then sit back and enjoy the ride, youngster. And start thinking of what we'll do when we get there."

She brought them down in his back yard. His home was modest in size but his yard was bigger than Russell had seen anywhere in the Lazaretto. What he wanted with all of that grass was anybody's guess.

Kwan was already sprinting up the back steps of the house. Russell had to push hard to catch up to her. She'd figured out the same thing he had; they could not give him time to slip away. They did not bother knocking. This was no friendly house call.

Kwan did not need Russell's help with the door. She kicked low on the door and it snapped off two locks when she did. To their surprise, Jenkins had not run. He was standing in the hallway, trying to wake up.

"What are you two doing?" Jenkins tried to sound firm but he failed miserably.

"Whether you know it or not, MacNally's still alive. So is Frank Dassin. But Spaeth has MacNally, so you're gonna tell us how you contact him."

"Russell, you must be out of your mind. Kwan, what are you doing here with this Arcobian *boutrach*?"

Russell unleashed a right hook that knocked Jenkins to the floor of the hallway.

"You made him my partner, remember Sam? So I'm with him now, and you're gonna answer his question."

"Or what?" Jenkins sat up and carefully put a hand over the soft tissue where Russell hit him. "I suppose you two are gonna work me over, is that right?"

"You aren't that lucky." Kwan sat beside him and tapped his

knee with the barrel of her service weapon. "You get to retire. You get to keep your pension, and you get a ticket out of this place. You get to just fly away."

"I like his idea better." Russell wasn't kidding. He stood over Jenkins and pleaded with him. "Come on, Captain. Please, *please* tell her you don't want to retire. As a favor to me, tell her."

90

Frank woke up when Russell shook him. The rain had slacked off, though it still fell steadily. He hurt everywhere. The most prominent pain was on his shoulders. Yes, his skin was rubbed raw from carrying the Bushmaster, but also his shoulders just didn't want to work right after he'd strained them by supporting MacNally's weight as they wandered from street to street.

By now, stiff and fresh out of the adrenaline that had kept him moving, he needed help exiting the vehicle. Though he might have been able to get up the driveway and into the house—he had no idea where he was—he allowed a powerfully built black man to practically carry him through the door.

"I've been getting to know your little boy. He's a good kid."

"Jett? He's here?" Frank was suddenly overcome with unease, sure that he was forgetting something. "His mother? Where's Lara?"

No one would answer him. It was important. He knew the answer he was looking for was unpleasant and no one was willing to say it.

"Take me to Jett," he demanded weakly. They didn't.

"He's asleep, and you should do the same thing. Give us a minute, I'm getting a bed ready for you."

The man left him on a sofa. Frank slid off to one side and tried to find a comfortable position for his head.

The room was full of people. They were talking in hushed tones. A man with a weary yet harsh tone was asking a lot of questions.

"You think he's alive?"

"I don't think they would have taken his body if he was dead."

"Let's hope not. We make that call, he's got to be part of the deal."

Several people spoke at once. A woman, the one who had found him at the SubTransit station, spoke loud enough to silence everyone else.

"Whether he's alive or not, we deal for MacNally and the Dassin woman."

Lara? Deal for Lara?

"Don't worry about that. I'm gonna handle that business."

"Who the hell is this guy to make the call for us?" asked the woman.

"Kwan, please, I told you, Lepov's got to do this. He's not a cop. Spaeth can deal with him. And Lepov knows how to handle himself. We can make promises all day long but it won't mean anything to Spaeth."

"So what does he mean, he'll handle it?" The woman wasn't going to go quietly.

"Do you trust me, Russell?"

"Sure, Lepov, you know I do. And she will to."

"Then stop wasting time and give me that. I'll make the call from the kitchen. And I want to be alone. I don't need all of you breathing down my neck trying to tell me what to say. Pete, is there any way you can trace this thing?"

"Let me see it." A long silence, the whole room seemed to be holding its breath. "No, I don't like to admit this, but I've never seen anything like this. This is new stuff. Way above my skill set. If it does what I think it does, I love it. It's beautiful."

"Okay, enough of that. You can keep this when we're done. Merry Christmas."

Someone tapped Frank on his shoulder and he looked up and saw the big guy standing there again. He pointed at Frank then pointed down a hallway.

Frank went where he was told. He stepped into a room that was lit by one small lamp. A double bed stood against a wall, and a small bundle lay on one side of it. Frank moved closer to it and the big man put a hand on his shoulder to stop him.

"Just go on and climb in there with him. You might wake him, but after thinking about it, I doubt that really matters. He'll be happy to see his father."

Frank knew he was filthy, knew he needed to clean up. He hated to think of the mess he'd be making. But messes like this could be cleaned up. The bigger messes, like the one he'd started when he first considered stealing from Jonnie Spaeth, might never be cleaned up properly. He just hoped that the little boy in the bed would find a way to forgive him one day.

He was almost asleep when his eyes snapped open.

Jonnie Spaeth.

Lara.

He had finally remembered. Exhaustion, fear, guilt and a mounting self-hatred burned within him as he lay in the dark for a year, trying desperately to believe that Lara would come out of this alive and well. He would understand if she hated him the rest of her life. Just as long as she could do it for a very long time.

91

Lilly had wanted to confront Gregor at the park, to walk up to him and Gloria and tell them she had seen it all. Had seen Gregor kill an unarmed man. Had seen Gregor toss the body into the lake. She'd started to leave the shelter of the trees but Shay hadn't let her. He had stopped her with just a few simple words.

"What a romantic rescue." His cruelty always reached its peak when he started cracking jokes.

She did not give him the satisfaction of a sharp reply. He might have been able to hurt her, but Lilly was already rebuilding her defenses. If she could appear stable and imperturbable, he would eventually leave her alone. Shay never liked to pick at a scab that wouldn't bleed.

"I can't imagine you need more proof that it's time to give up on the heroic Gregor Lepov. I would say the only question left to answer is whether or not we're leaving now or need we wait a few days while you pack a few things and say goodbye to old friends."

She held her tongue. She wished he would go away. It had taken her far too long to decide if she should confront Gregor or simply disappear. But now, as she rode the SubTransit car toward the southern edge of the city, she knew that disappearing was the wrong path to take. She needed to speak with Gregor one last time. After all, there were too many things they had left unsaid. Too many things that had been too difficult to say while the ink was still wet on all that IHS paperwork.

She had no way of knowing if Gregor would go back to Bril Abbot's house. She could only hope. She did worry that he and Gloria had gone into hiding. It was certainly possible. She hoped not.

Walking to the house as the rain fell over her shoulders, she decided that if he had come to the house, and if she could find no chance to talk with him privately, she would say what she had to regardless of who was able to hear it. Even if she had to say it in front of Gloria.

When she knocked on the door she was a little disturbed to find the house so full of people. They all seemed to be waiting. For a moment she had wondered if they had been waiting for her. But when they barely spoke more than a few soft greetings to her, she knew that something else entirely was bothering them.

Menya Russell was standing in the corner of the room closest to the door. A tall, strong-looking woman was standing close to him. She stared hard at Lilly, and did not stop until Lilly finally left the room in search of Gregor.

Pete Landon was sitting on a small, upholstered chair, his one leg resting on the arm of the chair, the foot attached to that leg bouncing nervously. He jumped up from the chair long enough to approach her and ask if everything was okay. After squeezing her arm affectionately, he went back to his anxious lounging. Gloria was there too. She was on the corner seat of the sofa, sitting stiffly with her knees together, feet drawn close to the sofa, and her hands placed on her knees with the greatest of efforts to appear effortlessly poised. The skin around her eyes was slightly swollen. It had taken her a long time to stop crying. Far longer than it had taken the man in the lake to stop breathing.

As she crossed the floor of the front room, Bril Abbot emerged from the hallway and looked happy to see her. He made the motion of sipping from a cup of tea then pointed at her. She shook her head, declining with a forced smile. He nodded as his eyes narrowed into a look of concern. She stopped when she reached him.

"I'm okay. I just need to find Gregor and speak with him for a minute."

"You need a towel, that's what you need." He pointed to a drop of rain that had been slowly traversing her temple.

"When I'm done. Why don't you let anyone else serve you a drink? It doesn't seem fair that you're always taking care of this whole crew.

"My house, remember? That makes me the host. No one else."

"I like you, Bril Abbot. You're an honorable man." She felt a sudden desire to take this poor, exiled man — an outcast who had once held all the worlds in his hand — and hold him tight, show him that there were still people with an inexhaustible supply of humanity coursing through their veins. It wasn't in her nature, she knew that. And it would be unwise to take the risk. This she knew with assuredness. But she also knew that taking the risk would be evidence of the humanity that so many people had assumed she lacked.

Yes, she'd been known for her cold nature, long before she'd ever even come to the Lazaretto. It had been a fluke when she'd met Gregor and she'd allowed a portion of herself to thaw, to melt until she'd revealed something other than a calculating, hard-nosed business woman. But even under Gregor's influence she'd never really learned to feel true compassion for anyone unless they had some tangible value attached to them.

She had certainly never felt compassion for Shay when she had discovered the extent of his crimes. She had never even felt an obligation to talk with him first, allow him a chance to explain.

Was that why she felt compelled to seek out Gregor? Had she

changed enough that she couldn't just walk away without an explanation? She suddenly understood Shay's mocking grin as he watched her leave the SubTransit station. Shay knew she couldn't walk out on Gregor as easily as she had walked out on their marriage.

In the kitchen, Gregor was alone, facing a window painted black with night. Lilly knocked gently on the doorframe.

"I didn't reach Spaeth. I'm—" he was surprised to see Lilly when he turned around. "I'm waiting for his call."

"And then what, a duel, perhaps?" she asked.

"No one knew where you were. I was about to ask Pete to use his magic tricks to track you down."

"I took a walk in the park, Gregor."

He knew something was wrong. She could see it. He watched her approach as if she were something dangerous. Finally, looking behind her, he took a step forward and spoke softly.

"Follow me." A door on the far wall led to a small, covered porch on the side of the house. They both stepped outside. He closed the door before he spoke. "Okay, you want to say something. I can see it. What is it?"

The porch roof popped sporadically in the cold as rain hit it. Out in the darkened yard the sound of thousands of raindrops washed the night with an insistent whisper.

"I'm leaving." She hadn't planned on saying it, but there was little else to say. She could see by the look in his eyes that if she asked about the shooting he would either justify it or deny it, depending on how much she had seen.

"Listen, this is about to be over. Once Spaeth contacts me I can make a deal that will protect us all."

"And what about her? Will she be grateful that you killed her husband?"

"Okay, so you followed me, you saw what happened. You know that I was only trying to stop him from breaking her neck. The man was a killer, I'm not ashamed of what I did."

"You really believe it, don't you?" Lilly could see it in his eyes. This wasn't a straightforward case of a man attempting to justify what he knows to be wrong. He had only done what any man might be expected to do when he saw someone threatening his wife. Spurred by this simple realization, Lilly could suddenly see what Gregor had seen. More importantly, she could see what he hadn't been able to see. He'd arrived too late. He had never seen Gloria and her husband walking through the park with her arm holding to his. He had never seen her calm, untroubled demeanor prior to all the shouting. He had never seen her sudden, unprovoked attack.

All he had seen was a man standing over the hysterical,

terrorized Gloria Lepov, his hands raised to strike her.

"Gregor, what do you mean he was a killer?"

"He murdered his partner yesterday after I told him where to find the man. I don't like being used that way. Dannen wanted the prize all to himself. He was killing off his partners, and he was going to do the same to Gloria."

"You're absolutely certain?" When he nodded, she decided to tell him what she'd seen. She told him how she' followed the Dannens through the park. How Gloria had never been in any sort of distress until she had started shouting at her husband. She didn't know if Gregor would believe her. All she could do was let him hear the truth. It was up to him to recognize it.

She could see he was trying. There was enough light coming from the kitchen window to allow her to see the uncertainty in his eyes. She put a hand on one of his.

"He's not going to believe you." Shay's voice drifted out of the dark. He was standing on the steps of the porch. She had not seen him approach. "Look at him, he'd rather believe her than you."

"I'm sorry Gregor, don't listen to him." She wasn't going to allow Shay to provoke Gregor into a fight. "And I'm sorry, I should have told you. I was with Shay. He knows. But he wasn't supposed to follow me here. I didn't mean to bring him here."

Gregor turned his hand so that he was now holding hers. He squeezed it tight enough to command her full attention.

"Lilly, listen to me. I need an excuse to go back into the city. Once I hear from Spaeth, I'm going to tell them in there that you will be taking the boy to stay with the Duvalls. And I'll drive you. Can you do that for me?"

"He's getting you out of the way, Lilly." Shay's derisive laugh angered her. "He doesn't want you here, muddying the waters. Not when he's got Gloria."

"Stop it, Shay! You're wrong! Tell, him Gregor. Tell him he's wrong." She wanted to push Shay away but Gregor held both of her hands now and he wouldn't let her go.

"Lilly, listen to me. I need you right now. I'm mixed up good but maybe I'll straighten this out. But right now I need you. So tell Shay to go, we'll talk about him later."

Lilly wished that Shay would stop laughing. She focused on Gregor.

"Tell him to go away, Lilly."

"Shay…" she said his name but didn't look at him. "You have to go."

For once, Shay had no witty remark to toss out. He did as he was told. He went away.

92

Collecting people was becoming a habit. The New Yorker had delivered the Irishman—a body that was just barely alive—to the Australian because he couldn't see the point in killing him. The man would die soon enough. There was no reason to speed up the process. Besides, it was a chance to irritate the Australian. He'd want to know why the Irishman hadn't been killed. And the New Yorker vowed to himself that he would make the Australian personally kill the Irishman if he was still determined that his brother's killer should die.

Once the Spaniard stabilized the Irishman, the New Yorker told him to check on the Ursuline again. The report was the same as before. She was alive. She would stay alive. She would need time to recover.

That was more than could be said for the woman at the bottom of the elevator shaft.

The number of people who had died as a result of this burglary was growing. Word had just come down that the Frenchman was dead. Counting the men who had died down in the tunnels under the Shipping Port, as well as those in the ambush on the street, he calculated that seven men had died. The German, and Frenchman and the Swede's wife were three more. The Australian's brother (including that other fool) made two more. A dozen people. All of them lost over an old relic that meant nothing to the Australian.

The Australian's dedication to his image was impressive. It was also disgusting. The New Yorker wondered how they could all work for a man who was so bent on revenge he couldn't see the cost of his rage.

Maybe, a few years ago, the New Yorker might have tried to temper his boss's vindictive streak. But he was experienced enough to know that it would do no good. No matter how many genuine points he could make in the argument, the Australian would not change his mind. It was even possible that he might see the New Yorker's interference as a sign that the New Yorker could no longer be trusted.

Was that it? Could he no longer be trusted? Had he begun to see that his employer was unworthy of loyalty? Could he, the New Yorker, look himself in the eye and admit that the Australian was so far gone that he needed to be stopped? Shot down like a rabid dog? Twelve people dead to protect one man's reputation—and more to come.

His men would not be the ones to stop this. They did what they were told. They might have wondered why some of their compatriots had died, but they weren't going to refuse the Australian's orders.

Such men were hired for their unwavering obedience, not their reasoning skills.

But the New Yorker was more than just hired muscle. He was shrewd enough to know that this situation had slipped out of control. And despite the fact that the Australian's brother had been killed, anger was no reason to keep throwing good blood after bad blood.

The worst of it was the way the Australian had forced his hand with the Ursuline. She hadn't deserved that. She'd had the decency to try and do one righteous deed in the middle of a dark and crazy world. And how had the Australian reacted? He had demanded she pay her debt in tears of pain.

That new God of hers might help her forgive him for the beating he'd given her, but the New Yorker sure as hell wasn't going to forgive the Australian for forcing him to do it. It would be easier to stick a knife in the man and leave him to bleed to death on the cold, dirty streets of the Lazaretto than forgive him.

He wasn't sure if that had been his intention from the start but he now knew this was what he wanted. To end what the Australian had started.

He spent a few minutes in the suite, watching the Ursuline. She was not aware he was in the room. If she was conscious it was impossible to tell. She had been sedated. More than relieving her of the pain, it also freed her from the misery of her memories.

With as much courage as he could gather, the New Yorker went to the Australian, unsure if he could carry out his plan. For once he didn't wait to be summoned. He also didn't bother to knock. He pushed open the door and searched his soul for the courage to stop the most powerful criminal in the Euxine system.

"You're just in time." The Australian stood up from his desk and waved him in. "I was about to call for you."

The New Yorker kept moving, afraid that if he stopped his determination would evaporate. They were alone, which meant he would not have to take down any bodyguards first. And the Australian was not armed, so he would not be forced to shoot from a distance. Instead he would be able to walk right up to the man and strangle him. He deserved nothing better.

"We received a call a few minutes ago. A very interesting call. It seems that someone wants to make a trade for the woman. They have my stolen property and are willing to deal."

"Who?" The New Yorker stopped, unable to suppress his curiosity. Had the Englishman double-crossed them?

"I don't know. He had an old Russian name. I do not know the details of his proposal. I said I would call him back. I haven't yet. But I think I am willing to listen. If only to get him to meet with us.

The meeting will not go the way he will expect it to, but that will be his problem, not ours."

He'd lost the moment. The New Yorker knew that his interest was piqued enough to delay his plan. For now he would wait.

"Of course," the Australian said, his voice dripping with condescension, "it would be embarrassing to admit to this Russian that the Swede's wife is dead because of that woman you brought along. But we'll just have to play along, keep this man happy until we can meet him face to face."

The New Yorker already knew he would regret not killing this man when he'd had the chance.

93

When Lepov had asked for the report on the body of Louis Jardyn, Russell had been sure it would not be available yet. And when he'd checked for it, the report was still pending, just as he'd expected. But when Kwan heard what he was looking for, she did her own checking and the report appeared almost immediately.

"How did you do that?" Russell asked without hiding his astonishment. "We never get reports that fast."

"Those guys down there like me a whole lot more than they like you and MacNally — perks that come with being a nice person."

Lepov had only scanned the report, looking for one specific detail. He must have found what he wanted because he grunted with disgust and handed back the report.

Russell, Kwan and Lepov waited in the kitchen until the call came back from Jonnie Spaeth. The one-sided conversation was not difficult to follow once a few meaningless pleasantries were exchanged.

"I'm willing to hand over the stolen Luger if you'll give us Lara Dassin." Lepov, Kwan and Russell had agreed that this was the best way to start the negotiation. Something that simple might be what Spaeth was after. They did not want to complicate matters unless they had to.

Lepov's eyes narrowed as he listened to Spaeth's response. He shook his head slowly to let the detectives know he didn't like what he heard.

"Now listen, Jonnie, you know she's got nothing to do with this. You let her go free, you get your little popgun and you can leave this lousy rock."

"Ask him," Kwan interrupted. She made a motion for Lepov to speed things up. Lepov put up a hand and nodded.

"Okay, that's good, Jonnie. Good for everyone involved. Just let me talk to her, I want to be able to tell the little boy I heard his mother's voice."

A long silence from Lepov as he shook his head again, this time as his eyes turned cold. "Sure, I get it. Don't wake her. Let her sleep."

"Ask—"

"Jonnie, before we decide where we'll meet, tell me something. Is MacNally still alive?"

Russell could not tell by looking at Lepov what Spaeth was saying. If he had to guess he'd say MacNally was—Russell really didn't want to guess.

"Okay, then here's what I would like to offer." He looked first and Russell, then at Kwan, then he finally spoke. "You give us MacNally and we'll give you Frank Dassin."

The granite stare from Lepov was enough to keep Russell from objecting. In fact, it helped him to recognize the logic in the trade. Spaeth still wanted revenge. He'd want someone. Maybe, if they gave him this choice, he'd only kill the thief and not kill the man responsible for his brother's death. After all, Dassin deserved to die more than MacNally.

A heavy silence ensued. To Russell, the offer was fair. Spaeth would get his stolen property back and he'd have the man responsible for this mess. All he was giving up was a woman who meant nothing to him and a man who was old and, most likely, severely wounded.

"Dammit, Spaeth!" Lepov jumped up from his chair and Russell thought he was going to knock over the table. "You kill Ed MacNally and I'll come back to Bukovina and hunt you down. You think I'm afraid of you? All you have to do is give him to us and you can have the man who stole from you in the first place. You can do what you want with him, I won't care."

Russell could see that Kwan was uneasy listening to Lepov bargain with a man's life, no matter how stupid and greedy he'd been. At one point she looked ready to intervene on Dassin's behalf but instead she quickly left the room.

"Okay, Jonnie, you win. I'll have to raise my offer." He shut down the audio connection long enough to look at Russell. "Give me a few minutes alone with Spaeth. Trust me, you really should leave the room."

"Lepov, he's my partner. If you've got something to offer him that'll save MacNally's life, quit fooling around and offer it. I don't care what it is."

"Okay." Lepov reopened the connection. "Jonnie, I'll tell you why you're gonna give me MacNally. Because I'm gonna give you Kry Dannen, the man who double-crossed you. Were you aware he murdered Jardyn to take the Luger for himself?"

It was easy to see by the way Lepov began to smile that Spaeth had been in the dark about Kry Dannen. But Russell could see that something else was making Lepov smile. And it wasn't anything funny.

"Where is Dannen?" Russell asked Lepov once he finished with Spaeth.

"Let that be my little secret for now. You'll know soon enough."

Later, Russell wondered if Lepov had been planning that all along. But at the time, he had felt it was a stroke of genius. As soon as the connection was terminated, Russell said as much to Lepov.

"It will only seem like it was a great idea if MacNally comes out of this alive. But I'm still gonna need something else from you."

"Name it," Russell said.

"I want you to take your new partner home. Now."

"Why not let her stay? I trust her and she could be a big help."

"I'll tell you why," said Lepov. And he did.

Minutes later, Menya Russell suggested to Pearl Lin Kwan that they both go home to get some rest.

94

It doesn't help to know you have a weak spot for someone. Knowing in advance that they can lie to you, manipulate you, pull your strings—none of that prevents it from happening. The knowledge only helps soften the blow the next time someone lies to you or manipulates you or pulls your string. And though you hate yourself for having that weak spot, at least you know why it happened. You know it wasn't because you were naïve or stupid or crazy. You were simply being true to your nature, and that someone was being true to his or hers.

And Gloria had certainly been true to hers. Russell's report on Jardyn's death was the first solid evidence he'd found. The fact that his death had been at night, not later that next morning, changed everything. Of course, it had been Lilly's story about what she had seen at the park that put him on the right track. All that remained was to check on one other item.

He had dropped off Lilly and the boy, Jett, at Georges and Maria Duvalls' apartment. He had called from Abbot's and they had been ready when Lepov had arrived. He had extracted a promise from Lilly—as binding as it could be—that she would not leave the Duvalls' until he returned. She had made him promise to return after he met with Jonnie Spaeth.

He assured her he had every intention of coming back.

But before the meeting he needed to check on one last thing. And so he returned to the rooms that Gloria and Kry Dannen were renting. He only needed to see one thing.

The Dannens were still renting the rooms. No one was aware yet that Kry Dannen was floating face down in the Terran Park lake. And Gloria had not been back to the hotel since the shooting. That was important. Lepov had to see that room before he met with Spaeth.

Once inside he went straight for the desk. The deskscreen where he had written the note for Kry Dannen was blank. It had been wiped clear as Lepov had known it would be. He moved to the desk and tapped in a command which brought up a maintenance menu. Casual users on this system assumed that if you wiped a screen message clean it was gone—irretrievable. But Lepov knew that this was not always the case. One simple trick was to kill the power supply to the unit. Restoring power to the system often allowed retrieval options for data recovery.

And as he had suspected, the last message that had been on that desk redisplayed. Lepov read the note left for Kry Dannen.

It was not the note he had written.

When some people make a mistake they are timid, hesitant to admit it. Some even go so far as to deny it. They'll become indignant. Vociferous. Others will look to share the blame, dragging innocent by-standers down with them. There are even those who will deflect the blame to someone else. Anything to keep from facing up to their mistake, no matter how big or little it is.

And then there are those people who just get angry. These people recognize their culpability in the mistake and know that only they can correct it. No one else can undo the wrong.

No one but Lepov could possibly make amends for the magnitude of his mistake.

Ultimately, it was a myth to believe that it was better to know that you had a weak spot for someone who did not hesitate to exploit it. Someone who *counted on it.*

Lepov erased the message and left. He might have already agreed to a deal with Jonnie Spaeth, but that didn't mean he couldn't sweeten the deal in Spaeth's favor. The crime boss would be surprised to hear Lepov's altered terms; it was unlikely he was used to being offered unsolicited bonuses.

He did not go back to see Lilly. He had time, the meeting wouldn't happen for another two hours, but he was not sure he could handle seeing Lilly right then. He had to keep his head, had to remain focused, and that would be nearly impossible if he were allowed to consider the ramifications of what he had discovered. And if he saw Lilly, he knew he would be tempted to tell her. And once she knew, there would be no way to prevent himself from dwelling on his failure.

That would come later, easily enough. There was no need to rush it. The only thing that was of immediate importance was the meeting.

Lepov had never intended to give Dannen to Spaeth for obvious reasons. All he had really hoped to accomplish was to get MacNally in sight, then worry about how to force Spaeth to give him up.

But now, he actually had something to offer Spaeth other than Dassin and the stolen Luger.

95

For Frank Dassin, life had come full circle. Having set in motion the plan to steal from Jonnie Spaeth, he was now about to face the man again. On the day he had first decided he would develop and carry out his audacious plan, he had always known he would have to get as far from Jonnie Spaeth as possible.

But incredibly, he was now about to meet with the one man in the Euxine system he never wanted to see again.

When he had awakened in Abbot's bed, Frank had not yet fully shaken off the sleep. He hadn't found it odd when he heard that the woman with the white hair had taken his child to another household. And as he listened to Lepov, that investigator, explain why he— Frank—needed to attend the meeting, Frank nodded as if it all made sense to him. But the more awake he became, the more odd it all seemed.

Why had they taken Jett somewhere else? And Frank could see no reason why he would need to be at the meeting. But then, as they came closer to their destination, Frank began to understand. Returning the stolen gun was not going to be enough to satisfy Spaeth. In order to get Lara back, and to keep Spaeth from seeking retribution, they were going to have to give Spaeth something extra.

Frank was that something extra. He knew it. He could tell in the way none of the others were looking at him. He was in the back of the TransitCar, between Lepov and the blonde woman. The Transit driver was in the front. The two detectives who had found him were no longer around.

That back seat suddenly felt awfully tight. As big as he was, and as small as the woman was on his left, he could have overpowered her. But to what end? The TransitCar was fully thirty meters off the ground now. Not a safe height from which to jump.

But he knew these were only the initial reactions to panic. When he really applied thought to what he was about to face he knew that Lepov had it right. If he had to be sacrificed to Spaeth to save Lara, then that is what should happen. For Frank, it was easiest to just focus on that one, simple, sweet goal. No matter what happened after everyone came together, it would all be worth it if Lara came out of it unharmed.

That was a goal worthy of commitment. Frank fought down his panic and forced himself to find the peace necessary to follow through with his part of the trade.

Lara. She was the only thing that mattered now.

And then without warning, Frank's stomach flipped upside down as the Transit driver ducked the car for a fraction of a second before pulling back to force the vehicle into a climb. A steel and glass grid slid past the belly of the car.

"This the right one?" asked Lepov.

"According to the instructions. Can I assume Spaeth owns this building?" Abbot watched the passing grid of the skyscraper slow as he braked near the top.

"Assume all you want. It's what I'm doing. If I had to guess, his ship will be up here. He insisted we do this here so that he could take off immediately.

And Frank saw that Lepov had been right. As soon as they crested the top of the building, they could see a sleek, silver ship sitting on the far edge of a landing pad in the center of the rooftop. The ship was not nearly as large as one of the transports that most people used for arrivals and departures in the Lazaretto. But it looked far more dangerous. Its predatory profile left them with no illusions. It was sure to be armed to the teeth.

Abbot dropped his TransitCar close to the center of the landing pad. At the touch of a switch, the sound of the engine ceased. From where Frank was sitting, he could not see Lara anywhere. But then an access panel opened on the ship and Frank recognized Tommy Towers standing in the gap.

"Abbot, you stay here, at the wheel. You aren't a part of this. If bullets start flying, how fast can you get off this roof?"

"Fast enough. I didn't shut it down. It still has power. I won't have to bail out right away."

"Hey," Lepov put a hand on the seat, close to Abbot's shoulder, "I mean what I said. You don't have a part in this. Do not wait for any of us if everything falls apart. My gut tells me Spaeth is gonna play by the rules because it's good business. And I've got a small insurance policy that should keep him in line. But if you don't get this heap off this roof in the event you hear guns being fired and you see us diving for the floorboards, I'll take the time to fire a shot or two your way so that you'll know just how disappointed I am with you. Got it?"

"Lepov, go do what you need to do. I drive a TransitCar in some of the worst neighborhoods in the Lazaretto. I know how to take care of myself. So go."

"We're going." Lepov, still sitting forward in the seat, turned to Gloria. "You stay here too, Lori. Frank, you come with me."

"Grey!" Gloria grabbed his arm. "You be careful. Jonnie can't be trusted. He's no good."

"People who can't be trusted are always no good." He patted her gloved hand. "But sometimes we end up trusting the ones we shouldn't because we just can't help ourselves. For some of us, hope is a sickness. As real as any disease that traps men in this Lazaretto. We just have to believe that things can't get worse or have to get better. We do it because the alternative is too messy. It means we've been living our lives for a lie. And if we have, everything we've done has been a lie. And I mean everything. It's a sad way to look at the world but it doesn't make any sense unless you do it this way. Once you do, once you know you had no option but to trust someone who was always going to betray you, it hurts just a little less. At least you can get back up and walk away in the hope that one day you'll finally meet that someone new who you'll not only learn to trust but you'll learn that the trust was well placed."

"I think you stopped talking about Jonnie Spaeth a few minutes ago. If you're feeling guilty that you trusted Kry and that he betrayed you by killing Lou, don't do it. You couldn't have known I was telling you the truth when I said he was dangerous. I understand. This Lazaretto has not been good to you. It's left you worn and unable to focus. You seemed sure I was going to lie to you. And from your point of view it was the right call. I have lied to you in the past. There was no reason for you to trust me."

"They're coming." Abbot reached out and touched the windshield.

"Let's go Dassin." Lepov grabbed Frank's coat as if he thought he would have to drag him out of the back seat.

"I'm coming, Lepov. You don't have to hold on to me. I know what this is about."

Lepov stopped and stared at Frank. "Do you really?"

"I'm a thief, not an idiot. I want Lara to get out of this alive. I know that the only way for that to happen is for me to go with Spaeth. Otherwise, we'll always be looking for him. One day, maybe while I'm at my new job, I get a message that says my wife and child were killed in an accident. I'll never know for sure, but I'll always believe it was Spaeth. We'll never be completely free of him. This way, if he accepts me as payment, my wife and son will be safe. I'm willing to make that trade. But I don't see her."

More than half a dozen men had stepped out of the ship. Frank could still see Tommy Towers, standing in front. He could now see Jonnie Spaeth as well. Jonnie was not as short as Tommy, but he was thin, his wide hat nearly extended beyond his shoulders. But his wiry frame did not mean he wasn't dangerous. He kept a cane with him, and one end of it could be used as a Shockhammer. And Jonnie enjoyed using it.

Nowhere could he see Lara.

"Where is she?" Frank felt Lepov put a hand to his chest to hold him back.

"Just keep quiet, Frank. Let me do this." Lepov pushed a little and Frank gave in, dropping back a few steps.

"You're Gregor Lepov. I'm Jon Spaeth. I'd shake your hand but I understand that's not always healthy to do in this town."

"Don't worry about it, I wouldn't shake yours for all the...well, let's just say I wouldn't shake yours."

"Where's the gun Frank stole from me?" Spaeth wasn't wasting any time.

"I hate to tell you this, Spaeth, but your gun's no good. I had an expert look at it. It's old, that's not the question. But my expert knows for a fact it wasn't the gun that killed Adolph Hitler."

"I know that," Spaeth waved a hand dismissively. "That's just a story I tell. People don't know any better. A harmless little fabrication."

"Then what have you been doing?" Frank nearly shouted his question. "Why have you taken my wife?"

"I've been protecting my reputation. What did you think I was doing? Did you think I'd let a few worthless boneheads like you steal from me? What am I? People don't take from me. I take from people. It can't happen the other way. If you couldn't understand that you need to demag your brain. So Lepov, give me the worthless gun or my men will shoot every one of you."

Frank couldn't understand why Lepov looked so at ease. Spaeth stood there with all those men, and could simply kill them all, without freeing Lara or even allowing the Transit driver to leave. But even as he was trying to guess at Lepov's calm, a small green triangle, the size of a man's thumb, appeared on the label of Spaeth's coat.

In the darkened swirl of the landing pad, it was very bright and Spaeth looked down at it immediately. His expression was much the same as if he had just spilled gravy on his favorite suit. When he returned his gaze to Lepov there was a cruelty in his slight smile.

"A solid response, Mr. Lepov. Is this when you say 'don't move'?"

"This is when I say you'd better tell me the truth now. Why

wouldn't you let me talk with Lara Dassin?"

Frank's eyes swung from Lepov to Spaeth several times as he tried to catch up to what was being said. "What's going on?"

"How are we going to do business like this? The first thing you do is insult me, withhold my property from me, then you aim a gun at my chest and imply that my end of the deal is crooked. I should ask you where is Kry Dannen?"

"There's a young man on the other end of that trig-sight who has been told to fire once a specific time has passed after he activated it unless I put a hand in the air to stop him. He's running out of time. Where's Lara Dassin?"

Frank watched Spaeth, who was no longer smiling. His eyes were impossible to see beneath his hat but a stray refraction of light sparkled out of one eye. Beside him, Tommy hadn't moved. He was content to just stare at Lepov, ignoring the green target. He had not even glanced down to see if one had appeared on his own coat.

"I was going to have to admit it anyway," Spaeth finally said. "It's just a difficult thing to do, Frank. I don't like to be the one to bring a man this kind of news. But when I really think about it, I suppose if anyone deserves this kind of news it's you. Your wife's dead, Frank. She killed herself."

Lepov raised his right hand. The target did not disappear.

"Where is she, Spaeth?" asked Lepov. His other hand snaked out and grabbed Frank's sleeve. He cautioned Frank not to do anything rash with just a look.

"I already answered you. I can tell you where your Irishman is, though. Go ahead, Tommy."

Tommy turned and waved at the ship. Two men carried MacNally out on a stretcher. They crossed the landing pad and dropped him in front of Lepov. Frank couldn't tell if the detective was alive until his head turned slightly.

"Lepov, you got a cigarette?"

"In a minute." Lepov let go of Frank and reached into his coat pocket and withdrew the Luger.

"I'll take that," Spaeth reached out for the gun.

"No deal." Now Lepov was aiming the gun at Spaeth. "We agreed, the gun for the woman."

"And him," Spaeth nodded at Frank. "But did you forget you agreed to give me Dannen for your Irish friend? I want to see him, now."

"If you want Kry Dannen you'll have to fish him out of a lake in Terran Park. I put him there. But it's your lucky day, Jonnie. I still have something you want."

Without another word, Lepov returned to the TransitCar and

opened the back door. He leaned inside and tugged at Gloria. Frank couldn't see what was happening but he guessed that she was resisting Lepov. He finally managed to yank her out of the car. She struggled against him, but he held her firmly as he forced her to join the group in the middle of the landing pad.

When they were close enough, Frank could see the terror in her eyes.

"I told you Kry Dannen had double-crossed you, Spaeth. But I was wrong. Here's the one you want. She shot Jardyn, and she meant to get out with this little trinket." He waved the Luger at Gloria. "So I think we can still end this so that everyone will be satisfied."

Frank stared at Lepov. How could he say that? He was acting as if Spaeth had never even mentioned Lara.

"Now hold it, Lepov. He's lying about Lara. She wouldn't kill herself. Don't tell me you believe that. Are we supposed to just walk away?"

"Frank, I'm sorry about your wife, but we'll discuss it later. Unless Jonnie here wants to change his story, or give us more details..."

"Calm down, Frank." Spaeth shrugged his shoulders. "If I had to guess, I'd say she was trying to escape. Maybe she killed herself when she saw she couldn't get out. Or maybe it was an accident. Who knows, right? But did we kill her? We did not. So back off, don't look so angry. And as for you, Lepov, I agree. Give me the gun, this woman of Dannen's, and Frank. For that, I won't make this dumb cop pay for killing my brother."

"Grey, don't do this." Gloria wrenched away from Lepov. He lost his grip and she would have run if she hadn't lost her balance. Instead of running, she fell to her knees. Lepov grabbed her collar. She began to kick at him.

Everyone was watching her. No one was paying any attention to Frank. Frank was watching Jonnie Spaeth. Spaeth was laughing at the woman's attempts to get away. Had he laughed at Lara the same way? Had he laughed when she'd died?

Frank looked beyond Spaeth, to the edge of the building, which was only about ten meters away.

"Stand up and shut up." Lepov jerked her back on her feet. "And I told you to stop calling me Grey."

He raised his hand to strike her when Frank decided to take his chance. He ran straight at Jonnie Spaeth.

96

Nothing had gone as he had planned it. The Dassin woman was

dead—no chance Spaeth was lying about that—and there were too many men on the roof for Russell to shoot. He might get half of them, but MacNally couldn't defend himself, and Abbot was unarmed. From the moment Spaeth had appeared with so many men, Lepov had been resigned to the one outcome he'd hoped to avoid; he would have to give up Gloria and Frank Dassin.

But as he struggled with Gloria, Frank Dassin surprised them all. Lepov had known the man was taking the news of his wife's death hard. He knew he'd been wrestling with the sudden grief and anger that was his due. But he had not expected this tall, lanky accountant to burst straight into Jonnie Spaeth. Together, the two men tumbled backwards, a crumpled mass of coats and shoes and hair and curses.

Lepov braced himself for the gun battle that was about to explode around him. He saw a green flicker streak across the bodies of Spaeth's men. Russell looking for a target. Ready to shoot the first man who raised his weapon. There was no reason to let Tommy Towers interfere. Lepov, the Luger still in his hand, shoved the barrel forward as he rushed at Towers. The little man was too busy watching Spaeth and Dassin roll around to notice Lepov's advance.

Too late, Towers looked down to see the barrel of the old pistol rammed into his ribs.

"Hey, watch it." Towers cautiously raised a hand and applied the lightest pressure to Lepov's arm.

The two combatants finally rolled apart; Dassin came up on one knee, fighting for breath. Spaeth regained his feet and faced his attacker. "Shoot this guy, Tommy."

Dassin tensed, stole a look at Towers. At the same time, both Spaeth and Dassin could see that Towers wasn't going to lift a hand to help. Dassin, aware that none of the other men were moving to interfere, tackled Spaeth again. In a matter of seconds, they'd rolled, scratched, and bit their way to the low parapet that ringed the perimeter of the roof.

Dassin wasn't strong, but his fury was sufficient to enable him to seize Spaeth by the collar and keep him from scrambling away. Dassin had rotated so that his back was pressed against the parapet.

Then, as Dassin began to push with his legs, Lepov realized what the man intended. Only the parapet was too short. He held Spaeth in a bear hug—Spaeth's back was pressed into Dassin's chest—and was trying to stand up. But with just three kicks of his heels into the surface of the roof, he was already high enough that his shoulders had slid over the top of the low wall.

Lepov had been wrong. Dassin wasn't trying to stand up. Instead, he was doing exactly what he intended. He was dragging Spaeth over the edge of the roof. But Spaeth wasn't finished yet. He began smashing his elbow into Dassin's gut. At any moment Dassin was going to have to let go, and when he did, without Spaeth's weight holding him down, he'd vault off the roof, alone. His sacrifice would be meaningless.

And then abruptly, they were gone.

Lepov still had the Luger pressed into Towers' ribs. But Towers didn't seem to care. Instead, he was laughing. It had begun as a low chuckle but had increased until it was a full-bodied cackle. By the time he finally stopped, Lepov was convinced the gangster at the end of his pistol had lost his mind.

"Do you know what I wanted to do earlier tonight?" I—" he looked down and paused, until Lepov withdrew the gun. Towers put two fingers on the tip of the barrel and gently pushed it until Lepov relented and dropped the gun to his side. "—I tried to kill that crazy fool. Well, I didn't actually try, but I had decided to do it. I just couldn't get up the nerve. And now look at what that number-cruncher did. He just knocked off Jonnie Spaeth. Like that."

He snapped his fingers and started to laugh again.

Lepov was still holding on to Gloria. He could feel the hatred emanating from her. Towers noticed her at the same time. He waved a hand at her. "And let her go. I don't want her. I've already got a woman. What would I do with two of them?"

"Well, take the gun, anyway." Lepov switched his grip on it so that Towers could grab the pistol grip.

"Keep it, you heard Spaeth, it's worthless. And I ain't got a reputation to protect. What I do have is a need to get the hell out of here. This place is crazy. I need to get back to some sunshine and warm weather. How do you people live here, anyway?"

Lepov shrugged. He couldn't deny it was a good question.

"You want my guys to put him in that TransitCar?" Towers was looking down at MacNally. He waved at one of his men and spoke a few soft words. The man pulled out a large handgun and passed it to Towers. Towers bent down and tucked the gun into the blanket next to MacNally. "Here's a gift for you, cop. That's a fine gun. It's yours, and I don't want to take it from you. It's my way of saying thanks for shooting that gorilla brother of Jonnie's."

Lepov turned to see that Abbot had not left during Dassin's fight with Spaeth. That was about right. No one had done anything Lepov had expected them to. At least Russell had provided cover as he'd promised. That he hadn't started shooting when Dassin jumped Spaeth spoke to his quick thinking. The roof would have turned into a kill zone—for all of them.

"I can walk," MacNally said. Lepov had barely been able to hear him and he simply ignored his friend. Instead, two of Towers' men lifted MacNally and put him in the back seat of Abbot's car.

It wasn't until MacNally was in the car that Lepov realized he was still holding on to Gloria. She was no longer fighting him. And he could see that she had recovered her controlled demeanor. That she had panicked in the face of Jonnie Spaeth had surprised Lepov. He'd never seen her lose her cool.

He hadn't realized how much he wanted Spaeth to take her, to punish her for her betrayal. But now, knowing that she would not be taken back to Bukovina, he had to make a decision. And he couldn't put it off.

The first thing to do would be to get MacNally to the clinic. After that, he'd deal with Gloria.

"Lepov, I'm glad we met. This couldn't have worked out better. I think it's safe to say I owe you one. If you ever need a favor, you let me know." Towers was laughing again. "Life's funny, isn't it? I tried to tell that sonofabitch to let this go. To get off this rock. He was an ass. Now, if you don't mind, I gotta go find this girl I know who likes to talk to God."

Behind the silent, black shape of the ship, a gleam of golden light split the black sky. Day was coming. For a moment it looked as if a real sunrise would light the morning sky.

Towers signaled the men who remained to follow him and they left the roof. Once the door was shut, Lepov and Gloria were standing alone beside the car.

The wind had picked up. Gloria's hair swirled into her eyes. She brushed it aside and said: "It's too bad about Frank and his wife."

"It's too bad for the boy." Lepov motioned for her to get in the car.

"Grey, you don't have to worry. I'll leave. I won't stick around. And I'll talk to Lilly, so she'll know I'm not in the way."

"Get in, Gloria. Just get in."

He put her in the front seat, next to Bril, then wedged into the back with MacNally. Peering into the darkness, it looked as if MacNally had either passed out or fallen asleep. Lepov saw the handgun poking out of the blanket beside him. He slid a finger over its cold, textured grip.

"Everyone ready?" Bril looked back at them and shuddered the engine.

"I thought I told you to get this thing off the roof if there was trouble." Lepov removed his hat; despite the cold night, he'd been sweating heavily. He needed to release a little tension.

"No you didn't. You asked if bullets started flying how fast I could get off the roof. I said fast enough. I never said I would get off the roof."

"You might not realize it, but that came very close to turning into a bullet-fest. You should have got out of here. But since you didn't, I guess that means you don't mind driving us a little while longer. So first of all, take us to the Duvalls. From there you can drive the Doc and MacNally to the clinic. You can leave me and Gloria behind."

"Hey, my pleasure." Abbot pointed at his meter. "I've had that meter on since MacNally first hired me. Someone's gonna have to pay my bill when this is over. I'll be able to take a vacation."

A vacation sounded nice, thought Lepov. It was just too bad that he'd never be able to take one.

The sky had warmed unexpectedly as the morning sun broke the dawn with a rare mix of reds, blues, and golds. The Transit driver spun them over and down the sides of the great glass building, and soon the fleeting vision of the sun over the Lazaretto disappeared from view.

97

"Don't worry about it, I've got it." Maria Duvalls grabbed a wet rag from the kitchen sink and quickly dropped to her knees as she began to wipe away the mess.

Jett, the sweet little boy that Lilly was rapidly getting to know, had knocked over his bowl of peaches. As soon as it had happened he had stiffened up, eyes wide and afraid.

But Maria was not at all bothered by his spill.

"I'm quite used to cleaning up after people. In fact, I've never really cleaned up after a little boy. Just older people usually. This is different, and even a little fun."

"You said you work in a clinic?"

"My husband works there. He's the head physician. I'm just a volunteer. So many people don't get proper care in this place. We just try to give them a little dignity, restore their humanity near the end of their life. There, now, see? All cleaned up."

The little boy relaxed by the time she was done. He seemed greatly relieved that no one was yelling at him over the spilled fruit.

"Now, what I think," Maria said, turning to look into Jett's eyes, "is that this little boy might enjoy a nice warm bath. Does that sound good to you?"

Jett nodded, his eyes searching from Lilly to Maria for a sign that it was okay to want the bath. Both of the women smiled and nodded encouragement to him. Once they did, his nod grew to a vigorous nod that gave them the impression he had lost control of the muscles in his neck.

"Okay, then, you come with me." Maria took his hand and

helped him down off the barstool. She put her other hand up to block Lilly from following. "You go and lie down in that spare bed I showed you. You didn't sleep much. I won't need your help with this little man. And he'll need to sleep too. I plan to relax him with the bath then put him to bed next to Georges. Georges is still asleep and it will be interesting to see his reaction to waking up next to our little visitor. Now, go!"

Maria pushed Lilly down the hall. A door on her right opened into the spare bedroom. A soft click of the door and she was alone. She could faintly hear Maria's voice and the muffled hiss of running water.

Lilly saw light coming through the edges of the heavy drapes that covered one wall. She probed the center of them until she found a gap and used both hands to separate the two halves of the drapes. She worked a gap that was just wide enough for her to step into. The window behind the drapes afforded a towering view of the southern end of the Lazaretto. It was less congested here. There were fewer tall buildings and further out Lilly could see smaller homes replacing the apartment complexes. Somewhere out there was Bril Abbot's home.

But off to her left, if she placed her head close to the cool of the glass, she could see a golden glow. One she'd never seen before in this city. A fire? Spot lights? She knew what it really was, though she hardly dared to believe it. Anywhere else—on any of the planets—she'd know it was the sun rising without its shroud of clouds.

Did Gregor see it? What was taking him so long? She forced herself to think of something else.

Though the glass was still cool she imagined she could feel the warmth of the Euxine's golden sun. Lilly shivered and felt tears forming along the rims of her eyes. She had begun to believe she would never see the sun again. Had tried to tell herself it was okay, that she had no need to ever feel its warmth kiss her cheeks. She had lied to herself, since the day she'd been told—

A soft knock on her door. "Lilly?"

"Maria?" She opened the door to find Maria, the sleeves of her robe pushed up high on her arms, her hands wet. "I can't leave Jett. Someone is knocking at the door. Could you go?"

Lilly rushed to the door but she did not unlock it until she examined the people in the outer hallway.

There were just two of them. Gregor was one of them. *She* was the other. Gloria. The wife—the ex-wife. Lilly knew what Shay would say if he were there. He'd tell her to keep the door locked. Don't let either one of them inside.

Lilly was made of weaker fiber than Shay. She opened the door.

"Lilly, get the doctor. Right away."

Lilly stared at Gregor long enough that he must have seen the hurt in her eyes. That he'd left her behind was problem enough. That he'd been out with Gloria at his side sickened her. The woman was poison. Couldn't he see that? Didn't he realize she'd conned him into killing her husband? And yet he was running around with her all night long?

"Lilly?" Gregor gave up on her and pushed her gently to the side as he hurried off in search of Doctor Duvalls.

Something did not look right with Gloria. She was folded into herself, as if she were terribly cold. Had she become sick as well? Would they be forced to live with her in the Lazaretto? Shay would absolutely love the irony of that. Before she could observe much more of Gloria, Gregor and Georges Duvalls crowded the foyer.

"From what I could see, they were able to patch him up alright. But he's lethargic," Gregor was saying as they came within earshot.

"And the soccer player, he is downstairs with him?" Georges was pulling on his coat and began searching for something in a small closet by the door.

"Right out the front entrance. I can't come with you. There's something I've got to do. I hope you don't mind."

"I'll be fine." Georges finally extracted a wool hat from the top of the closet and donned it with just a hint of care. "And Detective MacNally will be fine, I'm sure. I suspect he lost blood and these men were not able to replace it. But I must hurry. Miss Stewart, will you tell my wife I do not know when I'll be home?"

Lilly nodded but the doctor was already out the door without looking back.

And then all that could be heard in that entryway was the soft, whispered voice from Maria at the far end of the hall. Occasionally, a splash was heard as well.

Lilly could see that Gloria would not look at anyone. She kept herself withdrawn, unwilling to acknowledge Lilly's presence. "Gregor, what happened? Something's gone wrong, hasn't it? Is Jett's mother safe? Where did you take his parents?"

"I've got to go back out, Lilly. Just stay here a while longer. I won't be long. Do this one favor for me."

Lilly thought Gregor was reaching out to her, to embrace her, to show her he understood how hard it had been to be left behind and not know if she would ever see him again. She took a step in his direction but he did not advance to meet her half way. Instead, he angled away from her and put an arm around Gloria.

"We need some time alone. Please, Lilly, we just need a little time alone."

She should have seen it coming. Gloria obviously did. Even before he spoke those last words, her posture had changed and she was now standing up straight. Her head was uplifted, defiant and triumphant eyes shone out from under her uncombed hair. There was a hint of pity in her manner as she nodded at Lilly.

"Gregor, wait." Lilly had nothing to say to him. She just needed to keep him from going. Keep him from crossing that threshold.

"Lilly, it's okay. I'm just saying goodbye to my wife."

Glad to see them leave, she terrified to think that the sound of her heart breaking would simply draw out more pity from Gregor's first—and possibly his only—love.

Damn Gregor, his favor, and his wife.

##

For the first time since Gloria had realized Lepov had intended to turn her over to Jonnie Spaeth, she seemed to relax. They were in the elevator, the floor falling away, their bodies dropping with it. The heat of Gloria's anger had subsided. She no longer stared at him with those black, bitter eyes. As the elevator slowed, their bodies pitched forward just enough that they rubbed arms together. She did not pull away.

He saw the ghost of a smile on her lips. She wanted this farewell. She was ready to move on again. Ready to drop him for yet another new life.

They exited the building and he guided her around the corner of it, heading out into Terran Park. She stiffened a little when she understood where he was leading her.

"What are you doing, Grey?"

"I just want to make sure your husband hasn't crawled ashore. You don't want me be arrested do you? We were kind of in a hurry last night. I'd hate to scare any little kids who might be out for a frolic on the beach."

"I thought you were going to tell me goodbye."

"Oh, I am. I am. And why not out here, look at the sky. We may have ourselves a real sunrise."

He had his hand on the small of her back, nudging her forward. Once they cleared the trees and saw the lake she began to resist him.

"Tell me the truth, what are you doing?" She tried to stop walking but he pushed harder and she almost lost her balance. Stumbling on a few more steps she reached the park bench that they had used the night before. She gripped its iron slat and refused to go any further.

"Now listen, you've been playing pretty loose with me, since you tried to offer me up to that gangster. You not only had Spaeth fooled, you almost had me believing you were willing to give me up. What was your plan? Were you going to shoot us out of there? Because if that was your plan, it wasn't going to work. You were going to get us all killed. You got lucky when Frank lost his mind."

"Shut up, Gloria. I'm gonna do the talking. But for the record, I was perfectly willing to let Spaeth walk away with you and you know it. But that's not why we're talking now."

She lifted her chin and the black hatred was back in her eyes.

"You see, from the beginning I knew I shouldn't have taken this job. It smelled like spoiled milk from the moment you came into my office. But I let you in, I let you make your offer, and I accepted it. Not because I thought it was an honest deal but because I thought it was the only way to keep you in front of me where I could see what your real goals were."

"And you had everything figured out, did you?"

"Not at first. It wasn't until just a few hours ago that I finally put it all together. I've got Lilly to thank for that. Because without her on the outside looking in, I was designed to fail at this. I was too blinded by my own hurt and love and confusion to see you for what you really are, even as I swore you were an evil woman who couldn't be trusted."

"You're still cute when you're mad, Grey. But I'm not as easily charmed as I used to be. I'm not going to stand here and listen to your insults and accusations. Not from a man who has blood on his hands."

She let go of the bench, pushing Gregor aside. Instead of allowing her to move him, he pushed back. And after she'd regained her balance she looked down and saw the Luger in Lepov's hand, pointed at the belt on her coat.

"You're going to shoot me?" Her laughter carried out over the water.

"I'm going to keep talking and you're going to keep listening."

She didn't try to leave again. She folded her arms and that smug smile of hers contained just a hint of uncertainty.

"You had me with that pathetic plea not to tell Kry where Jardyn was hiding. Because you knew I wasn't going to trust you. So I let you lead me to Jardyn, I let you influence me to only tell Kry where he was. And I immediately knew Kry had to be the one to kill him. I just never seemed to remember that you were the one who first knew where he was."

"I didn't know. I only knew where he was supposed to leave his message. You took the message."

"I know, that was smart. Real smart. But he didn't leave the message. He tried to tell me that but I didn't listen. He didn't know what message you were talking about. What should have been clear to me was the fact that you knew where he was all along. I couldn't figure out why this message was waiting for you. If he could prearrange for you to get his message you could have just prearranged a new hotel if he had felt the need to move.

"But the message was for me. So that I would think you didn't know where he was. It was so stupid it was brilliant. Or I was just stupid. And then, when I called that morning, to talk to Kry, I was afraid you'd answer the phone, but he did. I was glad, I wanted you to keep sleeping, but I wonder, were you even there? He was already agitated when I called, maybe he was agitated because his wife had not come home that night."

He saw the anger in her eyes fade a little, pushed aside by a little fear, maybe a little pride even.

"Russell's report on Jardyn's body told me what I'd needed to know. He hadn't been killed that morning, after I talked to Kry. He'd been killed earlier that night. Probably just moments after I left. You were supposed to go back to your hotel, but you didn't. You were right behind me. And he let you in, which he shouldn't have, because he'd figured all of this out talking to me. But like me he had a weakness for untrustworthy blondes, didn't he? Or maybe he just gave up. Grew tired of the fight within—love her, trust her, fear her, hate her. Did he looked relieved when you put that bullet in him?"

"You're too tired, Grey. None of this is making any sense. You know Kry killed him. Kry tried to kill me. You of all people can't forget that—you shot him. You saved me from him. Remember?"

"Sure, a man can't ever forget his biggest mistake. And I never will. You see, when I left that note for him at the hotel, it was just bait. I wanted him to come after me, because I knew he was going to go after you. I thought he'd left the gun in the hotel room, and when he saw it was gone he was going to think it was you. Noble me, I was putting myself up as a target. But he never read that note. I saw the note he found. The one you wrote. Because again, you were right behind me, as soon as I left Abbot's place, you were out the door. And you rewrote my note."

It was the first time she allowed the truth to be seen in her face. She hadn't thought he'd be able to see the note she'd deleted.

"That's right. Your note. Not my note. Oh, he thought it was my note. What was it you wrote? My confession that I had slept with you, killed Jardyn, and was willing to give him the Luger if he gave you up? Just the thing a jealous husband wants to read. And so he brings you to the park, because he needs this gun." Lepov poked her in the belt with it to draw her attention. "He made a deal with Jonnie Spaeth and he can't let it slip away. And then you put on a show for me, and I played my part. I killed him. It's what you wanted."

"I told him I was tired of his money and his insufferable, boring life. I told him he was old, and I needed a younger man." She put a hand on the gun barrel, her voice softened. "I told him I was going back to you because you were twice the lover he could ever hope to be. Silly stuff, the stuff that gets under a man's skin. I wasn't lying when I said he was jealous and dangerous. So he played his part too. But you played your part to perfection."

"God, Gloria. You haven't changed a bit. This was all about your getting tired of another man. Like you were tired of me. And once again you used me to move out. But instead of carrying the furniture, this time I got rid of the body."

"I'm surprised you didn't have me kill Jardyn."

"You wouldn't have done it." She smiled as if amused at the thought.

"But I just might have put a slug of lead into Kry if I thought you were in danger?"

"I knew you would, if you were angry enough. And it was always easy to get you angry enough."

"But why kill Kry at all? He wouldn't be the first man to watch you walk out of his life."

"Kry wasn't the kind of man to let a woman walk out of his life. Not like you. He had more self-respect than that. Had more dignity. More...well. I couldn't walk out unless he was dead. I'd never get away with it. I'd be running the rest of my life. My motive was too strong. And then there was Jonnie Spaeth. I wanted that gun. I wanted the money that came with it. When Kry decided to double-cross the others, he thought I agreed to it. But he signed his death ticket with that decision. I had to get it from him. And yes, you had to be the one to kill him."

"But you don't have the gun, Gloria. I do. And Kry isn't the only Dannen I had to kill."

"You gonna shoot me, Grey?" Her laugh was soft and her smile was cruel.

"Don't, Gregor." Lilly's voice cut the morning air and Lepov was tempted to turn toward it. Instead, he stared at Gloria, who was looking over his shoulder.

"Lilly, get the hell out of here. I'm just telling her goodbye."

"I've been behind you long enough to know that isn't true. Listen to me. She's not worth this. You can walk away."

"She hired me to kill her husband and I did it. I'm not willing to walk away from that. Besides, it's my turn to say it: baby, I'm just tired of you."

"Gregor, don't!" Lilly came forward and put her hand on the Luger. Instead of struggling for it, he simply let it go.

"I don't need it, Lilly. Keep it." From his other pocket he extracted the Panther. "Lilly, go back to the Duvalls."

"You can't kill me, Grey." Gloria watched Lepov's hand.

"You thought I could kill your husband."

"Sure, and you did. But not because you're a killer. Because you still love me. And you wanted to protect me. I've known all along what kind of man you are. I've always known. I've always counted on it. I knew you'd do it. I knew your heart, and I know you won't kill me."

Lepov raised the Panther until the point of the barrel was touching her ribs just below her left arm. "Do you? Do you know how good a man I am? Do you know how good a man I'm not?"

"Better than even you know."

"I wouldn't bet on it, Gloria."

"I already have. And you aren't going to shoot me." She leaned into him, kissing his cheek.

"You're the Devil, baby." The Panther fit his hand perfectly.

"Maybe I am. But nobody shoots the Devil. It won't change the fact that you killed for me."

"I'm willing to give it a try."

Gunfire echoed across the lake. Gloria's eyes opened wide and she looked as if she might ask a question. Instead, she leaned against Lepov, her lips hit his cheek yet again, lips that would never lie or kiss again. Instead, she slumped in his arms.

Lepov caught and held her tightly. He could feel warm blood soaking into his coat and shirt. He slipped the cold steel of the Panther into his pocket as he gently allowed her to fall back onto the bench. Once she was down on her back Lepov turned his head to look at Gloria's killer.

"She made you kill for her once already. I couldn't let you do it again." Lilly wasn't crying. There was no tremor in her voice.

Lepov took the Luger from her and tossed it into the lake. As the morning sunshine warmed the air around them, Gloria was already cold to the touch. Lepov left her lying on the bench, put an arm around Lilly, and led her away.

99

MacNally looked a lot better. Russell had been watching him for several days. Each day, a little more color came back into his face, and a little more color came back into his speech. By the third day, he was able to raise his bed just enough to be able to see more than the ceiling.

"So what are you telling me, Russell? You'd rather stick with Kwan?"

"I haven't said anything close to that."

"You did. You tell me that she makes good conversation, that she's sharp, funny, and you said she's…I don't…you'd rather look at her than me. And then this thing about jasmine. What was that all about?" MacNally had been holding his head up but now he dropped it back against a thin pillow.

"All I was saying is she isn't so bad a partner. But you get better and you and I can go back to our lovely little special friendship."

"Damn it Russell, there you go thinking without my help again. The fact is, I'm done. I'm old."

"You aren't *that* old, Ed."

"Russell, I don't want to do this anymore. I'm done and I don't want to debate it with you."

"Well don't come looking to me for a job." The voice came from outside the door. Lepov walked through it. "Did this guy just say he was retiring?"

Russell nodded.

"That's good. Best thing that will happen to the police force in forty years." Lepov sat on the edge of the bed near MacNally's beltline and bent low to examine the recovering detective. "You feeling any better?"

"Lepov, you're killing me. It hurts my chest when you sit there."

"Your chest was hurting before I sat there, you're just being dramatic."

"So tell me why you're here. Then maybe you can stand up so I can breathe."

"Okay, I'm getting up. Russell, shut that door. We need to talk."

Russell closed the door and dropped into a chair. The room grew quiet until Lepov began to speak.

"I came to tell you two the truth. You deserve it. The both of you have been good to me when you didn't need to. And while maybe I could hide the truth from you, I just don't want to."

He had ended up standing at the lone window in the room, overlooking the gray, wet Lazaretto. That one, brief day of sunshine had not lasted. No one had expected it to. Lepov seemed transfixed by the rain. When he spoke, there was a gravity to his tone Russell could not remember Lepov ever using before.

"I need to talk about the shooting in Terran Park. You been told about that yet, MacNally?"

"I told him," Russell nodded.

"That was your ex-wife, right? That was one helluva fight. Whatever he did to her, it was enough. You're just lucky she shot him then shot herself and didn't include you in the bargain. Do you know what it was about?"

"You guys worked it all out, huh?" Lepov aimed his question at Russell. "You think she killed her husband then used the gun on herself?"

"Why not?" Russell's answer was purposefully vague. He didn't want to elaborate in front of MacNally.

"You're a better detective than that, Russell."

"What does that mean?" MacNally eyed Russell suspiciously.

"Maybe we're not better than that."

"So let me help you out a little."

"Lepov," Russell cut him off, "you might feel the need to get something off your chest but this isn't the place to do it. Go find a priest or a cheap psychologist. But don't come in here to confess anything or throw yourself on the mercy of a court that doesn't give a damn."

MacNally had had enough. "Somebody tell me what's going on!"

"What Lepov is about to do is confess to something that he doesn't need to."

"This isn't a confession. Not in the conventional sense, anyway."

"It doesn't matter." Russell had not spoken of any of this to MacNally. He had hoped to let the man recover in peace. The less stress the better. But Lepov was forcing his hand. "This isn't very complicated, MacNally. The official story is the one that is going to stay in the final report. That's the one I told you. We found the murder weapon, an antique gun that had been tossed in the lake."

"But your reports have come back, haven't they?"

"They have. And although a temporal dislocation was found between the two deaths that raised a question, we've been able to find a satisfactory answer for it."

"A temporal what?" MacNally asked.

"A timeline problem. Forgive my lawyer's language. Kwan thought it would look good in the report. You see, for most murder/suicides, you don't have a gap of ten hours. But we've decided that Mrs. Dannen only ended her life after a night of regret and self-hate, or whatever it was that led her to take her own life. Obviously the guilt of killing her husband was too much to bear."

"And how did you explain the fact that she shot herself on the bench but managed to toss the gun into the lake? That's a distance of nearly ten meters," Lepov pointed out.

"You know what?" Russell paused and nodded as if this were a completely new thought. "No one's asked that question before. But it is an interesting one. But I'm sure Kwan and I will be able to think of one if we're pressed to."

"And what about your Visuals? What did they tell you? Did Gloria fire that gun? Were her prints on it?"

"One of the problems with Visuals is that they're expensive to run. We weren't able to run the highest rates with them, due to the rash of deaths the occurred in that shooting that broke out in and around the shipping port. So we weren't able to firmly establish the answers to those types of questions."

Lepov shook his head. "MacNally, I'd say your training is finished with Detective Russell. He's about as honest as you are now. I'd ask how you convinced your boss to accept such shoddy work, but I have an idea what happened there."

"Jenkins is a little easy to handle, right now." Russell didn't need to add that Jenkins was only too happy to keep his mouth shut as long as Russell, Kwan and MacNally didn't report him for betraying MacNally to Spaeth. In exchange, Jenkins had agreed to announce his retirement in a few weeks.

"So Russell has this under control, though I admit I'm not too sure what he's doing. If I had to guess I'd say you're both saying Gloria didn't shoot herself. And if that's the case I don't want to hear the truth, do I?"

"You're going to," Lepov said.

"Why? As I recall, you weren't interested in telling me the truth the last time you knew a murderer's name that I didn't."

"That's because you didn't know who that person was and that person paid their due. But right now, Russell knows that the prints on that gun included Gloria's, mine, and Lilly's. And as I said when I started this, I could stay quiet on this and you'd never know the truth. But I want you to. Because if you speculate, you're gonna get it wrong. And I don't want that between us."

"Well, dammit, Lepov, if it means that much to you, just tell us what the hell happened and then we can forget about it."

And he did. Lepov began by explaining his role in the murder of Louis Jardyn and he didn't stop until he had finished with Gloria's shooting. He did not hesitate to give them the full details. Even when he had to admit that he had taken Gloria to the park with the intent to kill her. Even when he had to admit that Lilly had taken the job from him.

"You once asked me, MacNally, why Lilly and I are still here. Why we left Alpha Quadrant. I never told you but I think I'd better. We came back for the same reason everyone comes back: by invitation of the IHS. There was the little matter of a procedure that had to be enforced. Lilly was diagnosed with a pathogen: meningitis. It's more complicated than that, the word they used was much longer. Something to do with encephalitis. Anyway, as the doctor put it, there is pressure up here," he tapped his forehead several times, "and it has caused some hallucinations. She had good days and bad days. But the latter are beginning to outweigh the former.

"I think she knew it was getting worse. And she had an idea that she had less to lose by pulling that trigger. She also thought she was never going to get off this rock. But I've been talking to Dr. Duvalls and he says that there are things that could be done for her, to mitigate the damage, give her a chance at a little more normal life. Hell, I don't know all the science behind it. I just know that if she lived somewhere other than this damned place she'd be able to get some help."

MacNally and Russell exchanged looks. What sort of response was there for a friend in this situation? How could you tell a friend that the hope they yearned for was illusory?

"I'm sorry, Gregor." MacNally lay with his head back, staring at the ceiling. "We can do a lot for you. We can keep her out of jail, but the one thing we can't do is break open the Lazaretto. No matter how much we want to."

"I know. And I wouldn't ask it of you. I told you this wasn't a confession in the traditional sense. I didn't come here to confess to a crime that was already committed. I'm here to tell you that I'm about to commit one. And I'm asking you to understand. That's all. For a little boy and woman who thinks her life is over. I'm not even asking you to look the other way. Once it's done, you can arrest me. Just don't stop me."

Crossing to the door, Lepov opened it, but paused before leaving.

"It doesn't mean anything that she pulled the trigger. I'd already pulled that trigger dozens of times in my mind. From the day Gloria left me, the years that followed, and ever since she walked into my office. I didn't need a reason to do it. She gave me one, anyway. That wasn't a surprise. But I never really needed much of one. A man's pride gets torn out of him and if he's really honest with himself he'll see that it doesn't take much more than that to avenge a wrong. For all our belief in nobility, we're damned petty when someone sticks a knife in us. Especially if that someone was a woman we once loved.

"Lilly was trying to save me. She reckoned that if she pulled the trigger I wouldn't bear the guilt. But she only made it twice as painful. No, I'm not blaming her. Even if she hadn't been sick, if her head hadn't been lying to her, she might have done the same thing. I won't deny the grandeur of her sacrifice. I'll never understand why she would do something like that for me but that's not the issue. I only mean that I have to bear the shame of Gloria's murder and Lilly's sacrifice all wrapped into my petty little urge for revenge.

"And don't think that this last act of mine, this gesture of kindness is an attempt to redeem myself. This wouldn't cover the down payment on such a debt. Not if I managed to free every exile on this rock that didn't deserve to be imprisoned here. But just let me do this one thing, Mac. After that, I don't care what you do with me."

He was gone. Entranced by his words, Russell and MacNally stared at each other. Finally, MacNally spoke.

"Want to know a secret, Russell?"

"Sure, Pops."

"I wouldn't know what to do if I retired. So help me up. And I hate to say this, but I don't have a stitch of clothing on under this hospital gown."

100

Lilly couldn't sleep. She briefly wondered if the wind had awakened her; a storm had blown through earlier in the night. But she didn't hear one now. Having tried and failed to go back to sleep, she decided to get up and find some hot tea or maybe even some brandy.

She had not left the Duvalls'. They'd been kind enough to allow her to stay with them. Lilly knew she couldn't go back to her place, knew she shouldn't be alone, but the reason for this did not always stay in her mind where she could occasionally pull it out to examine it. Whatever the reason, she had an idea that it was a good one. It wasn't just Gregor's insistence that she stay with the Duvalls. It was the doctor's persuasiveness that kept her from leaving. He was both terribly kind and convincingly logical.

Lilly liked that about him.

She did not turn on lights so as not to wake the Duvalls. However, as she neared the kitchen, she heard voices and saw a soft glow. Closer, she recognized Gregor's voice.

"The offer is a complete package. She'll need someone of your caliber, and the boy will need parents."

"I never thought of leaving." That was the doctor. "There is so much work here. So much yet to be done."

"And if you stayed, would you ever catch up? Would you ever finish all the work?"

"No, of course not. And you are making a salient point. If we were to leave, there are men who could replace me. Younger men, schooled in the latest techniques. More fit to handle the hours. I won't kid myself. I know I'm replaceable."

"We all are." Lepov cleared his throat. "You realize what I'm proposing? For both the boy and Lilly."

"I understand," Doctor Duvalls' voice was almost too soft to make out. "But I know they do not pose any real danger to others. Not if we take precautions. Mr. Lepov, I think I would turn you down, if it was only to care for them. You could find others to do the job. Even in this I am replaceable. But you see, for Maria, I think I will tell you *yes*. Because I do not know how much longer she can take this place. She is strong—stronger than even I knew. I know that she does not draw much attention her way, but in a very real sense, she does more for the people in that clinic than I do. But every time she cares for a patient, it wears a little bit of her away, like rain, eroding the face of a stone angel. A little every day. But if I take your offer, I can remove her from this place. And maybe she could turn her attention to the boy and instead of taking from her, maybe he would bring something to her."

"I'm glad to hear it, doctor. But I'm sorry to say there is little time if we are to make it. Will you be able to do this quickly?"

"Now?" And Lilly heard the doctor exclaim softly, as if he'd just seen something wonderful and terrible all in the same glimpse.

"I have to leave. But I'll be back in thirty minutes. Don't wake Lilly. I'll get her when it's time. I'd rather she didn't have time to think about this. There's just no way to know what she'll..."

"She'll be just fine, Mr. Lepov. But we'll do as you say."

Lilly heard chairs scrape the floor and she drew away and glided back down the hallway as quietly as she could. In her room she shut the door, watching to see if Gregor would notice that her door was open before she could close it. He did not appear in the hall before the door was completely closed.

"Lilly—" She should have known Shay was in the room. At first she refused to turn and face him. "You've been avoiding me, my dear. Was it something I said?"

She held her tongue. She wanted him to stop talking.

"Was it maybe something *he* said? Oh yeah, how did he say it? *Tell him to go away.* That was rude. And then he said something about how he would talk to you about me later. Did he? Did he talk to you about me? You sent me away, you did as you were told. But he's not holding up his end of the bargain. Not yet your husband, but damned well acting like one."

"You are too," she whispered, her eyes closed, still facing away from him.

"Well, old habits, as the saying goes. Why do you think I'm here, Lilly? To whine about Lepov?"

"How should I know?"

"Why wouldn't you? If the remarkable Gregor Lepov is right,

you're the only one who would know why I'm here. You once sent me away, to prison. Now, you've called me back from something far more solitary than prison. *Why am I here?*"

And then she turned, saw him silhouetted with the light of the city illuminating the window in a silver screen backdrop. His black outline was flat as if he were only a photograph or a shadow on the glass. She was afraid to go near him, to discover he was only a shade, a ghost of what had once been her lover and friend. But it was impossible to stay away. She took a step forward.

"I was such a coward," she began.

"Not Lilly the Invincible." She could almost see his broad smile though his entire face was hidden by the dark. "Don't believe that."

"I never even had the courage to talk to you, after...I told myself I was afraid of you. But I knew it was a lie."

"Don't worry about it, it can't matter now. What good could come from talking, huh? Most of the time, when husbands and wives talk, someone gets hurt. Accusations are thrown, confessions are wielded like hammers, and worst of all, there's nothing like the guilt that tags along with an apology. Especially when there is no need to give one, though that is when they're most effective."

"When Pete told me, that day, about your shuttle..." Lilly tried to see his eyes but it was still too dark. She stepped closer. "I knew right then that I'd never get the chance—"

"Don't say it, Lilly. You shouldn't be apologizing."

"I think I know that now. At first, I just wanted to hear you say you still loved me. Or at least that you didn't hate me. But none of that seems important now."

"So why *am* I here?" Shay asked her. And this time, she could hear it in his tone. He wasn't asking to trap her with her own answer. He wasn't hoping to get a chance to shoot a sarcastic remark back at her. He needed to know why she'd brought him back. She needed to know why.

She wanted to say she had no idea. But the closer she came to speaking the words the more an image came to mind; an image she did not want to acknowledge.

Yes, there might have been a reason why she would conjure the presence of her ex-husband, but that reason had nothing to do with a need for resolution, no need for a last word of absolution. Nothing so dignified. She had only begun to see Shay after Gregor began talking of Gloria. And he'd never actually begun speaking to her until after Gloria arrived in the Lazaretto.

"You know why. We both do. I know why. And we both know you shouldn't be here anymore."

They were close enough now to touch. She felt him lean in, put out a hand and held him back. She could see his eyes now and knew she would never see them again.

Epilogue

The New Yorker had been surprised when the call came in from the Russian. It was true he had told the man that if there was anything he could do for him all he had to do was call. But he had not expected his offer would be accepted so soon, if ever at all. He could have ignored the request. He could have replied with a flat denial. The New Yorker certainly wasn't obligated to keep his word.

But his experience with the Ursuline had left him uncertain and willing to look at his world from a new perspective. He still had trouble looking her in the eye. Not because she despised him. But precisely because she didn't despise him. That awful, ridiculous, beautiful mantra of hers kept invading his mind — or was it really his soul? — whenever he closed his eyes to sleep or allowed his thoughts to drift.

The worst part was the way she looked at him. He could see no hatred in her eyes, no bitterness, no condemnation. She was not warm with him. Did not reach out for him. But neither did she flinch or retreat from him.

He knew he had failed her in too many ways to count. Now, this Russian was asking him to honor his word. It was an alien concept to him but he knew that it was an important step.

When he off-loaded the men upon their arrival on Bukovina and announced his intentions to meet the Russian's request, the Ursuline insisted on staying with him. He had no idea why she would want to. But he had known she would do it. He was beginning to recognize that she was no longer playing by the same set of rules most people observed.

And so as soon as the *Strike* was readied, it lifted off again. And this time, there were no secret communications, no plans for vengeance. Just the simple act of honoring a commitment. That it was such a novel idea disturbed the New Yorker. That it obviously pleased the Ursuline was a step in the right direction.

He left her alone during the trip, allowing her time to recover, grow stronger. Heal. As they neared the cloud-covered moon she was already showing signs of recovery. The Spaniard had given her several different topical creams that sped up the physical healing. The Biblical reading seemed to have a profound effect upon her emotional state. By the time they were in the Lazaretto's outer orbit, she was taking dinner with him in the galley, her manner surprisingly cheerful.

The brief tease of bare sunlight was just a memory now. They were standing on the same roof again, with only the boiling gray horizon of clouds as a backdrop. For Lepov, it made sense. That the sun had tried to make an appearance three days ago did not make sense. The Lazaretto knew it and had reaffirmed its commitment to the shroud it determinately wore.

The ship stood quivering in the cold wind. Once again, Tommy Towers stood at the ramp, this time without his men. A woman stood beside him. She leaned against him, using him as a means to keep warm.

Lepov was alone, but at his signal, the doors to Abbot's TransitCar opened, and Maria Duvalls stepped out, the boy named Jett holding her hand. Georges followed them to the ramp. Lepov closed on the ramp as well, and put a hand on Maria's shoulder.

"Thank you, Mrs. Duvalls. I know the Doctor says it is hard for you to leave."

"Only a little. For him," she looked down at the Dassin boy, "I'm happy to take him away from here. But don't thank me. You are the one..."

"...who's breaking the law." Lepov winked at the boy as they took a step onto the ramp.

"I will follow soon." Doctor Duvalls reached out to his wife and embraced her. "Don't worry. Forty days is not as long as you think. I can't leave illegally. I wouldn't be able to continue my work. Now stop that."

He lifted her chin and stole a kiss from her.

The boy, now an orphan, held tight to the Duvalls woman as if she were his mother. And that was, in fact, what she would become. Lepov was glad that she had been so willing to take on that role.

He turned to look back at the car. The doors were still open. For a brief moment, he wondered if she was going to be difficult, but then Lilly finally appeared. The buffeting grew around them and her white hair swirled in a sudden cyclone. Lilly put up a hand to bring it under control. She walked towards him slowly, in no hurry to reach him.

Behind her, he could see Abbot standing now beside his car, waiting.

"I don't think I can do it, Gregor." Lilly met him at the ramp, her hands shaking as she placed them against his chest.

"You don't have a choice." He pulled her close. "The Doc has made the arrangements, they're going to meet you when you land. And you heard what he said. There's a better than even chance they can make you right. Make you well. It can't be done here. And I won't let you stay."

"But why not you?"

"Don't ask me that, Lilly. We went over this before."

"You went over it. I didn't. I didn't get a say in this. That's unfair. I can't imagine what you're thinking. Do you think that you deserve to stay here? That somehow, because you shot Kry..."

"For a sick woman, you sure have a lot of energy for arguing."

Lepov motioned for Tommy to come closer.

"We'll take care of her, Lepov. Come on, lady. Let Shirl take your hand. She's a good girl. She'll make sure you're okay."

"Gregor," Lilly grabbed his hand, "for once, just listen to me. Can't you, for one time, quit being so stubborn? Whatever either one of us did here, it goes away when we get into this ship. None of it happened. And for the first time in our life, the two of us can be in a normal world, with sunshine, and snow, and warmth and the simple freedom to touch without fear."

"I'd like that. I really would." Lepov leaned over and kissed her forehead. "Now stop arguing. I once met a lady who willingly paid off her debt to society with forty years on this rock. I'm too old to make it that long, but I deserve to give it a try."

"You're a selfish ass, Gregor." He could tell she meant it, and he knew she was right. But it didn't stop her from kissing him one last time.

"Tommy..." Lepov pushed her away.

"Let's go." Towers gently tugged at her shoulders, and he guided her up the ramp. Lilly's last look was full of tears and a surprising amount of bitterness.

Lepov couldn't understand that. Might never understand Lilly Stewart. Why couldn't she see he was setting her free even as he recognized that he didn't deserve the same fate?

"I have no idea what's going on, pal, but good luck." Towers reached out to shake Lepov's hand. Lepov accepted his hand. "This is the completion of my offered favor. Don't think I'll come back for you. You don't step on this damned ship right now, you gotta get out of here like everyone else. But don't worry about the kid and the women. I'll get 'em where you wanted them. But after that, let's not meet up any more."

"Deal." Lepov took a step back.

Towers was about to turn around when he stared beyond Lepov with a flare of anger.

"What the hell?"

Lepov spun around and saw a black vehicle drop onto the roof beside Abbot's TransitCar. Towers let out a curse as the doors popped open and MacNally and Russell both appeared, guns drawn.

"What are you pullin', Lepov?" Towers demanded with a growl.

"They aren't here for you. Get inside and get this ramp closed. They'll let you go. Just hurry up and get out of here in case they change their minds. I'll keep their attention on me."

Lepov started moving forward toward the detectives.

"Just hold it, MacNally." Lepov put out a hand.

"Russell, don't let that ramp close." MacNally spit out the order as he reached out and grabbed Lepov by the wrist.

"Got it," Russell sprinted forward, his gun trained on Tommy Towers, who must have realized he would never get the ramp closed in time. He simply stood at the top of it, staring at Russell. The young detective climbed half-way up the ramp and stood still, his service weapon not quite pointed at the gangster, but not quite pointed away from him either.

MacNally twisted Lepov's wrist, and Lepov had no leverage to fight him. He let the big man spin him around, his hand and arm now folded up against his back.

"You're early. It was a simple request. Let her fly out of here. You know she isn't a danger. Just this once, Ed, be a human. Don't be a cop. Don't be an IHS employee. Just this once."

"How is it you and I ever ended up as friends?" MacNally asked, pushing Lepov towards the silver ship. "After all this time, you still don't understand the first thing about me. How is that possible? I figured you out from day one. You're a cheap detective who isn't above breaking the law — *my* laws — to get what he wants. How can I read you this easily and you can't see the first thing about me?"

"I'm just a private investigator, you know. I never said I was a good private investigator." It was surreal that they should be trading quips at this point. If MacNally prevented Lilly from getting out of the Lazaretto, Lepov was simply going to have to kill the man.

"Who's your new friend?" MacNally nudged Lepov in the back, pointing at Towers with the barrel of his Panther.

"He's nobody." Lepov lied. "Just a driver."

"He's Tommy Towers, that's who he is." Towers stood firm, tapping himself on the chest. He wasn't intimidated in the least by two cops. "Maybe you don't remember, but I saved your life."

"Relax, Tommy. I'm not here for you."

"I like the sound of that."

"So arrest me after this bird flies away." Lepov jerked his arm free and turned to look MacNally in the eye.

"Russell, what do you think?"

A tense moment passed as Lepov and MacNally eyed each other.

"I wouldn't do what he wants. Much like you, Lepov hasn't got a brain big enough to figure out what the right call is here."

"And you do?"

"Sure, Pops. Put that hand cannon of yours into his ribs, and shove him into this illegal ship. And then we both stand here and make sure he doesn't get back off it. And once it is on its way, we tell everyone we didn't find a ship up here, and whatever it was, it wasn't full of exiles breaking quarantine."

"You're forgetting one thing." MacNally waved to Abbot. "Get your ass over here, soccer player."

Abbot walked across the roof and stopped beside the big detective.

"Don't worry about me, Mac. I've got no reason to leave. I'm happy in my little house. I appreciate the thought, but I'll politely decline. And good luck, Lepov."

They shook hands before Abbot returned to his TransitCar.

"I'm not gonna thank you for this, Mac." Lepov allowed a half-smile.

"Of course you won't. Get in the ship."

"When this old guy gets too mean, just kick his cane out from under him." Lepov shook Russell's hand.

"I like that. I'll try it."

"Lepov," MacNally stepped in close, "get off my Lazaretto."

"Okay, Ed." Both men nodded. There was nothing more to say.

As the *Strike* rose into the cold air, Lepov stood in the open doorway of the cockpit, watching Towers as he pointed her nose at the angry slate sky.

"Stick around, Lepov. Let me show you something."

Lepov felt rather than heard someone approach him from behind. He saw Lilly's hands come into view as she wrapped her arms around his waist. She laid her head against his back.

"Look at this." Towers pointed into the mass of blackening clouds.

At first the clouds seem to grow darker as they passed through a thunderhead. But then, a tiny orange glow seemed to infuse the wall of clouds with a barely perceptible pulse of energy. In the next moment, the glow began to spread and the whole of the cloud bank switched from black to white to a vibrant gold. Then, as the clouds rapidly thinned, and the black of space began to replace the horizon, Lepov could finally see it.

He nudged Lilly with his elbow.

"Hey, take a look."

She stirred, and leaned to one side. She drew in a deep breath and let it out with a long, contented sigh.

She whispered: "It's *beautiful*."

And it was. The sun was coming up over Sinop. A brilliant, burning sliver of crescent bathed the rim of the Lazaretto's parent planet in golden tones. And briefly, still in the upper reaches of Aegean's stratosphere, they watched a sunrise over the Lazaretto that grew into a blinding glare that was impossible to keep in view.

Lilly's hands were entwined around Lepov's as Towers dialed down the cockpit aperture. As the view faded, Lilly pushed up as high as she could and whispered in Lepov's ear.

The End

About the Author:

Jason Phillip Reeser, having the spent the first half of his life traversing state lines in a nomadic life that covered ground from the snow-covered forests of Michigan to the sun-bleached sands of Florida, now lives and writes in Westlake, Louisiana. His ghost story anthology, *Cities of the Dead,* which Louisiana Poet Laureate Julie Kane called "a twist of Louisiana Gothic," is set in the cemeteries of New Orleans. He recently published *Room With Paris View*, a travel memoir with his wife, poet Jennifer Reeser. His short stories have appeared in such publications as *The Louisiana Review*, *Bewildering Stories*, and *Danse Macabre*. If you would like to contact him, send email to editor@rocketfirebooks.com. He welcomes comments and questions of any kind.

Visit his FaceBook page at:
FaceBook.com/Jason-Phillip-Reeser
Jason's blog, *Room With No View*, can be read at:
roomwithnoview.blogspot.com

Rocket Fire Books is a small publishing company. If you enjoyed this book, we would appreciate your willingness to mention it to friends who might also enjoy it. If you are active online, at sites like Facebook, Goodreads, Amazon, Shelfari, or similar sites, we ask that you remember us when reviewing and recommending titles. Look for us at rocketfirebooks.com, as well as our Facebook page:

Facebook.com/TheLazaretto.
Thank you in advance for your kindness.
RFB

In New Orleans, Louisiana, the dead refuse to be buried.

Praise for Jason Phillip Reeser's short story collection:

Cities of the Dead

"...a skilled and entertaining Louisiana storyteller." --*Lake Charles American Press*

"...powerful and compelling." --Neal Connelly, author of *St. Michael's Scales*

"Jason Phillip Reeser proves an expert guide to the necropoli of New Orleans, where some of his thirteen tales from these moldering crypts pay homage to the classic pulp magazines. Others, however, engage deeper philosophical questions of morality and mortality, as the dead try unsuccessfully to make their peace with one another and with the living, who are equally incapable of breaking through the time-worn yet timeless marble that separates two levels of being. As one hapless soul concludes, 'Death was not going to be terribly different from life.' "

R.S.Gwynn,
University Professor, Lamar University
Author of *The Narcissiad* and *The Drive-In*

from Saint James Infirmary Books

Turn the page for news on current and forthcoming books from Rocket Fire Books.

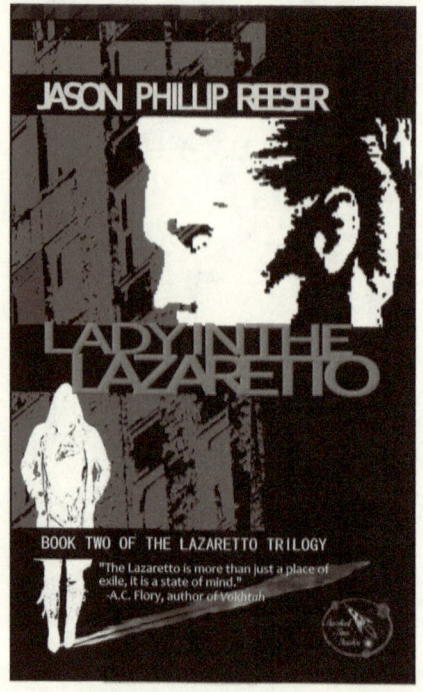

**Non-Fiction from
Jason Phillip Reeser
and Jennifer Reeser:**

*Room With
Paris View*

a travel memoir from
Saint James
Infirmary Books

*"The detail, the curious
footfalls of the Reesers are a joy
to follow, even when they are
regularly lost. There are many
confused steps, but none are
wasted. You see, this really is a
guide book for those who want
good ideas, but certainly don't
want   guiding."* – author
Richard Bunning

Jason and Jennifer Reeser arrived in Paris on a windy day in April. For the next two weeks, as rain fell every day, they explored the city of Eiffel, Rodin, Picasso, the Louvre, Notre Dame Cathedral, Sacré Cœur, Saint-Sulpice, and Père Lachaise Cemetery. Choosing to steer clear of hotels and canned tours, they rented an apartment on the top floor of a six-floor walk-up. Despite the cold and the rain, despite their lack of traveling experience, they were determined to see all they could of the city that inspired the likes of Vincent Van Gogh, Claude Monet, Charles Baudelaire, Victor Hugo, Oscar Wilde, Emile Zola, and Ernest Hemingway.

For anyone who has ever thought that a trip to Paris would be full of rude waiters, bad food, and insufferable crowds, this will set the record straight.

Full of advice for first-time travelers, literary and historical notes, as well as an entertaining account of their views on art, culture, cuisine, and the people of Paris (both the locals and the tourists), *Room With Paris View* will certainly give the reader a new perspective on the City of Light.